SPIRIT WRESTLER

Also by James Houston

Eskimo Prints
Ojibwa Summer
Songs of the Dream People
The White Dawn
Ghost Fox

Editor
Lyon's Private Journal 1821–23

SPIRIT

WRESTLER

JAMES HOUSTON

McCLELLAND AND STEWART

The Canadian Publishers
McClelland and Stewart Limited
25 Hollinger Road, Toronto M4B 3G2

Printed and bound in the United States of America

Canadian Cataloguing in Publication Data
Houston, James, 1921-
Spirit wrestler
ISBN 0-7710-4250-7
I.   Title.
PS8515.0868S65   C813'.5'4   C79-094797-8
PR9199.3.H675S65

To Black Donald Snowden
then Chief of the Arctic Division
who sometimes shared the
best and worst of it with me

Ayii, Ayii, Ayii.
That woman down there beneath the sea,
She wants to hide the seals from us.
These hunters in the dance house,
They cannot right matters.
They cannot mend matters.
Into the spirit world
Will go I,
Where no humans dwell.
Set matters right will I.
Set matters right will I.
Ayii, Ayii, Ayii.

ESKIMO SHAMAN'S SONG

THE
NORTHERN SERVICE
OFFICER'S REPORT

CANADA

Okoshikshalik Camp
South Baffin Island
Northwest Territories, Canada

I awoke in the middle of the night of January 17 and heard all fifty of our camp dogs howling their warning that strange men and dogs were coming toward us in the dark. I struggled from my sleeping bag, found my sealskin boots, pulled on my heavy pants and parka, and ducked out through the snow-block entrance of my tent. Hunters from our camp at Okoshikshalik were already there, peering into the freezing blackness of the night.

I heard the heavy thump of sleds and the straining sound of dogs and drivers, faintly at first, then growing stronger, as they forced their way between the jagged barriers of sea ice that the big moon tides had thrust up all along our Baffin Island coastline. Two dog teams came looming out of the night, racing toward us across the hard-packed snow. Our sled dogs, free of harness, tore into the new arrivals, and an immense fight erupted. These unknown strangers and our hunters waded together into the snarling turmoil of dogs, flailing out with butts of heavy whips, kicking with the deadly accuracy of Eskimo hunters.

The fight ceased as quickly as it had begun, and an ominous, wounded silence spread between us and the newcomers.

Even in the dark I could feel the tension, and sensed that everything was wrong. The men from our camp did not crowd in the way they do when friends arrive, but kept a nervous distance, waiting for someone else to speak.

I myself stood back until my eyes had grown accustomed to the darkness, and I could see the outline of a human body lashed on the nearest sled. Then I called out in Eskimo, "Who is there?"

One of the drivers flung my question back at me.

"Is that a dead man?" I asked.

"Who knows?" said another of the drivers.

I stepped forward, bent, eased the lashings, and felt cautiously beneath the stiff canvas.

"He is not dead," I said, and asked again, "Who is he?"

The three drivers looked away and did not answer me.

"Who is this man?" I insisted.

A voice from the darkness said, "Shoona is the name we know him by. He is no relative of ours. We were told by Kuni, the man who makes decisions in our camp, to bring him here to you."

"Hurry! Carry him into my tent with all his covers," I told them. "He is not dead, but I believe that he is dying."

As the drivers started to unlash the sick man from their sled, I ducked into the tunnel that protected my winter tent, and through the small wooden door with the hinges that squeal so badly every time I open or close it. The tent itself was just ten feet in diameter, low and double walled for heat retention, and rounded so the Arctic winds would not catch its corners. It was no good in cold weather, and the Eskimos had built snow blocks all around the outer wall for me. That helped considerably, but the tent was one of those clever white-man's designs that I would never try again. A Baffin Island snowhouse is much warmer.

I pumped up the small brass Swedish Primus stove and got it roaring so the rim turned cherry red. It wasn't yet warm enough in the tent to take your mitts off, but I knew that condition would improve. After I'd chipped ice into the kettle, I cleared some floor space, folded an old white bearskin, and covered it with a piece of canvas to form a makeshift mattress.

Three of the strangers lugged the dying man inside my tent, laid him down, and hurried out, not even waiting to see me take the covering off his face, but half a dozen children from our camp huddled curiously at the door.

I adjusted the lamp, bent down, and turned back the frost-stiff covering from Shoona's face. When the children saw it, they gasped in horror, backed out, and slammed the door behind them. Shoona had lost his human look. His face, like his wolf-trimmed hood, must have been soaking wet. Now, face and hood had both taken on a ghostly sheen of hoarfrost. Beneath the frost his skin was ashen gray, and I thought after all that he must be dead.

I pulled off one of my mitts and reached inside his hood. I could feel blood pulsing slowly through the big main artery in his neck. He was alive, though barely. I moved my hand across his view, but his eyes remained half open, glazed and seeing nothing, and his breath was not visible in the cold.

"Nylak! Nylak!" I shouted, holding my small door open.

I knew the girl could hear me call her. Everyone in camp must have heard me. But she did not come, or even answer.

Nylak was a young woman in the camp, with a handsome face and kind, warm, natural ways, who kept my tent tidy and helped me in other respects, too. Her father didn't mind our being friends, and her mother sewed for me and kept my sealskin boots in soft condition. But oh—I mean with strangers near us—Nylak was too shy.

The door opened cautiously and Nylak's uncle peered inside. He was a short, strong man with a wide brown face and narrow eyes that seemed to pierce through me. He had always looked to me like a warrior, a bowman, who should have been astride a half-wild pony riding in the forces of Genghis Khan. He had not even bothered to pull on his parka to walk through forty-below-zero air from one dwelling to another, but wore only a cheap plaid flannel shirt above his sealskin pants and boots.

He cleared his throat and squatted down beside me. "Her father says I'm the one who's got to help you. Not my little niece. She's so afraid, that little Nylak. No wonder. This one lying here is no ordinary man. That's what they say back at Trader's Bay," he told me, and I noticed that he kept his eyes averted from Shoona's deathlike face.

I rubbed the sick man's wrists and tried to pump his legs toward his chest to get his circulation moving.

"Tell me, what do you know about him?" I asked.

He sniffed and wiped his sleeve across his nose. "He is, well, sort of a religious man," he whispered hoarsely. "But the missionary who was here last summer told us that he and his church were moving forward, and that Shoona and his religion were old-fashioned, standing still, or going backward. This man comes from down the coast. We haven't seen him in this camp for a good long time. He knows he isn't welcome here."

The last time I myself had seen Shoona had been at least a year ago or more. He had been wearing caribou-skin clothing and a pair of those old-fashioned bone snow goggles pushed up on his forehead. One rarely sees them nowadays. He was a short, well-fed man then, perhaps thirty years of age, who wore his hair caught up and tied in some strange way that gave him a wild, uncaptured look. He had square, even teeth, and prominent cheekbones that seemed to force his black eyes into narrow slits. Just seeing those eyes staring at me had always made me feel uneasy.

Nylak's uncle coughed again and nodded his head toward the corpselike figure. "Look! He's still alive. He's breathing," he said. "I'm going back to sleep."

I thought about the flask of rum at the bottom of my grub box and I answered, "Yes, thanks—I don't need you now."

Cold steam burst into the warming tent, and then the frozen hinges squealed again as Nylak's uncle slammed the door. I squatted alone, staring at Shoona's slowly heaving chest. The Primus stove was giving off a steady hissing sound, and I could see a white cloud forming, drifting upward from my kettle spout.

I rummaged around in my battered box until I found my dented metal flask of overproof rum. I filled an enamel cup three-quarters full, but decided this was far too much for a man who might not make it through the night, and so drank off about a quarter cup, turning my head away from the Primus, fearing my breath might catch on fire. Adding hot water from the kettle, I knelt down beside Shoona, raised his head, and held the steaming rum beneath his nose.

His eyelids fluttered as he let out a painful gasp. I tilted up his head and poured a little of the precious liquor in his mouth. Some trickled down his chin, but I got all the rest inside him. I saw his throat constrict, his Adam's apple pumping, as he tried to swallow. He wheezed, then got it down and coughed. His eyelids fluttered and came wide open in an unseeing stare that frightened me and made me fear my cure might kill. He began to tremble violently and call out in a singsong voice.

"*Avo divio aksorutit kasuaktoarikgiortok kuksiatok kalaluktunga.*"

I listened to him carefully, but it wasn't proper Eskimo he was speaking. Those were words I had never heard before. They didn't fit together.

I put two cubes of dehydrated beef bouillon into my chipped enamel mug, and half filled it with hot water. Then I added just an ounce or so of rum, stirred the result, and tasted it. I could hardly bear to part with it.

I raised Shoona's head again and watched him suck it down.

7

I was surprised when he said *"Nakomut,"* thanking me in the Baffin dialect. *"Quianamik,"* he said, using another form.

His voice first seemed small, as though it came from far away, but suddenly it zoomed in close and heavy, filling my tent like the low groaning of a church organ. It surprised me that he had gained the strength to speak at all. The overproof rum and the heat from my Primus stove were having their effect. The hoarfrost on his face began to melt and run in sweatlike rivulets into the matted ruff of wolf hair around his hood. Blotched blue frost patches appeared on his cheeks, then turned a mottled red. He twisted and groaned and licked his lips. I felt his head, and knew that he was going to run a fever. I believed that I could easily lose him from pneumonia.

"Atkak! Uncle!" I shouted through the tent wall. *"Atkak,* come back and help me!"

I looked at my wristwatch, forgetting that it had been stopped for days. Guessing the time was difficult in the almost endless winter darkness, but I thought it must be midnight or beyond.

When Nylak's uncle came into the tent again, he squatted down and tried to work my flashlight, but the batteries were too cold to give out any power. He grunted, tossed it on my rolled-up sleeping bag, and lit a candle stub instead. He held it close for me while I opened the government medical box and got out the hypodermic needle and a precious vial of penicillin.

"Help me roll him over," I said. "Help me."

Untying the cord around the sick man's waist, I eased his sealskin trousers down. His body and his tattered clothes were soaking wet. I opened the trap door in the long gray winter underwear, swabbed the needle, and with the alcohol cleaned a tiny circle on one buttock. Carefully I plunged the hypodermic needle through the rubber cap and watched it as I drew up 100,000 units of the penicillin.

Shoona jumped as my blunt old needle pierced him, and

when I withdrew it he let out another gasp. I swabbed again, then rearranged his torn and sodden clothing.

Nylak's uncle, feeling bolder, reached out and touched the sick man. "His sealskins and his underwear, they're soaked right through," he said. "This man has fallen through the ice. He's been underneath the water!"

Together we drew off his knee-length sealskin boots. Sea water ran right out of them. His feet were blue and rimmed with salt.

"You go and get those dog-team drivers over here to me," I said. "The ones who brought him here. If you have to wake them up, then do it. I want to know everything that happened to this man. I want to know tonight."

It was not long until the three drivers came ducking through my door. They did not pull back their parka hoods or remove their mitts in the normal friendly fashion, and not once did any of them glance at the living person they had delivered wrapped in canvas.

"This man's been in the water," I said, studying their faces. "Look at his boots and clothing, sodden wet and steaming."

"*Agaiii!* No! He goes not near the fish lake. No!" they answered me together. "He doesn't go out hunting. He's done nothing since he left Trader's Bay last autumn. He won't even go out fishing through the ice with women. No. We get the food, he stays behind."

"That one hunts not at all," said the hawk-nosed man. "He's too busy with the women in the igloos, and the little weasels."

Teriaapik—little weasels? He could not possibly have said that, I thought. I was tired, and having trouble with the language.

"Everything is frozen down at our camp—lakes, river, sea—all frozen," the youngest driver added. "We found this man stretched out in his bed exactly the way you see him now."

"*Kowshiktuvingalook,*" they said. "Soaking wet and gasping in his igloo. Lying on the bed, alone, without a woman. Imagine him without a woman. Lately, that's the way he's been forced to live."

"What happened to him?" I demanded. "How did he get so wet?"

"*Achoolee*." The wiry thin man shook his head. "We don't know anything about such things."

"Well, you should know. You're Shoona's friends."

"We're not his friends," the short man said emphatically. "None of us know what happened to him. The camp boss at our place was angry when we got back from hunting. Oh, yes, very angry! He told us to get rid of this man, to lay him out to freeze. Then he changed his mind, not wanting trouble. He had us bring him here to let him live or die with you. Our wives said, 'You three hurry! Come back soon.' They're not angry at us, but they were afraid to have Shoona dying in our camp."

"If the weather's right, we will go back home in the morning," the thin man said. "He may be dead by then. He's always given trouble."

"*Imialooktipivunga?* Do I smell rum?" the biggest driver asked me, using their word for liquor, sniffing the air and drawing off his mitts. He smiled. "I would gladly drink some rum with you."

The others nodded, pushing back their hoods. I stared at all of them but did not answer.

The hawk-nosed man pulled a fistful of tattered cigarette butts out of his pocket. "Have you got papers?" he asked me. "We wish to roll a cigarette."

I passed them my tobacco and some papers. Each carefully rolled a bulky cigarette as fat as a cigar.

They glanced nervously at Shoona when they heard him moan and put up their hoods, preparing to leave.

"Wait," I said. "You know the male nurse? The white man, Corgy, who lives at Trader's Bay?"

"Yes," the dog-team drivers answered. "Yes, we know him."

I tore a blank page from my journal and wrote awkwardly in pencil: "I have here with me a man named Shoona who was brought in very sick tonight. He is running a high temperature, between 104°–105°. I have given him 100,000 units of penicillin and will repeat tomorrow morning. Am keeping him warm, hoping he will live. Please come at once."

On the bottom of the page I wrote "N.S.O." for Northern Service Officer, and initialed it, adding "January 17," hoping that date was right. I found it all too easy to lose the hours, the days, and even the weeks when I stayed in the camps with people who live in the long darkness of winter or the endless white nights of summer and regard time, and indeed their lives, in a very different way from ours.

"I want you to take both sleds," I said to the drivers, "and go early in the morning. Even if the weather is not good, I want you to take this piece of paper to the nurse."

Before I folded it, I wrote across the bottom, "Onward, Men of Harlech," because Nurse Corgy was a feisty little Welshman and proud of it. I hoped that last bit would help remind him that we were good friends.

"This writing tells the male nurse to come here quickly. Do you understand?"

They looked at me and then at each other.

"Yes," the hawk-nosed driver answered. "We understand. We will bring the male nurse here."

I folded the note and handed it to him. Corgy, like me, was a civil servant. Of course he would hate the long freezing journey down the coast and back again, and I couldn't blame him, but I knew that he would come. He was a rough, tough, broad-shouldered man from the rolling hill country of North Wales. He had been a medic with the Welsh Fusiliers, and, hell or high water, he would be here. I knew that.

It was a miserable time of year for traveling. The dog teams would have to make awkward land crossings of wind-blown plains with exposed boulders, then cross over ice barriers onto frozen bays. Two nights they would have to build igloos. I didn't envy them. Corgy would have to run a lot to keep warm, and he would have to help push that sled more than a hundred miles to reach this place. Then he would turn around and fight his way back again. You have to experience that in an Arctic headwind to understand how bad such a trip can be.

"You take that paper to the male nurse," I said again. "If you arrive at night, wake him up and give it to him right away before you go to sleep. Do you understand?"

They understood, all right, and they didn't look pleased.

As they rose to leave, I heard the sick man groan.

"Do you want to tell them something?"

"No," Shoona answered, and lay there gasping until they left the tent.

He stared wide-eyed at me, as though I were a ghost. "I don't remember coming here. I—I—It was as though I had been dead."

"You'll be all right," I said. "Don't try to talk."

I made a cup of strong tea for both of us and tucked one heavy winter caribou skin over his feet and another around his body. I lit my kerosene lantern and carefully polished the frost off its reflector. Only then did I crawl back into my thick eiderdown bag and pull off my own outer pants and parka. I put on my knitted woolen hat and thin cloth army shooting gloves, turned off the Primus stove, and stuffed a sock into my little air vent, which Eskimos call "the snout." I was grateful for the sudden silence.

Adjusting the light so that I could feel its welcome heat against my left cheek, I glanced at the four paperback books I kept on the empty ammunition storage box beside my sleeping bag. I picked up *Medieval People: The Common Man in the Middle Ages* and opened it with care, for book spines break easily in the cold. I was anxious to read English for a change, after straining to speak and trying to understand Eskimo all day long and half the night.

"*Peungitunga ishumaveet?* You think I'm bad, do you?" Shoona asked me in a broken voice.

I looked at him. He opened his eyes, then slowly turned his head and stared at me intently.

"I don't think you're bad," I answered. "I try to take care of you, don't I? I share my tent, my rum with you."

"Yes," Shoona said. "But still you do not like me."

I answered only by saying, "I think sleep will help you."

"It is said that you like almost every person on this coast. But I believe that you do not like me. The *neavirtee*," he said, meaning the trader, "he doesn't like me. It can't be helped. Most *Inuit* don't like me, either. Oh, well, I'm going to die. I'm not sure how it will be—where I am going. Maybe they won't like me in that place, either."

"I rarely hear people say they don't like you." I rustled the pages of my book. "I think you should go to sleep now. Let that strong medicine move inside you. Sleep. You'll feel better in the morning."

"No," he said, and sighed. "That's not the way it's going to be. I'm afraid to die, I'm afraid to go to sleep. I'm afraid of—of her!"

This time I didn't answer him. I pretended to read my book.

"There are some strange things I wish to say to you," Shoona whispered.

"Shhh. Shhh," I said. "Save your strength. We will talk about that in the morning."

"No!" he said, and rolled painfully onto his side. "*Nelunuktoalook*. It's too difficult, too difficult," he repeated. "Will you listen to me—now?" he asked.

Reluctantly I laid my book aside. "Yes. I'm listening. *Ataii! Ohaknairkeet.* You go ahead and talk."

Even in his weakened condition Shoona was a masterly

storyteller, made bold perhaps by the effect of rum and desperation. He did not hesitate to imitate the voices or the songs of other people, the sounds of animals, or even the whistling wind and driving snow. He used any device to give his story a sense of life. He spoke simply, using common words, making sure that I would understand. At first he had to fight for breath, but as time went on the strangeness of the tale he had to tell seemed to summon up his vital forces. At times an uncanny power seemed to emanate from Shoona. I could feel it. It was frightening. I don't know how long he talked that first night, but it was morning when, in spite of himself, he fell asleep.

So began a dreamlike troubled time for both of us. There were periods when he talked strongly again, staring at me or into the shadows, and others when his eyelids almost closed and his voice became remote, like that of someone speaking out of a trance. Occasionally he was able to take more tea or broth. When he slept, I went about my own business, though I was never far from him. Sometimes, of course, I slept.

I believe now that I, myself, may have been caught up in Shoona's powerful visions. That does not really matter to me. The important thing is that the story of Shoona's life was given to me. It will remain etched in my mind forever.

SHOONA'S
STORY

ONE
The Shaman

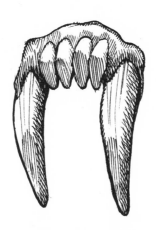

1

You look upon me now, a dying man. You may not know that I have had two wives and a strange childless family. Sorcerers, some called us. I have had wealth and power all around me. I could sleep in any family bed and stuff myself with meat caught by others. You well may ask yourself if that is possible. You may think I was born into some successful hunting family with a wise father who kept strong-minded women. Or at least, you will think, I must myself have been a splendid hunter, married to the daughter of some very forceful camp boss.

Wrong! That is not so. Everything for me began in a different way. My very life began in danger, while I was still riding in my mother's hood.

I was born up north on the Kogalik River during a time of desperate hunger. That frozen river and the shallow sea beyond its mouth are miserable hunting places, and they are not good for fishing, either. Some say the very ground was wounded by bad spirits. Years ago, they say, a white man walked overland and raised a high stone cairn up there beside the river's mouth. He left a box and ate his dogs. His broken skull and whitened bones were strewn everywhere. No human beings live there any more, and that is not surprising.

My father died up there, lost in fog and moving ice the very winter when I appeared out of my mother. Piak was her name. She told me, when I was old enough to understand, that if I had not been a male child, others would have taken me away from her and set me out to die between two snow blocks. No wonder. The hunters from our camp could not even feed themselves. What would they want with another hungry girl?

It became so bad in early spring that our people were glad to eat what frozen caribou droppings they found scattered on the snow. All our camp dogs were long dead, and eaten, and all the fish had gone down deep under the lake ice, and would not rise no matter how cleverly our women worked their shiny copper fishing jigs and sang their magic songs. Everything was going wrong for all of us.

When springtime finally blew its warm breath across our land, it destroyed the winter trails and any hope that other hunters might come with food and save us. Starvation in our camp was at its very worst, and the people lost all hope. But then, as if by magic, great cracks opened in the sea and provided us with a small beluga whale, washed up newly dead against the ice, near where we lived. No one knew who sent that blue-gray whale for us to feast upon, but we were grateful, for it saved the families at Kogalik who had survived the dreadful winter.

These few, my mother among them, struggled down here to the south coast of Baffin Island. She was skeleton thin, she told me, and scarcely able to believe that we were both alive. But the people of the first camp that we reached shared their tents and fed us generously, while we waited with all the others near the place called Black Whale Mountain.

Finally they came! The whalers! Their tall-masted ship had sails, and a smoking nose as well, and could twist and turn down leads in the ice, moving even when there was no wind.

It was remarkable, my mother said, to see the whalemen come off their ship red-faced, fat, and healthy, laughing as though nothing bad had happened. They took pity on us and shoveled a huge pile of hard round sea biscuits into the *umiak*, the women's boat, and gave each hunter a small sack of bullets for the rifles they had traded to us several years before. Then they sailed away toward Sharlo, searching for hunters and women better fed than ours who could help them with their whaling, and we knew we would see no other foreigners until another winter had come again and gone.

After that starving time up on the northern river, my mother said, she felt fearful about everything, and she could not bring herself to name me until I was in my third winter. And then she called me Shoona, meaning What-is-it? That is not a proud sort of name, and they say no one living here has ever possessed it before.

The year after I was born, in the brief time between the summer and the winter that we call *okiak*, three traders came to Black Whale Mountain in a small sailboat that had been dropped from the deck of a larger ship. They carried a pile of flat new wood and trade goods, which they landed on the shore, and then began to work like demons, trying to build a small house before the first snow. My mother said you could hear their hammers ringing from very early morning until far into the night; they even worked by lantern light until the roof was finished.

Five days after they had come, their boat sailed away with only two of them aboard. The third man, the one who could speak our language not too badly, they left behind with us. He stayed in the bay in the lee of Black Whale Mountain, and kept on hammering at the walls.

The people called him Keegutialook, Big Teeth, and they helped him store his precious trade goods safe inside the little side house. On the very night they finished the work, a raging blizzard came, and for three days nothing could be seen but whiteness. When it was over, the drifts behind the trader's house were higher than his roof.

The building of that trading post changed everything for us, and in the beginning the hunters and the women believed that it was all for the good. They had the feeling that they would never starve again, and they liked that first white man who came and stayed among us. Indeed, my mother told me that for the next four years our lives went well together. Because her mother had died, she returned to help her father at his camp. He was still taking seals at that time, and had two other hunters with him. But later, when I was in my eighth winter, my mother broke a taboo, or her amulets gave out, and the new ones that she bought lacked strength, so that her father, who had supported us so well at his camp, caught a fishbone in his throat and died a wretched death.

Once more my mother had no way to feed herself or me. But she was still young and strong and handsome in the face and good at sewing, and a hunter of importance offered her a chance to become his *aviliak*, to share his bed and his meat with him and his first wife. The first wife said she had no objection to my mother coming into the bed, but she was strong against any adopted male child entering into that powerful family if that child did not belong to her.

I could tell my mother was in deep despair when she said, "I can't go on like this. We must find another place for you to live."

She begged a ride for both of us with a dog team bound up north to a camp beyond Wild Bird Island. For four nights we rested there, and she spoke with all the families, but even I could tell that no one wanted to adopt me.

Early on the morning of the fifth day my mother had some violent kind of trouble in the bed, with a loutish hunter whom she greatly feared. Having no husband or relative to protect her, she rose in the night, and we set out together, running at first, toward the camp they call "Tall Clouds," the most northern camp of any of our people.

It was in the first spring moon, when the caribou drop their young, that we two went running. A harsh wind blew straight against us, driving sharp ice crystals into our faces, freezing our eyelashes, making it impossible to see the way. Even though we held each other by the hand, we often stumbled. I tried to walk as strongly as I could, but by the time the sun was sliding down toward the edge of the world I could not keep from crying, for my feet had lost all feeling and they would hardly move.

My mother, who was thin but strong, slung me up onto her back as though I were a baby. She made me lock my mitted hands around her neck, and staggered on in this way until it grew dark. Then we stopped, and I lay on the snow watching as she drew the short snow knife from her boot and began to build a small crude igloo for us. She forced me to help her, to chink the snow blocks, so that in this way I would warm myself.

Inside the tiny shelter we gnawed at half a frozen fish that my mother had snatched for us before we ran. We clung to each other for warmth, and slept exhausted. Somehow we survived the night.

In the morning we rose stiff with cold, and I saw that my mother had dark frost patches on her cheeks. She made me dance a joyless jig with her until some warmth returned to us, and then, with empty stomachs, we started out again in fear. It was stinging cold, and only the steady walking kept us warm enough to stay alive.

In the midday my shin muscles failed me and I started crawling on all fours. I was too slow for my mother, and when I called out to her, she was far ahead. She turned back and stood staring at me for a long time before she drew the snow knife from her boot and started to build a new igloo. When I crawled up close, I found that it was the smallest I had ever seen, the kind dog-team drivers build to allow a bitch to whelp her pups and protect them from the big male dogs.

She said, "This house is for you alone," but I was too worn out to understand her meaning.

When she finished, there were tears in her eyes. She brushed the hair away from my face and rubbed and sniffed her nose along the side of mine.

"Together we can go no farther," she said. "I can carry you no longer. All of my strength is gone. I am going to try to walk back to the south coast. Who knows if either of us will live or die?"

I begged her to take me with her, and she started weeping.

"I cannot," she whispered. "You rest here. Perhaps someone will pass this way and find you. Suck on this fish tail," she told me. "You will feel better."

There was almost no meat on it, but it was the only gift that she could leave with me.

"Son of mine," she said, kneeling and weeping, shaking me and pointing, forcing me to stare along her arm. "See that low hill with the little notch blown clear of snow? See it? They say that marks the way to Tall Clouds. Rest now, and then walk that way in the morning—if you can."

She pulled her hood to hide her face from me, but I could hear her sobbing. She turned and staggered south, moving like an old woman, her shoulders hunched against the cold.

I started crying out in fear. I called to her, screamed for her: "Annana! Annana!" But my mother never turned or looked at me again. She grew smaller and smaller, until she was only a speck on the flat white horizon. When all hope was gone, I crawled into the miserable snowhouse and curled up like a dog, shivering, feeling the tears freeze on my cheeks, afraid to go to sleep. But in my exhaustion I must have slept, for without my hearing it a huge storm came raging out of the north. It was the wind giants who waked me, cracking their whips against my trembling igloo. Then I felt stomach cramps, and to ease them I ate snow I scraped from the walls.

It seemed to me that I did not sleep through the rest of that awful night, and by morning I was so cold that I could scarcely move. But my leg muscles worked again, and I forced myself to crawl out, and raise myself, and walk north toward the notch between the hills. I reached that place in the late afternoon, and from there I could see the distant line of tidal ice where it was forced up between the land and the sea. Everything looked pink to me. I did not know it then, but I was going snow blind from the glaring sun of spring.

I had not yet learned to build a snowhouse, and I had no knife. In truth, I had no choice but to wander through that long and terrifying night, telling myself again and again that if I lay down I would surely die.

By the next morning I had almost reached the flat expanses of the frozen coastline. I could walk no more, and when I saw a meat cache built of stones, I crawled to it and clawed at it with my torn mitts and then with my bare hands. But whoever had made it had cleverly packed it with wet snow and let it freeze as a protection against hungry dogs and bears. Can you imagine that? Faintly I could smell the oily, rancid meat inside the cache, and yet I could not touch it.

After what seemed a long time I rose and staggered on along the coast, seeing nothing in the whole flat empty world save one lone raven that flew over me, huge but lean, with a strong cruel beak and blue-black feathers. It landed on a snowy hummock, observing me with cold and shining eyes, and croaked harsh words that made me know it wanted me to die.

I walked and fell and crawled again until I saw some yellow urine stains. Forcing myself on, I crossed numerous dog tracks and sled markings, and followed the drivers' footprints until at last I saw their camp. It was larger than I had imagined. There were six big igloos, with many twisting snow porches, all facing toward the sea, and there were several high meat caches and a paint-peeled whaleboat, almost buried in the snow. Everywhere there were big half-starved dogs roaming free, and when they caught my unfamiliar scent, they gathered into a pack and raced silently toward me.

I summoned all my strength and cried out to a young man and a girl, who turned and looked my way. They bellowed at the dogs and ran to help. I threw one torn sealskin mitten to the left and the other to the right, and the dogs, thinking I threw out meat, fought over them until the man and the girl drove them away from me.

"Who is this?" the young man demanded, looking at me strangely.

I was so weak and shy and stupid from hunger that I could not answer. But the girl took hold of the point of my parka hood and helped me stagger toward the igloos.

A woman called out, "You, there, foolish daughter, be careful. What is that thing you've got with you?"

"It is only a young boy," the girl answered. "Can we not feed him?"

"No, we cannot feed him. How could a boy who looks as young as that one live out there alone?"

The girl asked me if I had a family and a name, but still I did not have the courage or the strength to speak.

"You be careful," her mother warned again. "Evil things like that sometimes come up from under stones or out of cracks in the river ice at night. They only pretend to be human children until they have a chance to grab you!"

The girl looked frightened, but she half dragged me into the snow porch of the house, and I crouched there shivering, on all fours, grateful to be out of the glaring sun and wind. My eyes were sore, and everything had turned a glowing red. She brought me out some rich seal broth, which I lapped up like an animal, and some seal ribs, which I gnawed until every shred of meat was gone from the bones.

"Tell me your name," she said gently. "Where have you come from?"

"Shoona is my name," I answered. "I come not far from Black Whale Mountain."

"Oh, I think you might be a distant cousin of mine," she said, smiling. "Your mother must be Piak. I've heard of her. Where is she?"

"I do not know," I answered. "She had to leave me and walk south to look for other people. I do not know their names. There is a man there who wants my mother for a second wife. The wife he has won't let me stay with them."

"I will go inside and tell my family that," she said. "I knew that you were a real human being as soon as my eyes saw you. Look, I have an amulet," she said proudly, showing me one of several small bags sewn inside her parka. "It protects me from those other awful creatures, you know, the ones who make the snow creak and who cry out in the night."

After some discussion, her family allowed me to come inside, though they still eyed me suspiciously. Because of the warmth and the food, the shivering left me, and I slept all afternoon inside the igloo on some coils of sealskin line. I did not wake until evening, when the hunters all returned.

A big man—I mean a real brute of a man, whose cheekbones stood out like goose eggs blotched dark brown from freezing and thawing and refreezing—came into the igloo with the others.

"Look what we found," the grandmother said, pointing at me.

"*Ayii*. Yes, he must be the one," he grunted, and took me by the wrist and shouted: "*Unalook!* Now you're mine! Last autumn I traded his mother, Piak, a whole seal, skin and all, as well as a package of steel needles, for this boy. Her father had just died and she didn't have a man to help her. She said she couldn't feed her son any more. She promised she would try to bring him up here to me."

"I found him," said the young girl who had brought me in and given me the soup and seal ribs. "Could he not stay and live with us?" she asked.

"No! That boy is going to work for me. I traded fair for him. He's mine. Do you all hear me? That skinny wretch belongs to me!" The man's voice seemed more raucous than any raven's, though Tuluwak, meaning Raven, was his name.

He spat on the igloo floor.

He stood up, grabbed me by the parka hood, hauled me out of their igloo, and walked toward his own, giving a big male dog a savage kick when it strayed too close to us.

Raven's igloo was filthy inside and blackened from the oily smoke of two ill-kept lamps. I came to dread every person in that miserable igloo, and I hated Raven's sullen wife and the four cruel children she had reared. Raven himself, if he came in and found me sleeping, would snatch me up by thrusting two fingers into my nostrils, then take me by the throat and shake me, then fling me out into the blood-spattered snow porch, and I would have to sleep there with the dogs until his anger faded. He was a strong man, with power over others even though he was a worthless hunter. He greedily demanded his share of meat, and in this way he and his family stayed alive. Even when food was plentiful in the camp, he saw to it that I never got enough to eat.

He never called me Shoona, nor was I allowed to call him Father, like most adopted children. It was I who had to feed the dogs and strip the sealskin lines and empty every urine pot. Fortunately I was young then, and always hopeful. When I saw winter loosen its grip and patches of tundra widening against the melting snow, I would walk away from the camp and watch the whole flat world turn softly blue. It was easy for me to forget the hard parts of my life when I heard the snow geese calling in the early morning and felt the new warmth of spring as it spread over the whole land.

In the middle of the first moon of summer all the people of the Tall Clouds camp gathered together and skidded Raven's battered whaleboat out over the ice until it reached the edge of the open sea. Working together, the hunters and the strong-est women launched it with a shout of pleasure into the newly opened water. I was piled inside the boat with all the tents and pots and women and other children. The whaleboat's gray and mildewed sail was full of holes. But no one thought to mend it; no one cared. We were in no hurry. We were only moving along with life.

Everyone but Raven was in a joyful mood during our jour-ney south. The ice was thick, but we found open passages, and there was time for our two kayakmen to range wide in search of seals. They brought us all the meat that we could eat.

Each day I edged up closer to the bow and watched the straight strings of eider ducks winging their way just above the surface of the ice-strewn water. Throughout the long white nights, when we landed to sleep on the islands, it did not grow dark, and early in the mornings we would run ahead of the women over each island and make a game of finding the pale-green duck eggs lying in nests of softest eiderdown. They were delicious, those eggs. I would fill my parka hood with them, then crack and eat them until my belly would hold no more.

The sky was light at midnight when we arrived at Trader's Bay and anchored the boat in the shelter of Black Whale Mountain. Raven ordered us to pitch our tents only among those who came from the northern camps. Thus he made sure his tent was in the highest, driest place, yet close to the run-ning stream. A year before, this same campground had been littered with our leavings, but the lashing rains of autumn and the spring runoff of snow had washed the gravel sparkling clean again.

The older children climbed the hills and waited for half a moon, watching day and night before we heard the screaming *"Umiakjuak! Umiakjuak!"*—which meant they had finally sighted ship's smoke on the horizon. It was the trader's ship, and the women shrieked with joy.

A hunter's boat from an east-coast camp also arrived late that night, and next morning I met my mother, hurrying down toward the boxes and bales of trade goods that the sailors and our hunters had unloaded on the shore. She stopped and looked at me.

"It's no good at all," she said, "the way that awful Raven family has you dressed in filthy rags. Poor boy, you must be miserable. Look at your boots, just full of holes. Can't that woman even sew? Never mind. I'll make you a new pair myself—tomorrow."

But she never did. The next night, after the ship had gone, the trader gave a big dance in his empty warehouse. It lasted long into the morning, and I think my mother must have been tired, for she forgot to make my boots.

I didn't care. I was proud of my mother. She was always elegantly dressed, with a clean white trade-cloth cover pulled over her caribou *amoutik*. Her hood and pouch were large enough to house two infant children, though she carried none, and the back of her parka tail was so long it almost touched the ground. She had sewn a red wool ribbon of trade cloth along the border of her costume, and down the center of the long tail she had attached a clinking, twinkling line of copper pennies with a king's head on each one of them. And small brass bullet casings were crimped along her garment hem. I have no words to tell you how beautiful my red-cheeked mother looked, or how marvelous it was to see and hear her walking grandly up the trader's path to have a cup of tea.

Everyone said that in the splendid hunter's camp, where my mother was his *aviliak*, everyone was always well fed, and that they had so many sealskins with the fat on that they used to feed them to their dogs. I cannot tell you how I longed to live once more with my own mother in such a pleasant place, with skillful people all around me.

In the first moon of autumn, when a sleet storm came and coated all the tents with ice, Raven said it would soon be time to return to camp. Before we left he slyly traded another slave boy from a widow. His name was Pingwa and he was just about my age.

It was late autumn before we all sailed north to Tall Clouds, and the weather had turned sharply cold, but there was still no snow cover and I thought it the most frightful time of year. In my tattered clothes I was always shivering on the outside, but inside I was warmed by the fact that I had seen my own mother, and that she was alive and still cared about me and had said that she would make me boots. I used to dream that she would have her hunter send a dog team north and rescue me from Raven. That never happened, but my life grew better just the same.

I now had Pingwa to talk with and to share my burdens. Of course they gave us all the dirty work to do in camp, such as building heavy stone meat caches and helping haul up boats, and no matter how hard we slaved we never got our proper share of meat.

Pingwa was very short and runty, and I was skinny, with a head and hands that others said seemed too big for my body, but we both grew strong from all the work, and from wrestling and heaving heavy stones.

Pingwa could balance on his hands in a skillful way that I tried but could not learn, and he could run so fast that I never caught him. Even when he was cold and hungry and his teeth were chattering he could always manage a laugh or at least a smile, and when others were not looking he would perform one of two very different secret dances for me. The first was an imitation of our dreadful master, in which Pingwa perfectly imitated the raucous calling and greedy gestures of a raven. The second depicted the movements of a kind old woman in our camp whom we both liked very much. Pingwa could mimic anyone so well that I would sometimes fall down laughing.

One freezing morning during my fourth winter in that camp, the greedy Raven decided that he wanted more of the trader's goods—sugar, flour, tobacco, boxes of tea, and a fistful of iron nails as long as his forefinger, he said. Of course he was too lazy to trouble himself with the tedious and bitter-cold dog-team journey to the south and decided to send Pingwa and me to Trader's Bay. He reckoned that if they gave us only a few dogs we would travel far too slowly, so he let us take his own big dog team.

Before we left, he cut the labels out of an empty flour sack, a tobacco package, and a tea box. On each one he placed a mark—I for one, II for two, or IIII for four. Finally he made a careful drawing of many iron nails. He folded the paper around the labels, tied them all with a sinew, and ordered me to give it to the trader's Eskimo helper, Yannee, and to no one else.

Raven's family had been using two worn-out caribou parkas underneath the bedding to make it soft. These they grudgingly drew out from the sleeping bench and flung at us. They were huge, and after we struggled into them even Raven's surly wife laughed. She had to roll back the sleeves so she could see our hands, and tie sealskin thongs around our waists so we would not trip on the dangling fringes, but Pingwa and I strutted out of the igloo feeling like two full-grown hunters.

Raven took us roughly by the wrists and told us that if we lost his dogs there was no use in our returning to his camp. He said we would be far better off to stay out on the plains and freeze to death. He took a length of dog line and tied me to the sled and said, "There, now, they can't get away from you. But they'll drag you off if they smell a bear."

As we set out in a rush, the west wind swept his voice away. A pair of orphan boys, we drove south as masters of thirteen powerful dogs. We had expected to run a lot to warm ourselves against the deadly winter cold, but we scarcely took a step throughout the long and freezing journey. The dogs were lean and strong and ran so fast that we did not dare set foot on the snow, for fear of losing them. We clung to the sled, screaming, *"Rahh, rahh, rahh,"* for right, or *"Saoo, saoo, saoo,"* for left, but in truth the dogs seemed to know the trail south by themselves, running to urinate against one rock, and then against another miles away.

So swiftly did we travel that we had to build only two igloos on the way. This was fortunate, because they were miserable childlike snow huts that would never have withstood a blizzard.

We arrived at Black Whale Mountain in the midday. Inside the trader's store we tried hard to behave like grown men, flinging our two sacks of fox pelts on the floor as we had seen the hunters do. I gave Yannee the messages, and when we were finished trading and had our flour, tea, tobacco, cartridges, and nails, the trader gave us each a piece of bright-red candy. He said, "You two little lads had best hurry back to camp before it storms and kills the pair of you. They should have sent a proper dog-team driver."

We went straight out, and started our long cold journey north again. On the second night we picked the poorest place to build our igloo, and struck gravel with the snow knife. Sleeping on snow is warm, but bare winter ground is colder than a dead man's grave for sleeping. Of course we kept our pants and boots on and huddled close together, rolled up in the worn-out bearskin, trying to sleep.

"I wish we had our own iron traps," said Pingwa. "Then we could catch a lot of foxes, and trade them for a rifle and wood to build a sled. Surely the widow will lend us three young dogs. With them we could run away from Tall Clouds. We could set up our own camp, sew a little sealskin tent, and raise our own dog team. That's all we'd need. Then we could find a pair of nice plump wives."

That idea took hold of me so strongly that I sat straight up. "Yes! Yes!" I cried. "When we have wives, let's build our igloos and our tents together and live there side by side, in every season."

My fourteenth summer was like none of those that had gone before. I caught a girl. I mean I ran after her into the hills and did things with her that neither she nor I had ever done before. After that I started to think about my life in a very different way.

Some say they wish to know the future. But I am not one of those. For if I had known what a terrifying thing would occur to me, I might have killed myself to escape the pain. Even now I can scarcely force myself to tell you all that happened in the following year.

It began at the end of winter, when I awoke one morning with a fierce throbbing in my head, and a sickening dizziness. This feeling rolled over me like waves, and suddenly my vision blurred and the igloo walls went spotted gray, then black. People in the camp said that I fell down like a person head-struck with a heavy stone.

A long time later I awoke, and Pingwa had to help me rise. No one else would touch me. I looked around and saw others staring at me with a look of utter horror. At that time I did not know how much they feared me.

If I had had a living father, or even if my mother had been with me, I believe they would have called in an *angokok*, a shaman, and purchased a powerful amulet for me to wear, to fight against such deathlike sleeps. But I had no one—only Pingwa. He could not buy me an amulet, for between us we had nothing anyone would wish to trade. He was sorry for me, though, and told me that if I stood on my head, as often as possible, all such evil would run out of my ears. I tried that, and for a while we both thought it had cured me.

In the middle of the gosling moon Raven ordered us to break winter camp, and we journeyed south again as the winter ice was opening. My head sickness had caused me to grow even thinner, and I had lost all my taste for food. Sometimes my eyes saw things in double images, which some say is to see the real object and also its soul, its *inua*. It frightened me so much that I did not tell the others.

Our whaleboat was held out of Trader's Bay for nine days because of heavy ice that jammed the west cape. Finally we left the boat and walked in overland, arriving in the evening. The trader's ship had already visited and gone, and we would see no other for a year.

I heard the sound of the accordion, and girls laughing, and dancing feet going round and round the trader's warehouse. Our people were tired from our trek across the land but they did not want to miss a moment of that summer's dancing. Not me. I stayed away, for I wished only to crawl under the nearest upturned boat and hide myself from view.

Five nights later, in a crowded tent, it happened again. I mean—my soul flew out of me! I remember nothing of my falling down. I have come to believe that I was possessed by some frightful spirit for almost half that night. Pingwa told me Raven's wife stuck her sewing needle deep into my hands and cheeks to see if I was trying to fool them. He watched me carefully, he said, and he and everyone else could see that I felt no pain at all.

When the blackness went, I lay exhausted, not caring that a ring of adults stood around me, staring. As I struggled to sit up, some women screamed in fear and ran outside. Raven and the hunters, who remained inside, pushed Pingwa forward, forcing him to be the first to touch me, to see if I would claw or bite.

"Are you yourself again?" he asked me in a frightened voice.

"Why?" I asked. "Did something happen?"

"Oh, yes!" he whispered, as he held a tin of water to my lips. "These people here will tell you later. Even the trader came into this tent to see you. He was horrified. I know now that you were—that you were not you. I watched everything

‡

you did. A *torngak* or some other powerful spirit must have leaped inside your body. Some say it was Kukitorngaluasik, the one with long fingernails, because you tried to scratch people." He held his fingers up to me like claws. "Look what it did to me with your nails," he said, showing me his hands. "Poor Shoona! It did the same to you."

He wiped the blood away.

"Oh, it was bad," Pingwa said. "You had white foam around your mouth, and you showed your teeth like this." He snarled. "I saw you bite your tongue. Your eyes rolled up until we could see only the whites. I was like everybody else. *Kapiashukunga!* I was terrified—of you!"

Others started talking, and Pingwa whispered, "You be careful! When your mouth started foaming, that man who thinks he owns us wanted you thrown out of here. He kept yelling at Agiak and me to take you by the arms and feet and drag you outside. I was afraid of him and afraid of you as well. Agiak and I tried to pick you up. You were as stiff as a carving made of stone. Your arms and legs were stuck out straight as gun barrels. You know how strong Agiak is? He tried with all his might to bend your left arm. But he couldn't. I helped him, and together we could not bend it. I'm as strong as you are in wrestling, am I not?" he asked me, as he wiped the sweat away from my face.

"*Ayii,*" I answered him. "Most times, you are stronger."

"Well," he said, blowing out his breath. "Tonight you were many times stronger than Agiak and me together. You were something else—a bear, a wolverine, perhaps. Everyone will tell you what I say is so. You were an animal!"

I got up onto my knees and looked around. I had never seen such fear in people's eyes.

Pingwa said, "I saw strong hunters and their women put their hands over their genitals to protect themselves from you. Imagine—to guard themselves from you!" He leaned closer, whispering. "I will tell you something far more frightening than that. I heard Raven say to his wife that you have become too dangerous to keep around his camp. He plans to chase you out onto the thin ice far beyond us all and see that you never put your foot on solid ground again."

Pingwa's words terrified me so much that I wanted only to run away. But where had I to run to, with no dogs and no sled, and almost every human being I knew afraid of me?

2

After the *torngak* had got into me that second time, life became intolerable. My mother must have been ashamed of me and all that happened, for she kept to the rich man's tent and did not try to see me. I believe that in my fear and loneliness I could not have gone on living if it had not been for Pingwa.

That sullen Raven used to sit and stare at me as though I were some dangerous kind of louse. He would often snatch up a short caribou antler and threaten to hook its horn tips inside my nostrils if I did not instantly obey him. He warned me not to touch him or members of his family or any of their food, and of course he would not let me share the family bed. I had to sleep, always, on a coil of sealskin lines. I was like a starving dog, searching for meat scraps around the edges of his miserable dwelling. He, I knew, was waiting only until the new ice formed. Then would he decide the very day that I should die?

Autumn mornings came and hung above us, misting the tops of tents and the barren hills along the fjord, and the bleary sun cast frightening shadows. We slept restlessly on what we knew would be our last night near Black Whale Mountain until summer came again, and awoke and collapsed our tents before the sun had time to rise. The trader's house stood dark and quiet, as though it were deserted. What could we do but go? The last snow geese winged southward, calling high above our heads as we walked across the lonely tundra and climbed into our boat and set out northward.

Raven sat hunched over the tiller, hurrying because of the thickening shore ice that reached toward us with silver fingers. Our hunters killed eight seals before we reached Tall Clouds, and everyone believed that was a good omen, a sign of plenty for the coming winter.

A pair of *inukshuk*, big stones piled one upon another to imitate the forms of men, pointed toward the entrance to our bay. Almost nothing had been left at our camp except the dogs, now howling with starvation on their rock-bound island. It was that awesome time of year when the moon rises like a wind-burned face and sets the autumn darkness all aglow, and the heather on the tundra shimmers like the guard hairs on a wolf. With goose-wing brushes our women swept away the lightly drifted snow, and we all worked to set up the tents again. We sat shivering inside them, waiting, longing, for the true winter to come to us. We were eager to build real snow-houses that would withstand the wind and cold.

One morning I awoke and listened. I could hear absolutely nothing, no sound of wind or dogs or human beings. I crawled from my sleeping place and looked outside. The whole world was covered with the soft deep whiteness of snow and the sky above was dark with heavy-bellied clouds. I shook Pingwa and he followed me out into the new snow. It was above our knees, and we kicked and rolled in it for pleasure. Summer is too warm sometimes, or wet or windy, with the tents flapping and mosquitoes singing as they search for blood. Autumn, a time when children cough and die, can leave you trembling cold inside the tents. But in winter everything is right for us. The whole land and the frozen sea become our home, our open trail for traveling, and we build houses anywhere we choose. This is our time for hunting, dancing, feasting, and visiting our friends.

That same night a huge blizzard swept down upon us, tearing at every tent, and drove the snow into hard-packed drifts against the hills and wavelike patterns across the plains. The ice formed into small pads upon the sea, as far out as sight could reach, and in the morning they had frozen together strong enough for a dog to walk upon them. We marked this as the true beginning of our winter. Everywhere men were out pacing circles in the hard drifts, starting to cut snow blocks for our igloos.

Six days later I heard hunters shouting and their women screaming with delight when they saw the first two south-coast sleds appear. Even from some distance Pingwa recognized both drivers, young hunters from the south, each with another person sitting behind him on his sled.

"Why would they come so soon?" I asked him.

"I cannot guess," he said. "Traveling on the inland trail must have been torture for them with so little snow."

When the first sled came dragging up to us, I could see it had a woman on it.

"I have never seen her before," Pingwa said.

"I have never seen any woman look like that," I whispered, for she was as strongly built as any man. She had thick shoulders, sloping like a wrestler's, an enormous chest and mighty hips, and legs powerful for running. She made the dog-team driver beside her look like an undernourished child.

"*Ush, ush, ush!*" the young driver on the second sled called, not caring if he upset the man who rode behind him. He lashed out at his dogs and crudely rammed his sled through the rough ice, hating to be left behind.

Only when her driver had the sled in the very center of our camp did the big woman rise and stand before us, staring into all our faces. She pushed her hood back, and I saw that her hair was twisted in the old style, with tight braids looped around her ears. She had tattoo markings of long blue lines on her cheeks and chin, and on her hands, and on all her fingers. Her dark-brown face was dominated by her mighty cheekbones. They were wide, thrust forward, drawing the skin tight across her small nose, narrowing her bright-black eyes, which had smooth-skinned hoods above them to protect her vision from the wind and sun and blowing snow.

Suddenly she laughed at us, and I saw her squared white teeth. Most women's teeth are worn flat from chewing sealskins soft. Not hers, for she had never done such things. I must tell you now that she was not at all like other women.

This giantess came striding past me, heading toward the entrance of Raven's igloo, which was by far the largest, with meat porches, windbreaks, and twisting tunnels. She shook hands with Raven in the white man's style, as though she were the captain of the trader's ship, and also with the camp's three other hunters.

When she was finished, the man behind the second driver stood up and walked toward us. He walked strangely, leaning over to the left. His face was like a mask made out of driftwood, split open in a foolish, almost toothless grin. His cheeks and chin and forehead were dark brown as a gunstock, seamed with endless wrinkles, and his shaggy hair was streaked with gray and appeared to have been hacked off with a moon-shaped woman's knife. He had pale and bleary eyes, set wide apart, with a squint that made you think he could not see beyond his outstretched arms. His nose, which must have been broken long ago, twisted first one way and then the other.

"That's the one, the skinny man, who always travels with her," I heard one woman whispering to another. "She calls him Avo Divio. What kind of foreign name is Avo Divio? He used to look so much younger, that poor worn-out wretch. People on the south coast say that she almost killed him in the bed. They say he wasn't big enough to handle a woman with such enormous thighs, and when she gets excited she crushes him half to death. That's maybe why he walks all crooked."

The other woman held her hand over her mouth to hide

her laughter. *"Opinanee!* No wonder!" she whispered back. "I think she ruined his wrists as well."

I could see that Avo Divio did have curious wrists and hands. They dangled loosely from his parka sleeves, as though they were made from shark gristle without bone.

The big woman looked at him and said three words that none of us could understand, and thrust her way down into the entrance passage of Raven's igloo. I, like all the others from that household, followed her inside, watching as she boldly heaved herself into the place of honor, spreading her massive thighs across the very center of the bed. She sat like that and stared at Raven, silently daring him to challenge her position. Everything about her made me know that she was the boldest and most powerful person I had ever seen.

In the entrance passage I whispered to Pingwa, "Did you ever see such a giant of a woman? I wonder what made her come here. What's her name?"

"Kowlee!" he snorted. "Trousers! They say that she has changed her name five times. She had to because of the life she leads down along the south coast, at that place called Poisoned Ground."

We peered through the entrance and saw her reach into a whaler's trade-cloth bag and boldly offer Raven's wife a handful of her tea. That is not a thing that women do to other women. Only rich hunters, staying in some neighbor's camp, give tea, in return for the hospitality they expect. We share meat generously with our guests and neighbors, because it is given to our hunters by the animals with the understanding that it is sacred. It must be shared. But tea, tobacco, beads, candy, special things like that are beyond necessity. They are gifts that bring pleasure.

Raven's wife knew the big woman was acting like a man, but she was so greedy that she clutched the tea and gave Kowlee a simpering smile.

From that very first day, almost everything Kowlee did fascinated me. She had a curious way of laughing until her shoulders and her belly trembled, and you could imagine that the whole wide bed was going to collapse beneath her weight. She could smile and crinkle up her eyes and make herself well liked by anyone, and that is what she did to me.

I remember her at first the way she used to sit on Raven's sleeping platform, stuffing herself with fresh-killed caribou meat, talking boldly with the men, quickly slicing the red flesh with her moon-shaped ulu, woman's knife, and greedily sucking the grease from her fingers as she stared at the women in the igloo. At that time I believed she had not noticed me at all. So on the third day of her visit, when I came in with an emptied pot, I was surprised to hear her say, "Is he the one?"

"Yes, yes," said Raven. "He's the one you're looking for."

"Has anything strange happened to him since that night I heard about last summer?"

"No, nothing that we could see," Raven's wife said. "Except that he's often ill-tempered. And he's lazy, too. He hates to work."

"But still he does what I tell him," Raven told Kowlee, "or he gets nothing to eat."

Kowlee stared at me as though she wanted to see my very soul, but the expression on her face became almost kindly.

"What name have you?" she asked me in a gentle voice.

"Shoona," I answered her. "My name is Shoona."

"Has anything unusual happened to you since summer?"

"No. I used to have bad head pains and feel everything was going in circles. But now I feel well again. And my tongue is healed," I told her, sticking it out to show her the tooth scars.

She sucked up her tea and wiped her mouth with the back of her hand and sighed. Her sharp eyes did not leave my face.

"Last summer, when you were outside of your body—when someone, something, crawled inside you—what did you feel? Where did that thing take you? What happened? Tell me."

There was silence in the igloo as everyone waited for me to answer her.

"Nothing," I said. "I cannot remember any of it. I was asleep. That's all, asleep."

Slowly Kowlee picked the lean sweet bear meat from her teeth. Narrowing her eyes, she turned and spoke to Raven.

"That boy is either lying or the thing that entered into him—" She paused, and then went on: "That thing was very powerful, and froze his anus and his head. How else could he know it came into him, and bite through his tongue and feel no pain? We do not know if that thing has left him." Spacing out her words, seeming to spit them at Raven and his wife, she said, "I believe this boy is dangerous still. None of you know how to handle such a *torngait*-haunted person. If he is not cured soon, something else will surely burst out here." She turned her head quickly, as if she heard a noise that did not reach our ears. "Spirits rarely leave the bodies they use. They almost always appear again, bringing starvation with them— and sickness, yes, and death. I cannot believe that you would willingly keep such a person in this camp." She paused again.

"If you give him to me," she told them, "I shall remove the dreadful thing that hides inside him. I shall tear it out of him!" Her dark eyes glittered. "After that, if he is still alive, I shall try to turn him into something useful. That is not an easy task. It will take patience and countless seasons of hard work.

"What do you know of such things?" she demanded. "It would be madness for you to keep him here. You have all felt the power of the spirits that struggle to gain control—first of him, and then of *you*."

Even as she spoke I could imagine some loathsome creature writhing inside me, and for the first time since my sickness I felt truly terrified.

Raven stared at me, his eyes in shadow, so that I could not tell his thoughts.

"Maybe what took hold of him has gone away. Stayed near

the trader's house," Raven said. "Such evil things are said to be pale in color and prefer to dwell near white men." He pulled thoughtfully at his lower lip. "This boy said he feels well again. No head pains. Perhaps he's done with falling down. My wife and I," he said, glancing at her slyly, "we need this boy to do the work. And later, when we grow old, we will need him even more. Our sons are away," he said, meaning that they were dead, and fearing to use their names.

There was a long pause, with no sound but people breathing and the crooked man wheezing slowly in his throat. Kowlee whispered something to the young driver who had brought her to our camp. He went out quickly and returned carrying an old sealskin rifle scabbard, decorated with bold red ribbon from the trade store, and a well-worn canvas sack.

The big woman grandly untied the woolen ribbons and slowly drew the snub-nosed rifle from its case. It was a 44.40 Winchester, oiled to look well, but it was not new. This kind of rifle was believed by most of our hunters to be strong and straight shooting, its blunt lead bullets best suited for the killing of all kinds of heavy animals. Kowlee chuckled as she opened up the canvas sack and poured a cascade of bright brass cartridges onto the bed—more than two men have fingers and toes. That made Raven catch his breath.

"Last moon," Kowlee said, "when I arrived at Tugjak's camp, his wife was almost dead. He offered me this rifle and these cartridges if I would bring her dear life back to him. Of course I tried my best," said Kowlee, "and she did live for a little while. I tried everything to force the deadly weasel out of her. But they had waited far too late to call me. Avo Divio can tell you. He watched her soul run out of her mouth like heavy oil. But Tugjak gave me this rifle anyway, knowing that though his poor wife died I had done everything I could to try to save her."

She sighed and handed Raven the rifle as she reached out for some rich red ribs of seal meat.

Raven took the rifle from her and held it lovingly in his

hands. He worked the well-worn lever action, and sighted it above my head. He squeezed the trigger, and the rifle gave an oily click.

"*Neepipalo!* Sounds good!" he said admiringly. "I have heard that Tugjak had good fortune with this rifle."

"And so will you," Kowlee assured him.

"You offer me this rifle in trade for that boy, so that you may cure him of his sickness? Drive the wild things out of him?"

"No," Kowlee said. "I give you this rifle and the ammunition so that I will own that boy forever! He must be mine alone before I try to cure him. If I have the power to cure him, only then shall I try to teach him. If he cannot learn from me, then I shall rid myself of him."

She gave me a hungry look that might have been taken for a smile. "If this boy stays with you, I believe he will become truly dangerous!"

Raven glanced at his wife. I saw her make a crude gesture that could only mean he should get rid of me. He opened the lever of the rifle and closed it again, listening carefully as it locked in place. Once more he pressed the trigger, and heard its solid click. Then he stepped outside the igloo, and we waited until we heard the rifle fire a single hollow blast.

He returned and said, "This rifle and all these cartridges are mine. The boy belongs to you."

He leered at the other hunters in the camp, holding up the rifle, and said, "Imagine getting something good like this for nothing." And then he slipped a cartridge in its breech and aimed its muzzle straight at me.

"Be careful where you point that piece of iron," said Kowlee, in a voice as harsh as any man's.

Raven quickly flipped the cartridge out and heaved himself up onto the sleeping platform. He gathered all the bullets into a glittering heap between his outstretched legs, examining each round lead point with care.

"I cannot travel with this boy the way he is. We two must cleanse him first," Kowlee said, nodding toward the crooked man. "This boy will cause you no more trouble, now that he is mine."

No one dared to answer her, but Pingwa looked at me as though he was about to cry.

Kowlee grunted, lay back comfortably in the center of the bed, and said with a smile, "Tomorrow we shall build a special house for him. Shooonaah," she murmured, drawing out the sound. "What a silly name. Shooonaaah! You are mine! Bring me that slop pot quickly. Do you understand me? Bring it here to me!"

I was not used to hearing a woman speak in such a forceful way, but I jumped up and took the pot to her.

"That's a good boy, Shoona," she said, lying back once more, forming a small mountain beneath a covering of winter sleeping skins. It was not long before we heard her breathing heavily in sleep.

Huddling down on my coil of sealskin lines, I pulled up my hood and drew my arms out of my sleeves and hugged them to my body, for the night was cold. I heard the young hunter, Akbil, whispering in bed to his smooth-faced wife, wondering what the big woman would do to me, and I fell asleep imagining all sorts of awful things.

In the morning I stood shivering with the others outside our igloo, watching Kowlee take up a long thin *tauk* stick for measuring, and walk thoughtfully across the hard-packed drifts of snow. She moved east at first, head down, as though she searched for something. Not finding it, she turned around and walked cautiously westward, probing the depth of snow. The crooked man shuffled along behind her carelessly, his loose wrists dangling.

Suddenly the big woman stopped and fell on her knees, listening, holding back her parka hood, her ear cocked as though she heard a noise beneath the snow. She said something to the crooked man in words I could not understand, rose heavily from the snow, and drew a small circle around her with the wand.

The crooked man pulled out an old-fashioned snow knife shaped from whalebone, and smiled back at all of us as he licked both sides of the long thin blade to make the slicing surfaces icy slick. Carefully he cut each block, precisely following her instructions.

Kowlee was painstaking about every detail of the little house. Every hard snow block had to be fitted tightly into place, and she herself neatly chinked each one of them with finely powdered snow. The crooked man remained crouching inside until he had wedged the last key block in place. Then his snow knife came stabbing through the igloo wall as he neatly cut an exit passage. Thrusting this block away, he crawled outside.

The little house was strong enough to bear Kowlee's weight when she crawled on top to do the final chinking.

"Now everything is ready except you, dear Shoona," she said, and leered at me. "But first you must come back into Raven's igloo."

She took me gently by the hand and led me down through the passage. She waved her other hand disdainfully at all of Raven's family, meaning none of them could come inside their igloo until she gave them her permission.

She sat on the bed and good-naturedly drew me up beside her.

"There, that's better," she announced, and bent over the meat pot. "I'll find you a big one," she said, and drew out a luscious piece of caribou meat, far larger than any I would have dared to take myself.

"Eat this," she whispered, with her lips drawn back, her eyes glittering beneath their tight-drawn hoods. "Always listen carefully when I talk to you. Look straight at me, Shoona!

If you stare always at my eyes and listen, I will teach you many ancient things, thoughts and deeds that people in this miserable household and in this whole north coast have never once imagined. If you obey me, you will become a master, and not be a slave to others as you are now. Do you understand me, little Shooonaa?" she said, dragging out the sound of my name, pulling it out of my body.

I nodded, and began tearing the rich caribou meat straight from the bone, stuffing it into my mouth before she or someone else could snatch it from me.

"I want you to rise up, to live outside yourself. I want you to see with your own eyes what it was that robbed you of your body. I am going to wall you into that small igloo. Freeze its entrance block in place. You are going to stay there, Shooonaa, for as long as need be. Oh, I will stay here near you, little Shoona. I will feast for you while you are fasting," she said. "After this you must eat nothing. Do not fear. Many starving people have lived for one whole moon and half another without a bite of food. You may scrape snow from the inner walls and suck it into water. Remember, you need only water! All humans and animals die too quickly without water.

"I lived on water once myself. Oh, it was years ago," she said, and laughed. "I saw all sorts of things. You, too, will see your own tormentors if you are truly what I think you are. Some days I may come and speak with you. But mostly you will be alone, searching, searching for an entrance to the other world."

She rose from the sleeping platform, picked up a frozen dog skin from the igloo floor, and tossed it at me. I clutched it under one arm, and chewed and gulped and swallowed my last mouthful of food as she led me out the entrance passage.

The people in our camp stood in a half circle around the little igloo and watched curiously as Kowlee said, "Down on your knees, boy. Crawl inside."

The last person I saw was the crooked man. He bent with

both hands on his knees and stared at me. When he saw me look at him, he blinked and grinned, and whispered hoarsely, "I hope it isn't too cold in there for you. I hope you stay alive to see this lovely world again."

I hesitated, thinking I might jump up and try to run away from all of them, but Kowlee put her foot against my rump and shoved me through the narrow entrance, stuffing the dog skin inside after me. I watched as the crooked man fitted the snow door carefully into place.

I was horrified to find the inside of my igloo was so small that I could not stand fully upright or lie out straight. I heard children laughing, and the sound of Kowlee sucking up water from a pot and spitting it against the edges of the snow door, so it would freeze and lock me in the igloo.

3

During the late November moon our winter comes on fully. The sun grows weak and bleary and moves no higher than the horizon, and our days are short. Even at midday the lines between the snow blocks of my prison glowed only faintly. At first I heard Raven's children playing and dogs howling in the distance, but soon the night cold sent them running to their igloos, and I could not hear a sound.

It is not our custom to live in a house or sleep at night without a constant light of some kind, but I was left in the darkness, terrified and alone. I closed my eyes, wrapped the evil-smelling dog skin around myself, and cried until I slept, fearing I would freeze to death before dawn came again.

When the first pale light of morning turned the walls gray, I woke and heard the squealing of snow as someone crept toward my igloo. I heard heavy breathing just outside, and then a high, inhuman voice called out to me: "Shoonaaa! Dear little Shoona! I will snatch your very name out of your bones."

A short knife jabbed into the roof, and I could see the stare of Kowlee's glittering eyes.

"It's freezing cold this morning, but I see that you are still alive, lying there in your little grave." She giggled like a girl. "You stay there. Hear me, Shoona? Stay and listen. Hear the voices crying to you in the wind."

I did not even try to answer her.

"You're feeling angry with me, are you, Shoona? Well, that, too, will pass." She lowered her heavy eyelids. "You will be hungry for some days to come. Then that ache in your belly will go away. Do not worry about dying. Many young men before you have gone without food in order to seek visions. Do not worry about hunger. I shall eat for you," she said, and belched, and laughed at me, and sucked her big square teeth. "If you think of me eating for you, little Shoona, how can you die from hunger? But be careful of the cold, and keep that dog skin wrapped around you tight. I want you alive!"

She paused. "Try to remember when you fell down and something entered into you. You have seven body holes. Which one did that thing crawl through? Try to remember how it looked and felt and if it spoke to you. Do not waste your time thinking only of your hunger. Think wisely. Concentrate on the long-legged caribou that live in the giant white eggs beneath the earth. Think also of those half-human creatures that swim in the sea and those that flutter through the sky at night. Call out to all of them, and surely one at least will answer you. Oh, yes, more than one will answer. All you have to do is treasure up your hunger, and wait, and think, and all those creatures large and small will come to you!"

She rammed a piece of snow tight into the hole, and I could hear her breathing heavily in the cold as she turned and trudged away across snow. I tried to imagine the warmth of Raven's igloo, the food she was going to eat for me. My stomach puckered up with hunger and my mouth filled with the bitter juices of desire.

The first three days of my confinement were made tolerable by a caribou thighbone that I had hidden in my parka hood.

First I licked and gnawed every morsel of flesh from it. Then I took a whole day to wear a long crack in the bone with my thumbnail, and when it finally split I sucked out the soft marrow, savoring it, making the rich taste last till darkness came. That helped, but not enough. Besides, I worried because eating marrow out of bones is known to cause misfortune. In the freezing light of morning, the pangs of hunger gripped me once again.

On the fifth night I awoke suddenly and felt some strange thing happening to me, as if claws had pierced my clothes and were raking at my flesh. As I screamed out and lunged away in terror, I heard a high thin hawklike scream that set every dog in our camp howling.

I listened carefully, but I could hear no footsteps moving away. The dogs stopped howling and everything returned to deadly silence, but I do not think I slept again that night.

When morning came and faintly lit my igloo, I hauled up my parka and examined my body. I had four long red lines along my ribs, as though some creature had reached through the igloo wall and clawed at my side.

The camp sounds seemed far away and muffled, but I heard children calling *"Apoutialook."* Their words told me that heavy snow had fallen in the night, soft new snow that would silence human footsteps.

I examined the igloo carefully until I found four holes, no larger than a wolf's tooth, pierced through the wall. I looked at my long red wounds again and wondered.

Those first days of my confinement I remember almost with pleasure, for my true hunger had not yet begun and I scarcely knew the meaning of real fear.

I woke one night and heard the dogs moaning in a way that meant they smelled a white bear. The camp was on the shore of the frozen sea, exactly where hungry bears would wander, and I knew such a one could easily smell me out and collapse my igloo with a single blow. I imagined that I heard the soft pad of its feet, and I held my breath in horror. Then I heard three words spoken to me outside the snow walls—strange words, secret perhaps, that made no sense at all. Had a real bear come to me? The dogs could smell his musky odor. Had he spoken? I would never know the answer.

I lost all track of days and nights, for during storms my prison scarcely changed from light to dark. The walls had become sheathed inside with the ice caused by my breathing, and at times, when it was a little less cold, a gray fog clung to the ceiling just above my head. At other times I screamed and cried out until my throat was raw, because that seemed to break my loneliness and helped me to forget my hunger. Raven, for one, got tired of listening to me. He came over from the camp and grunted like an animal. *"Unalook,"* he shouted as he drove his harpoon through the wall, once, twice, thrice. I watched its sharp point in terror, and after that I stopped my bellowing, watching silent but sharp-eyed as a fox caught in a trap.

With the split bone of the caribou I scraped snow from the walls to ease my throat. I dug small pits when I needed to relieve myself, but that happens only rarely to one who is eating nothing. Often my stomach roared and rumbled like a spirit's voice that tried to speak inside me. To keep myself alert I tried to understand its words, but all it said was "Food, food, food!" I could feel my bones grow weak. I could feel myself shriveling up inside, and thought that I was dying.

One night I heard an accordion playing faintly and someone drumming in the camp, and I knew that they were dancing. I even heard their singing. It sounded like the soft hum of mosquitoes, far away in some distant land of summer, and the rhythm seemed to help me. I felt light-headed, and I clapped my hands to the beating of the drum. Soon I started singing, having a celebration of my own, creating clever songs that I had never heard or sung before. My body felt as though it had no weight, and I could fly. I flapped my filthy rags of clothing, and it seemed to me that I became a bird with hollow bones. I rose and soared about my house on clumsy leather wings. I kept on laughing, singing.

The drumbeats moved inside me and echoed like my thumping heart, and the igloo seemed to flare with all the colors of the setting sun. My hunger left me and my body filled with warmth, and for a while I knew a perfect ecstasy. That memory will remain with me until the last breath of my life.

When the drumming stopped I seemed to fall down hard on my icy igloo floor, and the cold and hunger struck again, doubling me over with frightful cramps. But even as I knelt shivering beneath my filthy dog skin, I knew that the soaring and the secret singing had been all mine. Although I could not remember the words or how they went, I knew that they belonged to me alone. It was as though I had been carried upward into some distant place, into a life far beyond anything I could ever have imagined.

Sometime later, days perhaps, I heard strange dogs and the voices of drivers arriving in the camp, then nothing more. I slept, and woke to hear the drum resounding and the muffled thump of dancing feet. With the split bone I drove a small hole in the roof of my snowhouse and lay in such a way that I could see one bright star glowing. The pounding rhythm seemed to enter into me and drive away all thoughts of hunger.

After a while I sensed that I was growing smaller, until finally I could see a tiny image of myself run up the wall and thrust its thumb-sized head out through the star hole. I could hear the rhythm of the drum more clearly and see the northern lights reaching out across the sea and probing downward to the plain with ghostly fingers. It felt good to draw the sharp, clean air into my lungs again, to stare up at stars that shone like ice chips from a giant's axe, and I laughed to see my small self clinging to the roof of the igloo. But when morning came I crawled down again and lay helpless, like a hibernating animal lost in winter sleep.

As I grew weaker, what could I do but rest, and toss, and turn, and dream? To eat snow, even to urinate, had become painful tasks for me, and sometimes the igloo went spinning around like the hollow wing bones whirled in play by children.

One night I awoke feeling light as air, and lay peering through my roof hole at the moon, now nearly full. I seemed to be suspended in some middle world, not feeling hunger or pain or pleasure.

"Shooonaaa! You dog turd!" Kowlee screamed, and she poured the contents from the house pot down upon me. "Think. Listen for the voices. Forget the moon. Learn first of simpler things."

She packed my observation hole with snow and walked away. Her cruelty had brought me to my senses, and my belly throbbed with the awful gnawing hunger. I pulled the dog skin over my head and tried to lose my thoughts.

When I awoke I heard strange gurgling noises beneath my bed. They turned into gentle bumpings, which slowly grew in strength until they set my igloo heaving like a storm-tossed boat. They frightened me, but slowly they made me understand that I was part of the earth and sky and sea, that I myself was moving with the measured rhythm of the tides, the turning of the stars.

That night I discovered a deep hole beside my head. It was just big enough for me to squeeze through. Imagine my amazement when I discovered that an underwater passage, a narrow river, ran beneath my igloo. It had been built on top of ice, river ice, hidden beneath the snow.

I slipped down through this hole, head first, and found the water very shallow. I held my breath, then slowly I began to change. I found that I could breathe, suck air out of the water! I waited near the hole until my fear of drowning left me.

There was scarcely room at first for me to swim beneath the ice. I started making clumsy stroking motions, trying to imitate a seal. I felt my vision extending until I could see for a great distance, even through the dark-green waters, and all my other senses sharpened, too.

The gravel bed that was the river's floor sloped northward under the ice. Stroking with my arms, I moved toward the river's mouth among long ropes of seaweed that wavered in the shadows, trembling with joy, blowing out great streams of bubbles, thrilled that I had learned to live beneath the sea.

A creature swimming toward me from the glimmering distance proved to be a seal, and hunger made me draw my sharp bone dagger and strike at him. He struggled only for a moment, then was dead. Pulling his body close behind me, I swam back toward my igloo. As the river narrowed, I could see the round hole in my ice floor glowing like a full moon.

I crawled into my house again, hauled up the fat seal, and sat down to enjoy my feast. I scarcely wondered why I was neither wet nor cold, but stuffed myself with the delicious meat, rolled myself in the dog skin, and fell into a dreamless sleep.

"Shoonaaa! You louse's rectum!" Kowlee screamed at me, and stabbed me with her stick. "Shoona! You've been eating. I can see the grease around your mouth. You will learn nothing that way. You will spoil your visions, blur your dreams."

"Wrong! You are wrong!" I shook my fists at her. "I have learned so much that I am frightened."

"Is that so, little Shoona? Don't you dare lie to me. Have you at last seen visions?"

"I saw myself," I said. "I saw myself climbing up this igloo wall."

"That is not a bad beginning," said Kowlee. "But is that the only thing that you have seen?"

"Oh, no," I told her, feeling proud and boastful. "I saw a hole appear in this floor right beneath me. You are now standing above a shallow river that leads down to the sea."

"I did not know that," said Kowlee. "Go on. Say more."

"The best way to swim is to move your body muscles and work your hands straight downward like seal flippers."

"So," she said. "Perhaps you are going to be a swimmer. That is unusual. Most shamans choose to fly or to climb down into stone cracks that lead to the caves beneath the earth. Only a few are swimmers. Tell me, how did you breathe down there?"

In a sudden rage, I shouted at her, "I won't tell you that unless you let me out of here!"

She gave me a sharp poke with her stick.

"Even that one dream feast of yours will ease your hunger and spoil your visions for a night or two. I hate willful stupid children," she muttered as she walked away.

One night I felt my head begin to whirl again with hunger. My empty stomach clutched itself in cramps. I flung back my dog skin and stared at the floor, expecting it to open, but nothing happened.

I saw a strange fire slowly kindle at my feet, and out of its flames a small round-headed bird appeared. It hopped onto the edge of my torn boot sole, ruffled up its feathers, and stared at me like an owl. Yet many of its parts were human, and as I watched, it grew, until it almost filled the icy dome. I could feel its increased weight. Its sharp claws pierced my boot. Its curved beak hung above my eyes. Its breath was foul.

Suddenly it whirled about, thrashing its wings against the roof. Between its legs I could see the face of a human, eyes bulging, lips puckered, and hear a voice speaking to me in a language I had never heard before.

The bird turned again, choking, and coughed up five owl pellets, which fell writhing on my dog skin and turned into living things, half animal, half human. I clung against the wall in horror while they became as large as crows, and crawled or hopped or flew about the igloo. Vile creatures, part bird, part fish, part human.

At dawn they went away and left me sweating in the cold. I began to scream for Kowlee, planning to tell her what I had seen only when she had given me food to eat, for now I knew that my feast of seal meat had been a dream.

"I have seen something!" I yelled. *"Arnakpuk!* Giant Woman! Something came to me!"

Perhaps Kowlee did not hear me, for the wind was blowing off the land and may have carried all my pleadings out to sea.

That night I woke when I felt a sharp jab from Kowlee's stick, and saw that she had again made a small hole in the roof for talking.

"Raven's children told me they heard something screaming in this house. Was that you, little Shooonaaa?"

"Sometimes it was me," I told her, "and sometimes it was others. Many others."

"Who were the others?" she snapped, and drove her stick down hard between my legs.

"You give me meat and I will tell you," I said, cupping my hands over my groin.

She stuck me sharply with her stick again.

"This place was full of birds last night," I shouted. "Birds with human faces hanging down between their legs."

After I had told her that I started crying. I could not help myself.

"Here," she said, and poked the short rib bone of a bear down through the hole, but tricked me by drawing it back and then waiting until I lunged at it again, once, twice, three times.

"You can't have this," she said, "until you tell me all you can remember."

When I had done so she let me have the bone. And she coughed and said, "Well, now, little Shoona, that's encouraging to hear. Do not forget the look of all those creatures you have seen. But think of wolves," she whispered. "Think of caribou and foxes. I find it strange that you have seen birds of the air and beasts of the sea, yet nothing from the land. And now give me back my bone," she commanded, and when I did not immediately obey, she hissed at me, "I wouldn't want to spoil your hunger."

So thoroughly was I in her power that I thrust the precious bone back up through the speaking hole.

Terrible dreams tormented me, and the next night, when I heard her footsteps squeaking in the cold, I howled like a wolf and yapped like a fox that's hot to find a mate.

"Shoona, have you been traveling?" Kowlee asked.

"Yes. Running free with all of them," I lied, and squatted with my teeth bared like an animal, hoping she would see me and believe me. I had lost all feeling for the truth.

"Speak to me," she ordered.

I let out a howl, half wolf, half human, that ended with the word *Kadang!*

"That is not an *Inuit* word," she said.

"It is a word that I heard when I went traveling beneath the sea." In truth I could not remember how the word had come to me.

"Kadang!" she whispered.

I said the word to her again: *"Kadang!"*

Instantly I saw the iron blade of a snow knife pierce the side of my house and start crudely hacking in a circle. She started shouting for the crooked man—"Avo Divio!"—and kicked in the new door hole she had made. I heard her grunt as she got down onto her hands and knees.

One huge mitt reached inside my miserable snow hut and caught hold of the point of my parka hood. I seemed to fly out through the exit, and blinked in the brightness of the starlight, gasping as the night air seared my lungs.

"Get on your feet and walk! Oh, Shooonaa, you smell awful." She held me out at arm's length. "Stop stumbling and walk, you filthy boy—but not too close to me!"

But I could not move or even stand upright unless she

helped me. When I tried to walk, my legs bent like seaweed, and even when she held me, I hunched over like an old, old man.

"Kadang? Kadang?" she said twice, slowly. "That is not a human word. You must have gotten that word from somewhere far beyond this place. Did you hear that word beneath the sea?"

Violently she shook me by the parka hood and cried out, "Stupid little Shoona! Do you expect me to stand out here watching the moonlight twist my shadow into dangerous forms because you've gone and lost the human way to walk and talk? Come with me, sea beast! I will lead you back to Raven's igloo and show you human comforts beyond your wildest dreams."

When we reached the entrance passage to the big igloo, she flung me down on all fours, snatched up a dog harness, and drew it tight around my neck and shoulders. Bending low to enter, she whispered to me, "Howl! Roll up your eyes and howl like something from the other world."

I obeyed her instantly, baying until my voice was hoarse.

"Again," she snorted. "Again! Again!" She kicked me, driving me forward. My voice was muffled and distorted in the curving entrance passage. I tried to bite a frozen seal's head, but she thrust her staff at me and forced me inside, groveling on my hands and knees and snarling fiercely.

"Be careful of him," she shouted at those in the igloo. "He is still dangerous. He may bite."

The children leaped up onto the wide sleeping platform, and the women, who had been sitting with their legs straight out, quickly drew their feet up under them.

"Kadang!" I growled. *"Kadang!"*

"Hear it? Hear it? That is a secret word," she told them. "A word he was given when he swam beneath the ice."

"Kaukpunga peeumavungawillanak tuktuvinik. I am hungry for caribou meat," I howled at Raven's wife.

In her fear of me she took her meat pot from above the

lamp and spilled half its steaming contents on the ice-gray igloo floor. I lunged at it, grabbing up pieces of meat and stuffing them into my mouth.

"*Agaiiwilluwak!* No! Never!" Kowlee screamed. "He is not an animal for you to feed like that. He is a human being, who now knows more than all of you. He has traveled into unknown places where the seals are hiding.

"Here, come here, dear Shoona," she called to me softly. "Stop biting. Get up off the floor, dear boy. Seat yourself here in the center of this bed by me."

My legs were so weak that I could not have risen if she had not taken me by my parka hood and jerked me to my feet. And certainly I would never have dared seat myself in such an honored position if she had not dragged me there.

I found myself next to the beautiful young wife of Akbil, who wrinkled up her nose because of the horrible smell that clung to me.

"Why are you doing that with your nose, you stupid heavy-chested child?" Kowlee demanded. "All of you here," she warned, "get used to the smell of this marvelous boy. He has become a swimmer. Do you hear me? A spirit wrestler from beneath the ice. He has been given a secret word. Think of that, you miserable sacks of bones. You know nothing! You understand nothing! I tell you to stare in wonder at this magic boy!"

I tried to sit up straight beside her and look as important as she said I had become.

"You, Red Cheeks," Kowlee called out to Akbil's wife. "Strip off this boy's garments. Wet a piece of trade cloth and wipe him clean all over. Then take off all your clothes and lie beside him in this bed and warm his front side, do you hear me? I will warm his back side. This marvelous boy has suffered as I was once made to suffer for you ordinary mortals. You have seen him walled up in that hut for one whole moon. Perhaps he has found a trail to travel on that leads between this land of Tall Clouds and that frightening world of spirits. He has searched and suffered so that he can help poor folk like you find food to let you live. He will be a shaman, a spirit wrestler, a sickness fighter, and if you pay him, he will not fear to go on dangerous journeys for you."

Kowlee helped the girl pull off my sealskin clothing, my grease-stiff parka, my tattered boots and sealskin pants.

"Throw those filthy rags of his outside," said Kowlee. "I know the sewing women in this household will not sleep tonight, but sit up making new clothes for this wondrous boy. Is that not true?"

"No," said the older women. "It is true."

I had never in my life heard talk like this. I could not believe my ears when Kowlee said, "Shoona, if you get thirsty in the night, she will suckle you. You hear me? She's yours alone while you are in this house. Remember that. You do with her whatever pleases you."

4

I woke with a start when Kowlee rubbed her nose against my ear and hugged me. I saw her dark eyes glittering as she stared defiantly at Raven and Akbil, and at their two women. All of them were silent, and so was I, for I found myself still clinging passionately to Akbil's naked wife. Both hunters rose from the bed to go outside, and I saw that each of them wore half a dozen bulky new amulets, which Kowlee and Avo Divio must have prepared for them while I was starving in the little snowhouse.

I came to observe that despite the amulets Raven and his wife were worried and sullen. Kowlee and Avo Divio had sat in his igloo and stuffed themselves for more than thirty days and nights, devouring between them at least half the meat in the winter caches. Pingwa told me that while I was away Raven and his wife had seemed like Kowlee's slaves—all for one worn-out rifle and a little sack of cartridges. That's the way it was with Kowlee. She always made the head man whose camp she visited feel that he was gaining everything. Only at the moment of her departure did he realize how much he had lost to her.

I had lived for only fifteen winters. It would be impossible for me to describe my feelings at the immense changes that had taken place. I had been like a starving dog, then suddenly I found myself stuffed full of food, lolling comfortably between two plump smooth-skinned women in the very center of the wide bed, occupying the sleeping space of the man who had bought me for his slave.

I clung to the warmth of Akbil's wife, and foolishly imagined that from now on my life would be one of endless pleasure. I had started to like Kowlee as soon as she released me from my filthy prison, and I wanted to believe her every word about my future. I welcomed her huge nakedness as she clung to my back like a mating whale, and rested comfortably in the warmth of those two very different women until well past midday. Then, like Kowlee and Avo Divio, I sat up and stuffed myself with food. In this way we three rested and ate and rested, until I felt strong again. Only then did Kowlee announce our departure.

I left Raven's household wearing new caribou-skin clothing and carrying a warm new sleeping robe. Everything fitted perfectly: parka, pants, mitts, and soft black sealskin boots, all carefully cut especially for me, and with the finest sinew sewing.

Raven gladly lent us two strong young drivers from his camp, his best sled, eleven of their strongest dogs, and half of all the meat that he had left—anything to get us out of his camp. When we finally did depart, the people of Tall Clouds stood there open-mouthed, staring at us, and not a soul but Pingwa waved good-bye.

When I got off to run and ease the load and help the drivers push the heavy sled, Kowlee grabbed my arm and pulled me back.

"Do only the things that Avo Divio does," she said.

He turned and winked at me, and I smiled at him. The thing I liked best about Avo Divio was his wide quick grin.

When he smiled at me, he would stick his pink tongue out, perhaps trying to hide the fact that five front teeth were missing.

"Don't strain yourself," the big woman said to me. "These two simple hunters' sons have been ordered to take us anywhere we wish to go. As long as we travel, they are our servants."

She put her arms around my waist and licked my cheek, and her wide tongue left a thin coat of ice there.

When I wiped my face, she laughed and said, "I really like you, Shoona! I want you to tell me about each of the strange creatures you saw when you went swimming. Speak quietly. Those two have pushed back their hoods hoping to catch your words. Try to remember all the unfamiliar things you heard. *Kadang*—that word has a strange sound! Think," she whispered. "I believe it may be a word you found beneath the sea. Was it a part of any song you heard down there?"

I did not answer her. I did not want to think about my time in the filthy igloo, or my dreadful visions.

After three long days of travel through rough ice and fog, we arrived at a camp built on a long arm of rock called Pointing Finger. Kowlee and I were invited with Avo Divio to move into the big, sparkling-clean igloo of a hunter named Tugait, which means Tusks. He was a tall, impressive-looking man, with two strong sons and one married daughter. He and his wife, Malya, had old-fashioned ways that I had never seen before, and it was easy to tell that they were very fond of Kowlee. They called her Kowleekudluapik, which is to say "Dear Little Trousers."

Perhaps their kindness caused her to act very differently inside their igloo. All the overbearing rudeness she had imposed on the people at Tall Clouds flew out of her. She laughed easily and was polite and kind to everyone in that house and to me as well. We stayed there for seven nights, and everybody treated me warmly, like a welcomed guest—I had a favored position in the bed and was fed abundantly. I felt sorry when the time came to move on again.

We left at midday, still using Raven's dogs and drivers, and arrived by nightfall at Trader's Bay. Our team heard the dogs from that camp howling, and raced wildly down the frozen fjord. As the five of us hurried to build our igloo in the frozen shadow of Black Whale Mountain, we could see a bright light shining from the trader's small north window.

In the morning Kowlee hugged me to her in the wide bed, then whispered, "Get up and come with me. We two are going to visit the trader."

Laughing at Avo Divio and Raven's two drivers, she said, "Look at me, a poor woman without a husband." She lifted me naked and kicking into the freezing air and added, "But I hope to have heavy treasures for this fine boy and me to carry back to you."

This second trader was a man whom the hunters and their wives called Round Eyes, because his pale-blue eyes looked always as though he was surprised. He was a lean and wiry man with a face as weathered as a piece of gray driftwood, and he had short brown hair on his head, raggedly cut by Yannee. Two deep lines ran like knife cuts from the edges of his nose and disappeared beneath his jutting chin.

He and Yannee had built a wooden wall, with a door in it, that cut the building in two, and he slept in one half and traded in the other. And they had made a wall of snow blocks all around the outside to keep the wind from sneaking in. In his stove, he burned black stones that came in rough brown bags, and pale smoke could be seen at all times streaming from the thin iron chimney. His house was so hot, some said, that it was enough to make a person sick.

I followed Kowlee as she tried to peek through the frosted windows, one after another, but the whole house seemed deserted. She listened. No one was in the trading store. Then she coughed violently and kicked at the walls, to let the trader know she had arrived.

"I hear him now. He's getting out of bed," she said, and hurried around to the door, which suddenly jerked open. The hot air turned to steam as it rushed out, half concealing Round Eyes from us, but I could see that he wore long gray woolen underwear.

"*Watchioupik!*" he called, meaning a little later, and ducked back inside. When he opened the door again he had pulled on thick pants and a caribou parka.

He shook hands with Kowlee and with me, then shivered, slammed the door behind us, and shoved his hands deep inside his trousers pockets.

"*Ekeerahlook!* Very cold!" he said in Eskimo, and made a little bow to Kowlee. "You arrive, dear trouser woman. Good to see you. This little lad is growing," he went on. "Has he had any more of those crazy fits of his? How is it that you brought him here?"

The trader spoke Eskimo well, but he said everything in a mixed-up, unfamiliar way that I found hard to follow.

"He has no father," Kowlee answered, "and his mother lives—with someone else. I'm going to take care of him, keep him as a son. Who knows? He might become a husband. Isn't that so, little Shoona?" she said to me, and laughed uproariously.

The trader chuckled and asked her if she had anything to trade.

"No fox skins, no sealskin boots, no fur mitts. I never sew," said Kowlee. "But I have ideas to trade, for whatever they are worth to you."

"*Isumaalook?*" he asked. "What big ideas have you today?"

"What ideas do you need?" she asked him.

"People here say you are wise," he said, and tapped his finger to his head. "Oh, yes. I do have a problem." He laughed. "It's sitting right down there beneath this shelf."

He bent, and grunted at the weight he heaved onto the counter. It was a square yellow wooden box, nailed shut, with black markings on it and four metal straps, two going this way and two going that.

"What's inside?" Kowlee asked him.

"*Imialook,*" he answered, using our word for strong drink. "Whisky from my own dear homeland."

"What's wrong with it?" she asked.

"Wrong? Nothing." He coughed, and rolled himself a cigarette. "Only one thing bad. That whisky does not belong to me. I drank up all of mine last autumn. The whisky in that box belongs to my company. It was supposed to go on the ship across the straits to Sugluk, but the purser made a bad mistake and left it here with me. And that the company knows. The Sugluk trader is mad as hell because it did not reach him."

"But why not drink it, if you wish?" Kowlee demanded.

"I cannot afford it," the trader told her. "The company would take seventy-six dollars from my annual pay if they found out that I drank it."

Kowlee stood staring at the square wooden box.

"Perhaps I know a way," she said. "Dear Shoona, you bring that box along with us."

"Aw, no. He's too small to handle it. He might break the bottles." The trader heaved the box carefully onto his shoulder. "What do you have in mind, witch woman?"

Kowlee opened the door to his house and made her way into a little room so hot you wanted to strip off your parka and your pants.

There was a large tin bathtub painted green, the first I had ever seen, and the trader had a lot of his clothes stored in it. Kowlee flung all of them out, scattering them across the floor, and then she pulled off her own long-tailed parka.

"What are you going to do?" he asked her. "Have a swim?"

Ignoring him, Kowlee looked around until she found a round plug, which she stuck firmly in the outlet hole. With her finger she picked at a paper glued to the inside of the tub, and said, "No one has ever had a swim in this."

She took the box from Round Eyes, raised it up in her powerful arms, and smashed it down into the green tin tub.

"Jesus, woman! Stop that! You'll break up all those whisky bottles!"

The trader grabbed her by the arm, but she was strong and shook him off. Again she raised the box, laughing as she saw the pale-brown liquor flooding out and splashing into the tub, and again she hurled it down.

"Woman, have you gone crazy?" the trader yelled at her. "Spilling all that whisky! Just listen to the broken glass. The bloody tub's half full."

Cautiously she raised the sodden case, and shook it. "How many bottles are in there?" she asked.

"*Kolitlomukolo*. Twelve." The trader's face turned pale and crumpled as though he was about to weep. "Every one of them smashed to bits."

"I believe you're right," said Kowlee. "And all the whisky's lying right there in the tub. I can scarcely stand the smell of it." She cringed and held her nose.

She sent me to the porch for a pail, stretched one of his undershirts over the top, and then with his water dipper started bailing up the whisky and straining it into the pail. You could see bits of glass caught in the wool, gleaming like chips of ice.

Round Eyes ran and got a cup and held it underneath his undershirt until it filled with whisky. He closed his eyes and took a long drink, gasped with pleasure, and said, "That's a queer way to get a drink of whisky. Why didn't we just open up the case?"

"If you had opened up the box and then each bottle, you would have had to pay for it."

"That's right." He nodded.

"This way you get all the whisky," Kowlee said. "When

the ship comes, you give them the smashed case. They will see that it was never opened, and so they won't take away your money."

"Oh, my God, you are a smart one," Round Eyes said, and took another long drink. "They'd never dream of this. When they open up the box, they'll see every seal on every bottle untouched by human hands."

I held the undershirt for them while they strained a second pailful. In the hot room even the smell made my head reel.

"You deserve a drink yourself," he said to Kowlee.

"No, never again," she told him. "I tried liquor once. It spoiled my thinking."

We put on our parkas, all three of us, and went back into the trader's store.

Kowlee looked him in the eyes and said, "Lay out as many tokens as my idea was worth to you."

He laughed, and winked at me as he sipped whisky from his cup. He spread five brass tokens along the counter, looked at Kowlee, took another drink, then reluctantly laid down one token more.

"I want tea," Kowlee said, "and sugar, tobacco, raisins, flour, matches, socks, a sharp knife." When there was only the one token left, she sighed and said, "Give us the rest in red and green candy, the sticky kind."

He stuffed everything except the flour into a wooden box. I carried that. Kowlee slung a hundredweight of flour on her back.

"I like that trader," Kowlee said as we walked away. "It's easy to make him happy."

Next morning we made the short dog-team journey back to Pointing Finger. We carried our heavy treasures into Tusks' igloo, laughing together with delight. Kowlee shared generously with Tusks and his wife, and with all the others from that camp who came to visit. I watched the women knead a raisin bannock, adding just the right amount of seal fat. Baked hot in an iron pan, it was the most delicious food that I had ever tasted. After the warm feelings of that feast I felt my life had truly changed, and I liked Kowlee even more. I was proud to have her as a friend.

With our dog-team drivers we departed in the morning, built one lonely igloo in the wastelands where no humans dwelled, left before it was light, and traveled along the south coast, watching the stars fade into morning. Ahead of us we could see mountainous country.

We turned northward, and hurried up the frozen fjord as darkness spread its wings. Before us a cluster of igloos glowed faintly in the night. I was truly afraid to arrive, for this was the place called "Poisoned Ground." High rock cliffs blown clear of snow towered above the camp, and I had heard that this rough rock country was a breeding place for dwarfs and demons with long flesh-tearing fingernails. A dreadful fear surrounded me as I saw the pale winter moon cut through the clouds, casting shadows beyond the huddle of igloos. Their dogs set up a ghostly wailing, and our teams hesitated, as though afraid to move any closer to such a place.

When our two sleds finally entered the camp and halted, nothing happened. We five remained on the sleds, staring into the gloom. Usually when a sled arrives, people come running out to welcome visitors. Not so at Poisoned Ground.

At last one old, old hunched-over man appeared out of an igloo's entrance tunnel and limped toward us like a wounded animal. Without speaking he helped unharness our team. He showed Raven's two young drivers where to carry our possessions and where to cache the meat that remained after they had fed our dogs.

As we went inside the igloo, the largest in the camp, Kowlee said to me quite loudly, "That old man you saw, his name is Wolf Jaw. He was once the most famous shaman on this coast. He taught me everything, and he could fly like a bird when he had all his senses. Now the poor old thing is deaf and snow-blind. When he is feeling well enough he pounds blubber for my lamp. You and I and Avo Divio can say or do anything we wish in front of Wolf Jaw. Sometimes he may seem to hear or see you, but he has few thoughts, and no one listens to them any more."

In the darkness I saw the old man turn his head with animal quickness and stare at me with pale unblinking eyes. I felt certain he had understood every word that Kowlee said.

Avo Divio laughed when I told him I could not imagine an igloo owned by a woman. He said that the hunters living at that camp had supplied Kowlee with all the meat and skins she needed for as long as I myself had been alive. We three, he told me, were not expected to provide meat and clothing for ourselves.

Kowlee's bed was the widest I had ever seen, perhaps because of her enormous size. I watched her heave herself up onto it and tend her big stone lamp, shaping the wick to encourage a long white flame.

Strange designs, all frozen to the igloo walls, flickered in the lamplight. I saw dark sealskin cutouts in the shapes of unknown winged creatures, and double images of whales and caribou with widespread antlers. In front of these, suspended on the ribs of dogs, hung skin masks that seemed to stare at me, their expressions changing in the shadows that the lamp flame cast, turning with some weird momentum of their own.

Kowlee looked around her house and sighed. "This is the place where we shall live together, Shooonaa!" She laughed and ran her big hand up beneath my parka. "Will you like that, little Shoona? I call you little Shoona, but by the time summer comes and we go tenting, you will have learned to be a man in many ways."

I watched her as she reached into the wooden box and took out two red candies from her sealskin pouch. She held them up for me to see.

"Poor boy," she sighed. "You must be cold. Come, crawl

into bed and warm yourself beside me. Take off your nice new parka and lay it over you. Now, pants off and roll them tight to make yourself a pillow. Yes."

When I lay down, she smiled.

"Open your mouth. I have a gift for you. No, no, don't touch it, Shooona!" She tucked the piece of candy underneath my tongue. "Now, doesn't that taste good?" She hugged me tight. "Dear little Shoona. You are mine—even that strange name of yours is mine. It has a sound like singing. Shooonnna." She blew my name out like a breath of wind in summer. "I'm going to plump you up a little bit and make you strong. Then I'll teach you all you need to know. Will you be quick to learn?" she whispered, and I felt her big teeth gently bite my ear. "I'm going to take good care of you. Then later—much later—when I grow old, you'll take good care of me. Shoona, is that the way it's going to be with us?" she murmured sleepily. Her grip around my hipbone tightened, and her voice took on a knife-edged sharpness. "Shoona, do you understand what I am saying?"

"Yes, yes," I mumbled, sucking the sweet candy in my mouth. "That's the way it's going to be—with us." Her grip relaxed, and I lay there like a small child in her arms, my body lost in her huge warm folds of flesh. But I wasn't thinking of our future, I was remembering the wild hot pleasures I had had with Akbil's wife. I closed my eyes so I would not see the moving shadows of the masks, and I slept untroubled by any dreams.

When I awoke, the seal-oil lamp was smoking and the flickering shadows danced around the ice-glazed dome. I lay on my back and studied the skin cutouts, which were not as frightening as the masks. One placed in the most important position on the left side of the entrance was much larger than the rest. It was red, made from the trader's blanket cloth, and in form it was half woman, half seal. This curious creature had only chopped-off stubs for arms.

I felt Kowlee wake and stretch, then hug me to her.

"Even in my sleep," she said, "I could tell by the way you twisted your head that you were looking at all those sealskin scraps I put up there. I cut them out to amuse myself when there's a blizzard. I lick their backs and freeze them to the wall. I hope they'll frighten people living in this camp, and other visitors as well. Perhaps make the children realize all the evil things they'll have to face, remind them that they'll need our help if anything troubles them."

I watched the old man rise from the far end of the bed and slowly make his way outside.

Cautiously, Kowlee tilted the lamp so that the glistening pool of seal oil would seep more freely to the wick, increasing the light and heat. "There is no need for us to leave this nice warm bed. I'll teach you what you need to know right here," she said.

Reaching out, she grasped a fistful of seal ribs from the pot and tore them apart, using her hands and her big square teeth.

"Here," she said, her own mouth already full. "We are going to start learning a very ancient language, one that almost no one else can understand." Slyly her eyes appraised me. "It is an old-fashioned way of speaking that belongs only to the *angokait,* the shaman. I know most of the words from that language," said Kowlee. "That old man, Wolf Jaw, used to know all of it very well. He taught me how to speak. But now he has forgotten almost everything."

She waited until he came back in and seated himself wearily in his place. "I know the poor old thing looks stupid sitting there," she said. "I mean with all those trader's safety pins pierced through his ears and hanging down onto his chest. He told me long ago that it made his hearing better, but I don't believe it does now. He's so old that when he walks I can hear his thigh bones creaking. But when he bought me as a poor girl from my family, he was still very strong and lively, a splendid dancer and a lovely singer. His powerful thoughts made people here respect him. Yes—and fear him."

"Why did your family sell you?" I asked Kowlee.

"Because I was born on an autumn night, at the very moment when our southern sky was being torn in half by lightning. The people were terrified, and hid their heads each time they saw the sky light up and heard the deadly crash of thunder. Wolf Jaw told people later that the storm was only sent to mark my birth, to warn everyone that a special person had appeared among them on that very night. Have you ever heard thunder or seen lightning?" Kowlee asked me. "It is rare!" Kowlee cupped her hand around her mouth and shouted, "Wolf Jaw. This boy has never heard the sound of thunder. Did you hear that?"

The old man just went on rocking his body slowly back and forth, staring blearily at his shapeless sealskin boots, and smiled. It seemed to me that his mind had gone out of his body and was wandering pleasantly in some distant place.

"He is nearly dead," said Kowlee, "and yet life clings to him. When he was still wise, unlike others here, he could see far into the past and future."

I asked how he had become a shaman, and Kowlee said, "He was the first of twins, born out of the same mother. He was the real human being, but immediately after him appeared his soul, like a reflection seen beneath him in still water, a perfect image of himself. Naturally the people in that camp were terrified of what had happened, and they put the second child, a visible soul child, out between the snow blocks. To let it live on earth would have robbed Wolf Jaw of his soul.

"Long ago Wolf Jaw used to have another name," she said. "He only took his present name after he fasted one summer in a tent with a tight-sewn entrance, and saw his vision, and knew that the wolf was his *sakavok*, his familiar spirit."

She nodded down the bed to where the crooked man lay huddled beneath a ragged bearskin. "Avo Divio also knows the meaning of many secret words," she whispered. "He's quick with his hands. You'll see how swift they are. But he's not smart the way you are going to be. He never had a vision. Look at him," she chuckled. "You'd think that he was dead if you couldn't see his breath go steaming up toward the ceiling.

"Now, speak to me of that word you heard—*kadang*. Can you not guess its meaning? Think hard. Remember everything."

"I have been thinking. It's no use. I do not know the meaning."

"Too bad," she said. "That word should come to you again. *Kadang!* I believe that word belongs to you alone." She paused. "*Udlakoot*, the dawn comes. It is now that I shall start to teach you the secret language. Listen carefully. I will begin at the beginning."

Kowlee stared into my eyes. "*Saunik* is the *Inuit* word for bones. But when we talk in our secret language, we use the word *avek*, which means roof beams, so no ordinary person will know that that word means bones. *Niahok* is the word for head. But shamans use the word *kanersuk,* the upper end. Do you understand that?"

"Yes," I said.

"Here is an easy one, because you have heard the name. *Seela,* spirit of the weather, is called *Narsuk* by us. Two words, *nanook* and *teriak*, are related in our explanation. *Nanook*, white bear, we call *orksulik*, nice fat. And *teriak*, white weasel, we call it *orksuliapik*, meaning nice little fat. *Annana*, mother, we call her *pona*, the one who enclosed.

"Now, my name is Kowlee, which means trousers. That is my *Inuit* name. My secret name is Sadvik. Our friends also have secret names. The common name of the old man is Wolf Jaw. His secret name is Sinaktok, meaning the flattened one.

The common name for Avo Divio would be Sinew Puller, but that is a name that must be kept secret—soon you will know why. *Angokok* is a shaman. Everyone says that. But our secret name for a shaman is *tarijuk*, one who turns things into shadows."

She laughed. "*Angokarsuk*, shaman's pupil, that's you," said Kowlee. "But your hidden name is Tariunulitok, one learning to make shadows. And when you speak of white men, you must use our secret word for them, *taujuk*."

She took a deep breath and said, "The last word I will tell you today is *tikliniuk*, which means pointing weapons. We use that word when we speak of guns and harpoons."

She sighed. "Shooona, am I not a thoughtful teacher? *Koli-atloo-mukoloo*, twelve words. Enough for you to learn today." She reached underneath the covers and gently smacked me on the buttock. "There! That's to make your memory sharp! Now say each word carefully after me and give its real and secret meaning. Tomorrow morning I'll make you repeat every one to me correctly before I let you go outside to make your yellow pictures in the snow."

Next day I almost wet the bed before I remembered *Sinak-tok*, meaning flattened one, the old man's secret name.

When I got back in beside her we ate some marrow from inside the bones of caribou. It is a delicious food that is de-clared taboo to almost everyone but shamans. Even they eat it carefully, for the marrow is known to be the dwelling place of souls.

That morning, before she started teaching me more secret words, Kowlee rolled over on her belly, rested her chin on her hands, and peered across the igloo as though caught in a dream of some past pleasure.

"I remember when I was young," she said, "though grow-ing to be a good-sized girl. We made a late spring journey to the inland, seeking caribou with the Chorkbok people. I was traveling with my teacher, Wolf Jaw. You should have seen him then. Oh, he was handsome, and a powerful walker, admired by everyone.

"When we reached the high plateau, we met the listeners at the breathing places. That's what they call those people from beyond the eastern range of mountains. Working together we and the listeners built a dance house and had a joyful feast that lasted more than half a moon. Together our hunters killed more than forty caribou. Imagine sending all those sensitive souls of animals out wandering dangerously near our camping place. We girls were so excited by the presence of the handsome east-coast hunters that we all forgot about the old taboos.

"Believe me, Shoona, when I tell you that I was excited then. It was the first time that I had ever lain with strange young hunters. Not one or two, but many of them. What a feast! And all that was mixed in with feats of magic, which I watched most carefully.

"Slowly I came to understand that their poor shaman was nothing but a simple trickster, a conjuror like Avo Divio. But the shaman and his apprentice from across the mountain were in no way as clever as Avo Divio. They knew hardly more about the workings of the sinew threads than you do—but you will learn, little Shoona." Kowlee laughed. "Have you ever noticed that Avo Divio walks like a sailing ship heeling over in the wind? But he is surely the quickest sinew puller you will see in all your life. But never call him Sinew Puller in the common language, for people here would understand."

"But is there nothing the shamans know except clever tricks and secret words?" I asked Kowlee.

For some time she studied my face with half-closed eyes, then whispered, "That will be up to you. If you are content to be a simple trickster, then that is all that you will ever be."

When Kowlee said that, I only partly understood her meaning. But I worked hard with her and used my memory. I could see that she was pleased because I learned the secret language quickly. She hugged me to her in the bed at night until sometimes I thought I'd die from loss of breath.

Four winter moons came at that place called Poisoned Ground, and by the first spring moon—*nourait*, we call it, the moon when the caribou drop calves—I found that we three could speak together in the secret language. I believed no other person except Avo Divio understood what we were saying. We used to go into the other igloos in our camp to see if anyone could comprehend our rapid slurry conversation. Kowlee offered candy or a pipeful of tobacco to anyone who could guess our slightest meaning, and we were delighted that not one of them ever did.

The four hunters and their families who dwelt with us at Poisoned Ground were our helpers, though perhaps they scarcely knew it. They provided us with food and clothing, and we shared with them the fancy payments given us by others. I mean the trade goods we earned from our séances held in neighboring camps. Our few families at Poisoned Ground were a part of us, and we a part of them. That was why we all continued to live in a place where it was known that evil creatures hid.

Secret words were the least of all I had to learn at that time. I shudder when I think back on all the countless things I had to memorize, such as the taboos for women of never sewing caribou skins on sea ice and not letting another's shadow cross you in the moonlight. I had to learn to be an actor, to create exciting illusions. I had to learn to make my voice sound very near, then far away. Avo Divio taught me how to do that. He showed me how to imitate the walk of others, in case I wanted to leave the camp and did not wish to be observed. He showed me how to mimic a woman's movements. He said that there was a time each evening before the darkness settled when every common object became a spirit-ridden shadow. And one night, as he spoke, he made what seemed like such a shadow dart between us, so that I caught my breath in fear.

"All you need," he said, "is a lamp placed just right, and a quick hand. I do little tricks. You will see how I do them with the sinews. It helps that big woman fool the innocents. But I could never be a shaman like Kowlee or Wolf Jaw." He shuddered. "I wouldn't want to be an *angokok*. I'd be afraid to be one!"

5

Seven winters came to me at Kowlee's camp as I learned all the practices of shamans. We had one special feat of magic that we three shared, after I knew why Avo Divio's secret name was Sinew Puller. Kowlee and he used to perform it just between the two of them, but they said this trick took three people to perform it properly. My part in it was very important, and I tried hard to do everything just right.

One day when the worst of the winter's blackness was starting to slip away, we heard that Supa, who was a headman, was sick, flushed and ill with fever. The Sinew Puller came to the igloo and told Kowlee. She said to me, "This is your first real chance. We're going to jump the weasel tonight for Supa. Be on your guard. There will be a lot of sharp eyes watching you."

Supa's snowhouse was small, but his relatives had built a larger igloo adjoining his so that everyone at Poisoned Ground could come inside to witness our success or failure.

I borrowed the small accordion from Supa's wife, for this instrument had now become much more popular than the drum at all séances. I could not really play the accordion, but I could make strange sounds come moaning out of it, which made listeners think of the howl of *torngait* ghosts and demons.

The young wives sat there all eyes, but saying nothing. Kowlee and the Sinew Puller and I waited in the passage, and entered the house only when everyone was settled.

Supa lay sick, with a stone lamp placed close on either side of him. Kowlee carefully rearranged him so that he lay sideways on the bed. Then she and the Sinew Puller started their hypnotic singing, and I made groans come trembling from the squeeze box. Many persons joined Kowlee in the monotonous chorus, and twice the Sinew Puller made a movement near the lamp too swift for human eyes to see. It sent a soul-shaped shadow flickering across the snow dome, causing the watchers to gasp in fear.

Kowlee held Supa's nostrils closed and bent to listen to his mouth. When he opened it to breathe, she fanned his lips with a ptarmigan wing and threw herself back, crying, "I haven't the strength to draw it out of him."

I played more ghostly chords, and leaped up, dancing, weaving back and forth before the watchers, so that soon they were swaying to my rhythm or trying to see behind me.

When I heard the Sinew Puller cough and sniff, I knew that he and the big woman were ready to set the weasel. I whirled around and shook it down my sleeve, crooked my smallest finger, and hooked the weasel onto Avo Divio's waiting noose of sinew that lay hidden somewhere between Supa's legs.

Although Kowlee had her back to me, she knew we had the weasel in place. She clapped her hands together with a sound like a rifle shot, and screamed and reeled away as though she had been wounded. Everyone jumped up and stared at her, expecting to see blood flowing. At that moment we were all three in our exact positions, and everything was ready.

Kowlee bellowed. *"Teriak! Weasel! Up his rectum, weasel. Drive the sickness out.* Out! Out! Out!"

The white weasel raised its head between Supa's knees and

looked around as all the women screamed. I myself would have sworn it was alive as I saw it scurry up between Supa's legs and disappear beneath his parka.

"Teriakpalo. Hunt the sickness. Chase the evil sickness," Kowlee screamed.

The sounds I forced from the accordion made the whole house tremble. Every infant started to bawl, and the dogs outside answered with a fearful howling.

Kowlee grabbed Supa's nose again, and when he needed breath his mouth flew open, and every person in that room saw the white weasel leap straight from between Supa's teeth. Then a sudden shadow passed over it, and it had vanished into the air.

Kowlee whirled and spread her arms and screamed at the audience in triumph, holding out the dried-up weasel-skull amulet that was strung around her neck as though it were a precious living thing. As she waved her right hand, I saw her lean back and poke Supa in the groin. He gave one sharp cry of pain, and started moaning.

"Hear that?" shouted Kowlee. "He's feeling better. My weasel drove the evil out of him." She whirled her amulet round and round above his head.

"Oh, thank you!" Weeping, Supa's wife handed Kowlee a sack of sugar and a box of tea, which were the two best things she possessed.

We three left the house in triumph, singing in the secret language.

Kowlee hugged me when we entered our own igloo and were beyond the sight of others. "That was the best weaseling we've ever done," she said, laughing, and the Sinew Puller agreed with her.

I felt like one of them. And, strangest thing of all, poor Supa did get back his health.

In the late spring, when the sea ice opened, the hunters in our camp gathered up their tents and families, and with the four of us journeyed west by whaleboat, zigzagging through the leads of open water toward Trader's Bay. It was a joy for us to see so many people, so many tents rising up along the shores. Trader's Bay held fewer than ten persons in the winter, but in the summer everything was different. If you counted all the families and the infants in their mother's hoods, there would be almost two hundred souls gathered on the windless side of Black Whale Mountain.

I was shy at that time in my life, and almost never took part in the dancing in the trader's warehouse. That suited Kowlee well—she did not wish me to appear like others, but to stand aloof from them. I used to lie in her tent alone, listening to the thump, thump, thump of the dancers' feet, and make endless fantasies about myself and all those eager girls. That summer the ship arrived very late at Trader's Bay, and it remained only one night to offload cargo before leaving us for another year. Almost before it was out of sight we took down our summer tents and left Black Whale Mountain in a freezing autumn rain.

"These long cold boat trips make my bones ache," Kowlee grumbled. "I'm tired of wandering. I am losing my strength."

Perhaps it was the cold rain and the smell of the wet dog-skin ruff around my parka hood that made me feel bad tempered. "I wish you'd never brought me south," I grumbled. "I could have run away with Pingwa and lived in a real camp with honest people and learned to hunt and trap like others. Look at me," I suddenly shouted. "I'm growing older, too. I'll soon be just like Wolf Jaw. I haven't got a wife to sew my boots. I'll never have a wife, the way you make the girls think I'm some sort of an animal—half dog, half stupid lout— belonging to you alone."

"You're going to be a shaman," Kowlee said in a voice as cold as the slanting rain. "You're not supposed to hunt or dance or trouble yourself with thoughts of young girls. Forget about them. Save your strength for more important tasks."

"Shaman?" I said scornfully. "What can a shaman do? What

can any of us do but play tricks on these people so they'll give us food and clothing? I've heard that long ago a shaman had the power to make real magic instead of pulling strings to make a puppet hop."

"Oh, you think so?" Kowlee's voice, colder yet, froze my rage. "Later, if you are still alive, I will show you how those ancient shamans made their magic."

It was a long and lonely winter for us at Poisoned Ground, and I cannot tell you how glad I was to see spring come again. But with the first summer breezes I could feel the old, dull, never-forgotten pains moving through my head. Dizzy spells left me weak and trembling. I would wake in a cold sweat during the white nights and hear loons calling on the fish lake behind our camp. A feeling of sadness would come over me, and I would remember my mother's face as she turned away and left me, believing that I would die.

On the very morning when we were preparing to go to Trader's Bay I felt terrifyingly weak, and when I got out of bed my muscles collapsed and a great light burst inside my head. It dulled to blood red and then to black, and I fell a long way through the darkness. When light returned, I found myself still sinking through a shimmering sea of pale-green water. Long wavering rays of sunshine rippled down, like moonbeams penetrating heavy clouds. Everything at first seemed soft and pleasant, but then the flames of the seal-oil lamp turned into sharp cruel teeth, and I sank into even lower depths, turning, twisting, rolling like a helpless worm.

I saw a shadow swimming toward me from the distant gloom, moving sleekly as a fish. It swooped beneath me, and as I twisted to defend myself, I saw its beak, pointed like a long black dagger. I saw its red-rimmed eyes. It was a great northern loon, black and white, the kind that wears the fancy tattooed necklace of a shaman and cries on summer lakes in such a sad and lonely way. It was not afraid of me, this swimmer. Indeed, I reached out and clutched its oily feathers, and rode easily on its back.

When I saw a kayakman approaching, I hid my face, for I could not bear to peer into his sightless eyes. The loon shook me off its back and called out, *"Piyu! Piyualoeet!"* meaning you must wrestle, you must fight him. I snatched the ghostly hunter by the point of his hood and dragged him from his kayak. At first we struggled fiercely, and he tried to strike me with his double-bladed paddle. But when my hands touched his throat he went boneless and sank downward, disappearing like a shadow in the gloomy depths of the lake.

"Hurry," I implored the loon. "Swim to the surface or I shall die."

There was cold wind on my face, and I opened my mouth to suck in air, only to feel Kowlee grab me roughly by the shoulders.

"Breathe deep," said her voice, and she shook me hard. Then she said, "Speak! Tell me all that happened while you were away!"

"Some of it is fading," I whispered. "The beginning is almost gone."

She hissed into my ear, "Use the secret language. Tell me all that you remember. Tell me now!"

I was so weak that I had to force each word out of my mouth, but I believe I was able to tell her all that I had seen beneath the lake.

"Ahaluna! That is so!" she said. "Many people saw you wrestling, saw you take the breath that saved you." She pointed to the Sinew Puller and to Wolf Jaw and to all the others who had witnessed my struggles.

"I saw you fall with your face lying in the flaming lamp beside our bed," said the Sinew Puller, "and lie there feeling nothing, though I myself could smell your burning flesh."

Slowly my consciousness returned, but at first I could make no distinction between the real things around me and the visions that had filled my mind.

Gradually, though, my human thoughts returned, and I could feel the pain in my face.

"Remember everything that happened here today," Kowlee cried out to the people crowded round me. "Tell others of the visions that Shoona has seen and shared with you! Shoona is a swimmer."

Kowlee was the first to call me Swimmer. I hated the name, for the last place I wanted to go was anywhere beneath the sea. I wanted to regain my strength so that I could leave Kowlee and Wolf Jaw and the Sinew Puller and go to some decent hunting camp and live with the plainest kind of people, not as a slave, not as a shaman, but as an ordinary hunter. I wanted to convince some girl's father that I deserved to have her for my wife. But I did not tell Kowlee, and, as before when I had suffered strange visions, I felt better afterward. It was as if a great weight had been lifted from my neck and spine.

Three days later the ice opened and offered us a dozen sparkling leads toward the open sea. Our hunters launched the old whaleboat, and we picked our way cautiously west toward Black Whale Mountain. I felt no bad effects from my strange journey except that I was afraid to look down into the water. Kowlee was healing my burned cheek with fresh raw lemming skin, and I was glad to be alive.

That night we beached the whaleboat in a cove, and quickly prepared our tents for sleeping. It was in the egg-laying moon of early summer. At that time stars do not appear because the sky does not grow dark enough at night. There is only a cold blue gloom, which comes and stands between the evening and the dawn, while the sun creeps crablike into the east, hiding just below the shoulders of the hills.

I heard a laughing sound, and looking out across the still reflecting water I saw a loon, a real one, not a ghost. That's the way one's helping spirit usually appears. I squatted on the lonely beach and watched him gliding smoothly over the oily surface of the water, then diving so that he caused not the slightest ripple.

I heard gentle footsteps on the gravel of the beach, and a young boy from our camp came near me. He squatted down and said not a single word until the loon reappeared. Then he asked, "Is that the one? Can you tell if that's the loon that saved you when you were drowning in the tent?"

"I cannot tell," I answered honestly. "Sometimes I believe my visions are only bad dreams, like dreams anyone can have from being sick or starving or from overeating."

"That's not true," the young boy said. "My father says you are a spirit wrestler. I wish I could be something. A flier, maybe, like Kowlee. Some say she goes walking on the moon. Or maybe I could be Godee or Jesusee—somebody, even Satanasee."

I went back into the tent and lay among the others, listening for the loon to call to me again.

In the morning Kowlee told our hunters to travel along the ice edge to a jutting rock she called Big Toe. The two of us left the whaleboat and made our way across the ice to the gravel beach, and then a short distance inland. The sky was a deep blue and the sun had cleared great patches on the south slopes. The ptarmigan were calling. It was the nicest time in all the year.

"Shooonaa, dear! Shoona!" Kowlee crooned. "What do you see there?" She pointed to three round hollows in the snow-cleared land.

"They look like holes scooped out of the ground. One, two, three holes. That's all I see."

"What are they?"

"I don't know. Maybe old meat caches."

"No," she said. "Those are old stone houses where the Tunik people used to live. Those houses are so very old that the tundra moss has grown over almost every stone. No one knows how long ago it was when the Tunik people built them or why they ran away from here.

"See how carefully they made their deep entrance passages?" she said, as I followed her toward the first hollow. "The Tunik used enormous whalebone ribs to form their roof domes, but those collapsed long ago with age. Some say they used to cover the ribs with walrus hides and sealskins, weighing them down with stones and sod. Maybe they didn't know how to build an igloo out of snow, as we do. Some say the land was warmer then. Maybe they used houses like this only in the summer. I have heard that the Tunik were surrounded by so many land and sea beasts that they did not have to move around as our hunters do in search of food. Some say the Tunik caches were always jammed with whale and walrus meat, and their blubber lamps were bright with clear white flames.

"One thing that was certainly the same as ours," she said, "was this wide, raised sleeping platform. See how it faces the entrance and takes up more than half the house?"

She seated herself upon the old stone sleeping place, and I stood close beside her.

"Watch me, Swimmer," Kowlee whispered. "I will show you something to remember, a secret from the past!"

She reached down between her outstretched thighs and carefully removed a stone from the sleeping bench. I looked inside and saw a small dark chamber.

"Now, pay close attention."

She held out both her hands, then quickly reached inside. I heard the stone glide back in place. When I looked up at her, she drew back her lips and snarled at me. I leaped back in fright, for she had grown enormous teeth and had two long fangs pointed like a wolf's.

When she saw my look of terror, she snatched out the teeth and laughed at me. "Swimmer, you must be growing stupid. Did you not see me take these shaman's ivories out of that hiding place and slip them in my mouth?"

She chuckled and handed me the teeth. They were so old that the carved ivory had turned deep yellow.

"Countless winters past," she said, "when the Tuniks used to hunt the big whales here, some shaman sitting in this very place must have practiced our same religious tricks on these simple people. Think of that, Shoona. The tricks that we performed last winter were well known all that great time ago."

She placed the teeth in her mouth once more and snarled at me in triumph.

"What else did they hide there?" I asked, and before she could stop me I reached inside the chamber.

A number of small objects were piled together in the far corner. My fingers selected one and drew it out.

"What is it?" Kowlee asked me nervously.

Holding it up to the light, I said, "It's an ivory carving of a woman. Well, the front half of her is woman, the back half is seal. She has small holes cut into a design on her back, and her hair is piled on top of her head in a knot and looped in braids around her ears. She has no face at all, just a flat blank where her face should be. She is like the largest cutout in your igloo at Poisoned Ground."

I held the carving up so she could see.

"Of course that woman's got no face," said Kowlee. "No carver would be so foolish as to carve that woman's face!"

"She must be Taluliyuk," I whispered.

"Yes! Some call her Sedna. She, too, is a swimmer, the one who terrifies the kayakmen. Put her back. Quickly put her back where she belongs!"

"No," I said. "I'm going to keep her. See, she has a hole cut in her tail. You say we are swimmers, both of us. So I shall wear her strung around my neck."

"Don't be a fool," said Kowlee. "Put her back, I tell you!"

"No!" I said again, and clutched the carving in my hand. I was growing bolder, and I did not always obey Kowlee. To distract her, I reached back and snatched up a second carving. "What's this?" I asked. "Why is the hole that suspends her at her feet? Does that not mean that she would always hang up-side down?"

"What's wrong with hanging upside down?" Kowlee snorted. "That's the way you and almost every other person came into this world, head first, upside down, attached by a cord.

"This is a woman's fetish," she whispered as she took it from me. "I believe a woman shaman sometimes wore this human image tucked up inside herself. In that way it would become a part of her, could seem to be reborn through her. She could then give this amulet the name of anyone she wished to help or harm."

"Do you mean," I said, snatching it from her, "that those whose names were given to this ivory figure fell under her power? There was no escape?"

"Of course there was," sneered Kowlee. "If they were well advised by some other shaman they would simply change their name—as I have five times changed mine. Then all this fig-ure's power to hurt would swiftly disappear. Give that Taluliyuk carving back to me."

Kowlee's eyes glittered as she grasped my wrist in her pow-erful right hand. Slowly she exerted an unbearable pressure, until I feared my bones would snap. Only then did I look away and release my grip on the precious carvings.

Reverently holding them, she rehid the wolflike teeth and the fetishes within the chamber, and replaced the secret stone. She watched me with mistrust until I turned and left the ruins, but when we started down toward the waiting whale-boat, she seemed to grow impatient and pushed past me. I could hear her mumbling, "You will get the four of us in trouble."

When she was some paces ahead, I turned back slyly and crouched in the passage to the ruin, watching as she strode down to the sea ice. Then I slipped inside, pulled away the bench stone, and snatched out every ivory fetish and hid them all in my boot top. I knew I had to pay for them or they would not bring me any power. But all I had to push into their place was a comb and an iron pocket knife. I hoped those would be enough.

When I reached the boat, the hunters had already raised the sail.

"What took you so long?" Kowlee demanded, and we set out in angry silence, ignoring the richness of this summer day that had been sent to us for pleasure. But after a time she said tauntingly, using our secret language because others in the boat were listening, "It is as I told you. Shamans have always used conjuring tricks like ours. It is a necessary part of all religion."

"You showed me that shaman's carvings," I said. "Were they simply tricks? When I tried to take them, you almost broke my wrist. Tell me, old woman. Those ancient shamans —were they all like me, or did they have wives, real wives?"

I saw her flush when I called her old woman. It was the first time I had ever done so. She turned her face away and looked out over the water, and nodded, answering truthfully, "Yes. Sometimes they had wives."

"Well, I want one, too," I shouted out—in our common language, so that everyone could understand. "I want a young wife soon! I am old enough. I am not going to spend the rest of my life warming the bed for you!"

That was the only time I ever saw rage and tears appear together on a human face. I should not have said that to her. I had been nothing, an orphan slave, and she had helped me. She had taught me everything. I sat there, my belly stuffed with meat, wearing a new sealskin parka. My hood was handsomely trimmed with young dog fur. My trousers, like those of the greatest hunters, were made from elegantly joined strips of light and dark fur. My waterproof boots were of dark rich *kasigiak* sealskin, sewn by an expert. Kowlee was training me to become an important person. But being young and ignorant, I was eager to defy and even wound.

Kowlee and I did not speak again until that night, when we dropped anchor in a bay and set up our tent within sight of Black Whale Mountain, just one day's sail from Trader's Bay. She waited as the Sinew Puller unrolled our sleeping skins, then suddenly turned and said to me, "You want a wife? Well, if you're sure of that, I shall buy you one. Oh, yes, a pretty one, with a nice flat face and strong legs and a smooth belly. That is all you want, isn't it? You don't care if she has any goodness in her, do you? You don't care if she has a head on her body so long as she has hot young ways and will thrash about the bed with you."

I was excited to hear her words but I pretended to sulk and did not answer her.

On the following evening she seemed to have forgotten my unkindness. I hoped she had not forgotten her promise to find me a wife. She talked gaily to the Sinew Puller and to me. She laughed and spoke of the good old times when we three together had first sold out magic to the people in the camps. And then she lay down in our tent and offered me one of the last pieces of red candy, saved for almost a year. I could not resist. I took off my clothes and lay down beside her. She sighed and held me in her massive arms as though I were a baby, and as the candy melted in my mouth I winked at the Sinew Puller, but he did not smile at me in his usual way. Instead he lay hunched unnaturally, not far from Wolf Jaw, and cracked his knuckles, coiling and uncoiling a braided piece of sinew with his long sensitive fingers.

"I have something wise to teach you," Kowlee whispered. "Turn your head and look at me. Stare into my eyes."

She raised her face above me until the lamplight was reflected in her eyes. "Can you see yourself, your smallest image?" she asked me, pointing at her shining pupils.

❖

"Yes," I answered, thinking only of the sweet red candy juices that trickled down my throat.

Kowlee started slowly moving her head in lazy circles, whispering to me, "Watch your little image. See your own small image moving in my eyes."

I grew warm and sleepy, and I was glad that the bad words I had spat into the air were forgiven.

"Are you feeling tired?" she asked me. "Your mouth is sweet with candy. You need to sleep, dear Shoona, sleep. There, lie quietly beside me. Sleep."

I felt her easing off her clothes.

"I will hold you," she whispered gently. "I will help you rest. You don't need any other woman, Shoona. I will make you rest, dear Shoona."

Her head had disappeared behind me, and the moment I could not see her eyes some instinct came to wake me. The Sinew Puller slithered like a weasel across the bed toward me, and from between half-closed lids I watched his right hand shoot out and slip his deadly little noose somewhere on my body. As he rolled back into the place where he had lain, I reached down just in time and slipped the pointing-finger of my left hand between my testicles and his sliding noose.

Kowlee's hot flesh pressed against my back and her power-ful arms moved stealthily down my arms until they loosely held my wrists. She raised her head behind me and I could feel her hot breath on my neck. The Sinew Puller's head was up, watching for her signal.

Suddenly her powerful hands caught my wrists like bands of iron. "*Attai*—now!" she commanded. "Now, pull!"

He gave his noose a violent jerk, and I screamed in terror, lunging upward. But the sinew merely stripped the skin off my knuckle before slipping harmlessly away.

Kowlee clung to me, her mighty legs locked around my thighs, her crossed arms crushing the breath out of my body. I stopped struggling and felt her grip relax.

"Dear Shoona, that didn't hurt you too much, did it?" she whispered. "That pain you feel will go away before you know it. You'll be far better off without those two little stones that have troubled you so much. We'll have good times in other ways—just you and me and the Sinew Puller. You'll see," she said. "Open your mouth and let Kowlee share her nice red candy with you."

Wolf Jaw sat up at the end of the bed, grunting, and peered unsteadily at us with his pale unseeing eyes. He started singing crazily, using a song made up of words from our secret language.

"You be quiet," Kowlee ordered him, and Wolf Jaw lay down again, still humming.

"*Unalook!*" I screamed at all of them as soon as I could find my voice again. "I know what you tried to do to me. I will never trust you again."

6

After that I tied on two pairs of trousers and lay with my head at the foot of the bed, and when Kowlee tried to speak to me I only kicked out at her. That summer I refused to help them with their conjuring, knowing that the times when we were camped in Trader's Bay had always been the best for selling amulets. We three had become so used to working together that they now believed just two persons could not jump the weasel well, for fear of watchful eyes. Kowlee thought they could not even hold a séance without me. She was desperate.

"One day," she said in a wheedling voice, "we three should go to the fishing place for the autumn run and perform some feats of magic for the people there. They will feed us well, and give us handsome things, and take us with them out to Kovik Island, where they are going to hold an autumn feast."

I lay on the bed with my eyes closed as though I had not even heard her words.

"Shoona, do you hear me? While we are there—" She paused and sighed. "While we are there, I shall help you pick a wife."

I opened my eyes wide when I heard that. I still did not

trust Kowlee or the Sinew Puller, but I did at that moment decide to help them with a séance. I started talking to them again, and good feelings came back to us. Then at the river's mouth the weasel jumped as it had in the old times, and we stuffed ourselves with fish like three starving ravens, and went on with all the others to perform at Kovik Island as Kowlee had promised that we would.

We arrived in four aging whaleboats loaded down with hunters and their wives and children, all eager for the conjuring and feasting. The occasion was the final planning of a marriage between two important families. Every detail had to be just right, and these final arrangements were undertaken only after the young couple had spent an agreeable winter in a trial marriage.

I spent my days and nights on Kovik Island slyly observing every eligible young girl, sorting them out in my mind like a child arraying pebbles on a beach. Which one would I choose?

On the fifth evening of the feasting I whispered into Kowlee's ear, "I want that one over there. The one called Annee."

Kowlee watched Annee delicately licking her fingers. She had a broad and handsome face with narrow shining eyes and bright red cheeks, and seemed so full of life that she could scarcely keep her feet upon the ground.

"Annee!" Kowlee snorted. "You can't have her. She has been promised since before her birth to that young hunter standing by the entrance to the tent. He is the son of Anowtok, the most important man in the camp at Egalaksak. When I promised to find you a wife, I meant I would have to search around for some simple sop of a girl, or an anxious widow who has no young hunter waiting for her."

"*Ahalee?* Is that so?" I said. "If I do not have that girl I shall leave you here at Kovik and go up north and live with others."

"Shoona," she said, "you have such strange ideas! Go yourself and tell that young hunter you plan to take Annee away from him. Then wait and see what his family will do to you."

Kowlee's words did discourage me, and I thought, Yes, who am I to demand as a wife the most handsome girl on this whole coast? I buried my passion for Annee, but I refused to perform or even to speak with Kowlee for I cannot recall how many days.

Perhaps on the seventh or eighth day, when the feasting was drawing to an end at Kovik Island, word came to us that Annee's young hunter had gone out sealing on the summer floe ice with his father and two brothers, who had all seen him slip and disappear. A great search by all the hunters went on for several days and nights, but he was never found.

Everyone was sad for this young hunter's family, and for Annee. Everyone but me!

As soon as I knew that the hunters had given up their search, I went straight to Kowlee and spoke to her in the secret language. "Now you can easily trade for her," I said. "Go to her family and speak for me. If you do not get Annee for me now, I shall go and work for that northern shaman whose name you will not even speak. I will teach him to jump the—"

"Swimmer," Kowlee broke in, "I am not thinking about whether I can get that simple red-cheeked child or not. I am thinking about you. I believe that even now you possess some deadly power. I believe that you have learned how to use your secret word. I believe that it was you who caused Annee's young hunter to disappear."

She stared wide-eyed at me, and I looked back at her slyly, but gave her no straight answer. I was delighted that she believed I had such power and hoped that it would frighten her.

"You call me Swimmer." I laughed. "Well, you are right! I am a swimmer. You and Avo Divio and even Wolf Jaw should all be very careful! If you try any more treacherous tricks, I swear to you I'll melt the marrow in your bones. Do you believe that now, you sly old bitch?"

She nodded her head slowly, but did not look at me or

speak. I knew that she and Avo Divio had in truth been frightened by my words.

"Go and do exactly what I told you," I commanded, my heart pounding with excitement.

Kowlee made me promise in front of Avo Divio that I would go on helping both of them. Only after that did she reluctantly get up and leave our tent. Through a peephole in the canvas by my bed I watched her walking slowly toward the tent of Annee's father. She stood unwillingly beside its open door, as though she could not force herself to take another step. Then, ducking down, she entered quickly. She remained inside for a long time.

She returned at last, in silence, and when I asked her what the father had said, she answered coldly. "He despises you. But in the end I made him agree to let his daughter come down to our camp instead of your joining his household, as you should. Annee herself screamed when her father said she must live with us at Poisoned Ground during the trial marriage."

"I will go to her father's camp and live with her," I said. "I'll be glad to go to a decent camp, and stay there always."

"Oh, no, you won't," said Kowlee. "We need your help to work the weasel. Why else would I have arranged this dreadful marriage? But listen to what I say now. Although I frightened him into letting Annee come with us, he warns you that he will send Annee's brothers' dog team traveling often to Poisoned Ground to see that their sister is well treated. And if Annee ever asks to leave you, they will gladly take her home with them. He says nothing will prevent that."

"Once I have her she will not go back with them," I said.

Kowlee rose, and just before she went outside the tent she curled back her lips and said, "Bullets fly straight from the rifles of her brothers. You will see."

On the very morning when we were to leave Kovik and return to Poisoned Ground, while our hunters and their women were loading the whaleboat, Annee ran away into the hills. Try as I would, I could not find her. I was not a hunter, clever at finding footprints, and of course no one offered any help. I trembled and grew pale with anger.

Finally I turned to Kowlee. "I am not going back with you to that dreary camp," I told her. "I am going to stay here and find Annee and take her north with me."

Kowlee stared at me and sucked in her breath. "You wait right there," she said. "Don't go anywhere."

She strode along the beach to Annee's father's tent and stood outside, talking to him. Whatever she said made him hurry back behind us into the hills, and after some time he returned, hauling Annee by the wrist. He flung her into our whaleboat, and she huddled in the bow, staring at him, too miserable even to cry.

I tried to thank her father, but he ground his teeth and turned his head away from me in rage.

Kowlee snatched up a long pole and helped the hunters push the whaleboat away from the land before Annee could leap out or her father change his mind. We heard her mother and her sisters wailing along the shore.

None of us looked back, not even Annee, who crouched in the boat half senseless, as though she had been dealt a crippling blow. The wind filled our mildewed sail and carried us out to sea. We had low scudding clouds and a fair breeze behind us, and we did not even stop to make a camp or really sleep. In such weather it is the custom for hunters and their families to take short seal naps in the boat, one lying against another's shoulder for the warmth and comfort.

When I tried to sit near Annee, she leaped up angrily and moved to the other end of the whaleboat. Kowlee and the other women looked grim, and our hunters stared at the line of ice on the horizon.

It was well past midday when we arrived at Poisoned Ground, but by dark our hunters had all the tents erected, and lashed down with heavy stones against the violent winds of autumn.

At first Annee seemed not to know us, and stood by herself, staring out across the cold gray straits. When she came inside, Kowlee laughed at her and immediately began to give her noisy instructions. Our big bed had to be arranged just so for Kowlee, with every last box and bag exactly in its place. The wives of hunters brought in armfuls of dry heather, which they spread thickly over the gravel. Old worn sealskins were placed hair down above that, and next our two white bear-skins, hair side up, and then the trade blankets, red to the right and blue to the left, and finally the caribou sleeping skins, hair side down, spread carefully on top of everything else.

I was very nervous for Annee and myself on this first night of our trial marriage, with Kowlee watching over us. Not knowing what to do or expect, I went outside for a while. It was good to see the neighboring tents aglow, and to hear the familiar sound of our camp dogs snarling at each other in the darkness.

When I judged that all the inside work was done, I ducked in through the entrance, and saw Wolf Jaw already curled up on the farthest corner of the bed. Avo Divio was next to him, pretending to be asleep. Kowlee glared at me with unfriendly eyes, and Annee sat hunched up on the bed, staring sadly at the gravel floor.

"I'll sleep here." Kowlee pointed at the right side of the bed. "You'll sleep there." She slapped her hand on the place right next to her. "And that one—she can sleep over there, somewhere between you and Avo Divio. Tell her not to sleep too soundly," she said. "Avo Divio is full of nasty tricks, isn't he?"

Kowlee chuckled, and made the lamp glow brightly so she could study every movement we made. We lay down together nervously. Annee did not take off any of her clothes, not even her sealskin boots or outer parka. She lay on her back as rigid as a corpse staring at the gray tent ceiling. Kowlee took off every stitch of clothing, and lay very close to me with one huge breast resting on my shoulder, her head propped on her hand. She stared at Annee balefully.

So desperately did I wish to claim Annee that I trembled from head to toe. But when I cautiously reached out and touched Annee's hand beneath the covers, she snatched it away as though she had been bitten by a fox. What could I do with Kowlee hovering over both of us? Finally, exhausted from our traveling, I fell into a fitful sleep.

I woke early in the morning, when I heard the Sinew Puller get up to relieve himself outside, and found that Kowlee was breathing steadily. After watching us for half the night, she had at last gone sound asleep.

Annee's eyes were open. She turned her head and looked at me. I smiled at her, and when I touched her hand again she did not draw it away. I laid my hand upon her chest and she did nothing. I rolled toward her and she lay there staring upward, scarcely breathing. I touched her again and she did not resist. I gently rolled her over on her stomach and raised her hips. She let out a long sigh. I was trembling beyond belief as I got up onto my knees.

"Annee!" Kowlee's voice boomed out behind me. "Get me a drink of fresh water—now! You take that kettle and walk up to the fish lake behind the camp and fill it up and bring it back to me."

Annee, who was shaking all over, collapsed on the bed for just a moment, then rearranged her clothes and climbed out from underneath the covers. Without speaking, she took the soot-blackened kettle and went into the early-morning darkness to search for water.

"You thought I was sleeping, didn't you, little Shoona? You two thought it was a good time to pull off your tricks."

"She's my wife!" I shouted at her. "Do you think I'm going

to sleep beside her all this autumn, all this winter, and do nothing?"

"Yes," said Kowlee. "I have lain beside you comfortably for seven winters without young girls jumping around you in this bed. Why start that now? You know," she said, and hesitated. "It's going to spoil everything between us."

"Well, then, that's the way it's going to be. I've got a wife now, and I'm going to lie with her, here or somewhere else!" I told Kowlee. "You are not going to stop us from being together. If you don't agree, I will have the widow sew us a separate tent, and you and Wolf Jaw and Avo Divio can go traveling with your magic tricks and live the way you did before you ever knew me."

Kowlee sat in the bed and stared at me, but before she could say or do anything to me, Annee came back inside and set the kettle down. After that she went and sat on the far end of the bed, beyond Wolf Jaw, huddled into herself as people do when they are feeling miserable.

Until the rising of the winter moon I did not once lie properly with Annee. That was my fault as well as Kowlee's, perhaps, because I did not move out into a different tent as I had sworn that I would do. Throughout that coldest moon before the winter is reborn, Kowlee rarely slept. Even when she seemed to, she was only faking, and would suddenly sit up at the very moment before our coupling, and order Annee or me to do some minor chore.

Annee made friends with none of the other women in that wretched camp, but Kowlee's plaguing drew her close to me. She would grimace behind Kowlee's back, and mimic her in a grotesque pantomime that only I could see. Those were the first family feelings that we shared.

In the end I secretly bribed our neighbor, Supa, to build an igloo for me while Kowlee was out walking. He and his old father obliged, though nervously, and when they were done, Annee and I gathered our few things together and flung them

✸

104

into that igloo of our own. We lit Annee's smaller lamp, and spread our bed, and sat there waiting for the sound of Kowlee's anger. But there was only silence. Avo Divio told me later that Kowlee was so enraged that she flung herself on the bed and refused to speak to him or to Wolf Jaw, and even to eat.

Annee and I spent only one night alone in our new snowhouse, but in some ways it was the best night of my life. I felt like singing, dancing, flying, for I was certain that our lives together would go on like that forever. I believed that Annee would always want to be my wife, to live with me alone until we died. On that first night alone she shyly called me *uingasak*, which means material for a husband. It was the most wonderful word that I had ever heard.

So eager were we to share the warm exciting pleasures of lying alone together that we laughed like children, and did not go to sleep until far into the morning.

When I awoke, it was to the sound of children running outside our igloo, calling, *"Komatchiat, komatchiat!"* Two dog sleds were coming to us from the west.

Like everybody else, I went outside, but when the travelers arrived, Annee had to push me forward to greet them. They were her father and her three strongest brothers, and my heart trembled.

I noticed that her brothers loosened the cinch line that held their rifles on the sled but did not unhitch their dogs. This made it plain that they had come for more than simple visiting.

Annee stepped forward and shook hands with her father and her brothers, politely, without speaking—as I did then, and all the others in our camp—before she hurried back to our new igloo to be ready for her father, Poota's, visit.

Kowlee laughed, and shouted to Poota and his sons, "That little house is far too small for big men. Come into my house. I have seal meat and some strong tea boiling. Come on, Shoona, you, too."

Annee's father and her brothers gladly turned away from

my house, and Annee and I had no other choice except to trail after them.

"The mother misses the daughter," Poota said to no one in particular, once we were all inside.

"*Ahaluna!* That is so," his three sons echoed.

"*Oo-pin-ann-ee!* That's no wonder," answered Kowlee. She drew out the word, making it sound sad, as though she was in deepest sympathy with Annee's lonely mother.

I did not like the way their words were going, but I was so nervous I could not think of anything I should say. Kowlee and the brothers and Poota sat on the bed and stared at me as though I were a louse that needed crushing. And when Poota spoke to Annee, she answered only "Yes" or "No," which was all any girl should say at a time when something important about her was being decided.

When Poota and his three hulking sons rose to leave Kowlee's igloo, Poota said, "Daughter, do you wish to come with us?"

There was a painful pause. I could not clearly see Annee's face because of all the kettle steam and the broad backs of her brothers. Poota stared at Annee for a moment, then turned and went outside, but the brothers did not move.

Kowlee just crouched there on the edge of the bed. Then she said, "You had better get your things together, Annee, dear. I'm sure your father and your brothers want to take you home."

Annee still stood silently beside me, staring at the hard snow floor. After a while two of her brothers, ignoring me completely, said to Annee, "Our father is ready to go. Come home with us."

Annee was already moving, propelled by her brothers toward the entrance. She turned and looked at me and started to speak, but Kowlee's voice drowned out whatever she might have said.

"You keep that chubby little face of yours out of the freezing wind," Kowlee shouted into the blast. "Stay on the sled, don't run, and if we're not dead by summer, we shall probably see you when the trader's ship arrives."

Panic seized me. How could I stop Annee's family from taking her away?

Kowlee caught me by the arm and whispered, "You be careful of those brothers. Hear me?"

I hurried out and saw Annee and one brother go into the new small igloo. *"Kigveet!"* her father commanded. "Come here, you!"

I went like a good son-in-law and stood before him.

"Have you been hunting this fall?" Poota asked.

"No," I answered.

"Fishing?" asked the oldest brother in a high feminine voice.

"No," I mumbled, and wiped my nose and did not look directly at them.

"Was it you who built that little igloo?" asked the younger brother.

"No, I didn't build it."

"Tell me, how do you live down here?" Poota asked. "How do you feed my daughter? Some say you don't own traps or a gill net or a rifle."

"Oh, well—others help me. I give them things—sometimes. They give me meat. They built my house for me."

"Unalook!" Poota snorted. "That's no way for a husband to feed a wife. Imagine my daughter having to live here with you on poisoned ground." He stamped his foot as though to hurt the land beneath the snow.

Annee came out again. This time she had on her mother's long-tailed caribou *amoutik*, and her winter boots. She looked elegant as she adjusted the big striped fur hood against the rising wind.

Annee's brothers did not so much as glance at me while they tightened the lashings across their rifles. "Ush! Ush!" they yelled at their team, and the dogs started off fast, racing for position as they pulled the long sled out through the barrier ice onto the frozen sea.

I ran beside the sled, following Annee for as far as I could go. She looked into my face, but did not speak, and soon I could no longer keep up with the running dogs.

"Stay with me!" I called out.

If she answered me, her words were carried away by the wind, drowned by the harsh voices of her brothers, urging on the dogs.

I fell to my knees and watched them until they disappeared into the night. The flat sea ice was now invisible, hidden in a swirl of drifting snow.

To keep the sweat from freezing on my body, I stumbled back to camp. My small igloo had disappeared, its sides kicked in and slashed to pieces. In the gloom I saw a shadow standing motionless in front of Kowlee's igloo.

"Little Shoona," she crooned. "You must be cold, and hungry, too. Come in here and visit for a while. I have thawed caribou meat and marrow and tea, and something else for you."

What else could I do? I followed her inside the big igloo, hating myself for feeling that in a way I was coming home again.

7

We spent that dark and fitful winter traveling as a group of conjurers, or lying idle in our camp at Poisoned Ground. I continued to eat Kowlee's food and sleep in bed with her, but I did not enjoy myself. Even the red candy had lost all its taste for me. Night after night I had wild hot-blooded dreams of Annee.

In the freezing cold of early spring, when the long light returned, we got a widowed woman to stay and care for Wolf Jaw while we three went out again and did our healing weasel trick to cure the sick. Kowlee also sold fetishes, to make the seals appear upon the ice, and in this way we survived and even prospered. Each day passed for me with painful slowness, but finally summer came and the sea ice that had barred our water route for nine long moons was broken by the tides. Great blue cracks yawned open and sparkled in the sunshine. Once more we eagerly patched and launched the ancient whaleboat and set out for Black Whale Mountain.

Even after we arrived in Trader's Bay, it was some days before I saw Annee. Finally, as I waited on the path one still evening when the mosquitoes were unbearable, I saw her coming toward me. She stopped when I spoke, but hung her head and scarcely answered. She had lost all the warmth she had shown me on that one night in our igloo, and I turned and walked away.

"Son of mine," a voice called out to me, and I turned and saw my mother. She told me that she was still the second woman of the famous south coast hunter, and I said I wished he would have me in his camp. My mother did not answer. She held me affectionately by the hand, and I tried to forget that terrifying evening when she had left me, believing that I would die.

On the following day I met Pingwa, carrying meat for Raven, who had brought his whole camp for the trading. Pingwa was thin and hollow-cheeked and dressed in rags. His hair was long and uncared for, his hands and face were greasy, and I felt ashamed of my own fine clothes.

After those three encounters, Kowlee asked what was wrong with me.

"I cannot get my thoughts away from Pingwa," I told her. "Raven has been starving him in Tall Clouds while I sit here belching from all the rich food I eat. Just look at Pingwa, slaving down there on the beach. How could we help him?"

"That is not an easy thing to do. Who knows how much Raven would want for such a person, if I tried to trade for him?"

But on the very next day, when the sun was high, we heard a child calling, "*Arnakpuk!* Giant woman! My father is hurt. He needs you!" It was Raven's daughter. "My mother says you should come now with me."

"There," said Kowlee, smiling. "It is as I told you. If you wear the right amulets and have patience, things often seem to happen by themselves."

Kowlee and I hurried to Raven's tent, and when we went beneath its gray and rotting canvas we saw him lying helpless, with a crowd of northern hunters and their women squatted around him.

"It's his leg," his wife said.

He had fallen among the tide-slick rocks and broken it, and it bent out from his body in a way no human limb ever should. His eyes were closed; his face was pale and drawn with pain.

"Can you fix the leg?" his wife asked.

Kowlee sat there and nodded her head, wisely saying nothing, staring at the awful angle of Raven's broken leg and thinking hard. Finally she said, "If I fix it perfectly, so he can walk and run on it and feel no pain, what will you give me in exchange?"

Raven opened his pain-filled eyes and stared at her. "What do you want?" he asked.

"I want Pingwa as my helper," Kowlee said so all could hear her.

"Oh, that's hard," said Raven's wife. "You got Shoona away from us and now you want the other?"

Raven groaned, and gave his wife a sharp sign to keep her mouth shut.

"Yes," Kowlee said. "If I fix your leg for you, you must give me Pingwa. I won't take him until you are able to run on it and jump on it and feel no pain."

Raven said, "If you can make my leg whole and strong again, after that you will be welcome to take Pingwa in exchange."

Kowlee ordered Pingwa and me to hold Raven by the shoulders while she straightened out his broken leg, and when he screamed, she said, "You lie there. Don't you move! Your wife will care for you. When the lemmings are running and the moon is right, I'll bring a boat for you."

And so she did. Four days later the trader's ship appeared on the horizon. Kowlee had me take up two tent poles, with a heavy blanket lashed like a narrow bed between them. At high tide she got into the whaleboat, and I rowed her to the beach in front of Raven's tent. Pingwa and others helped us ease Raven onto the stretcher and down to the boat, and we rowed out toward the slowly moving ship.

The captain looked down at us from the ship's rail and

slowed the ship until it was hove to. He had a sling lowered, and we were lifted, small boat and all, onto the enormous deck. The ship's doctor was waiting in a white coat, with a single amulet hanging around his neck. He had an Eskimo interpreter.

"His poor leg is broken," Kowlee cried out like a grieving wife. "Can anyone help me fix it?" She repeated the question loudly so that Raven would surely hear it.

The interpreter told us, "The doctor says take him into the sick bay."

Kowlee smiled at him as she started to follow Raven and the doctor through a strong iron door, though she had not been invited.

She called out in the secret language, "You and Pingwa row ashore now. I'll take care of this myself."

This ship time was like the others I had witnessed, except for one fact. The trader we had had with us for seven long years was leaving, and another one had arrived, ready to take his place among us.

Down on the beach our old trader, Round Eyes, shook hands with most of us, but you could tell that all his thoughts were already somewhere else. He hurried out and aboard the ship, never to be seen by us again. When the barge that took him to the ship returned, it brought in a very different kind of white man, one who called out cheerily before he even reached the shore. Short and plump, he had a wide smile and a bright and cheerful face. When he first pulled off his hat, he gave us an awful shock, for he had yellow-colored wavy hair. Years before, people here had called a young white whaler Kakuktak because his hair was yellow, too. Kakuktak had died here, executed by our people, so we wished to choose for this new trader a name that had nothing to do with hair. When he came ashore, he was wearing knee-high boots of a kind that holds out water, and they had a wide red edging around the soles. People started calling him Kumiaupuktok, Red Shoes, and that name stuck with him.

Red Shoes was strong and handsome in his plumpness, the way a man should be. Our people were amazed at how much caribou and fish and seal meat he could eat. He laughed a lot, too, and our people liked him very much for that. He was kind to all the children, and he was even kind to me, at first. I will be ashamed when I have to tell you what happened to that poor man.

He told us he was glad to see so many cheerful-looking people, and we believed he meant those words, for he did much that pleased us, and we did all we could for him. Even in the course of that brief summer, Red Shoes became forever famous among our people. He allowed us to have big dances in his flour house. He was so rich that he gave gifts of biscuits to everyone. And almost from the start he was able to keep two of our women in his house at once, which in itself made him an important man.

Also, he arrived among us already speaking quite well in our language. He told Kowlee that he had had a beautiful young woman at the place where he had last been trading, and that she had taught him to speak Eskimo while lying in the bed with him. As soon as he could, he said, he planned to send for her to come and live with him, but he never did. Instead he got involved with our women, which caused a lot of trouble.

More than a moon after the ship had gone, I went with Kowlee to see Raven. He was stretched out comfortably in his tent, smoking a fragrant pipeful of the doctor's best tobacco. His broken leg was in a hard white shell. Beside his head stood a brand-new pair of yellow wooden crutches. Anyone could tell that he was getting better.

Kowlee took him hobbling to the trader's house, and asked if he would help her. Together she and Red Shoes carefully cut the hard white shell off Raven's leg, and bathed it. A few days later he was out walking with a cane, and just before he left for his winter camp up north, I saw him trotting to his neighbor's tent as swift and spry as a youth of twenty summers. Kowlee hurried over and hid herself in Raven's entrance until he returned. He went inside, and after a short while Kowlee came out of his tent pulling Pingwa close behind her.

"Here is your friend. He's free," she told me in the secret language, and she held up his arm in triumph. "It is very difficult for an *angokok* to heal broken limbs," she admitted, "so I decided to let the doctors and the trader do it for me. You remember that," she said.

"Danasee! Danasee!" That word had come to us from the whalers. It had a joyful sound, for our people here have always been passionately fond of dancing. It is our way of expressing our feelings about life, about all of nature's creatures. We believe that dancing may somehow link our movements with the animals we seek for food.

To prepare for this strenuous celebration, most adults lay on their beds and slept till it grew dark, and so did I. When I awoke, the trader's warehouse door was open. A bright beam of light from his two pressure lanterns cut a sharp path through the autumn night and shimmered across the black waters of the fjord.

"Danasee, danasee," the children shrieked as they darted like shadows over the first new patches of snow.

I made my way toward the light and the sound of exciting chords as the wild old woman we called "the Wanderer" warmed up her accordion. Every other woman would wear her hair in neat tight braids, but the Wanderer's hair would be tousled and her greasy parka inside out to give the appearance of cleanliness.

There was a hiding place among tall stones beside the path, where I waited until Annee came along with four other girls. Silently I followed them in the darkness, scarcely noticing the newly falling snow until I reached the path cut by the trader's lantern and walked into a brilliant swirl of big flakes. Annee hurried with the others into the brightly lighted warehouse, which was large but already crowded.

The first person I saw was Red Shoes, standing flush-faced and smiling just inside the open door. He was wearing a fancy parka with green and purple stripes of braid and wolverine around the hood and hem. It was strangely cut, not at all like our women shape a parka, and there was no point on the hood, which to us shows a lack of pride. He wore a handsome black sailing captain's cap with a heavy red-gold badge, tipped so rakishly that you could hardly see one eye, and iron-hard leather boots with nails, which made a wondrous sound against the floor and caused clouds of flour dust to rise around him when he danced.

I had been inside only a short time before I saw him cross the warehouse floor and stand laughing and whispering with one of the young hunters from the north camp. The hunter rolled his eyes toward Annee, and I knew that he was saying something about us he should not have said to Red Shoes. Then to my surprise Red Shoes marched boldly over to Annee, reached down to take her hand, and lifted her up from where she sat among the younger women. Annee pulled back and tried to refuse, which is what all of our young girls must do, but as soon as the music started she gave in to him. The two of them joined a dozen other dancers in a circle, and everyone held hands and went racing round and round the floor in imitation of the whalers' wildest style of dancing. The Wanderer played her music faster and faster, until the dancing became a feat of strength. It only ended when several of the older folk, unable to keep up the pace, dropped out from the strain.

The Wanderer used an empty flour sack to wipe her glistening face and her chest and underarms, but Annee and Red Shoes went outside together with all the other dancers to cool their sweat in the freezing darkness. It was a long time before

※

they stepped inside again, and when they did, Annee's face was flushed and her eyes were shining in a way that I had never seen before.

"He took her up inside his house," I heard somebody say, and I swear every other person in that warehouse could smell what was on their breath.

I moved close to Annee and asked her if she had been drinking *imialook*. I meant rum or whisky.

She only laughed and wrinkled up her nose at me, and ran unsteadily across the warehouse, almost falling. She bent and started whispering to her sister, whose dark eyes flashed, and when she saw me watching her, she held her hand across her mouth to hide her glee.

Kowlee walked over to me and said, "Look at that thoughtless Annee. She must be telling stories of your weakness in the bed. You can tell by looking at her that she has made up her mind to go and lie with Red Shoes. I told you she was useless. *Nuliungasak!* Material for a wife, you called her!" Kowlee snorted. "Annee's never going to be a wife to you. You watch her. She's going now to that trader's house and make her winter bed with him."

What Kowlee said was true. I found that out because I stayed behind and watched the two of them when the dance had ended. They went together into the trader's house, and Annee did not come out until the dawn was showing strongly. When she passed me, I remained shivering behind the whaleboat on the beach. I guessed that many women's eyes were watching her go home, through the peepholes in the tent.

On the following day I found a hiding place near Poota's tent and waited there hoping to talk to Annee. But Poota came out of his tent and saw me crouching among the rocks, and I could tell that he was angry by the stiff-legged way he walked toward me.

"My daughter left you in the middle of the winter. How can it be that you still chase after her?" he said. "Still follow her in autumn like a lusting dog?"

I stood up quickly, shocked by the rudeness of his words, and ashamed, too, so that I could only stutter like a child.

"This I have to tell you," Poota said. "The trader has asked me if my daughter could stay and help him keep his house this winter instead of going back to our camp. He has given me a fine new rifle and a green canoe with paddles. I have agreed that Annee can stay here and help him. You be careful not to spoil that!"

Before I had a chance to say one word, he took another step toward me and said, "I will stand for no trouble from you. All arrangements made for you and Annee are now finished. Do you understand me?" He aimed his finger at me like the muzzle of a rifle. "Never let me or my sons see you sneaking around our camping place again."

As Poota moved toward the door of his tent he kept his eyes fixed on mine, and I thought I knew why. He believed I had used my shaman's magic to destroy Annee's hunter, and for all his bold and angry talk he was afraid to turn his back to me.

I believe now that Annee must have warned Red Shoes to be careful of me, saying I might try to hurt him. Something had caused a great change in Red Shoes and his feelings toward me. Two days after the dance he sent a small boy to my tent to say that he would like me to visit him at sunset, because he had a gift for me. I told Pingwa that I was not going, but, finally, being very curious about the gift, I walked up along his path just as the sun went down beyond Black Whale Mountain.

When I reached his door I stood there in the darkness not knowing what to do. There was a flickering light inside, but I could see no one through the cloth that hung across the window. I coughed very loudly.

"*Pudluriakpunga,*" I called out softly, meaning I had come to visit.

Red Shoes came to the door and said, "*Iteree*—come in."

I swept the light snow off my boots and followed him

through a dark passage into his dimly lighted room. It was thick with tobacco smoke and reeked with the high sweet smell of rum. Red Shoes sat down on the only chair, beside a small wooden table, and grandly waved his hand, showing me that I was welcome to sit anywhere I wished upon his floor.

I noticed for the first time that a young girl was leaning up against the wall, half hidden in the shadows, and recognized her as a distant cousin. Her name was Luviluvila; that word means Sandpiper. When I sat down near her, Sandpiper giggled and allowed her tin mug to roll loosely in her lap.

Red Shoes rose unsteadily and went over to a cupboard and took out a bottle and a tin mug. He poured liquor in his cup and in hers and in the mug, which he then held toward me. "Have a little drink," he said. "It's good for you."

Peuseeunigitunga. It is not my custom to refuse food or drink or anything that's offered me; so I tipped back my head and choked down most of what was in the mug. I felt it burn my throat and stomach and had some trouble keeping it from coming up again. But soon my head felt light and I was warm all over. I pulled off my parka, and Sandpiper pulled off hers, too. Her family was poor, and all she had on underneath was a worn-out man's shirt, too large, with all the buttons torn off the front, so that it hung gaping open.

The trader had a window by his table made with six pieces of glass set between narrow wooden ribs. Someone had taken a nail and sucked it with her mouth until it was warm, and then had drawn images in the white frost, creating a different person or creature on each of the six panes of glass. The trader's flickering lantern seemed to make the black lines tremble as though they were alive against the glittering frost. Among our people hunters do the carvings, but women are the ones who cut out images and draw lines to show you all the things that they would have you see. These drawings in the frost, I thought, could only have been done by Annee.

But Red Shoes didn't care about them. He just sat there

drinking, humming to himself, and staring at Sandpiper's smooth plump breasts.

Suddenly he looked at me and said, "Annee gone home. This new girl, she is my girl. You, my friend."

I started laughing because I was so pleased that Annee was not there, and that everything was going to be friendly again.

I said, "*Ahaluna*, yes, certainly. I am your friend." I wondered what his gift to me would be.

He poured us each another cup of rum, and I drank mine, and both of us started singing, humming the sounds of a whaler's tune we both knew well. Sandpiper tilted over sideways, eyes closing, falling off to sleep. Her empty cup rolled away from her across the floor.

Red Shoes got up off his chair and said, "Here, you help me get this little girl of mine to bed."

I jumped up and nearly fell over in my eagerness. I was glad to give a helping hand to any man who showed such generosity.

Red Shoes got Sandpiper by the shoulders, and I got her by the legs. She didn't even wake when we started lurching toward his bedroom, knocking into things and laughing at each other. I bumped the door open with my hip, and as I turned and looked inside I saw Annee. She lay naked on the bed, and tried to hide herself beneath the covers.

It was easy to see that Red Shoes had finished his talk with me, for he laughed and shouted, "*Tagvaotit*. Good-bye to you. Good-bye."

He sat down on the bed beside his two girls and, reaching out his boot, he slammed the door between us.

I was left alone in the kitchen thinking about Annee lying in his bed. The lamp was smoking, but I did not stop to fix it for him. I felt so bad that I drained off the last of the rum in my cup and all that was left in the trader's before I went out and slammed the storm door behind me. I was angry because of Annee, and because Red Shoes had forgotten about the present he said he had for me.

The cold night air sent me reeling. I slipped and sat down hard on one of the white-painted skull-shaped rocks beside the trader's path. I blew out my breath to make my head stop whirling.

I began to walk through the snow-filled pass beside Black Whale Mountain, a thing I had not done since I was young. There was no wind now, just lightly falling snow starting to cover the black outcrops of rocks. At first I had no feelings but soon I started laughing and singing. My song had a dead sound out there against the mountains, and soon I started crying, yes, weeping and thinking of my mother until the tears froze on my cheeks. I fell down several times. I lost one mitt and could not find it, but I didn't care. "Who minds about a mitt?" I shouted, and drew my hand inside my sleeve. I'd lost Annee and everything was going wrong for me.

When I reached high ground, I could easily view the sea, and began staggering toward it down the long white valley. The clouds pulled apart as I reached the lonely shore and showed me the running moon, and by its light I discovered the very rock I needed. The walrus, it was called by hunters, because of its headlike form and massive shoulders.

I climbed up onto the walrus rock quite easily and sat down, though I expected to see nothing in that wide expanse of new black ice. Emptiness surrounded me, and a silence broken only by the eerie howling of the camp dogs far away.

I took a smooth stone from my pocket and held it in the palm of my right hand. It was warm and ready to work its magic. Gently at first, then with increasing force, I began tapping it against the walrus rock. Click-click. Click-click. Click. Click. Click-click.

Slowly I spoke to it in the secret language, repeating the monotonous rhythm, nodding my head in time with the stony beat, staring intently along the shining path of moonlight. I began the chanting, using words Kowlee had taught me.

>*"Ayii, Ayii, Ayii.*
>Come to me,
>Sakavok, Sakavok,
>Helping spirit,
>Helping spirit,
>Come to me."

I begged the loon to come to me. The tide was rising. I could hear the pressure on the ice that strained against the walrus rock. My head was still spinning as I looked up and saw stars appear through drifting winter mists.

"Come to me, swift swimmer. Come to me now, now, now!" I chanted.

Then I stopped and whispered the word, *"Kadang! Kadang!"*

I listened in the silence to the silence.

"Unalook!" I shouted out in anger as I hurled the useless tapping stone along the moon's bright path.

The sea ice heaved and shattered. I gasped in terror and my drunkenness seemed to fly away. I saw a dark form floating before me in the broken ice, a pair of eyes peering at me with a phosphorescent glow, and I could hear this creature breathing heavily, refilling its lungs with air. It lay there in the water, watching me and listening.

This was no loon of mine, no helping spirit. This was some unknown monster from the world beneath the sea. I tried to call up powerful words in our secret language, but none would come to me. I was too terrified to make a sound.

Suddenly the creature arched its back and dove, splashing me with icy water as it plunged into the blackness of the sea.

8

Winter was closing in upon our autumn days and still we clung to Trader's Bay. At night you could hear the cold wind sighing high against the stars. The dawn was late, and darkness came in early afternoon. In the evenings we could see the last big flocks of snow geese drifting into the valleys behind us. They would rest there for the night, then rise into the morning sky, circling as they gained height above our camp, and calling down to us, "Kungo, kungo, kungo." I would hear Wolf Jaw sit up in our bed and call back to the geese, "Farewell, farewell winged people," wondering, perhaps, if he would be there still to greet them when they returned in spring.

Our hunters were anxious to get back to the camp and build up the winter meat caches with seal and walrus or whatever food they could find before the sea froze solid. And even Kowlee, who liked being near the trader, at last seemed anxious to go. I believe she wanted to set as great a distance as possible between Annee and me.

It was the worst time of the year for a journey in an open boat. The autumn nights, which kept us pinned inside miserable stony inlets until daylight came, seemed all but endless. We sailed only when our helmsman could clearly see the surface of the water, for the tides were enormous, six times the height of a man, and we had to thread our way through new-formed ice that hid the sharp-toothed reefs. One moment it was safe to pass over them, but the next they would tear the bottom from your boat and leave you drowning.

When you are traveling in the deadly cold of winter you can at least get off the sled and run beside the dogs to warm yourself. But in an open whaleboat you have no chance to move. You only sit and tremble in the freezing sleet or wind or rain.

We had waited at Trader's Bay much too long, and when at last we arrived near Poisoned Ground we found a great expanse of ice stretching from the shore far out to sea, too thin for a man to walk on and too heavy for our boat to break. We were forced to remain unprotected throughout that night on the open sea, where the smallest storm might have killed us all. The wind rose at dawn, and we cast off and sailed back to a long jutting arm of rock whose south face still protected a stretch of open water. There was only one place there to beach a boat, and in desperation we laid down blankets of precious seal fat and used them to slide the heavy whaleboat up above the tide line. We had no choice but to leave it there and to take only our most treasured possessions and backpack them across the rough terrain to the camp.

I can hardly bear to tell you about Wolf Jaw. He had been sick all summer and had scarcely walked a step. Now, if he wished to go on living, he must endure a two-day march that would tire even the strongest hunter. He sat on a scrap of caribou skin that Kowlee had spread out for him, and I believe that if he had been able to make decisions and speak, he would have asked us to leave him there to die. But it is the duty of younger people to help the old, and when all of us were ready to set out on the march, Kowlee knelt down beside

Wolf Jaw, put her arms around him, and shouted, "Get up! We will have to walk a while."

I was surprised to see him rise with Kowlee's help, smile blankly, and set out walking. Oh, he was pitifully weak and stumbling when he began, but slowly a new strength seemed to come into him, and his legs were still moving at the end of half a day, when we rested and ate some meat. After that I took his other arm around my neck, and with both of us helping we moved a little less slowly. That evening when we stretched the piece of canvas to make a shelter, Wolf Jaw sat there on the scrap of skin, swaying gently, and singing in a soft quavering voice. It was a rare and lovely thing to hear him. Even our tired hunters and their wives and children squatted in silence around him, carefully listening to his words.

> *"Ayii, Ayii, Ayii.*
>   No more am I one who goes wandering,
>   One who wears holes in his boots
>   While wandering way up inland,
>   Following my soul up inland.
>   *Ayii, Ayii, Ayii.*
>
>   Fondly I remember the wandering,
>   Following the ones with wide antlers,
>   While the tundra whitened,
>   Joyfully I followed the inland trail.
>   *Ayii, Ayii, Ayii."*

That night it snowed, and next day the walking was far more difficult. To make our journey as short as possible we chose a passage across endless stretches of tumbled boulders. Kowlee and I walked with Wolf Jaw between us. She told me that she remembered a time when she was young and he had carried her, following the caribou on the inland plain beyond the mountains.

"That's the way life is," said Kowlee. "At first the adults must carry the young, and later the young must support the old. Almost everything I know," she said, "came from the thoughts of this old man. Now I have only this small way to repay him for all his gifts to me.

"One thing he told me," Kowlee said, "was the difference between man and the animals. Man knows his death is bound to come, but we believe the animals are not burdened with such thoughts. That is their good fortune."

The long chains of safety pins Wolf Jaw wore suspended from his ears swayed back and forth across his chest. Between them dangled the amulet that he wore around his neck, which had come out of his parka.

Kowlee whispered, "He has bear claws sewn inside that amulet bag. I believe it is from those that he recalls his strength. Look at his feet moving as well as ours. He is walking more powerfully now than he has done for a dozen winters.

"Another thing he told me," Kowlee added, "is that our amulets themselves do not possess the strength. Only the soul of the animal from which that amulet was made gives out its power. He told me that long ago he found a great whale floating freshly dead in the long fjord, and traded it to the captain of a whaler. In exchange, the captain gave him a fast white wooden chase boat that would hold as many people as I have fingers and toes. When he was young, Wolf Jaw knew another famous shaman, who had lived long before the day that I was born, and he gladly traded the new boat to him for that pair of little bear-cub claws."

By the last half-day of our journey, our sealskin boot soles had split open or had worn away altogether, and when we finally staggered into camp, I could see my naked toes against the snow.

It was not hard or deep enough, that snow, for a proper igloo. The hunters built the best wall they could, in a circle, and we stretched the canvas carefully over the top. We all got inside and huddled together, so exhausted we could not even eat, and fell asleep.

An immense wind came the next day, driving snow across the frozen sea with a sound like countless little animal claws scratching, begging to come inside. But the day after that began in silence, and our hunters hurried out to build Kowlee a strong round snowhouse with meat porches and twisted windbreak tunnels. When everything won her approval, they built igloos for themselves.

The hunting went well in that season, and we three went out conjuring only once before midwinter—the time we call *Koviasukbingmik*, when the Christian missionaries are said to hang up their amulets on curious folding paper trees. It was about then that a dog team came to us one evening. The driver did not even stop to visit but dropped a single person off, then turned his sled around and drove back to Trader's Bay as fast as the dogs would take him.

The person who had been left behind walked up slowly toward our camp, and when the parka tail blew out in the wind, we saw that this was a woman. She came close to where I stood, and she raised her head and looked at me. My breath caught in my throat. It was Annee.

"What are you doing here?" Kowlee demanded in that voice she could make as cold as ice. When Annee did not answer, Kowlee turned her back and went down inside our igloo without even saying "*Pudluriakpeet*—will you come to visit?" which one is obliged to ask all guests.

We could not stand out there forever, so I took Annee by the hand and started to lead her inside. Kowlee stood at the other end of the snow porch, spreading her arms to bar our way, and we crouched together in the entrance passage, shivering and uncertain, then turned away so that she would not hear us speaking.

❈

126

"Do you still have friends in this camp?" Annee whispered. "Friends who might build another igloo for us?"

"Yes. The Supa family. They built that house for us before."

"Could we not sleep with them tonight?" She took my arm and hugged me to her.

"I shall ask them," I said, and together we ran to their snowhouse and ducked inside.

"*Kenukiat?* Who are they?" the father asked us from his sleeping place. I could tell he was surprised.

"It's me, Shoona," I answered, "and my—my wife, Annee."

"Wife?" asked Supa's wife, Nulia.

"Yes. May we sleep here with you?"

"Well, yes," said Supa. "Nulia, move over, and roll those children. There. That ought to be enough room for the two of you, if you lie close."

The children never woke, and Supa and his wife fell back to sleep, twitching pleasantly now and then, their bellies nicely rounded up with seal meat.

The lamp glowed weakly, sending shadows flickering across the smoke-stained igloo dome. Annee's shyness with me now was gone. She was cold and eager to pull off her clothes and lie beside me.

I waited for a while, and when she said nothing, I laughed a bit and hugged her to me, and whispered, *"Nuliungasak*, tell me all that happened."

Annee said, "It was that awful trader, Red Shoes. Oh, how I hate him!"

"Why?" I asked, rubbing my hand very gently down the whole length of her naked back.

"When I first—when I moved into his house, that nice old woman who washed his clothes and dishes was still living there, and so was that cousin of yours called Sandpiper. Soon Red Shoes said there was not room for all three women, so he had Yannee set up a little double winter tent beside his house.

Oh, it was warm enough, with heather in between the canvas walls and snow blocks placed around it. The old woman said she liked it better living out there by herself. That's because she couldn't stand Sandpiper. I don't care if she is your cousin," Annee said. "She's a wretched little slut and I hate her! Yet that ignorant trader could not see the difference between us."

"That is too bad," I mumbled, running my hand along her hot smooth thighs.

"I stood it as long as I could," said Annee. "I thought, oh, well, tomorrow he will throw her out. But she stayed on and on.

"Then Red Shoes made that wine of his, right after the first heavy snow. He used dried raisins, prunes, apricots, whatever he could find. It stood for one whole moon before we drank it. It wasn't too strong, but still, you know how bold I am." She giggled and pressed her belly close to me. "When Sandpiper went out to chip some ice into the kettle, I told Red Shoes that she was no good. I told him I wouldn't go on living in his house with her. I said to him, 'You send her back to her family, or I'll go back to mine.'

"He didn't answer, but Sandpiper had crept back in and heard me. She pulled off her parka and sat down wiggling on the trader's lap. He laughed and told her I had said that she or I would have to go. She pointed at me and shrieked, 'She goes! She goes!' And she started rubbing those enormous pointed breasts of hers against him.

"He just sat there humming, sipping his wine, enjoying himself, and didn't answer her or me. After a while he took first her hand and then mine and he said, 'Well, let's the three of us forget all this foolish talk and go to bed!'

"I snatched my hand away from his and I went out to the porch and pulled on my parka. I waited there for a while, for him to come out after me. He never did, and I was just as glad.

I didn't want him anyway, and I certainly didn't want to live in the same house with that wretched little slut.

"I was afraid to go wandering in the dark, so I crouched there in his porch until I saw the first faint light of dawn. Then I set out toward my father's winter camp. It's a long way, but I moved fast and arrived there just before dark.

"My father and my mother and all my brothers came out to welcome me. They gave me all the food that I could eat, and after I had slept and rested, my father asked, as you did, what had happened to me.

"I told my father just what I have told you, and when I came to speak of your dull-witted cousin, he said, 'Oh, you mean that beautiful, heavy-chested girl, the one who rolls her eyes.' I was angry at my father for saying that, but he just lay there in the bed sucking his teeth and staring into space, the way he always does when he is thinking of women. After a while he looked at my mother and said, 'I suppose by now that trader must be getting mad at me.'

" 'Why should he be mad at you?' my mother asked him.

" 'That new rifle he gave me is standing in our meat porch and that lovely green canvas canoe and paddles are on my rack out there. Red Shoes must be thinking that in our agreement I have got everything, and what has he got? Has he got my daughter? No. He has got nothing. That would make me mad!'

"My mother, who is always very respectful to my father, said not one word but turned and stared accusingly at me.

"I said, 'You don't know what it's like living in that house, so hot it makes me sick, and eating that pale food out of tin cans, and having to listen to that stupid slut go on and on, talking about nothing. This is my proper home!' I said. 'I will stay here and live with my own family.'

" 'What does that mean?' my father asked. 'Am I to send the trader back my rifle and the lovely green canoe?'

"When I did not answer, my father said, 'I believe you

should go back to the trader's house. My nephew is going that way in the morning. He has got a pair of skins to barter. Give Red Shoes my greetings and soon he will forgive you.'

"My mother looked at me and nodded her approval.

" 'Stay with Red Shoes at least until the summer comes,' my father said. 'That way he will not take back the rifle and the lovely green canoe.'

"Of course, I couldn't argue with my father, but I did pull the covers over my head so he would know I disliked his words.

"My mother woke me early in the morning," Annee told me. "I ate nothing. I went outside and saw that my cousin already had his six dogs hitched to my father's fastest hunting sled. My father came out to see me off, but we said nothing to each other.

"It was almost dark when we reached Black Whale Mountain. I told my cousin that I was not going to see the trader, that I wished to travel with him on the following day as far as Poisoned Ground. He had not heard my father's words about the trader, but still, he was nervous and suspicious of me. It took me almost all night to urge him to undertake the journey. Next morning early he did his trading, and we set out to travel toward this place."

I hugged Annee to me and said, "I'm glad to have you back with me."

"Aren't you glad we came here to this bed instead of going with that monstrous woman?"

"Yes," I said, and rolled Annee closer to me.

"Will you ask them to make us another snowhouse in the morning?" Annee whispered as I clasped her tight to me.

"Yes," I replied. "Oh, yes. Oh, yes!"

Supa and his old father built an igloo for us next morning. We did not spend one night with Kowlee, but that does not mean that we lived without her all that winter. She was angry with Annee for daring to return to Poisoned Ground, and raging mad with me for leaving her to share another woman's bed.

Most of the young hunters and their wives were afraid of Kowlee and did not like her angry ways. For that reason they started coming to visit us, hoping she would not notice.

A young wife came and complained of pains behind her eyes. I had a boy bring me a fresh dead lemming, and made its skull into an amulet for her, and also two small ivory knives to place beneath her head to cut the pain when she was sleeping. Her husband gave us one whole pound of tea, a blanket, and the best part of a seal for bringing his wife back to health.

After that every young woman living at Poisoned Ground came to me with one complaint or another. This brought Annee and me more trade goods, meat, mitts, and boots, and seal oil for our lamp, than we could ever use. Annee was delighted and astounded at our new wealth.

Kowlee laughed rudely when she met me walking near the meat cache. "Don't tell me. I know about it all," she said. "I see them coming and going as busy as bitches moving pups. I hope you don't think those young wives really believe in your childish little amulets and cures. They come to you instead of me because it's their only chance to make friends with that wretched girl you hide in there. Why?" She spat. "Because she was born into an important family. You will never learn to use your power so long as you waste your time with that greedy highborn slut."

There was truth in all that Kowlee said to me. The young wives were interested in knowing Annee, and by that time she was insisting that if they wanted to visit her they must bring their ailing children to me.

"I need new winter boots," said Annee.

So she told the best sewer in our camp that her baby looked thin and sickly, and that woman's husband asked me to make an amulet for the child. I did, and Annee got a handsome pair of sealskin boots in exchange. That is how our healing helped provide for us, and it would have gone on, yes, except that Kowlee became enraged.

One morning, early, when the strong spring light was coming back to us, I heard heavy footsteps creaking off across the snow. I looked up quickly from the bed and saw that a peephole had been cut into our wall. Someone had been watching us.

Three nights later Annee found an ivory dagger lying beneath her in our bed. It was not the kind that cuts away all sickness. It was shaped to bring on pain and sorrow. I hammered that spirit weapon into finest powder and went out at dark and flung its dust back toward Kowlee's igloo. But I had bad dreams that night because I was still afraid of her.

An old man in a neighboring camp had been ailing, and his family sent word through Kowlee saying that I should be the one to come and cure him. Can you imagine that? Already my fame was spreading. Kowlee was wrong. I was myself becoming famous. Even the Sinew Puller admitted that this was so.

But the invitation given to me made Kowlee very jealous. She sent word that the three of us should go together and put on a séance for one Anaktok, a hunter I did not know.

I sent word back by the Sinew Puller, saying that I would gladly join her if Annee was allowed to travel with us. Annee knew Anaktok and his people and wished to visit a cousin of hers in his camp. That took Kowlee one whole night of thinking, but in the morning she did not say no.

We left early, using two dog teams, which allowed Kowlee and Annee to remain some distance from each other.

Darkness had come before we arrived at Anaktok's camp, where his sons had built a new igloo for us. It was nicely heated, with two large oil lamps, and a whole seal carcass was thawing for our evening feast.

Anaktok, whom we hoped to cure, had been a man of power all his adult life, and if we could make him well, who could tell how generous our reward would be? A man like that might offer us the use of his meat caches for all the rest of his life.

While Annee went visiting her cousin, we three were alone in the igloo. Kowlee opened her loonskin bag and said, "Now you two listen carefully. This is how it's done."

Even after seven practices we did not have it working to our satisfaction. But Annee came back and told us everyone was gathered in the big igloo, waiting for the healing to begin.

Kowlee rolled her eyes at us and said in the secret language, "You two be careful!"

In that uncertain way we left our igloo, nervous and unready to perform.

Annee followed us inside Anaktok's igloo. He was sitting up in the center of the sleeping platform, pale as death, supported on one side by his wife and on the other by his eldest daughter. They told us that if he lay down, he became sick and the igloo seemed to spin around him.

"I believe that some monstrous thing is trying to eat his bowels out," Kowlee said. "Something that waits beyond these igloo walls. Lay him backward in the bed," she ordered.

Anaktok's wife and daughter turned him around and laid him so that his head was propped up against the back wall of the igloo.

"This is going to be very dangerous," Kowlee said, making her voice booming and hollow. "Where is his eldest son?"

When the son stepped forward Kowlee asked him, "Have you a gun with two barrels?"

"Yes," said the son, and brought out his father's shotgun.

"Can you load it?"

"Yes," said the son. "But I don't wish to in this crowded house."

"Well, if you wish to save your father's life," Kowlee intoned, "you will do it. Now!"

The son obeyed her.

Oh, I was nervous, and I can tell you that the Sinew Puller was twitchy as a fox. One of the complications of the trick was that the Sinew Puller had to play the accordion, a thing that he had never done before.

He played it terribly. I do not know how the people in that camp had the courage to stay in Anaktok's big igloo with the sounds he dragged out of that box. I pulled up my hood to try to deaden the awful moaning, but I soon forgot those hideous sounds because I myself had such complicated duties to perform for Kowlee. One of them had to do with an old bring-close glass Kowlee had been given long ago by a trader, which was now hidden up my sleeve.

I could see Anaktok's relatives squint their eyes in pain when the Sinew Puller hit the high chords. That may have helped us, and so, I believe, did the overcrowding of the igloo.

Kowlee, as I have said, had a way of making her voice change. She could make it seem far away or close beside you. She could sound like a whimpering baby or a gruff old man. This greatly added to everyone's confusion as she sat by the lamp and began to cast her spell.

"The seals and the walrus have always given themselves to Anaktok," she said in a voice like that of a sea beast granted human speech, and a small dark image of a walrus appeared above Anaktok's head and hung there against the snow wall, trembling like a lost soul. The people in the igloo gasped.

"Now Anaktok will have no sea beasts because the monster eats them," Kowlee went on in the same sea-beast voice, and I secretly moved the bring-close glass toward the oil lamp's flickering flame. Bright yellow jaws appeared around the walrus, and as I moved my hand they opened and closed, causing the walrus to disappear. That made several children scream and run from the igloo.

Now the dark image of a bird appeared and seemed to fly about the room until it came to rest above Anaktok's head. When the terrible jaws appeared again and went snapping at the bird, Anaktok himself twisted his neck and strained to peer above his head, to see why the watchers cried out in such fright.

"Look!" Kowlee's voice became a shrill cry as a new specter appeared, racing upward from Anaktok's open mouth. "It's a soul! A human soul! It's Anaktok's soul!" said the high shrill voice. "Help me! Help me frighten off the monster!"

Anaktok's relatives cried out again in terror, trying to drive away the terrible teeth. But everyone could see them slowly reappear against the sweating igloo wall. They ground together and grew brighter and more terrible as the image of a human soul left Anaktok's open mouth and started up toward them.

Kowlee leaped up from her place, shouting, "The gun! Give me the gun!"

I watched her as she snatched it from Anaktok's son and whirled and fired both barrels at the terrible grinding teeth.

The noise, which had seemed unbearable, was followed by dead silence. Above Anaktok's head, where the huge grinding fangs had appeared, there was nothing except two head-sized holes in the igloo wall.

"It's gone! It's gone! It didn't get his soul," Kowlee whispered, and the sweat stood out across her forehead. "Is it lying dead outside? Or can you see its tracks?"

Anaktok's sons ran out with the bravest of the hunters and when they came back they looked amazed and horrified.

"It's not out there now," the son said to Anaktok, who was sitting up without the women's help. "But it left strange tracks like none that we have seen before. Oh, it was something big—and heavy."

Our igloo was cold when we got back to it, but we didn't care because we were all three sweating with excitement.

"Oh, that went very well," the Sinew Puller said, laughing, and he pulled out two great foot pads made of sealskins.

Kowlee said, "And you, dear Shoona, give back that nice thick bring-near glass."

She wrapped the sealskins and the bring-near glass in softest eiderdown, and tucked them carefully in her loonskin bag along with the skin cutouts of the teeth, the walrus, the bird, and the man-shaped soul.

Kowlee chuckled. "I was nervous firing that gun in a crowded room, but did you see how it shook Anaktok out of his sickness? Did you see him sitting up as perky as a young boy? Best of all," said Kowlee, "we left nothing behind. No strings, no holes beneath the igloo. All we needed was a little of their lamplight and a nice clear wall."

Annee, who had been watching at our entrance, said, "Quiet! Here they come."

Anaktok's sons came in, each carrying a new red wool blanket. They set them on our bed.

"These are from our parents, who thank you, and wish us to tell you that our father is standing up and feels much better. You will be welcome to take meat from his caches whenever you pass his camp."

We thanked them humbly enough, and when they went outside again, Kowlee made us all a cup of tea half full of sugar so that we could celebrate.

She was too excited even to notice Annee, but spoke just the same in the secret language. "That was the best that we have ever done," said Kowlee.

"What did you think?" I asked Annee.

"I never saw anything like that," she said. "Where did the monster come from? I never saw a human soul before. How did it escape the jaws? Where did it go to afterward?"

Kowlee laughed and clapped her hands together. "See! She lives with us and yet she doesn't know a thing."

The Sinew Puller said in the secret language, "I must admit that Shoona has a skill of hand. He made those jaws snap in such a lifelike way that I almost had to jerk away for fear that they would bite me!"

Annee was never one who liked to be left out of things, and she could not bear to hear the three of us talking in a language she could not understand. I know that is why she now said to Kowlee, "One of those two red blankets we were given will look lovely spread across our bed and will keep us very warm at night." And she held out her hand.

At first I feared that Kowlee might strike her, but instead she tossed her one of the blankets, saying, though in the secret language, "I wish she would stuff it in her mouth."

Annee did not even thank her but looked around and picked up Kowlee's comb. "Is this quite old?" she asked, holding it against her head.

"*Ahaluna. Petohavingalook.* Certainly it is very old," said Kowlee. "It's a Tunik comb. See how handsomely it's carved. See how that walrus ivory has turned brown with age. That comb was worn by some Tunik woman long ago."

"Tell us about Tunik women."

Kowlee said, *"Tichiminivingalook . . ."* That is how stories begin. "The *Inuit* people, our ancestors, came into this country, and the Tuniks, who had lived here in earlier times, ran away into the northeast. In these parts around here only two Tuniks remained behind, a huge surly beast of a man and his wife. She was almost as large and strong as he was, and just as loutish and stupid, and just as bad tempered."

Annee was silent for a moment. Then in a small girl's voice she said to Kowlee, "You know a lot about the Tunik. You are so big and, oh, so awkward sometimes. Perhaps you are descended from someone who was born of such a giant woman. Perhaps you are a Tunik."

Kowlee's eyes narrowed and her face grew tight. "Awkward, did I hear you say? Tuniks were loutish and stupid, I told you. What do you mean, calling me a Tunik?" she shouted at Annee, as she leaped like a wrestler from the bed.

※

"We'd better go," I said.

Kowlee snatched up a dog toggle and an old flint fire maker and started striking them together, making sparks that flew toward Annee, which was her magic way to cleanse the house.

We turned and hurried out.

"No use running," Kowlee screamed after us. "You can't get away from me. I've got a way to fix you, you troublesome little bitch!"

9

It was storming in the morning, but Kowlee was gone. When I asked the Sinew Puller where she was, he said he didn't know. He had heard her raging around the house for half the night, but long before dawn she had dragged one of the young dog-team drivers out of his bed, and in spite of the drifting snow they had driven out together, heading eastward along the coast.

"Oh, she was angry!" the Sinew Puller said. "And she was in a hurry! They took eleven dogs with them. The trail must be hard and the wind was at their backs. They were moving fast." He sucked in his breath. "I think Kowlee was chasing after something."

I did not like the sound of that, and later told Annee that she should not have asked for the red blanket or said Kowlee was like a Tunik. I warned her that Kowlee was dangerous, but Annee just laughed and said, "What could she do? If she even dares to come near me, I will warn her to watch out for my father and brothers."

"That could be too late," I told her. "You don't know that woman or the things that she might do."

Five days later, when the sun was down and the long pale

light that comes near winter's end was casting shadows through our camp, I heard Supa's children call out, *"Komatik! Komatik!"* They had seen a single dog sled coming toward us on the sea ice.

"It's Kowlee, and they've got some other person with them," said the Sinew Puller, who was watching them through Kowlee's long brass telescope. "I think the one behind her is a woman. Big hood, and not helping in the rough ice. Yes, a woman."

The sled drew up and halted in front of my igloo, and Kowlee rose from it in triumph. She reached back and grasped the wrist of the girl she had behind her.

"Here she is!" Kowlee shouted. "Look at her, dear Shoona —and you, too," she sneered at Annee. "Here is my *tunivoapik*, my little gift to both of you."

The girl held her hood so that I had only the slightest side glimpse of her face, but that was enough to show me she was young and tall.

"Take her! Teach her! Use her up!" Kowlee laughed and went on speaking loudly, wanting everyone crowded around the sled to hear her words. "She's yours," she boasted, pushing the girl toward me. "You need a nice warm novice of your own to teach."

I took the strange girl by the hand, and there was something about her that made me not let go.

Behind me Annee said, "Who is she? She should go and stay with Kowlee, who brought her here."

Kowlee ignored Annee and whispered in my ear, "Awful things have happened to this poor orphan girl. I'll tell you all that later. She wants to learn our ways. She'll be a perfect one for you to teach. You'll see what a gift I've brought you. Look at her face," said Kowlee, pulling back her hood. "Look! She's almost a *kaluna*, she's half white! The missionary gave her the name Elisapee. Her grandfather was a whaling captain who anchored close to Savage Island, where they used to come before the trader built his house. You can say, if you like, that I'm a distant relative of hers, and that it's all right with me if you take her into a trial marriage."

Kowlee said all this aloud so everyone could understand. "Go ahead," she urged me, "feel her breasts, her hips. She's plump enough, and look how tall she is. She's got strong legs for running in snow, or for pushing other girls who might try to crowd her in your bed. You'll see. You'll find that everything I say is true. She's just the kind you like best. Why don't you try her?"

Kowlee pushed past Annee and thrust the strange girl into my igloo passage.

"There! Don't you worry," she said, using our secret language now. "I'll stay out here and talk to this bitch you sometimes use while you go inside and lie with Elisapee. Be good to her."

In ordinary language she called out mockingly, for all to hear, "Annee, why don't you come and have some tea with me?"

Annee turned away from Kowlee, looked at me in a grim unsmiling way, and followed close behind Elisapee into our own entrance.

She made tea but offered none to the new girl, and did not speak or even look at her. When I was finished with my cup, I refilled it from the kettle spout and passed it to Elisapee. She gave me a shy smile and began sipping the tea.

I asked her where she was from and she told me Big Fish River, but I was afraid to ask her anything more because of Annee, who sat in furious silence at my side.

"May I sleep here with you two?" the new girl asked presently in a polite but timid way.

"Oh, yes," I told her, but at the same instant Annee said, "No! You go and find some other place to sleep."

"The big woman told me to stay here," Elisapee said, still politely and timidly.

Looking straight ahead, Annee said, "You are not sleeping in this bed with us."

I left the two women sitting rigid on the bed and went to Kowlee's igloo.

"I've got trouble," I told her.

Kowlee laughed and said, "That Annee has always caused you trouble," but when I told her what Annee said, she went out and called Supa. He came right away, followed by his father, and Kowlee said, "Get your snow knives and build a nice little igloo attached to Shoona's. Cut an inside entrance between them, and make a strong sleeping bench just big enough for two. And hurry! It's getting dark.

"There," Kowlee said. "They'll soon be done. You go and tell Annee that Elisapee is going to have her own little igloo." She giggled like a young girl. "Shooona, it's nice to have you as my friend again."

Elisapee gladly moved into her small new side igloo with its entrance opening into ours, made up a nestlike bed of caribou skins, and lit a small lamp Kowlee sent her. We could hear her humming as she went to bed, and this seemed to drive Annee wild. She would not even speak to me.

Annee had grown up in a house surrounded by a powerful family, and that had made her into a sound sleeper—so sound, in fact, that on many mornings shaking would scarcely wake her. But on this night she tossed and turned for a long time before she relaxed and I could tell that she was truly sound asleep.

I saw Elisapee roll over and look at our bed through the entrance passage. She smiled at me. I nodded and pointed at the tea kettle hanging above the lamp.

She raised her eyebrows, meaning yes, and I slid cautiously out of bed. I took the kettle and one cup, watched Annee's eyes until I was certain that she was sound asleep, then stepped across the igloo's icy floor and entered Elisapee's small side chamber for the first time.

⁑

I examined the dome, and seeing it was tight, I whispered, "*Namuktopaluk?* It is good enough?"

"*Ayii*, yes," she whispered back. "It was a good idea."

I poured out a mug of tea and took a gulp and passed it to her. She took a sip and passed it back, and so we shared it.

"Are you all right?" I whispered. "Do you need anything?"

"What do you mean?"

"Are you warm enough?"

"Yes. It's nice and warm in here," she said, holding back the covers just a little bit.

I could see that she was naked. I shivered, and she said, "You're cold, poor thing." Then she raised her head and looked at Annee.

"Annee's asleep," I said, and I was truly trembling, not so much from cold as from excitement.

"You be sure," she whispered.

I stepped back into our house and waited a little. Annee's breathing was relaxed and regular, and her eyes moved fast beneath closed lids, the way they do when a human being is having dreams. I left the kettle near the lamp and ducked back in beside Elisapee. "She's sleeping soundly," I whispered.

Elisapee held back her bedcovers, and I stripped off my boots and slid in beside her. She was giving out so much heat that I pulled off my shirt, and then I started learning a thing about Elisapee. When I moved close to her, she seemed to run right out of words. And so did I. She would smile and move her body in a way that left me speechless!

Can you believe that after we had lain together not once but twice, I felt so pleased and so contented that I fell into a deep sleep? How can any man's sense of danger move so far away from him?

When I awoke, it was to what sounded like the high-pitched screaming of a female hawk who finds her nest attacked. Annee was up and pulling on her parka, stamping on the hard snow floor, jamming her clothing and sleeping skins and blanket into her canvas woman's bag.

"Don't dare say one word," she spat at me. "Take him, you slut!" she screamed at Elisapee, and in her fury flung a battered cup at us. She ran her bare hand along her lamp flame, snuffing it out. "I hope you freeze," she said, and marched furiously from our house.

I started to scramble out of the bed, but Elisapee held me tight. She smiled.

"Let her go," she said in a soft and coaxing voice. "I'm sure that big woman will arrange to have some driver take her back to wherever she belongs."

That's the way it was. When Annee left me for the last time, I did not even rise out of the bed that I now shared with Elisapee. As the dog team left, I rose on one elbow and fished a shoulder of seal meat from the pot and shared it with Elisapee. She believed that I must be a hunter, and I did not say anything to change her thoughts.

To celebrate we stayed in bed all day. Kowlee sent a small girl over with a gift of some tobacco in a twist of paper, and a length of nice blue ribbon. I was as truly pleased as Kowlee that she and I were friends once more.

Elisapee! What can I say to you about her? She was the most wonderful person in my whole world. Just knowing her caused me endless joy and trouble, but there is no way of changing one's own destiny. Only a truly powerful shaman might change that, and I did not feel I had such power.

Elisapee told me that her grandfather had been a foreign whaling captain. Her mother's name was Punik. Because all the young males were promised at the time, Punik was given in marriage to an old widower named Nuvok and bore him two children. The male child died. Elisapee survived. Taika was her Eskimo name, but the missionary baptized her Elisabeth. That sound is unpleasant in our language, so we soften it to Elisapee.

Later I will tell you more about Elisapee and how my life was changed.

The main difference I noticed after Annee left was that Kowlee and the Sinew Puller became best friends of mine again, and accepted Elisapee as though she were their favorite daughter. Can you explain that? Why would Kowlee be enraged at me for sleeping with one girl and encourage me to sleep with another? I am not too clever at understanding any women.

When Elisapee and I had eaten our evening food and were stretched out side by side, we tipped back our heads and let the tea steam wash our faces.

She said, "I do not remember my real parents, for they died when I was very young from the sickness that comes from tins of fish that have frozen and then thawed. The tin cans don't care who they kill. But that year my parents died was a good one, with lots of seals, and everyone had all they could eat. Relatives of mine said they wanted to adopt me, but the missionary came to our camp from Big Fish River and took me away soon after my parents died.

"The next thing I can remember is other children, white children, shrieking, laughing, playing all around me, and a stern new mother who frightened me."

"Did you live with the missionaries all the time?" I asked.

"Oh, yes. But I don't want to talk too much about that family. It was not at all a good time in my life.

"The trader over there had a wife, and she was Eskimo. She was my only friend who understood the whites. She said, 'Don't worry. When you grow a little older, everything is going to get better for you.'

"But it got far worse. I had been studying a school course sent to the missionary by ship's mail. He taught me with his other children, and I reached grade nine. Then a letter came by dog team from the Bishop. He was our boss down south. The letter said that the missionary and his whole family

✸
***

would have to go to England for a year, or two years, maybe three.

"I was as excited as all his other children. I wanted to see everything I had been told about: elephants, and soldiers riding horses, and little King Georgusee in his castle, and the *auyahuktuivingalook*, the huge archbishop, with his tall hat, sitting on his enormous throne in the cathedral. I was certain they were going to take me with them. But just as the ship arrived the missionary told me that I would have to stay behind. I had no other family. I felt lost, and I started shuddering and weeping, and could not stop myself for a long time.

"The missionary had given me to one family, but they only waited until the ship was gone before they gave me to another, to Okalik's family. Okalik took me west along the coast and kept me at his camp. He had a wife, a little timid thing, afraid of him, and he no sooner got me there than he tried to do awful things to me. When I realized we were alone out there and screaming would not help me and no one seemed to care about the things that Okalik did to me, I lost my power to speak, and I feared that I would lose my mind.

"I had wanted for so long to get back near the place where I was born and live an Eskimo life, and yet when I did, that winter was the worst time in my life because of Okalik. Finally he tried to make me do something so unbearable that I screamed and screamed, telling him that I'd tell the policeman in the red coat, the young one named Martin.

"After that I had to leave. I hugged Okalik's little weeping wife and ran two days and nights along the coast until I came to the next camp, the one they call Big Boulders. People were normal there and kind to me.

"I was angry with the missionary for leaving me so that I would fall into the hands of Okalik. I thought that he hadn't cared what happened to me. The people at Big Boulders asked where I was going, and I thought of what would make the missionary angry. The person I'd most often heard him say was bad was Kowlee. He used to tell us that she was a daughter of Satanasee.

"So I told everyone I met that I wished to go and live with Kowlee. People were surprised at that, but the first dog team that traveled west along the coast carried my message to her.

"She came right away to see me, and I told her I had hated living with the missionaries. 'I'm *Inuk*, not white,' I told her. 'I want you to teach me how to be Eskimo again, and how to find my helping spirit.'

" '*Opinanee!* That's no wonder,' Kowlee said to me. 'You get your sleeping skins and we'll go back to my camp. You live with us,' she said. 'I cannot teach you because an *angokok* is supposed to teach only one person. Then that person in his time must teach another.'

"Kowlee told me all about you, Shoona. She said that you were clever and kind and knew the secret language, and would help to teach me. She told me you had been living with a stupid thoughtless girl, but that this girl would be leaving just about the time I arrived. And so she did."

I found that Elisapee was wonderful at remembering the words of the secret language, and we lived together in a state of happiness. It never bothered her that other people said our winter camp was a howling place for every kind of *torngak* demon. Sometimes, outside our house at night, Elisapee and I would hear the snow creaking and something sigh or moan. Most white people would have said that the sound came from one of our dogs outside, but not Elisapee. She would lie close to me, and listen, and whisper, "There they are. They're coming close. Help me to learn to see them, speak to them."

"When I told Kowlee what Elisapee had said, she nodded. "That girl is quick and clever and she wants to learn. I am pleased to see you pass on the knowledge that I gave to you while I am still alive. Are you telling her the stories she must know? About the coming of the white raven, and how tufts of grass turned into humans? About Taluliyuk, and Igtuk the boomer, and the *torgaasit* and the *kikukiaks*, and all the other deities?"

"Yes, yes. I'm telling her," I said. "But it takes time. Remember—" I held up all the fingers on both hands. "It took you ten winters to instruct me. And still there's more to learn."

"Not from me," said Kowlee. "You know all I know—and more. You possess a word."

I lived joyfully with Elisapee that winter in the best companionship that I had known with any woman. Supa's son came to help us as often as we needed him, and his wife did all our sewing. Elisapee went often to visit Kowlee and they practiced speaking together in the secret language, and the people at Poisoned Ground were pleased that I was trying to teach her to be a healer.

Elisapee used to curl up close to me and whisper that her mission life was too straight in a line, and she would draw a line with her smallest fingernail down my chest. Then she would say that life at Okalik's camp was too wild and bad and crooked, and she zigzagged the line along my belly. Then she would make a curving line and say that our life together was exactly right. I used to twitch with pleasure when she said that!

One night as we lay together in the bed I whispered, "I've got something for you. It's a present."

"Let me see," she said.

"No! You guess first. I've got it hidden in my hand."

"Oh, I'm no good at guessing." Elisapee laughed. "Did it come from the trader's store?"

"No," I said. "It's something better than that."

She felt my clenched fist. "Did you make it yourself?"

"No. It's old. Very old."

"Oh, I can't guess. You've got to tell me."

I rolled over on my stomach and leaned toward the lamp. She did the same. Slowly I opened my hand.

"It's a small carving," said Elisapee. "It's ivory—from a walrus tooth?"

"You're right," I said. "It's a carving of a half seal, half woman. You can tell that by her hair, all gathered up into a topknot."

"But why does she have no arms, no face?" Elisapee asked.

"Because she's magic. She's the sea goddess, the one the kayakmen call Taluliyuk. Look back here. The carver drilled a hole so someone could string a piece of sinew through and wear it as an amulet."

"Me! Me!" said Elisapee. "That charm was made for me, all those long years ago."

I was prepared for her to say that and gave her a piece of sinew I had left beside the lamp. She carefully strung it through the ancient ivory hole and tied it around her neck, sitting up naked in the bed. I must admit that she looked beautiful in the lamplight with the little pendant hanging between her breasts.

"Do you mind that it's hanging upside down?" she said.

"I don't mind at all." I sighed and reached out for her. "It looks just right on you."

On the following day the hunters brought us some delicious young seal liver and the tender rib bones thick with dark red flesh.

After Elisapee had put them in the pot above the little Primus stove, she turned and said, "I wish you had been the one to hunt this meat."

"Why?" I asked. "I have no need to go out for meat. These hunters do all such things for us, and we do other things for them."

"But is it right?" she asked.

"How did your missionary father get his meat?"

"Oh, he received donations just like you. My white mother told me that in England they passed a plate around and people put money on it for him. But I would like us to be just like other, ordinary, people. Help them, but live like them, too. Hunt with them."

⁑

149

"Kowlee says that's wrong," I told her, "but I have often wanted to live in an ordinary way. It would be easier to make friends. You are my friend. Pingwa is the only friend I have who is a hunter. After that, Kowlee is the closest, and then there's Avo Divio and Wolf Jaw. I have no others."

"Let's be ordinary. Will you let us try to be?"

"Yes. But don't tell Kowlee."

I didn't really mean yes when I said it, because the idea was too new to me. I agreed with Elisapee because we were lying warmly, playing in the bed, and I did not wish to change her mood.

"How could we be like others?" I asked her later.

"That's easy," she said. "We'd just do ordinary things—like going hunting, or fishing with the gill net my uncle gave to me."

"I don't know how to hunt or fish."

"Supa's wife said that as soon as the moon is right she is going hunting with him on the island. Almost everyone is going hunting caribou together. Could we not go with them?"

"I've never hunted," I told her. "I've fired a rifle no more than once. I hated the way it kicked and banged my shoulder."

"We could borrow a rifle and practice. I'd like to learn to shoot."

"Women don't fire rifles," I said, laughing.

"Malee does. She hunts ptarmigan. You and I could learn together."

Winter gathered all its dying strength and blew against us in a violent storm. After that you could feel the new warmth of the sun, and when you pushed back your parka hood you could sniff the air and tell that spring had come.

"Komatik! Komatik!" I heard the Supa children calling.

I was almost afraid to go outside, because visitors brought sudden changes, and I was having such a splendid life with Elisapee that I didn't want anything to change. But when I heard a familiar voice calling my name I rushed out, and there was Pingwa—my best friend in the world, returned from the Bird Island camp up north.

I ran up to him, and he hit me a blow on the side of my head, and I hit him in the same way. We both struck hard, for among our people this is the custom of best friends.

"Come sleep in my poor house," I said, and only then did I look at his long thin hunting sled with five fairly well-matched dogs. A girl was standing beside his sled, with Kowlee and Supa's wife and all the other women crowded around her.

"Who's she?" I asked him.

"This is Kigavik, my wife," he said most proudly.

I shook hands with her. She had a smooth and well-formed face and gentle manners. Pingwa and most others called her by the Christian name Josie.

Elisapee came out smiling, shook hands, and asked them into our igloo, where she made tea. I noticed that Pingwa had a new white canvas parka cover with red braid and a fine black dogskin ruff. The hood of his parka had the high steep point that we call *kokokpak*, the point of pride, and I knew that Josie or her mother must have designed it. It meant that she was very proud of Pingwa.

"You look like a rich man," I said.

"You and Kowlee made that possible," he said with a laugh. "We had lots of foxes in the early winter. That changed everything for me."

Although I had no rifle and no dogs, I was pleased that there was enough meat and cached dog food so I could invite Pingwa and his wife to stay with us. We four shared the bed and talked together as though we were all one family. Pingwa told us they were traveling to the nesting places where Josie used to spend the egg moon with her family.

"We will pitch our tent and fish through the ice and wait for the geese to come," Pingwa went on. "Josie says there is an old boat belonging to her father at that place, and he says it's mine if it will float."

"I would like to go traveling," said Elisapee, "and live in such a way. Could we not go somewhere like that?" she asked me.

"Come with us," said Pingwa. "Remember? It is what we always said that we would do, when we were young."

Kowlee was delighted when she heard our plan to go and camp near the nesting places.

"You will both need a second pair of boots," said Kowlee. "I will tell the best sewers to hurry and make them for you."

Supa's old father lent me his rifle, and Supa showed me how to aim and fire it. We spent only one bullet and I didn't hit the mark, but Pingwa and Elisapee and Josie all said I came quite close, and assured me that I would do better when I aimed at an animal we really needed. That set me to worrying about sending lead to strike into living bodies and disturbing souls. But I said nothing to the others, for they were the hunters who had kept me alive with meat.

Kowlee lent Elisapee and me a little canvas tent, which we lashed with our other possessions onto Pingwa's narrow hunting sled. The Sinew Puller came up leading two middle-sized dogs that he had borrowed for us.

"These two are not much good," he said. "They're skinny, and they won't eat much. Good hunting to all of you." He smiled at Elisapee and me. "You both look glad to be alive. Good traveling!"

"Tugvaosi! Good-bye!" we called to everyone as we set out. After that the four of us were always moving, sometimes running, sometimes sitting on the sled, enjoying the sun and the sparkling hard-packed snow, looking forward to our first hunting camp together. It was the first time in my life that such a thing had happened.

From the moment that they met, Elisapee and Josie were the best of friends. We lived and laughed and ate and slept like brothers and sisters, sharing everything we had.

That evening there was not the slightest breath of wind and every drift of snow cast a long blue shadow. I helped

Pingwa unhitch the dogs and feed them with the walrus meat we carried, and together we tipped the sled on its side in case of a sudden storm. Josie and Elisapee spread our tent flat on the snow and laid out our sleeping skins, and after we had made tea and eaten meat, we lay like four young foxes out before the den, whispering together as we watched the night sky deepen into azure and heard the gabbling of the king eiders that stood like bright-dressed dancers along the white edge of the ice.

"Did you hear about the white man?" Pingwa asked me. "The one we all saw walking up at Tall Clouds in the early spring?"

"No," I said. "Who was he? What was he doing there?"

"No one knows," said Pingwa. "It was deadly cold on that morning when we met him. He had no sled, no dogs, no pack-sack and no rifle. He seemed to be going nowhere. We squatted with him on the snow beside our sleds and tried to talk with him, but we couldn't understand each other. Finally he just stood up half smiling and walked away from us. Later, when the women urged us, we turned our sleds and doubled back to find his camp. But we found nothing. He'd disappeared completely."

"What did you do?" I asked him.

"Well," said Pingwa, "in early summer, when we came south to Trader's Bay, we told the government man about that stranger. He was very much disturbed. He traveled north himself to Tall Clouds with some hunters but they found not a trace of him."

"That's very odd," I said. "How could a white man remain alive out on that freezing plain with nothing?"

"I couldn't do it," Pingwa said. "Not without a snow knife."

I laughed and said, "Perhaps the lot of you were dreaming. Such a thing could never really happen."

When the snow on the land began to disappear, we decided to separate for half a moon. Pingwa and Josie wished to try for the big red trout that slowly circled beneath the ice of the fish lakes. Elisapee and I thought that we would rather collect eggs and eiderdown from the island nests—enough, we hoped, to make a great wide robe that would cover all four of us.

We were not sure about these plans, and talked back and forth about going together here or there, or separating.

On the following evening, Josie said, "Shall I sew up a bag to collect the eiderdown?"

Pingwa jokingly said, "Are you going for eiderdown with Shoona?"

Josie blushed and laughed and said, "I forgot who was going where."

But Pingwa kept up the joke and said, "I suppose that means I'm going inland to fish with Elisapee."

"I wouldn't mind," I said as a compliment to Josie, but Elisapee had become a part of me and I could not imagine life without her.

Elisapee laughed and said, "There would be nothing wrong in that."

Out of this joke among the four of us, which caused wild laughter, we decided to part and travel in just that way. On the morning that our separate journeys began, I still thought someone would refuse. But nobody did.

We laughed nervously as we parted. Pingwa and Elisapee took the dogs and sled and headed inland; Josie and I walked down along the inlet carrying our tent and sleeping skins until we came to the place where her father's boat was cached.

I looked at her and she glanced back in a shy unsmiling way and said, "I miss them both already. *Keetapik*—but only just a little." She seemed beautiful to me then, not only in her appearance but in all her warm and gentle ways.

We found the boat and launched it. I rowed, and Josie sat in the stern, humming a song as she paddled and steered and bailed out icy water. In this way we crossed the smooth narrows of the sea and landed on the eider island.

At evening, after we set up the little tent, we watched long chains of female eider ducks flying low across the ice-strewn surface of the sea. Then Josie went inside and unrolled our sleeping skins and spread the gray army blanket and covered it with two winter caribou skins that she and Elisapee had stitched together.

By the time I crawled after her, she was already asleep, or pretending to be so. My hands shook as I took off my clothes and crawled quietly into bed beside her. Josie was fully dressed. That disappointed me.

I lay still, wanting her. I cannot tell you how much I wanted her. And yet I did nothing. And finally, because of our long trek down the inlet and the rowing across to the island and setting up the tent—well, I, too, fell asleep.

I woke when I heard geese calling overhead, and looked over, expecting to see Elisapee at my side. Only then did I remember that Josie and I were alone together. I turned to her, and as I did I felt a glow of warmth and guessed that she had taken off her clothes. Gently I reached out and touched her. Josie's soft flesh seemed to burn my hand.

Lying alone with her there in that small tent was something too exciting to describe. We could hear beluga whales whistling and blowing as they rose to cross the reef, female eiders cooing, snow buntings calling and answering. Down by the shore some male herring gulls laughed, and others cursed them for it. Everywhere the sounds of early summer burst around us, and our nostrils were filled with the rich smell of the tundra.

As each new day came to us, it seemed that Josie had been lent to me in special celebration of this arrival of our new year. I tried to think of Elisapee and Pingwa, but their images were vague and far away.

In the midday we gathered eggs and eiderdown. If the sun was warm in the afternoon we would lie in the shelter of the rocks and watch the bearded seals come up to breathe among the skeins of outgoing ice, and the endless flocks of sea pigeons, with blood-red feet and white patches on their blue-black wings, whirring past above us.

Most of our nights were sensuous and quiet. But some were wild. Once Josie leaped right out of our bed in the early evening and ran along the whole edge of the island, clutching her arms about her in the cold still air. I chased her, and she laughed and screamed as loudly as she could, and I let out loud roars until I caught her on the high ground. The nesting gulls set up a raucous crying, but no humans heard our voices. Every human being in the whole world was far away from us.

By the time the moon waned we had filled two huge bags with eiderdown, and had eaten eider eggs beyond all counting. Still, we packed another hundred eggs into a sealskin bag carefully, with down laid between them. Then we collapsed our tent, rolled up our bed, and stowed everything inside the rowboat and made our way back to the coast of Baffin Island. It was raining there, and the rain turned to heavy sleet, so our long walk back was miserable.

When we arrived, Elisapee and Pingwa came out of the larger tent and stood together, watching us as we moved toward them across the mushy rain-soaked tundra.

We formally shook hands, all of us unsmiling, then eased our packs down and sat exhausted on the tent floor. At first we did not speak.

Finally Pingwa asked, "Did all go well with you?"

"Oh, yes," I told him. "We got a lot of eiderdown and eggs. You two can have them all. We do not wish to eat another egg."

They laughed and pointed to the place where they were caching twenty big red-bellied char and said they did not even wish to see fish until the moon had faded. This set us all talking together at once.

I smiled at Elisapee, and said, "Did you have a good time?"

Elisapee came and sat near me, and Josie sat beside Pingwa. And so our celebration for the coming of summer ended, as it had begun, in friendship.

Late that night, when the other two were asleep beside us and we ourselves had lain together, I whispered to Elisapee, "How was it? I mean, being with him?"

Elisapee said, "An old woman told me once that one person married to another should never tell the other anything about lying with someone else. She said it only causes trouble. Endless trouble."

"Oh, never mind that old woman. Tell me!"

"No!" Elisapee smiled. "I'll ask you nothing, and I'll tell you nothing."

And about that she never did.

TWO
The White Stranger

10

We returned to camp in the fullness of the berry-ripening moon. Strong north winds had swept away the floating fields of ice, driving them south to rot in the warmer sun of Hudson Bay, and vast expanses of blue water stretched to the horizon. After the long winter you could feel your soul singing deep inside you.

Kowlee gladly took Pingwa and Josie and their dogs and crowded them together with all of us into the whaleboat. With a fair wind at our backs we sailed for two whole days until we came under the lee of Black Whale Mountain. We beached our boat in Trader's Bay and joyfully drank tea with families we had not seen for one whole year.

Pingwa and I helped Supa and the Sinew Puller erect Kowlee's enormous tent, and then put up our smaller ones. We placed the three well apart from one another, though I cannot tell you why, because we all remained the best of friends.

In the morning, when we hurried up to the store, the old woman who took care of Red Shoes was hanging up his clothes on a sealskin line. Annee came out and gave the woman a pair of her sealskin boots to dry, and when she saw me coming up the path she turned her back, stamped into the trader's house, and slammed the door.

The trader had been watching from the window, and he laughed when we went inside and hunched his shoulders like an owl. "*Arnait!* Women! They never change!" he said. He waved his hand toward the empty shelves and asked us what we had to trade.

"Not much." Kowlee shook out only three fox skins from the almost empty bag.

"Well, that's fair enough," he told her. "I've only a little left to sell you."

He counted out exactly fifteen matches from the last box in the store, and one meager handful of tea. When Kowlee asked him for tobacco, he said he hadn't had a smoke himself since early May. "It's seal meat, fish, and seagull eggs for all of us until the trade ship comes again, and that will take forever! She'll go to Sugluk first."

But he was wrong. Two mornings later, as the sun was burning through a white fog that drifted out across the sea, we could hear the children on the hilltops screaming, "*Umi-akjuak! Umiakjuak!*" At high tide an unfamiliar ship, with two swept-back yellow noses and a low sharp knifelike hull, came steaming into our small bay. It was a new government icebreaker, and she looked enormous, like a huge black whale. When the captain ordered both her anchors lowered, the chains made an enormous clamor. Everyone who could find space crowded into our small boats and wheeled round and round her. I myself went aboard as quickly as I could, and stood on the broad, fresh-painted iron deck beside other Eskimos, who had arrived before me.

Pingwa, Sarki, and other hunters from the north camp hurried over, and Pingwa said, "Look there! That's him. That's the *kaluna*, the white man we saw up north. See him standing over there, all by himself. He's the man who had nothing with him."

Sarki said, "He's the very man we saw walking all alone near Tall Clouds, with no dogs, no gun, no woman. He was just wandering, leaving those strange footprints of his strung out across the snow. Now we can ask him what he was doing up there. We tried to speak to him but he still shakes his head and cannot understand us."

"Where is Elisapee?" Pingwa asked. "She could interpret for us. We really want to know how he stayed alive up in the north, alone with nothing, and how he disappeared."

I waved to Elisapee to come up the ship's ladder. She is not at all shy with the whites, and after I explained to her, she went straight up to the stranger and spoke to him. We could see that his answer to her was short. He smiled at her, and then at us, and spread his hands and shrugged.

When Elisapee came back, she told us he had never in his life been up north. "He doesn't even know where Tall Clouds is," she said. "He has never been anywhere in the Arctic before, so you must mistake him for some other person."

"We made no mistake," said Pingwa. "It was him. *Ahuluna.*"

"Certainly, it was that man standing there," Sarki agreed, and blew out his breath in an angry way. "We can all remember the strange sweet smell of his pipe tobacco, and he was wearing those same boots."

Sarki's wife nodded firmly. "*Ahilah.* Yes indeed."

"Look at that little half-moon scar on his upper lip. We even remember that. He is the man we met," said Sarki. "Why would he lie and say that it is not so? Ask him how did he disappear in that flat snow country."

When Elisapee told this to the white man, he just shook his head and shoved his hands into the pockets of his summer anorak.

"Ask him where he was during the moon when the seals come on the ice," said Pingwa.

Elisapee turned to him, and then back to us.

"*Tavanivingalook*—far, far away. You-rope," she said. "He says he comes from Europe. I have got no other word for that place. Later in the same moon, he says, he came to Montrealmee, then went far down south. He says he was half working, half learning at a school I've heard of. It's called Yaa-le. Yes, Yale or some such name."

I kept my eyes right on the white man's face, and he kept looking straight at me, his eyebrows raised, as though we had known each other in some distant place beyond our memories.

He was not tall as some whites are tall, but he was lean. Though his shoulders were not wide, they sloped in a way that made you know that he was muscular and strong. His face was more deeply tanned than that of any white I had seen before, and his nose was longer and straight as a wolf's snout. His eyes were round and set deep in his head, and a cold ice-gray. His hair and the rough beginnings of a beard were a changing brown in color, like the back pelt of a summer wolverine.

He was not as restless as most whites. You know the way they usually hop and jump about, and twitch their hands, and swiftly change their face expressions. Not this man. He just rested there against the rail, quietly watching Elisapee and me, not looking at any of the other hunters and their wives. He stared just at the two of us, as though he was studying the movements of our eyes.

Suddenly a huge booming spirit voice echoed over the whole ship. Our hunters and their women jumped with fright, and the whites all ran to the ship's ladder. But Elisapee laughed and told us it was the captain speaking.

"He has a box to blow his voice up like a giant's. He's saying that the white people can go ashore now."

We could hear iron squealing against iron, and saw a big flat barge being lowered over the icebreaker's side.

The strange white man suddenly turned away from us and slipped through a heavy iron door that led inside the ship. He returned some moments later, carrying a sleek blue kayak balanced on one shoulder and holding its paddle in his other hand. It was not a sealskin kayak such as we use, though it was similar in shape, fully decked and long and slender, and you would not wish to give it any other name.

We watched him weaving his way cautiously through the crowd of people on the deck. Leaning over the rail, he stared at the sloping ladder that two seamen had lowered until it almost touched the water, and began to climb down, balancing the kayak carefully, watching that it did not strike against the ship's iron side or the sharp zigzag steps. Eskimos above him on the ship and others drifting in their boats watched intently as he bent and launched it in the water.

When the captain saw the bright-blue kayak, he bellowed harsh bad words down from his small house perched high on the ship. His giant voice gave off such an awesome roar that flocks of frightened birds went skittering down the whole length of the fjord, but the stranger looked up and smiled, and waved his paddle at the red-faced captain.

The Eskimos enjoyed it all, admiring the expert way the stranger stepped from the iron monster of a ship into the eggshell thinness of his kayak so that his feet put no weight at all upon the bottom.

Poota shouted, *"Inuktak!* The new Eskimo!" It was something strange to hear. Poota did not know that this kayakman told lies, which in our minds is a sin as great as stealing.

He paddled easily toward the shore, and Pingwa and I followed him in the whaleboat, as did many others. A crowd stood on the gravel beach to meet him as he landed.

"Kabubawak takoveet?" Kowlee's old friend Tusks called out to him, and he pointed to the ancient kayak landing stones. The white man changed the direction of his craft, as though he understood Tusks' words, and his method of disembarking was almost exactly like ours—he rose and stepped onto the stones and then to shore as gracefully as any of our own best kayakmen.

Old Tusks greeted the white man in exactly the way that he would greet a fellow kayaker who had returned from some distant place: *"Tikipeet,"* he said. "You have arrived."

"You speak as though you know him," I said.

"I don't know him at all. But I can see that he is a real kayaker, one who cares. That kind of person is becoming rare."

From the moment Tusks said that, standing by the landing stones, we admired this new white man's skill. He stood shyly and politely on our shore, and as we came near him he shook hands with every one of us, even the smallest babies in their mothers' hoods. That was as it should be, for these children would one day tell their children and their children's children of their first meeting with this man. All through these greetings his face stayed calm, but his steady, ice-gray eyes seemed to look inside our heads.

"*Inuktitootkauyimaveet?* Do you understand our language?" Tusks asked him.

He did not answer, or seem to understand in any way, but he smiled politely before bending to lift his kayak from the water.

"*Tamna,*" I said, without pointing to the high stone kayak rack, and he made no response. It was true. He could not understand our words at all.

Old Tusks took him gently by the arm and led him to the rack, telling his wife to bring some skin line.

The white man upturned his kayak and placed it with utmost care on the rack. He drew two small pieces of fur from his short parka pocket and laid them at the exact two points where the kayak touched the stone. Tusks' wife came with the sealskin line, and the old man showed him how to lash the kayak quickly and easily so that no ordinary wind could blow it down.

"*Teamik?*" Tusks asked him, and made a drinking motion.

He nodded, and Tusks' wife hurried up the beach toward their tent. The new white man followed Tusks, surrounded by a flock of silent children, and when one of the watching women called him "the man who tells lies," Tusks turned and growled at her.

"That is the bad kind of name those northerners all too

quickly give to others," he said. "This new Eskimo's name is Kayaker. Do you hear me? Kayaker!"

From then on that was our only name for him.

Early the following morning, though Elisapee always liked to sleep, she jumped out of bed and propped our tent flap open, made tea, and jumped back in beside me so we could lie on our bellies side by side and look out and admire the wonder of the sleeping ship that lay at anchor in our bay.

Elisapee said, "Do you think that man with the blue kayak was really the man Pingwa and the others saw walking on the north coast?"

"Yes," I told her. "I believe he was. All those hunters and the two women with them would not make the same mistake. And yet it is difficult to believe he would lie to us and say he was not there." I remembered his cold and steady eyes, and a strange thought came to me. "Maybe his lies are not lies, for him," I said to Elisapee. "He is not like any white man we have ever known. Why should his truth be like that of other white men?"

Elisapee looked at me as if she did not understand what I was saying. I do not know if I myself understood, although even among us some of the things our shaman do and say would seem like lies to white men.

Still looking at me, Elisapee said, "I wonder where he really comes from. And if those others are right, why was he near Tall Clouds?"

I had no answer for that, so we lay and drank our tea, and brushed away mosquitoes, and watched as the icebreaker's crew lowered the cargo barge. They piled it with heavy wooden boxes, then sent it moving in toward shore. It left a long pair of shining ripples, like a swimming duck.

The noisy coming and going of barges continued throughout the pale-white night. In the early morning fog appeared, rising like slender ghosts along the fjord. We heard the cap-

::

tain's voice bellow something through the spirit talker. The ship's anchors clanked up noisily on their chains and the exhausted voices of the sailors called out to one another as the last barge was hauled inboard and lashed into its place.

Most of us stepped outside our tents and stood watching quietly. The weather had changed, and big wet flakes of snow came spiraling through the early-morning air. We could see black smoke rising from the middle of the ship.

The ship's bells clanged, and she slowly turned and eased down the fjord on the rising tide.

We went back to bed, and I fell into an exhausted sleep. It seemed to me that my eyes were neither fully closed nor fully open. Dogs howled far across the fjord, and soon they were answered by our dogs, as though they had all seen something that alarmed them. And then I heard big claws rattling against the gravel as some unknown creature stalked toward our tent, pausing, it seemed, between each step. The rattling stopped, but the sound of its breath came clearly through the canvas.

As I twisted and turned, trying to wake and warn Elisapee, the tent door opened, and I heard the creature cross our threshold and crawl toward the bed. I thought I shouted in terror, but only faint cries came out of my throat from the dream world. Whatever it was, the loathsome thing crept like a newborn demon into our bed, and lay between Elisapee and me. I could feel its wet wings trembling, smell sour milk on its breath. It began to crawl over me, and at that I screamed out loud, waking Elisapee.

"You've been dreaming," she said, shaking me. "It frightens me when you have bad dreams like that."

Later that morning another and quite different visitor surprised us. Elisapee had just been wondering where Kayaker was going to stay when—as though she had magically called to him—he raised the flap of old Tusks' tent and came walking straight along the shore toward ours. Tusks' youngest grandson held his hand and skipped along beside him.

We waited quietly inside the tent until Kayaker bent and looked inside.

"Eetiree," I called to him.

It was good having Elisapee as my interpreter. She said, "Please—come inside."

The grandchild lost his nerve when he saw me and ran away. Kayaker came in, and stuffed his little woolen seaman's cap in the pocket of his anorak. His neat-fitting parka gave him a strong, bold appearance, with the heavy-shouldered, narrow-hipped look of a true kayakman.

We moved over on the bed to make space for him, and he sat down comfortably between us, with a pencil and a small book in his hand. He spoke in English, of course, and I know all the things he said only because Elisapee told me later. He began by saying to her, "Your name's Elisabeth. We talked together yesterday." Then he asked me mine, and Elisapee helped him say it as he opened his book and wrote it down. "I've been a long time traveling, and I'm grateful to be here," he said. "I don't like noisy ships, but last night I slept well in your Arctic silence." He smiled at both of us, and I thought his gray eyes no longer looked cold. But neither did they look like the eyes of a man who would lie.

He asked her if the sea here was often as calm and smooth as it was just now, and she said, "Oh, yes. It's true that we sometimes have terrible storms, too, but people can usually see warning signals in the clouds."

He told her she spoke excellent English and that he was sorry he did not speak Eskimo. "I wish so much to learn," he said. "Will you help me to speak your lovely-sounding language?"

More boldly than I would have dared, she told him that it was not an easy language and that some people were very hard to teach.

"Oh, I speak several languages already. That usually makes it easier," he said, "and of course I'll pay you if you help me.

But, to begin with, I'll need a good interpreter, someone who can also give me information about the life here." He explained that he had come to Baffin Island to learn everything possible about our type of kayak: how hunters built them, how they used them, what part they played in our life. There were Eskimo people west of here, he said, who never had used kayaks.

Elisapee had been told that kayaks used to be everything here, and said they were still a little bit important to some of our older people. Then she told him about the women's much larger skin boats, the *umiaks*, and she spread her hands to show their size. "They were big enough to hold forty people as well as dogs and children. But they're all gone now. There is only one old skeleton frame left, and it is all broken."

"Yes, I've heard the *umiaks* are gone," Kayaker said. "And most of the kayaks, too. They're disappearing fast, so I want to study them while kayakmen who hunted in them are still alive to talk with."

Elisapee asked me where the kayaks were, and I said, "Tell him old Tusks has got a very good one down at his winter camp. And Blue Fox, he's got a slender beauty, but it's rotting up near the fish lake. It needs a sealskin covering. They say there's another in the north, on Wild Bird Island, though few have ever seen it."

Through Elisapee he asked me, then, what man here knew the most about kayaks, and I said that we would have to ask the older hunters. I really knew old Tusks would be the man, but it was such an important question that it should not be answered easily by a young person like me.

"Will you ask the old men for me?" He looked at me and at Elisapee. "When they agree who is the wisest kayakman, we will try to use that person as our main informant. That is, Elisabeth, if you'll be kind enough to interpret for me."

She told me later that those were the very words he said. She stared at the gravel that we had spread for drainage before our wide low bed, and said, *"Yuksavok,"* which in our language does not mean yes or no. It only means it should be so.

"Thank you," said Kayaker, and he reached into his hip pocket, took out a folded leather square, and drew from it a piece of paper, the kind with a face and numbers on it that we call *keenaoyuksak*. He tried to hand it to Elisapee.

She shook her head and would not take it. "I have done nothing for you," she said. "Maybe I can't be a *tusiyee*, interpreter, for you. I have so many other things I want to do."

"Oh," he said, and now his eyes had a strong dark look of disappointment. "Is there anyone else here who speaks English well?"

Elisapee thought a while and then said, "There is Yannee, but he works for the trader. I speak it only because I was forced to go away and live with white people. That's the way I learned it, not because I wanted to."

"Please, it's important," he said. "I hope you will interpret for me." He stood up and smiled at us once more, but I could not tell if this smile reached his eyes. "May I come and see you again tomorrow?"

Elisapee translated, and I answered, "Yes, certainly." I went on thinking Kayaker was strange in himself and strange in the way he looked at me, but I was growing used to that and could not help liking him.

For a few minutes after he was gone, the two of us just sat together, staring at nothing. At first I was sure that Elisapee would not help him because she did not like the whites. But now she said, "Look! I thought he might do that. He left the paper money where he sat, even though I told him I didn't want it."

She picked it up disdainfully and looked at both sides of it.

"Inuabuk. This is ten," she said, using our word for half a man, meaning the fingers of one man's hands but not his toes. "This piece of paper is worth one summer white bearskin."

"That will trade a lot," I said. "Why did he leave it when you said no?"

"Because he really wants me to help him about the kayaks. He needs my help."

"Do you want to help him?"

"Maybe. What do you think?"

"It might not be too bad. Will he give you one of these every time you help him?"

"I believe he will," Elisapee said.

"Well, then, I don't see any harm in it."

"He's white," she warned me. "I usually get in awful trouble when I'm near the whites. Missionaries, traders, government men—they all make me sad. They make me mad, and then they say I start acting as if I were crazy!"

"If that's how it is, I don't want you to work for him," I told her. "I don't want you feeling sad or crazy."

"Yes. But maybe I should help him. It's not nice to refuse people when they really need your help."

"No," I urged her. "Don't you work for him. Even now, before you start, I can tell that it's going to make you angry with him, and then perhaps with me."

But what I hoped would not happen did happen. You know how women are sometimes. As soon as I started to say she shouldn't work for Kayaker, right away Elisapee became determined to help him. She started getting a bit mad at me for telling her she couldn't work for Kayaker. I thought we could use that money coming every day, so I pretended to be getting jealous. Then I realized that maybe she really did want to work for him, right from the start, and she only said no at first so I would urge her to work for him. Perhaps it was she who tricked me in the end.

After a long while Elisapee said, "Oh, this is foolish. I won't translate for him, or help him, if that will please you."

"Oh, go ahead," I said. "You help him all you want."

Elisapee didn't look at me, or speak for a moment. Then

she said, "You'll have to promise me that if I do try to help him, you won't get angry at him and hurt him in any way, as you did—"

She clamped her lips tight shut and said no more.

"You think I hurt that young hunter who was going to marry Annee? Well, I did not! And look at Annee. You saw her on the shore this morning walking around laughing, feeling fine. I didn't hurt her either, did I? And there's nobody in this world who made me feel worse than she did."

Elisapee nodded. "Yes. I know. But just promise me that if I work for Kayaker you won't hurt him, or me, or anybody else. Then I will give you every piece of paper money he gives me, and you can go and trade it for the two of us. I don't care anything about the money. But I would like to try to help somebody. I am really ashamed of the way I hate certain kinds of white people, when half of me is white."

And so it was agreed between Elisapee and me and Kayaker that she would act as his interpreter.

Kayaker told her he was writing a paper for Yaa-le university. He said he did not know how long it would take him to gather all the information he needed, but he would stay on Baffin Island until his work was done. When he came to me, quite humbly, and asked me through Elisapee if he might be allowed to pitch his tent near ours, I laughed and said I had no right to tell any human being where he might pitch his tent. The land in Trader's Bay was free, like all of our land, and people could live wherever they wished to live.

I was so curious to see him unpack that I offered him my help. He had brought some strange and wonderful things into this country with him. Just one example was his tent, the nicest I ever saw, rounded like an igloo so that any wind would leap across it. The back half was colored black to keep light out for sleeping during the pale summer nights, and the front half yellow to let in daytime light strong enough for a woman to do her finest sewing. Kayaker also had a curious little rifle that screwed apart like a pipe to hide inside his pack. He had brought a large pile of books, some for reading, some with pictures, and others just blank or with lines of blue, meant for drawing or writing in. He had all kinds of thin metal tongues, as long as a whaleboat, that rolled out or back into themselves, marked off with lines like the joints between your fingers, that he used for telling the size of kayaks and other things.

He had lots of food with him, and Kowlee came over and sampled some of this with us. There were little silver packages with a fine dust that turned plain water into rich blood soup, and we all thought that was delicious. But when Kowlee tasted something called powdered cheese, she ran outside and blew it into the wind. He also had dried chips of ptarmigan and caribou, sugar, tea, coffee, tobacco, and everything else a man could want. I told Kowlee and Elisapee I hoped he'd never go away.

Elisapee and I were still helping him unpack boxes in his tent on the second night after the ship had gone, and we saw the moon rise full across the bay. We left our work and went outside. Kayaker sat down and studied the sky, then searched through his large packsack and pulled out a wooden stick about as long as my forearm. It was of a kind that I had never seen before. It had eight holes for his fingers, and when he blew into one end, it made a low-pitched sound, or a high sound, or any other sound his mind and fingers wished to make. He leaned back against his new stone kayak rack and faced the moon, whose light was strong enough to make the long skeins of snow glow blue as they spread like crooked fingers down the side of Black Whale Mountain. He blew gently through the wooden pipe and sent out a slowly spreading sound that made you shiver, made your blood run hot and cold, made you think of winter nights, and far-off howling dogs, and stars that hang above you waiting for you to learn to come to them. The music that he blew out of that piece of wood was the saddest sound I ever heard a human make. It sent shivering messages into every living part of me.

I turned to look at Elisapee. She was lying flat on the tundra, arms and legs spread wide, mouth open, eyes tight shut. When the music came to an end, she slowly opened her eyes and raised her head and stared at Kayaker. I had the feeling that I was already dead, and that in this world of ours, only Kayaker and Elisapee existed.

11

When I went outside next morning, I saw that Kayaker had already gone. He had placed a heavy box in front of the entrance to his tent to keep stray dogs from entering, and his kayak rack was empty.

A small breeze set the whole sea dancing lightly, as though wide patterns of silver fish were flashing all along the blue-green waters, and on the far horizon beyond Trader's Bay long broken chains of white ice were slowly drifting southward.

I steadied the telescope against a man-sized rock and watched the blue kayak coming up the fjord. Kayaker drove it smoothly through the water, the double-bladed paddle dipping and flashing in the sharp cold sunlight. Anyone could see how much he enjoyed the summer morning. As he paddled toward our tents he turned his head to admire the weird rock forms carved by the weather on the steep cliff faces. And now he began testing his kayak, letting it drift sideways in the light cross wind, turning it easily back on course with one short sure backstroke, paddling it in a tight circle. After that he paddled straight to our beach, but before his bow could touch he turned the kayak sideways, placed his weight on the paddle across the wooden cockpit, and lifted himself up and stepped

⁂

out into calf-deep water. With one swift motion he lifted the kayak to his right shoulder and carried it up to the rack.

Elisapee sat in the entrance to our tent, combing out her long black hair. She squinted in the sunlight, and said, "He's very clever with that boat of his. The way he carries it around you'd think it weighed no more than a paper cup."

"It's not so light," I said. "I've picked it up myself. It has many ribs, and its wood is hard and heavy. He's stronger than you'd think."

"What a marvelous day!" Kayaker called. "I'm hungry. Elisabeth, please tell me how to say 'I'm hungry' in Eskimo."

"*Kaukpoonga*," she told him, and he repeated that word to me.

"*Uvungaloo*," I answered, meaning "me too."

Kayaker opened his food box and came up with three small packages wrapped in shiny paper. He gave one to Elisapee and one to me, but when I took a bite there was no flavor good or bad, just a dryness that gritted on my teeth like sandstone.

"*Eeeukk!*" I said, and spat it out.

Kayaker smiled and spoke to Elisapee.

"He says it's healthy for you." She laughed. "It's all you need to eat to stay alive. Go ahead, take another bite. I'm going to. They're like those sandy little dried-up biscuits they used to send to the missionary. You get used to them."

"I'm not crazy and I'm not starving," I told her. "I'm going over to Pingwa's tent for some decent seal meat. Are you coming?"

"No," Elisapee said. "Kayaker paid me to stay here and help him. Josie will surely send me back a little rib or two. I'll see you later in our tent. Don't forget, if they offer you some extra meat, you bring it here. We need it."

So I went away, leaving Kayaker and Elisapee alone together.

Old Tusks' summer tent was not so very far from ours, although we could not see it because of the stand of rocks between us. Tusks was known to have made great sea journeys in the past, but by that summer he had grown old and rarely moved a stone's throw. Next to Tusks lived a boyhood friend of his named Tadlo. He, too, had been a splendid kayakman.

In the old days, when the winter ice let loose, Tusks and Tadlo would have paddled their kayaks on a three-day journey to the place between the islands where they knew the seals came in abundance. But now they were too old for that, and their kayaks rotted on the racks at their winter camps, the sealskin coverings splitting in the summer sun.

We three talked it over carefully, and because I was a man, Kayaker and Elisapee decided that I should be the one to hold up five fingers and ask old Tusks if he would accept one green face every day in exchange for telling this new white man all that he recalled about kayaks. Tusks said that he knew nothing of the power of five green faces, but that he would be pleased to teach the stranger the little bit he knew.

I had never had the slightest interest in kayaks, but by listening to Tusks and to Elisapee as she interpreted Kayaker's questions, I learned much about kayaking, and about the thinking of the whites as well.

I remember the simple things about width and length and speed, and the subtle differences in paddle blades. I also remember the important, almost mystical words Tusks had to say:

"A kayak is like a woman. A young hunter enters a kayak in excitement and by instinct, and when he leaves its manhole he is like a child emerging from his mother's womb. Sometimes a kayak seems dangerous and lonely, a place occupied by just one human being, a man's own grave, rolling on the edge of an endless sea. In a kayak a hunter faces his greatest perils—and also, out there alone on the sea, experiences his greatest joys. The hunter and the animals he seeks seem to join and become part of one another and of all the life there is.

"I know the words of an ancient song sung by our kayakmen," Tusks said, and he began to sing them out:

> *"Ayii, Ayii,*
>> The great sea has set me in motion,
>> Set me adrift,
>> And I move like a weed in the river.
>> The arch of sky
>> And mightiness of storms
>> Encompass me,
>> And I am left
>> Trembling with joy.
> *Ayii, Ayii."*

Elisapee interpreted the words that he had sung, and Kayaker swiftly wrote them down in his thin flat book.

Now Tusks' mood seemed to change. "My first kayak was— about as long as this tent."

But Kayaker interrupted him, saying it would be easy to find out about the length and width and depth of kayaks. He wanted to know more about the feelings and ideas of a kayak-man and to hear more of the songs.

Kayaker's very words, his boldness, seemed to drive away the magic from Tusks, and for the rest of that meeting he would tell only the most ordinary things about a kayak. Though Kayaker wrote everything down, and sometimes made small drawings, I could see that he was disappointed.

But on the next day Tusks held up a caribou antler and said, "This is just as good as wood for kayak ribs. Some old people believed it was better. They said bones and antlers possessed more spirit than the logs of wood that get caught and turn in the northern ice, and drift to us from no man knows quite where."

Tusks moved his hands as he spoke. "Oh, we know how to shape that wood, to score it with long shallow grooves, then with a wedge-shaped walrus tusk hammer it carefully until it splits exactly on the line that we have marked. As to bending wood, some say we learned that as a gift from the creatures living beneath the sea."

From the swiftness of Kayaker's writing, I could tell that he had begun again to treasure every word.

"Old dried wood is impossible to bend," Tusks said, "unless you boil it first in seaweed and salt water. After that it becomes quite soft and yielding. Then one by one we place the kayak ribs between our teeth. Using our two hands, we bend the wood, slowly forcing it downward until it takes the exact shape we desire.

"When you see one of our kayaks today," Tusks boasted, "you are always looking at something old and valuable. As long as a kayak survives it is passed down from father to son to the son's son. The skins of our kayaks are replaced by our women every second or third year, but the frame, the keel, and the cockpit, and the ribs beneath the skin, may be old beyond telling.

"When I inherited my great-grandfather's kayak I replaced ribs because they were split or broken, but also to understand that kayak and make it mine. I cut pieces from the antler of a huge bull caribou that had given its dear self to me. To use this in my kayak was a dangerous and yet a wondrous thing, for parts of land mammals are known to help you, and yet they are taboo on the sea. To make this right I gave the antler parts to Wolf Jaw, and he sang to them and licked them very carefully. In that way I was able to build the forces of the land into my kayak. That is why good fortune on the sea most often comes my way.

"I used two seal shoulder bones as well. Lastly I shaved a walrus penis, which is solid bone and almost as hard as iron. I shaved it carefully into a new prow for my kayak. That kayak carries the feelings of many of my ancestors, but it is mine now. It belongs to me."

Tusks sat nodding in the entrance to the tent, looking out across the fjord and remembering times long before we had been born.

"Our hunters do not nail wood to wood, like the whites.

That seems to us a painful thing to do. Iron nails are sharp as arrows driven into flesh, and also they resent the sea. They rust and pull out all too quickly. Our kayak ribs and frames are each one notched or gently drilled, then lashed together with sealskin line cut thin or thick. Damp sealskin line stretches and snaps back like a living muscle. Our women sew the skins for kayaks with long tough sinews—usually the spinal cord drawn from the backs of small whales.

"The true strength of our kayaks is that they can bend and twist and stretch. Good kayaks do not fight the sea. They yield to the force of every wave. A well-built kayak is like the skeleton of a living man—bones linked with sinew moving easily within the skin.

"Men grow old long before their kayaks," Tusks said. "Look at me! I am old and tired and need to rest."

Kayaker agreed but asked Elisapee to say to Tusks that he would like to talk with him some more.

I went down with Kayaker on the following day and waited while he untied the ropes and lifted his own kayak off the ancient rack of stone. As we walked across the long gravel beach toward the water two women came toward us. They had their hoods up, covering their faces from the cloud of mosquitoes that had followed them across the tundra, and talked together softly in the way of married women. Although they did not look up as we approached, they surely must have seen us. As they passed us, one of them whispered to the other, "There he is! The white man we saw walking up near Tall Clouds."

"He says he wasn't there."

"Don't you believe it. That was the one. I saw him clear as I see you."

Old Tusks was sick for three days, but when he was well enough to come again, he gave Kayaker more useful knowledge. He tried to use Kayaker's small blue craft to show him how a hunter's parka bottom must be measured, and made to fit tightly over the cockpit's rim to keep out water in a heavy storm. He tried to show Kayaker the way a hunter rests his double-bladed paddle on the cockpit gunnel and rolls it on a chunk of seal fat to ease his labor and make the paddle silent. He explained how a hunter holds the paddle high and works it across his chest when he wants to move with greatest speed.

Kayaker wrote down every word. But still it was difficult, because they had no sealskin kayak to examine.

"Where can I buy one?" Kayaker asked Tusks. "I will be glad to pay whatever you think is fair. Would you sell me yours?"

"No," said Tusks. "I am going to keep that kayak while there is one breath left inside me."

"Will Tadlo sell me his?"

"He will not," said Tusks. "I knew you'd want a kayak, and I asked him. He says that he can never sell it, even though he has not paddled it these last four summers. Maybe—" He held up his right hand and spread all its fingers. "I think maybe it is five or six summers since he paddled, though he will not admit that."

"Is there no other good kayak?" Elisapee translated.

"No. Not near here," said Tusks. "Only the old one out on the grave."

"Who owns that one?"

Tusks squinted in the sun as he looked at Kayaker. "Nungo owns it from his father. Nungo's widow put that kayak on his grave for him because he told her he might need it in some other place."

"Well, it's not needed. It won't do him any good," said Kayaker.

Elisapee paused and tapped her teeth before she translated that.

For some time Tusks just stared at the ground between his boots. Finally he said, "How do you know that?"

When Kayaker did not answer him, Elisapee translated

Tusks' next words: "That kayak rests on Nungo's grave, and it is going to stay just where it is."

Kayaker closed his notebook and asked Elisapee if Tusks would consent to walk out there and show the kayak to him. Tusks said in reply that he didn't see how that could cause Nungo any harm.

Next day there was fog and rain, but just at evening the sky cleared and we four set out, walking slowly. Tusks had to stop quite often, breathing heavily and resting on his stick.

When we reached the brow of the hill, we could see the grave. It was in no way unusual except that it stood alone, a pagan grave, with skull-sized stones and larger ones piled waist high above it, and only long enough to hold a human body with its knees half bent.

The long slim kayak lay upside down, weighted carefully with stones so that it balanced on the grave. Most of its sealskin covering had split in the rains and summer sun and hung in tatters thin as paper, exposing the delicate-looking frame.

Kayaker exclaimed in delight at the beauty of its graceful lines, at the smooth way the frame converged at bow and stern, and then flared sharply upward. After that he stood staring at it silently, as though he had lost the power to move or speak.

But, I said to Elisapee, it was too bad the kayak was such a wreck.

When she told this to Kayaker, he turned on me almost angrily. That didn't matter at all, he declared. Any small part of a watercraft as pure as that was still a treasure.

We three stood back and watched Kayaker as he walked toward the grave. He moved cautiously, as though stalking some rare waterfowl that might spread its wings and fly away. When he reached the kayak, he knelt down and ran his fingertips admiringly along the curves of the bone-white ribs. On all fours, he peered underneath at the cockpit and then looked up at Tusks and said, "This kayak did not come from Baffin Island."

"You are right." Tusks smiled and pointed south, across the Hudson Strait. "That kayak was paddled here by the great-grandfather of the one who lies beneath it now."

"Across the Strait? Why, that must be at least a hundred miles of open water."

"A whole camp of hunters migrated here with a dozen kayaks and two big *umiaks*. They stopped at Tugjak Island," Tusks said, pointing south toward two blue cloudlike shadows on the horizon of the sea. "Two of their women gave birth to babies there, then placed them in their hoods, and rowed on with the others until they reached this coast."

Tusks asked him how he knew the kayak was not one of ours, and Kayaker explained that its whole shape was somewhat different. It was longer, with a slightly wider bottom, and the stern was less tapered. The cockpit was round in back, not squared like those of our kayaks, and its angle was much more extreme.

"They must hunt big bearded seals or walrus over there," Kayaker said. "This kayak is built to carry several tons of meat."

Tusks nodded as Elisapee translated all of this. "Whole families could fit within its skin. We could scarcely believe our eyes when a hunter would visit us in a kayak such as this, and five or six others, guests and children, would come wriggling out after him."

I said to Elisapee, "Tell him to look there. The loon's-skull amulet is still tied and hanging in its place, and so are the small knives to cut the weather. And look here, the broken wooden ribs across the deck have been replaced by bones."

Kayaker asked if they were seal bones, and when Tusks assured him that they were, he asked also if they were used just because wood was scarce, or for some magical connection with the seals.

"Those seal bones serve two purposes," Tusks said. "Seal and walrus shoulder bones both are very strong, and they have a natural eyehole in them. For short spans they are stronger than the best of wood."

Kayaker then asked how many sealskins a new cover for the frame would take, and Tusks told him eight or ten of those our women used.

Kayaker wanted to know if there were many women here who could still do such work. Tusks answered with a proud yes, and Elisapee added, "Almost every older woman here knows how to sew a kayak cover."

Now Kayaker asked in a pleading voice how he could own such a craft. "This must be one of the very last real ones," he said. "Oh, I know there are others tucked away against museum ceilings. But almost all the rest are gone. How I would love to own it! Imagine the thrill of paddling a kayak like this. Look at those bottom ribs!" He ran his hand expertly down its long flat keel. "I could roll such a kayak."

Tusks snorted when Elisapee translated. "And drown yourself," he said. "We do not roll a kayak here, and neither do the people living south or west of here. They say the Greenlanders roll those round-bottomed kayaks of theirs but we have never seen such a thing, and we do not know why they do it. But they say that the sea where Greenlanders hunt is often plagued by huge waves that rebound from the rocks so strongly that the hunter has to roll his kayak over to protect himself, and that may be why the Greenland hunters have learned to tip themselves upright again with the power of their minds and paddles."

"I could do that with a slim craft such as this," said Kayaker. "Perhaps the hunters on the other side used to roll these kayaks like the Greenlanders."

"Never!" Tusks said positively. "If such a thing had been their practice, we would have heard of it. Endlessly! Those people over there are tireless storytellers. They forget nothing of their past. They love to tell you of their prowess as hunters, their skill as kayakmen. They had some clever tricks. But for them, as for us, an upturned kayak marks the end of life."

Kayaker stood there studying Tusks' face. "Do you think, after all, that I could buy this kayak frame? I hate to see it rotting here."

"Certainly you could *not* buy it!" Tusks stared down the river to the sea. "This kayak," he said, placing one hand upon it, "belongs to the man whose bones lie underneath. I do not know where his soul has gone. The last words this man said to his wife were that his kayak should be placed here above his grave, lashed and weighted down against the winds. It will stay here until it rots completely."

Kayaker asked if the widow was still alive, and Tusks nodded. "Her name is Sea Bird. She is an old, old woman now, and would never allow that kayak to leave her husband's grave."

Kayaker knelt at the stern and wrote something quickly in his book. He closed one eye and sighted along the kayak's keel.

"Straight as an arrow," he whispered. "This kayak should be saved."

In some ways Kayaker seemed gentle as a woman, but I could see that underneath his shy and quiet ways he had a will as hard as black ironstone. That is the way with many whites. They smile at you like loving children, but if you look closely you will see the cunning in their eyes.

He came into our tent the next morning, bringing with him a handful of those little shiny silver packages full of coffee that we think look like flatfish. I had tasted coffee only a few times before I met Kayaker, but now I liked it almost as much as tea, and Elisapee said that in the morning she liked it even better.

Kayaker asked where Nungo's widow lived and if Elisapee and I would take him to see her before Tusks had a chance to talk to her about the kayak.

"I hope you are not going to try to get that kayak," Elisapee said. "I would not want to translate such words."

But we set out for the gray and tattered pair of tents belonging to the widow, and while we were walking Elisapee said, "This is not a sweet old lady you are going to meet. You should hear what she has to say about the young people and the way they live today." Elisapee held her hands over her ears. "Sea Bird says that most girls can't sew at all, and only care about running in the hills with boys and dancing in the trader's warehouse. She says that sons today are idle, not hunters, that they don't know how to throw a harpoon straight enough to stick their foot, that they borrow their father's rifles to make lots of noise but bring home nothing. She says the seals and caribou are safe. She goes on and on like that. You'll hear her!"

Elisapee coughed outside the old woman's rickety door, and when she heard an answering cough she bent and stepped inside.

Sea Bird was hunched beside her lamp, smoking on her husband's pipe. The air was rank with the smell of harsh tobacco, and of fish and seal meat well beyond the eating stage.

"*Kenukiak?*" she called out in her cracked old voice. "Who is it?"

"*Pudluriakpusi,*" Elisapee shouted. "We come visiting. We and this new white man that some call 'Kayaker.' "

Elisapee sat close to Sea Bird and indicated a place for Kayaker beside her on the bed skins that covered more than half the gravel floor.

"*Taktooalook,*" Sea Bird said to be polite. She meant that her tent was dark, unworthy of our visit.

"*Kowmijualook,*" Elisapee answered, meaning that it was bright enough inside.

With these politenesses over, Sea Bird shaded her good eye and squinted at Kayaker. "Who did you say this one is?"

"He's a kayakman," said Elisapee. "He likes to talk about

kayaks. He brought on the ship a little toy blue boat of his own."

"So this is the one! I've heard about him," said Sea Bird. "The blue kayak toy. Hunters told me it's a silly little thing, but they say the white man is good at paddling it. Is this that man?"

"Yes," said Elisapee. "I can speak with him for you."

"No need of that," Sea Bird said, and turning to Kayaker she began talking in rich old-fashioned Eskimo. "My husband was a kayakman," she said. "Hunters here say he was clever with the paddle. But all that's going now. The kayaks are disappearing fast. I used to see the hunters stroking past this tenting place in early morning. How many men?" She held up both her gnarled hands and started counting. "*Atouasik, muko, pingasut, sitamut . . . sitamaruktok*. This many. Eight of them out, all hunting together. Today what does a body see while looking out on that bay? A few of those clumsy noisy trade canoes all painted red and green to scare the animals. No wonder it's hard for me to get a feed of seal ribs. These young people live on the trader's hardtack biscuits. It's disgraceful. They'll turn themselves into white men if they don't change their ways."

"Tell her I saw her husband's kayak yesterday when we went walking up the river," Kayaker broke in.

"Yes, I heard that you were up there looking. You and Tusks and these two. That's a real kayak," Sea Bird said proudly. "You saw a real good one when you saw my husband's kayak. It didn't even come from around here. These people here, my husband said, make awkward-looking kayaks." She laughed and swayed her body wildly on the bed, as though she might tip over.

"Did you ever hear your husband or any of the hunters from the other side talk about rolling a kayak over and then coming up on the other side?" Elisapee interpreted for Kayaker.

"Oh, yes, I heard them speak of that. But whoever did roll over got himself drowned dead. I never heard of any coming up on the other side. I lost one of my brothers that way. Oh, yes, but it was a long time ago. Hunters say it's difficult to get your legs out of a kayak, once the sea water's pushing and squeezing you tight inside the cockpit."

She coughed hard from overtalking, and we had to wait until she held a wooden splinter into her lamp and relit her husband's pipe. She puffed it hard to soothe her throat and lungs, and when she was breathing easily again, Elisapee asked for Kayaker if she knew women here who could put a new skin on a kayak.

"*Ahaluna*. Certainly." She laughed at such a foolish question. "I could do that with my friends, if somebody brought me some decent sealskins. We have plenty of women's knives to scrape the hair off them." She slapped her loonskin sewing bag. "I have good tough sinew, and I remember all the strongest stitches, and most of the songs a woman has to sing. Kowlee must know every one of the kayak-sewing songs."

Kayaker told Elisapee to ask Sea Bird how many green faces she wanted for the kayak frame.

"This old woman doesn't even know what money is," Elisapee told him, trying to hide her anger. "If you gave her dollars, she might roll them up and light her pipe with them, or just scatter them and let them blow away in the wind."

"Then ask her what she does want."

Elisapee sat in sullen silence, looking at her fingernails, and when Kayaker grew tired of waiting, he ordered her in a cold tight voice to go ahead and ask Sea Bird. That's what he paid Elisapee to do.

Sea Bird said to Elisapee, "I only want things he cannot give me. I want not to be sick in bed the way I was last winter, with all my bone joints aching. I would like my teeth back," she said with a laugh, showing only gums, "and I want meat to eat, not just right now, but in the winter and the early spring, when meat is hard to get. I want fresh seal meat to eat until I die."

Elisapee smiled when she translated this for Kayaker, delighted that Sea Bird had asked for impossible things.

But he looked at his black wrist clock, got up quickly, and said, "All of you wait here for me. Don't go away!"

He was gone for a long time.

Sea Bird said, "I like the looks of that young man. I never heard before of a white man who cared about the kayaks. Is he a hunter?"

"No," I answered for Elisapee. "He's like me. He doesn't hunt at all."

"Why would he want a kayak if he doesn't hunt?"

In answer, Elisapee shrugged.

When Kayaker did at last come back, he was carrying a small but heavy wooden box. He set it gently down in front of Sea Bird and borrowed her blubber axe to pry one side open, spilling out more than twenty boxes of ammunition. He showed her that there were twenty shining rifle cartridges in each flat box.

Sea Bird laughed again and said, "I don't even have a rifle. Besides, I'm getting kind of old to learn how to shoot the meat."

Kayaker himself laughed at that. "You don't have to shoot the meat," he said. "Young hunters here are always short of ammunition. You give them only this many"—he held up five fingers—"and you tell them they must bring you one whole seal or caribou or you'll find a different hunter, who shoots straight."

Sea Bird started chuckling to herself and weighing the shining cartridges in her gnarled old hands. "For five bullets I'll want two whole seals." She wiped her nose. "They can miss with their own bullets. I want two seals for every five bullets or they don't get any more from me."

"Will you let me have the old kayak frame if I give you these cartridges? They will bring you more meat than you can eat for all the seasons of your life."

"Oh, yes," she said agreeably. "You can have my husband's kayak. He was my provider. He would like it—knowing that kayak would go on providing me with seals. Would you like me to get some women friends and sew a new skin on for you?"

Kayaker smiled and patted her bent shoulder and said, "*Ahaluna!*"

Sea Bird sucked her pipe and said to Elisapee, "Speaks a little Eskimo, does he? Too bad he hasn't seen a few more winters. He might be looking for a good wife like me!"

Old Tusks showed no real emotion when he saw Nungo's kayak frame resting down on the beach in front of the white man's tent, where it had been carried by Kayaker and me. Tusks turned around and walked straight toward the widow's tent and went inside, and for a few days after that he refused to see or speak to Kayaker. He believed that this white stranger had done something so completely wrong that no pile of shining cartridges could ever set it right.

I saw him watching Sea Bird as she went about on her two hobbling sticks, asking for sealskin sewers. When his own wife said she was going to help Sea Bird sew the kayak's skin, Tusks reluctantly gave in. And Kowlee told me she planned to be there with the other women to make sure the words in the sacred singing were exactly as they should be.

Kayaker watched the old women standing together, talking secretly, and then, with their hands clasped beneath the apron fronts of their long-tailed parkas, walking in single file toward Nungo's boat. Eyes cast down, they appeared to search the ground, though their stride was open, with a rolling gait, not at all like the smooth graceful walk affected by the young un-married women of our camps, but more like that of men traversing ice.

They stood by passively, staring out to sea, as old Sea Bird said a few thoughtful words to them about the kayak covering.

She was old enough to be open and bold with other women, yet at this time she was humble, for thoughts more than words pass between such women. Everything is known, and little if anything need be said. The women huddled together like geese, not even glancing at the kayak frame, nor did they speak. It was as though what they needed to know had been understood and taught by them for countless generations.

The old women worked with the dried hairless sealskins throughout that day, first unlashing them from their stretching frames, then weighting them in the stream to soak once more into softness. Now the hunters, young and old alike, kept away from the sewing women, who were known to be very short tempered during this reflective period. They were engaged in women's labor, entirely separated from the work of men.

But they did allow Tadlo to go and give instructions to the older men, who came cautiously to the beach with coils of bright new sealskin line. In silence they cut away the ancient lashings, and carefully rebound the frame at every joint, tightening holes with slender plugs of bone. When they stepped back from the kayak frame, every part was strong and ready.

At some unspoken signal all the women turned and walked away, whispering together, their shoulders touching. They drew the entrances to the tents tightly closed behind them. Everybody watched and waited, knowing that in the morning, if every sign was right, they would begin to cover the kayak frame.

I heard them, not long after dawn, and saw them walking along the gravel beach again, this time carrying their loonskin sewing bags. They were soaking strands of sinew in their mouths and rolling them into short lengths of strong waterproof thread. From incised ivory needle cases they took out their favorite trade needles and sharpened them rapidly on small hand stones. I watched them test the points against the small soft blue tattoos upon their wrists. I saw them working still with the soaking sealskins.

⁑

Only the men and boys lay sleeping in the tents. I pulled up my hood to ward off mosquitoes, and went to fetch fresh water from the stream, for on this day the younger women and all the girl children had gone to watch the ritual denied to men.

On the edge of the beach all the young girls and the newly married women who could not yet sew skillfully squatted in a tight group. Their backs were toward the tents, and yet they remained a respectful distance from the sewing. They had only the small girl infants on their backs.

Nine of the older women crowded around the kayak frame, and Kowlee helped two of them fling several wet sealskins over part of it. Four women squatted on each side, ready to lock-stitch the soft wet skins together.

The weather was dead still. The tide had drifted a chain of white ice to shore along the whole length of the fjord, and it hung there motionless in the distance, like a snowy mountain range. Each woman had her hood drawn up, for the mosquitoes were drawn by the rich smell of the new sealskins and descended in starving hordes. But windless weather is good for seal hunting, and the men gathered on the opposite shore and set out in their clumsy trade canoes.

On the beach the women began their singing, led by Kowlee, and softly humming the choruses. They were supposed to be singing sacred songs, and yet I heard them chanting "*Anorah, anorah,*" begging the wind to come and drive away the mosquitoes. But I imagined I could hear the rattle of the little knives that hung inside the backs of the canoes as each hunter tapped them gently with his foot. These amulets have a greater and a smaller power, and the smaller power is one to frighten off the wind, threatening the woman who controls the weather.

So here we had a conflict between our hunters and our women. And even as I watched, a light breeze whipped across the fjord, driving away the mosquitoes, ruffling the smooth surface with short sharp waves, giving every seal a place to hide his head. The women together let out a loud moan of pleasure and flung back their hoods in triumph, sewing swiftly, driving their short needles through the tough skin, using shiny store-bought thimbles. Still they were foolish to beg for wind, I thought, because seal hunting had been poor this summer, and the women would pay with their hunger for the wind that they had brought to us.

Oh, yes. Our women have power. The idea that they are ruled by men is a myth that they created to make men good natured and easier for them to handle. Men need women! Only after a man's mother or his sister or his wife has finished sewing his clothing and his kayak, and preparing his harpoon line, his dog harnesses, his mitts, and his boots—only then may he go hunting. When a girl is married, bears children, and matures, regard her closely. She may kneel in humble silence on the bed and yet rule every member of the family. She may hold her husband before her like a mask, speaking her words through his mouth. She may even decide, by whispering to him in the bed, where he and others with him should conduct their hunt. Have you not wondered that so many of our spirits that rule earth and sea and sky are women? The sun is a woman. Talislusk, Nuliayuk, Sila, Arnalook—and Taluliyuk, the sea dweller, the enemy of hunters. All of these powerful spirits are women!

Kayaker I watched intently that morning. Round his neck hung a heavy camera with a large and evil-looking eye. He was interested in making photographs of the women as they sewed, but he was careful not to get too close to them.

Kowlee made them change their pitch at high noon, when they turned the kayak over. After that their singing had a wavelike sound. Light clouds came in the afternoon, but still the breeze kept off the insects, and the men returned with nothing from their long day's hunting. When the wind tails in the sky turned flaming yellow, I could see the women's *ulus* flashing in the long low light. With the approach of darkness heavy clouds drifted across Black Whale Mountain, and raindrops splashed the gravel, but still the sewers did not leave their work. Their hands darted furiously in and out as they tried to outdistance nightfall, and when Kayaker walked too close, they hissed at him like nesting swans.

They used magical cross-stitches as they closed the bow and stern, and at the very last they carefully knotted small amulets into place. They hung a fish jaw beneath the back of the cockpit, and sewed a hawk's claw near the bow, and hid a bundle of tiny ivory knives where the paddler could tap them with his foot.

When they were finished at last, the tired and hungry women rose in silence and walked stiffly back toward their tents. The wet skins dried and tightened like a drumhead in the strong wind that came rising in the darkness.

When I got up in the early dawn and went outside to make my secret yellow lucky signs, I saw Kayaker standing in the half light, hands on hips, admiring the grace and sleekness of his reborn watercraft. I knew that he could scarcely wait for morning, and when it came a crowd of excited people gathered, men, women, and children.

Kayaker picked up his slim black craft and carried it down and placed it gently as an eggshell in the water. I watched him ease his narrow hips into the cockpit, supporting himself on the long narrow-bladed paddle, which held the kayak steady between the waters of the fjord and the well-worn landing stones.

When he was ready, he took one gentle stroke, and then another, and paddled smoothly through the shallow water and down the bay, with a crowd of hunters and their women following him along the shore. Then he turned and paddled back toward the landing place. Sometimes he went fast, raising his paddle breast high and stroking powerfully. Other times he rested the paddle on the high comb of the cockpit, and rolled it slowly, letting the ancient driftwood frame of the kayak bear the weight, using an old style that allows a hunter to travel all day long without tiring.

When he landed, he slipped out skillfully and took up the bow of the kayak. Old Tusks, his anger at Kayaker gone in his delight that the ancient ritual had taken place again, waded into the water and lifted up the stern. The women proudly watched the young man and the old one as they carried this masterpiece up across the beach, and carefully rested it right side up near the stone rack built for the small blue kayak from the outside world.

Elisapee asked him what he thought of it.

"It's as smooth as flying," he told her. "But far better than flying. It's the greatest thing that I have ever owned."

He unlashed the small blue kayak from its rack and handed it to the nearest children.

"Elisabeth," he called, "will you please tell these young boys that this blue boat is now theirs? Tell them to share it and enjoy it."

He stepped close to the skin kayak and ran his hand along its side. "Just look," he said. "You can see the morning sunlight shining through her. You can see every rib." He paused and spoke to all of us. "This one I will roll," he said. "I swear to you that before I leave, I'll roll this kayak over and come up again."

12

We held a dance that night to celebrate the launching of the old kayak. We made the trader's warehouse tremble with the pounding of our sealskin boots. Kowlee said that Sila, the woman in the air, must have been listening, for in her gladness she had sent a cold breeze to us from across the ice floes, and it had withered the hordes of mosquitoes. This, said Kowlee, was Sila's way of thanking our people for not letting old traditions die.

I believe that she was right. The breeze fell when the last mosquitoes were gone, and for six whole days and nights the sea lay silver calm. Icebergs that drifted in the Strait caused strange mirages, which sometimes appeared as huge reflections, then seemed to melt and disappear before our eyes, then reappear again like monstrous ghosts that stand at the very edges of the world.

I awoke early on the last of those white and breathless mornings, for I could hear a pop-pop-pop-popping sound echoing all along the stillness of the fjord. I roused myself and went outside the tent and saw a small Eskimo boat approaching. This is something very rare for us to see. Small boats almost never cross the Strait because of the grinding ice fields that choke our summer waters, and out to the west the ice is even worse.

I left the tent door open and crawled back in bed beside Elisapee. "You might as well wake up," I told her. "Some new people out there are putting down their anchor. *Inuit* people we have never seen before."

That made her open her eyes. You must have noticed that women feel a burning curiosity about anything new that happens. Tell them that strangers are coming and you'll see them scramble out of bed.

The strangers' boat rested not far from shore, fairly near our tent. She was wide and high and stubby, with too much cabin on top, painted like a house, all buff with purple trimmings, and had a short, thick, chewed-up mast that must be used mostly for loading and unloading awkward cargo. She was so overloaded now her hull was almost under water, and she rode lopsided, like a wounded gull.

Kayaker turned from in front of his tent and called up to ours, "Elisabeth! Who's that?"

"We don't know," she said. "Some people from Big Island, maybe?"

I could hear our people talking in all the tents as they got out of bed. The comings and goings of the whites interest us only a little. But real Eskimo hunters from some other place whom we have never seen? That's different! We could scarcely wait to meet them and hear all the strange things they would have to tell. One of our canvas canoes put out for them and brought back a tub-headed man and a younger hunter, with their first load. This included a big brown army tent and sleeping bags and two grub boxes, which meant they intended to stay by themselves, and for some time. They smiled and shook hands with everyone, but stayed close to their grub boxes, as though to guard them. According to our way, they should have come ashore with nothing and waited for an invitation to live among us. But different people have different

‡

customs, and only our oldest people now refuse to accept this.

I walked down to greet the two strangers, and was studying the curious cut of their pants and parkas and their boots, which were sewn not at all like ours, when I felt Kowlee touch my arm.

"Look who's come up out of the engine housing," she whispered.

I shaded my eyes and stared out at the overloaded boat and saw a white man on deck. He was not overdressed in new and fancy Eskimo clothing, like most whites, with woven woolen caps and belts and rows and rows of brightly colored braid around their sleeves and parka bottoms, and big lush trims of wolf or wolverine around their hoods. Oh, no, this white man was dressed like a hunter. His parka cover was of blue canvas, rough and faded, with holes and oil stains and a tattered sleeve. His pants were of the cheapest kind the trader sells, patched and worn and baggy in the seat. His boots were good but tied at the knees with seal thong instead of bright red or yellow ribbon. His face was narrow and darkly tanned, and his brown hair was bleached on top by the sun. He wore thin steel-rimmed spectacles, whose glasses caught and flashed back the morning light.

He reached down and pulled out a purple bag, which makes you know you are looking at a missionary. In this bag they carry all their amulets, and their ideas and songs written into three black books of different sizes. Still, the way he slammed the engine hatch tight shut, unshipped the rudder, and leaped down into the canoe made me believe that I was looking at one of our best young hunters.

"Is that a white man?" I asked the tub-headed stranger.

"*Ayeee,*" he said. "He's a missionary, but he also knows a lot about running the engines in the boats."

A third, broad-shouldered, man stepped down into our canoe with the missionary and stowed some other bags and boxes, and when the canoe came close to shore, it was the missionary who swung himself easily over the bow and prevented the keel from grinding against the rocks.

He did not clutch his bag of purple amulets like most missionaries, nor did he make a big affair of saying "*Kunowipisee*" to everyone, or shaking hands by pumping up and down and up and down as though each stranger were his best friend whom he had not seen since childhood. No! This white man had dignity. Perhaps that was because he was short and compact, like one of our people, not long and gangly, like most whites. He nodded to people shyly, and worked as hard as anyone to move the heaviest things they'd brought ashore. With his hood up and his back to me I could not tell him from one of our hunters, so naturally did he walk across the tide-slick stones.

This *ayahoktoyeegee*, this missionary teacher, was completely new to us. We had never seen him, never heard a name for him, but we could easily tell that he had learned our language in the west. He spoke it well, but with a sound that made you think he had a hollow goose bone in his throat. Our people believe that one missionary is very like another unless you travel with them or work in their houses and really get to know them. Most of the people who have done that say that some of them are quite nice, but there are those who would not always speak so kindly.

Sarkak, our catechist, the man who helps the missionary read the books to us, was late in coming down to meet the new arrivals. That was because he and his wife had paused to change into their best clothes.

"Who lives in that peculiar-looking tent?" the missionary asked him.

"A new white man," Sarkak answered somewhat proudly. "He's living here with us and learning all about our kayaks and how we use them. He does not speak our language, but he's a good strong paddler, and if you talk to him he'll pay you well. Come, I'll take you over to his tent so that you can see and speak to him."

"Oh, no, thank you. Not just now," the missionary said. "I'm bound to meet him soon enough."

I asked Elisapee why he wouldn't want to meet with Kayaker, and she said that she'd tell me later.

I went to the open entrance of Kayaker's tent and stepped inside. He was rattling the cups and tearing open his little silver packets, and the whole tent reeked of coffee. Elisapee went to the stream to get fresh water for him, and when she returned I asked her if Kayaker knew a missionary had come ashore. She said he did but didn't want to see him.

"Well, that's the way whites are," I said. "Two of them an endless distance from all their own people, two white men who have never met—yet they have already decided they dislike each other. You wait and see. Probably the new trader won't like him, either, and later this missionary will tell us that the trader is a man we should not trust. That's the way whites are. Do you understand why they act like that?" I asked Elisapee.

"Yes, I understand that much about them. Both of these men want to be here alone, with only *Inuit*. They have come a long way to be alone with us. Each wants to talk with us about only the thing that interests him. They want us to join them in their thoughts about religion or our kayaks, nothing else." She nodded toward Kayaker. "He thinks I know missionaries because I used to live with them. I don't really like them, and I don't want to talk to that missionary any more than he does. That missionary over in Sarkak's tent will be thinking that Kayaker is one of the crazy people who waste time and government money coming in here studying Eskimo boats, paying them far too much for information, spoiling them with new ideas. That's the way the whites think."

We shouldered our small packs and followed Kayaker behind the hill, carefully avoiding the missionary. I spent most of that day holding the other end of one of Kayaker's long unrolling steel tongues while he wrote down the exact measurements of every rib of Nungo's kayak frame. Elisapee interpreted and I answered as many of his questions as I could. Then we went to Sea Bird's tent, and Kayaker entered into his book all the things that she told us. He tried to be cheerful with all of us, and yet I sensed that he was in a nervous mood. I believe that he was worrying about the missionary, wondering if he could somehow avoid ever having to speak with him.

But as we were returning to our tents along the narrow path, we saw the missionary, followed by Tusks and Sarkak, coming straight toward us.

Kayaker and the missionary looked up at the same time and saw they could not avoid each other. They stopped and nodded, and then, because we were watching them, they shook hands violently, as though they planned to break each other's bones. We are shocked when we see white men shake hands like that.

Elisapee told me later of the words they spoke. I like to hear the strange things that foreigners have to say, especially when one white is speaking to another. When they talk to us they almost always use the simple words of children, but even in translation, their talk with one another sounds quite adult to me—except when they talk about the weather. Unfortunately, these two began by speaking of the weather.

"It's been a splendid day, with just the right amount of wind," the missionary said.

Kayaker asked the missionary if he'd had a smooth voyage, and the missionary said they had had a violent windstorm off their island coast, but smooth sailing after that, with only scattered ice. With that, they had used up all they had to say, and Kayaker sighed and kicked the gravel. He apologized for being in a hurry, adding that the missionary could come and visit—sometime—if he had nothing better to do. That was the worst kind of invitation, as the missionary understood, and he said that visiting would be difficult because he had to hold services in his tent and unload the lumber from the boat and fix the flywheel on the engine. Still, he might come for coffee sometime.

Then he asked if he could bring along his two friends, Sarkak and Tusks, using the word as though they really were best friends of his, persons scarcely known to us.

Three days later the missionary actually did make his visit, accompanied by Sarkak and Tusks.

"I say, this is a most unusual tent," he said as he straightened up inside. "Quite a little novelty. Have you tried it in a wind? I mean a really roaring, tearing Arctic wind?" He laughed.

"I suppose not," said Kayaker, and then just sat and stared at him.

I bent and lit Kayaker's small Swedish Primus stove and pumped it up until it roared, and Elisapee filled the kettle to make coffee. That seemed to change their mood. Kayaker nervously rearranged his rucksack against his sleeping bag and leaned with his back against it, his long legs crossed. His sharp-nailed hiking boots were pointed at the missionary.

The missionary laid down his purple bag of amulets, pulled off his tattered parka, and rolled it tight to sit on. He removed his glasses and wiped away the steam, and I was surprised to find his eyes were not so large and piercing as they had seemed, but really rather small. Tusks and Sarkak squatted, staring uncomfortably into space. Elisapee and I slumped beside Kayaker against his bag.

The missionary rubbed his hands together and said, "Well, well. I must admit this is not too bad a little tent. You must have government grants or be a wealthy man to afford such luxuries. Where do you come from, Mr.—ah—?"

"Morgan," Kayaker said. "Victor Morgan."

"And where have you come from?"

"Somewhat south of here," said Kayaker.

"You must be connected with a university, then."

"Oh, I've taken courses and taught here and there. Here and there and everywhere."

⁑

"I'm right, then. The government has given you a grant to carry out your studies."

"You might say that."

"Canada or the U.S. or Britain?"

"Actually, I've had a little help from various sources," Kayaker said.

"Well, well," the missionary said, and pushed his glasses in against his nose. "You're quite a mystery man. You don't admit to anything, and you don't have any sort of accent I can detect, and you—"

"That coffee smells good to me," said Kayaker, and he got up on his knees and poured it from the kettle into six tin mugs. "Will you have some powdered milk and sugar in your coffee?" he asked.

The Primus flame made the missionary's glasses flash like icy pools of water. Although I scarcely knew him, I knew how angry he was as he banged down his mug and said, "Oh— that's much too hot for me!" He turned to me and asked, *"Kenouveet? Puyukpunga.* What's your name? I've forgotten."

"Shoona," I told him, and he sat for a while, staring at Elisapee, before he asked her name.

"Taika," Elisapee said, not looking at him.

I had almost never heard her use her Eskimo name before.

"Oh! Others call you Elisabeth. Won't you please use English? I have heard that you speak it very well indeed. You did not grow up here among these people?"

Elisapee did not answer.

"Then where?" he asked.

"Big Fish River," she said almost rudely.

"I've heard a lot about that place," he said. "What camp did you live in over there?"

Elisapee paused for a moment and then said, "I grew up in the house that is painted the same color as your boat."

"You mean you grew up in the mission house? Oh, bless my soul! Then you must be *that* Elisabeth—the one old Willy and his wife adopted. Well! I hope we'll have a chance to talk about that later." He paused, studying us all through those eyes made large again by his glasses.

"It seems to me we're quite an odd collection for such a small community! A man who comes from nowhere. A man who some say is a shaman. And Sarkak, an Eskimo so powerful that he buys his own church buildings. And you, my dear," he said to Elisapee, "hiding here from the missionaries."

"And then there's me," he said, rudely leaving out Tusks. "I've come here to help Sarkak raise his church. With these two hands," he said, spreading his short blunt fingers, "and Sarkak's firm determination, we shall build a strong and lasting place of worship."

He went to the entrance of Kayaker's tent and held it open. "Look over there," he said. "We are unloading lumber on the opposite shore. Sarkak and I decided to build the church over there, as far away as possible from the trader's. Some of them are rather sinful men."

Next morning we could see many hunters hauling bags of gravel to make a pad on top of the permafrost, and by noon of the following day a white grid appeared that would support the floor, and we could hear the hammers ringing. That evening the missionary came along the path toward Kayaker's tent again, with many children running around him and calling out, "Candy! Candy!"

Kayaker had been in a good mood all day, but his face was a mask of gloom as he stepped back to give the missionary room to enter, and waved his hand toward the grub box.

The missionary stepped across the tent and sat above us as though he occupied a pulpit. Some of the children came crowding in, and Avinga, who was the boldest of them, held out a piece of paper with a pencil drawing on it. All the children knew that if a white person accepted something from them he must give them something in return.

The missionary, perhaps caught by this before, seemed reluctant to take the drawing, but he reached out for it in the end and examined it with care.

"Well, well," he said, "this little child has drawn an angel for me. Would you like to see it, Mr. Morgan?"

After Kayaker had examined it, too, he said to Elisapee, "Will you ask Avinga if this winged creature is one of God's angels?" But the missionary broke in and asked instead.

"Oh, no," the boy said seriously. "That is a *torngak*. A very bad one. Her name is Silakudluk. She is the other weather spirit. She has wings, and she goes 'Whoee, whoee, whoee' at night."

The children began to imitate the moaning and screaming of Silakudluk's voice.

The missionary said, "It is remarkable to hear children speaking so openly and knowledgeably about those old-fashioned spirits. You'd never hear anyone speak like that where we've established a mission."

"You should know more about the spirits," I said boldly. "Don't you know that the *arnalook* seek endlessly to gain control over the animals that human beings hunt for food? These *arnalook* were not born as we are born," I told the missionary. "They just appeared at dawn one morning. They were simply tufts of grass that suddenly turned into the first men and women."

The missionary coughed, as if he did not like my words, but then he surprised me by saying he would like to know more about what he called "the wicked little *arnalook*."

"Old Wolf Jaw saw them himself a long time ago. He told Kowlee it was in the fullness of the winter moon, in a time of hunger. The *arnalook* were lying on their backs in a neat row along the edges of the big tidal ice crack, beyond our winter camp. They kicked their legs in the air, open and closed, open and closed," I said showing Kayaker and the others with my fingers. "Wolf Jaw saw them clearly in the moonlight. They made a high humming sound that must have been their way of singing, and because he had heard them clearly, he was given a brief power over the *arnalook*. One by one they slipped down through the crack into the icy water and released the seals, and on the following day the bad hunting was ended."

Kayaker stroked his jaw, and his eyes seemed not to be looking at any of us but at something far away or deep inside his own thoughts.

"I believe that survival is still at the heart of all Eskimo thinking," he said now. "Survival in a world governed by dreams. We think it's odd that you seem not to fear death itself. You fear hunger and sickness, and unseen spirits that may do you harm, but you do not fear death. You say of death, '*Iyonamut*. It can't be helped.' "

"But death is not frightening," I said after Elisapee explained what he was saying. "It is only a short journey from one place to another."

Kayaker asked her how I knew there was another place.

I told him I had been there. "After a long period of fasting," I said, "I crawled through a hole and entered that other place and saw some of its creatures and heard some of the words that are spoken there, before I came back again into this place."

"You are fortunate," Kayaker said. "The whites believe that most sickness and even hunger is something that can be controlled. But death they fear tremendously."

I said to Kayaker, "Many *Inuit*, too, are not sure there is an afterlife. But some shamans have said that they have briefly died and gone into a different place, down through a crack beneath the stones. In that place, they say, you are neither warm nor cold, neither sad nor happy, neither full nor starving. These shamans have peered into that other place and seen animals and human beings wandering together as though they were all friends within one family."

Kowlee came over when we sent for her, but she was strangely silent. Finally the missionary gathered up his purple bag of amulets and made one parting attempt at conversation.

"I think you need some Christian teaching here." He rose to leave. "Have you ever noticed," he said to us, "that those Eskimos who attend our church services have good fortune when they go out hunting?"

"Yes, that's true," said Kowlee. "But we have also noticed that on those same calm days the wicked ones who miss your services, they have good luck at hunting, too." That ended the conversation.

Elisapee, Kowlee, and I stood with Kayaker outside his tent and looked at the reflection of the leaden sky in the long fjord.

"I'll tell you why that church is being built," Elisapee said to Kayaker. "It has nothing to do with white people. It is being built because Sarkak is the head of our most powerful hunting family. When he was young he was not Christian, but a walrus tore apart his kayak, and as he was drowning he called out loud so all could hear him, 'Save me and I will go with Godee and with Jesusee!'

"At that moment his hunting companion reached out and grasped him by the point of his parka hood and pulled him to safety on the back deck of his own kayak, and he was saved. What could Sarkak do but go with Godee and with Jesusee as he swore he would?"

"I would have done the same," I said, and Kowlee and Elisapee and Kayaker agreed.

13

The bad time for me started in the early autumn. Tadlo became afraid that this strange new white man would somehow find a way to take his kayak from him. Kayaker had measured it and examined it with care, so to put him off the scent Tadlo had Elisapee tell him about the splendid frame of an even older kayak, a true Baffin Island type, that was weathering away up north at an abandoned camp on Wild Bird Island.

Upon hearing about that almost forgotten skeleton of a boat, Kayaker grew restless and then seemed in a desperate hurry, and went with Elisapee to hire the hunter Ikhalook to take him up there in his whaleboat.

"He has asked me to go with him," Elisapee announced. She looked at me very seriously and said, "Do you think that it's all right? He really needs me to interpret, but he wants you to come, too, so you can answer some of his questions about shamans' amulets and charms to cut the weather. Maybe later, when he is gone, you can start teaching me again. The other day he asked me about Taluliyuk and how she lost her arms, and I couldn't remember whether you had told me or not."

Next morning early we left with Kayaker in Ikhalook's whaleboat. I made room for Elisapee up in the bow, but she settled herself amidships, with Kayaker, and Ikhalook and his son sat steering in the stern. None of us could hear a word above the pop-pop-popop-pop of the ancient engine, and so we said nothing to one another but stared out at the still blue morning.

We reached Wild Bird Island the following day, and we searched along its southern shore until Ikhalook's sharp eyes spied the tent rings of the long-abandoned camp. As soon as we landed, Kayaker went running toward the kayak's graying skeleton. It was resting upside down above the gravel, carefully supported and properly weighted down with stones. Every scrap of its skin had been torn away by hungry foxes.

I could tell Kayaker was delighted by the way he jerked out his sketching book and his steel measuring tongue, and started to make drawings of the frame.

"It's very different from Nungo's," he said. "See—it's smaller, lighter, wider bottomed, with a square-backed cockpit. This is a true Baffin Island kayak. Think of those men adrift out there who would give anything to have it."

I did not know what men he could mean, or what use the naked skeleton of a kayak could be to them, and Elisapee was confused, too.

"Men adrift?" she asked him. "Where?"

At that his eyes took on a blank look, but his cheeks flushed. "Oh, well—out there," he repeated, and after that he did not speak for some time.

Of course he could not wait to possess this kayak for himself. "If we can find a relative, I'll gladly pay for it," he kept saying, and Ikhalook and his son helped him to lash it across the whaleboat.

I came back from Wild Bird Island with questions in my head. I wondered why Elisapee had sat beside Kayaker on the whaleboat, and why he had said that thing about the men adrift, and why he was curious about Taluliyuk. Why should a white man be curious about that woman beneath the sea?

It may seem to you that much of this was Kayaker's doing, or even that Red Shoes and the missionary played a part in it.

But I turned all my anger against Kowlee. I believed she was doing something secretly that was ruining me.

My new mistrust visibly affected her. It was as though I could see her shrinking, fading before my eyes. One morning when I felt the first cold wind of autumn, I saw her leaning on a stick in front of her tent, watching the heavy storm clouds roll over Black Whale Mountain. Her face had become a wrinkled mask and her once powerful shoulders sagged like an old woman's.

"Swimmer!" she called out to me. "Why are you letting that white man share Elisapee? Are you going to lose her? Will you lose her to the first foreigner who tries to touch her?"

"Don't talk like that," I said angrily. "You stand there sneering like the others. Why don't you help me?"

"I have been trying to help you, but it's not easy. I think something strange is happening to your soul," she said, and bent down painfully and went inside her tent.

But later, when I met her on the path, she said, "I know now how I can help you. Come, return to my big tent. Bring Elisapee and live with us in safety. You, me, Elisapee, and Wolf Jaw and Avo Divio—it would be the way it used to be. Remember those good times we had, lying together, eating red candies, and laughing in the bed when it was storming?"

"Oh, yes, I remember."

"We could all go out together visiting the camps again," said Kowlee, "living well, selling amulets, and holding those séances that made people scream. Remember those nights, little Shoona? Remember how good it used to be with all of us together?"

I laughed at her and walked away. But I did start thinking of those old times, and believed they had been good, and a great sadness started to rise in me.

For the next six days the weather was full of wind and icy rain, and we saw little of Kayaker, who was busy with his writings—thinking, he said, and writing up his notes.

❇

I didn't miss him, I can tell you that. Elisapee was very different when Kayaker was not around. She was with me all the time. We stayed late together in the bed each morning and shared all the simple joyful pleasures we had known.

Sometimes, though, Kayaker did leave his tent, even in the fog and rain, but only to go walking across the tundra by himself. We would not see him coming back until dusk. The waters of the fjord pounded against our shore and coated every stone with ice, and the wind and rain continued.

They lashed the coast for another five long days and nights, and then the rain turned to sleet that drummed against the tents and made us shiver and huddle together, covering our heads for warmth.

Oh, it was boring. Sometimes we held sealskins over us and ran to visit Kayaker or our other neighbors, and sometimes Kayaker came to visit us. You could tell that the weather made him restless and short-tempered, the way it was making us. When I told Elisapee that Kowlee had invited us to come and live with her, she refused, saying that she had to stay and kelp Kayaker, perhaps even through the winter.

We visited him on the last night of the rain, after the wind had died. Everything was cold and damp and sweating in his tent, and the lamplight shivered in a way that made you want to blink your eyes.

A strange thing happened between Kayaker and me before that night was over, but it all began in the simplest kind of way, as we three were eating dried meat from a package, and sucking sugar fruit out of some little cans he had brought with him. He turned suddenly to Elisapee with a question, and she told me he wanted to know if this was a good time to ask me something special.

"*Achoolee*. I don't know," I said, "but I am feeling good because the wind is gone and the moon is showing through the clouds. So tell him to go ahead and speak."

"He says that today he asked Tusks some questions about

⠀

212

amulets, and Tusks told him that you or Kowlee knew far more about amulets than he did."

"What does he want to know about them?" I asked cautiously.

Kayaker spoke to Elisapee, and even made a small drawing in his book for both of us to look at. She interpreted.

"He wants to know exactly what those eight little bone knives are for, the ones tied into the kayaks that sway and jingle when they're paddling."

"They are to cut the weather. You know, to prevent violent storms, like the one that passed this morning."

I noticed that he wrote nothing in his book. "What about that ivory peg I see on the side of most harpoons?" he went on, instead, and made a drawing. "The kind with those two round things that look like testicles on the side."

"Oh! Those are for—for holding the harpoon in place so it won't slip off the kayak deck and fall into the water. I suppose the round things are carved that way to make them look good."

Kayaker rubbed his lightly bearded chin, but still he did not write a word of what I'd said. He spoke softly to Elisapee, who nodded, and laid aside his thin green book.

"There comes a time," he said, "when a little sip or two of *imialook* will help us relax, feel good, and remember things more clearly."

That set Elisapee laughing. She said to me that whites call rum "a devil" and refer to all strong drinks as "spirits," as though drink itself possessed some magic.

Kayaker dug around in his special box and took out a short round black tube. He cut the top with a knife point and pulled the tube apart, revealing a bottle full of red-brown liquid that glowed in his lantern's light. Then he took out three metal cups and carefully filled them to the brim. He passed one to Elisapee, and one to me, and raised the third to his lips, saying some word I did not understand, and drank. Elisapee and I did the same, and felt the spirits burn our tongues and throats and set our stomachs afire.

I blew out my breath, and the warmth spread all through my body. Giggling, Elisapee examined the label on the bottle, and asked, "Is this drink just for navy men?"

Kayaker smiled and said, "Let's have another, shall we?"

We each drank that one, and then a third, and I began to feel like an entirely different person—myself, yet not myself. I started whistling, trying to imitate the sounds Kayaker made on his wooden stick, and when my lips seemed thick and made no real sound at all, I laughed until I fell over sideways, bumping against Elisapee, splashing most of her drink down on her boots. I started singing, forgetting all about the silence, and the moon that listened to me just outside the tent.

"One more for luck," Kayaker called out; his voice sounded far away.

I noticed that he took only half a cup himself, though he had filled mine completely. Well, I liked generosity in a man. One could tell that Kayaker would share a seal or caribou with all his neighbors. For us, that was the finest thing that we could say of any man.

He had almost filled Elisapee's cup, too, but when she started singing mission hymns in Eskimo and English, he took it from her and spilled more than half of it into mine. Elisapee was not pleased, but I drank it down and said, "Tank-yoooo!" showing off my English.

That made Elisapee giggle again. Then she told me he wanted to know the real reason, the important one, for the little knives that hang inside the kayaks.

"Oh, that," I said. "Well, tell him to listen, because I am going to tell him. Those knives are hanging there to threaten her, you know, the woman beneath the sea, the goddess Taluliyuk, if she comes near the kayak. Yes. She can hear those bone knives rattling. Click, click, clicking. That sound frightens her. It reminds her of the awful night in the storm when her father had to throw her overboard because he thought they all would sink, and how when she tried to crawl back in, the eight men in the skin boat chopped her fingers off, just at the first knuckles. And then all ten knucklebones turned into seals. She screamed, they say, and grasped the boat again, and the hunters cut off her hands, and they turned into a male and female walrus. After that they chopped her arms off at the elbows, and they became the parents of all whales."

"Oh," said Kayaker when Elisapee told him that, "then those knives have nothing to do with cutting the weather."

"Oh, a little something." I laughed, proud of the wisdom Kowlee had given me. "But that is not important."

Kayaker was writing furiously in his notebook. "We are getting somewhere now," he told Elisapee, and asked again for the name of the goddess.

"Ta-lu-li-yoook!" I said. "But she has got a lot of different names. People west of here call her Sedna, and in other places a few say Tikanakamsilik. But one shouldn't call her Puyee, Sea Beast, even though she is half human and half seal. You are not supposed to notice that, if you see her swimming out there in the fjord."

Elisapee said to me, "You talk too much when you've been drinking *imialook*," but I had more things I wanted to tell Kayaker.

"Those little walrus-teeth carvings from long ago, the kind you find in the old ruined Tunik houses, they are all of her. So is that ivory carving hanging around Elisapee's neck."

I wiped my mouth to see if my lips were still there. "Well, that's her. That's Taluliyuk. I mean she's the head of everything. She's the most powerful of them all. All the other creatures, all the ordinary sea beasts, they are below her. They are like her children, because they began from her, and she protects them. She has a husband, a dwarf, a hunchbacked man named Unga, and even he is far beneath her. But still his words can make her change her mind."

Kayaker, who was writing every word I said, asked me to pronounce Unga's name most carefully. I showed him how Unga's back was twisted. I even drew a little picture of Taluliyuk and Unga in his book, and of the monstrous dogs that guard their house.

Elisapee told me Kowlee would be furious if she knew what I had done, but Kayaker started pointing at the writing and my drawings, speaking rapidly to Elisapee, and she paid no more heed to me. So I picked up the bottle and turned my head away and took a long strong drink. This time it did not burn my throat but went down like water from an ice-cold stream, and made me start to sing.

"Lucasi poksinga ki lau lo li, Ayii.
Lucasi poksinga ki lau lo li, Ayii."

I almost collapsed with laughter at the sound of my own voice.

Kayaker took the bottle and placed it well beyond my reach. I didn't care, because I had slyly filled Elisapee's cup as well as my own. I wished that Kayaker would leave, so she and I could go to bed and get some good out of the wild way I was feeling. She must have felt like that, too, because now she smiled at me and rubbed against me, and everything was getting better until I noticed that we were still in Kayaker's tent instead of ours. I laughed at my mistake and felt too happy to think that we were the ones who should leave. And when Kayaker picked up the seal harpoon he had bought from Tadlo and asked again what the two round things were, I cried, "Testicles! Those are the likeness of a pair of hunter's testicles!"

"Why are they there?" he asked. "To excite Taluliyuk?"

"No!" I shouted. "To frighten her. To make her remember the dog man who got her pregnant. She was only young then, before her father found out, got angry, and threw her from the boat. Ever since then Taluliyuk mistrusts every man and dog she sees."

"Are people here afraid of her?" Kayaker asked.

"Oh, no! When our hunters see her out there in the fjord with her half arms upraised, or moving along the open tide cracks in the sea ice, they call out to her, saying, 'Come, come, come!'" And I held the harpoon up as though I were the kayakman who threatened her.

"She's afraid of that ivory sticking out on the harpoon shaft," Elisapee told him. "She remembers the dog man's awful passions and dives from the kayakmen and swims away in terror."

"But if you yourself fall overboard, watch out!" I said. "Once you are in the water she has power over you, too. Stay in your kayak with your harpoon," I said and drew back my arm and aimed Tadlo's harpoon at the door.

"You put that sharp thing down." Elisapee laughed and snatched it from me. "I don't blame that poor sea woman for being afraid, with kayakmen all trying to stick their harpoons into her, but maybe she's not afraid of those little ivory things." She giggled and said, "I wouldn't be afraid of them."

"Oh, no! Not you. You're bold!" I laughed, too, and looked into Elisapee's cup, thinking that I would drink up what I had so generously given her. But no, the cup was empty. She had finished all of it herself. And now she started singing:

> "Good King Win-een-cel-has
> Looked doubt on the feastey
> Stephen brightly shown
> The moon about,
> Deep and crisp and EEE-VVEE-AANNN!

"Oh, I love that song," Elisapee cried. "I like Christmas. It's my favorite time. You want me to sing some more for you?"

Kayaker was busy writing, and Elisapee had her hands clasped round her knees and was rocking back and forth, the way children do in a game they sometimes play. Finally she rocked too far and fell helplessly back upon the bed. Laughing at herself she tried to rise, but changed her mind and went to sleep.

Kayaker took his notebook and his almost empty bottle and went out of his tent. I called to him, but he did not turn or look at me. He was gone, and that was a pity, because I had many other things to tell him. I shook Elisapee hard, but I could tell by the way her head rolled back and forth that she would sleep for a long time.

I got up and staggered to the entrance of the tent, which had become so small I could hardly get myself outside.

The night above my head was still, and clouds stood away from the moon and showed their softly shining edges. I could see Kayaker walking down toward the water in the blackness. All the tents across the bay were little glows of light. The trader's house shone white in the moonlight, and so did the stones along his pathway, lined up like two even rows of teeth.

Kayaker pulled out the cork, poured the rest of the liquor on the ground, and set the empty bottle on a rock. I watched him as he walked down the beach in a slow and careful way, putting one foot in front of the other, like a woman. Yes, I remember that clearly: he walked just like a woman.

I felt so dizzy that I squatted on the stones and held my head to keep my vision steady. Kayaker kept on walking, but he paused at the water's edge and peered at the dark image standing upside down beneath his feet. When he slowly walked out over his boot tops, up to his thighs, I could not believe what I was seeing. Even in summer our sea water is deadly cold, but although he hunched his shoulders when it touched his groin, he kept on going. The moonlight caused it to shimmer in bright circles, moving out from around his waist, his ribs, and finally his shoulders.

I shook myself to make certain I was not asleep and dreaming as Kayaker's head sank below the surface. I saw him raise both his hands, perhaps clenched into fists, because they seemed to have no fingers. Still he kept walking forward, until even his stubby arms disappeared beneath the dark water.

I waited for a moment. When he did not thrust up his head to breathe, I was frightened and lurched to my feet and ran down to the water's edge. But by the time I got there the ripples had spread wide in the moonlight, leaving the surface undisturbed.

He was gone, I thought. There was nothing I could do to help him. His body would float up when the stomach gasses started to work.

I lay down on the beach and curled up tight against the cold, and I remember that I had no feeling of either gladness or sadness. Kayaker was gone. It was as simple as that. I let my dizziness wipe away the night, the moon, and all my thoughts.

I awoke at dawn still lying on the beach. More rain must have fallen, because I was wet and freezing cold. I looked out at the fjord and saw chilling mists spread across the water and come edging along our empty beaches. I heard dogs howling and answering one another all around our bay, with a sound as sad as that of a lonely woman crying.

I went up to Kayaker's tent, unzipped the zipper, and peeked inside. He was lying in his bag alone, asleep. I stood there a long time, pressing my hands against my head. But I could not push out the pounding pain. I thought it was the pain that confused me, so that I could not tell what had really happened last night and what I might have dreamed.

Elisapee, too, held her head in her hands that morning and told me she had never felt so sick in all her life. After that she did not wish to talk. So when I had drunk my tea I went outside again alone, to think my thoughts. The sky was ominous, filled with low scudding clouds that crept over the top of Black Whale Mountain and slithered down its cliffs like wet gray smoke. The summer tundra over on the hills of Sangirut had a hoarfrost sheen, and flocks of sea birds came crying into the bay. These were bad signs that meant foul weather was surely coming.

I went back inside the tent and climbed into our bed. Elisapee lay on her belly, close beside me, fiddling with the kettle that hung above the lamp, trying to hurry up a second cup of tea.

"We could buy a new Primus stove with the money we are earning," I said.

"Oh, this one will do," she said, and threw a half handful of tea into the kettle.

Elisapee wanted to be *inularik*, truly Eskimo, and do without all the white man's things. Living with a missionary's family, I think, had taught her enough about *kalunait* ways to last her all her life. Just the same, she wore a big wrist clock now with a black face that glowed green in the dark and showed the number of the day and moon. It had buttons all around it and could be thrown in the water and still keep the time of day or night. Kayaker had given it to Elisapee so she would be on time when he needed her.

I wouldn't want a watch like that. It seems far too wise to me. A man has every right to be nervous of such a thing. But Elisapee just laughed at it and said if its hands moved too fast she'd break it with a rock.

She looked at it now, though, and said, "I have to hurry."

I tried to make my eyes focus on her as she pulled on her boots and parka and went outside. I knew she and Kayaker were planning to talk with Tusks about *talos*, which is a drumlike drag to slow down a seal after the hunter harpoons it. I thought that they might return sometime after midday. But I was wrong.

I tried to sleep again, hoping the pain in my head would go away. A little of it did, but most of it stayed, still throbbing, and I rolled around in the bed, always half awake. I went out once, just before dark. The rain was turning into sleet again, and the wind was moaning out of the north across the inland plain, so I turned back and sat alone watching the wind press in the tent wall as though some heavy spirit leaned against it.

After a long time I heard a squish, squish, squish on the wet tundra. Then our little wooden door flew open and Elisapee stepped inside. The sky behind her was pitch black.

She sat on the head log of our bed to pull off her rain-soaked parka cover and her sodden sealskin boots. Still without speaking, she cleaned the carbon off the wick of the lamp and re-shaped the flame with the handle of a broken spoon. After that, she poked through our supplies to see if there was any food left.

"Lucky you!" she said at last. "You've been in bed all day."

"I've had a pain inside my head all day," I mumbled.

"Do you want anything to eat?" When I did not answer, she put her hand on my forehead and said, "Poor you, poor you."

"What were you two doing over there?"

"Just talking. Talking till I'm sick of it," she said. "He wants to know everything about sealskin floats and drags and harpoon lines. He writes it all down and then asks the same questions over again in a slightly different way. It takes so long."

Elisapee squeezed beside me in the sleeping bag. I could feel her wriggling out of all her clothes. I shut my eyes to block the increased light from the lamp and lay there imagining all sorts of disagreeable things. I heard her place a cup beside me, and it smelled delicious, but I could not bring myself to raise my head and drink the tea.

Some time later I felt Elisapee rise on one elbow and touch me lightly. "Shoona," she whispered. I kept my eyes closed and pretended I did not hear her.

She eased cautiously out of bed, pulled on her high duffle socks and her least damp pair of boots, and slipped into her outer clothing. I heard her cross the gravel tent floor quietly and ease open our little wooden door. I raised my eyelids narrowly, just enough to see her as she looked back to make sure I was asleep. Then she crept out of the door.

My headache was gone. I sat up in the bed and quickly dressed, crouching cunningly away from the lamp so that I would cast no shadow against the tent wall. When I peered outside, the tundra moss was sodden but the sky had partly cleared, and in the north stars winked and disappeared and winked again among running clouds.

I moved cautiously across to Kayaker's tent. It was dark inside, and I stood for a long time, listening. Then I jerked open the zipper, leaped through, and struck a match. It flared up, illuminating the whole inside of the tent. They were not there. I ran my hand inside his sleeping bag, and it was cold, not slept in for some time.

Outside again I stood not knowing what to do. Then I saw that the kayak rack was empty. I looked along the dark fjord, but could see nothing. I walked down to the beach and found the empty rum bottle standing where I had seen Kayaker leave it. I weighed it in my hand, cold and smooth, and suddenly flung it toward the water with all my strength and heard it smash to pieces on the rocks.

Finally I went back and lay in the bed. I don't know whether I slept or not, but much later, when Elisapee crept in, I made my breathing regular, so that she would believe that I was sound asleep. After that I kept my secret knowledge buried deep within me.

Several days later I went over to Pingwa's tent early, because I had word that he'd had good fortune with his gill net and was saving two large fat trout for us. When I got back, I found Elisapee stuffing some of her clothing into a canvas sack.

"I have to go right now," she told me. "They say I have to go with them." She bit her bottom lip the way she does when she is nervous.

"The trader offered Kayaker a chance to go with him along

⁑

---

the coast in his Peterhead boat," she explained. "To see the place they call '*Inukshukskalik.*' "

That was the place where stone likenesses of men stood, dozens of them, pointing the way west to Sharlo.

"Well, let them go," I snorted. "You don't have to go with them."

"Yes, I do," Elisapee insisted, and went on looking for the little yellow-handled brush she rubbed across her teeth. "Red Shoes says they may sail all the way to Sharlo if the ice has opened up. He says if that missionary can do it, he can, too. They expect to meet people on the other side, and Kayaker will need me to interpret for him."

"Oh," I said. "Then may I come along with all of you? I have never been to Sharlo."

"Well, no," said Elisapee. "I asked about you, and they said there was no space aboard. And besides, you don't have a rifle, and the trader is hoping to get some walrus, enough dog food for the winter."

"*Yuuuk!* There's lots of space on that boat. It has a hold big enough to carry more than a dozen full-grown walrus. They just don't want me along. Red Shoes doesn't like me, and Kayaker will probably be glad to have you to himself."

Elisapee shook her head at me. "Don't say that! You agreed that I should take this job. I give you all the money. Shall I say to them that I can't go, my husband won't let me?"

"Oh, go then! Go!" I shouted. "If you want so much to be away with him." I did not want to say more, but couldn't stop myself from asking, "How long will you be gone? Tell me. How many nights?"

"I don't know. They say if we see too much moving ice out there we'll turn straight back. We may be back tonight or early in the morning."

"Yes, but if the sea is open? Then how long?"

"Oh, how do I know?" Elisapee sighed. "Two days, three. That's all."

"Oh, no," I said. "It will be six days, eight days, ten!"

I jumped up and ran out of the tent and headed straight inland. Believe me, I was furious with all of them, and when I heard her call good-bye, I did not turn my head or answer her in any way.

At low tide I strode over the narrows that cross to the next island, and walked slowly up to the place where some ancient Tunik house ruins stand. When I looked down into the bay, Yannee and his brother were hauling in the anchor and running up the sail on the trader's boat. She was thick-hulled and strongly built to endure a heavy pounding from the sea, and freshly painted, white with a dark-green trim. I watched her make a long tack down the fjord and head out to sea, and even at that distance the dark sleek kayak lashed across her afterdeck was easy to see. I thought of Elisapee laughing gaily, making coffee for all of them. It made me hate her and Kayaker and the trader, and everyone else aboard his boat.

Beyond them on the western horizon there was a long white line of ice. It seemed unbroken.

"I hope it's heavy." I stamped my feet in rage. "I hope it—"

I closed my eyes and clamped my hand across my mouth. Not another word, I told myself. There had been too much trouble lately.

I scarcely slept for the five long nights that they were gone. At dawn on the sixth day I went and sat shivering in the hills, afraid that something might have happened to Elisapee. For a long time I stared through the glass, watching a small white patch that I told myself was surely no more than ice.

My heart pounded when I knew for sure that it was the trader's sail. I closed my eyes and said aloud, "Well, Elisapee's coming back. That's what you wanted, isn't it? So don't be angry with her. She was only doing the work you agreed she should do. She's giving you all the money, too. Remember that!"

Kayaker paddled ashore with Elisapee stretched out on the

kayak's back deck, and I had the feeling that she had ridden there several times before. I was down at the shore to greet her when they landed, and she and Kayaker shook hands with me but did not look at each other or even speak.

We three walked back up to our tents. Kayaker was silent, but Elisapee talked incessantly. She told me they had seen nine polar bears and countless walrus and a good-sized herd of caribou on Sharlo. They had brought back a lot of fresh meat with them. Their faces were dark brown from the sun.

When they finally spoke together, they did so only in English, and Elisapee did not bother to translate a single word for me. Somehow they seemed like a married couple, and I saw myself as a ragged stranger trying to push in where I wasn't wanted.

I didn't say much until that night, in bed, when I asked Elisapee where she had slept aboard the boat.

"Up forward in the little fo'c'sle cabin," she answered, staring blankly at the ceiling.

"Where did he sleep?"

"Who?" she asked.

"Kayaker."

She paused. "He slept there, too—in that forward cabin."

"Who else slept there?"

She answered that in a cautious voice. "The trader and Yannee and his brother slept back in the hold or in that little engine room. Where we slept was their idea, not mine. I slept where they threw my sleeping bag. What's wrong with that?"

"Nothing," I said, and we were both silent for some time.

"Did you lie with him?"

She turned her head away from me. "Why do you ask me such a question?"

"Because I want to know. Did you?"

"Yes. I lay with him," she said. "What's so wrong with that? Last spring you went away and lay with Josie and I lay with Pingwa. Why is this man so different?"

"Why is he so different?" I shouted, sitting up in bed and

pulling on my boots. "You mean you don't know why he is so different? Well, I'll tell you. We four all agreed to do that *tivivok*, that wife-changing. We talked about it, took time to think it over, and then in warmest harmony we all agreed! Together we agreed!

"But this? This is not at all the same. Who asked me? Did Kayaker ask me if he could sleep with you? No! Did you ask me if you could sleep with Kayaker? No! Neither of you care about me. You do anything you want!

"Now the gossip will spread through every camp about me. Even the children will whisper that the new white man and my wife lay together alone in a little cabin on that boat, while I was sitting back here worrying, counting my poor unlucky amulets until you decided to return to me. Our exchange with Pingwa and Josie was agreeable to all of us. But not this secret lying together between you and Kayaker. This is going to cause all kinds of trouble!"

And it did. Next day I could not bring myself to speak to Elisapee or go near Kayaker, but I had to get outside. I had to talk to someone.

I went to Kowlee. I always went to her if I had troubles. She did not look well, but we shared some hot blood soup to cheer us up, and she listened to me carefully.

"What shall I do?" I asked.

It was a long time before she answered. She just sat hunched over, picking and poking at her long lamp wick, making the flame far worse than better, so that it threw long shadows around her tent.

Finally she said, "I'm not worried about the white man lying with Elisapee. Surely you're not such a fool as to care about a little thing like that!" Kowlee glanced sideways at me. "I'm worried about that man himself. He's very strange. Do you believe that Pingwa and the other northern hunters really saw him walking up at Tall Clouds all alone—with nothing?

⚏

They all swear they did. And yet he swears he was not there at all. What is the truth of that? I stood near that white man at the trader's not long ago. We looked straight at each other. He worries me. I cannot tell you why. I don't like the look of those big sensitive nostrils of his. And I certainly don't trust his dead pale eyes."

I was just going to tell Kowlee about seeing him walk out and disappear beneath the water when without warning Kayaker himself jerked open the door and stepped inside. Wolf Jaw, who I had thought was asleep, sat up stiffly in the bed and pointed his trembling finger straight at Kayaker's face.

"*Unalook!*" he shouted. "Get out! Never come into this tent again!"

I was astonished. I had believed for a long time that poor old Wolf Jaw had lost the power to see or hear or even speak.

Kowlee stared viciously at Kayaker, offering him no word of welcome. He narrowed his eyes, examining all three of us, then turned and left, going as stealthily as he had come.

We sat listening for some time, until we were sure that he was gone. Then Kowlee whispered, "He heard every word we said."

"Even if he heard, he didn't understand," I reminded her. "He does not understand our language."

"I believe he knows all languages." Kowlee scowled at me. "Even our secret language, his ears understand. I am afraid of him! I believe Wolf Jaw is afraid of him as well. *Kapiashuk-peet!*" she shouted across the tent. "Are you afraid?"

Wolf Jaw did not turn his head or seem to hear her voice.

THREE
The Woman
Beneath the Sea

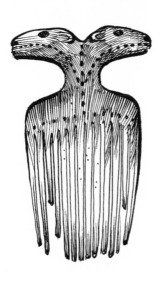

14

Only a short time after the voyage to Sharlo, I heard from Pingwa that Red Shoes was sick. I had not really looked at him, but only at Elisapee and Kayaker, the day they all returned. And because he did not like me, I always sent Elisapee to do our trading at his store. So what Pingwa told me was a great surprise.

"These days he almost never seems to leave his house, but I saw him last night," Pingwa said. "And I could not believe my eyes. At the winter dances he weighed as much as any two men here, but now, I tell you, he weighs less than any one of us." Pingwa hunched over and pulled out his parka. "His clothes just hang on him. Yannee and his brother say he has something wrong inside of him. He may be dying."

"But he's not old at all," I said. "Why would he be dying?"

"I don't know," said Pingwa. "Red Shoes radioed the ship that he is sick, and they will come here to take him south."

Soon after that, the ship did come but stayed hove to, waiting beyond the broken, tight-packed ice for a northeast wind to come and open up a passage. When the wind came, the ship worked her way slowly toward us up a long lead in the ice, belching black smoke high in the air. She tried her best, but she was not an icebreaker, and the lead kept closing with the wind and tide. After two days of desperate effort, she relaxed and hung there like a tired whale held captive in the ice.

Sarkak, the catechist, who was thought to be the wisest man among us, solved the problem. He picked six of our strongest hunters, including Pingwa, and then Yannee and his brother helped them lash the trader's big green freight canoe upright onto the largest sled, and hitched it to Sarkak's dog team. Together the hunters carried Red Shoes down and laid him in the canoe, with his soft bales of white fox packed under him and all around him.

The broken ice had jammed together, forming dangerous ridges and wide pools of open water, over which the dogs and sled and men must pass. Sarkak walked out ahead of the dogs, testing every step of the way with his long ice chisel, moving slowly in a long, zigzag course before he found ice firm enough to cross. The men made better progress after that, sometimes passing through rough ice that had been forced up far higher than their heads, sometimes having to jump and to make the dogs swim, but always they kept moving.

I know all this because, with many others, I was up in the hills watching through the long brass telescope. I kept thinking about the poor sick trader, and telling myself that he was a good man who had done me no great harm, and that Annee was nothing to me.

When I looked up to rest my eyes, Kayaker and Elisapee were standing right beside me. Kayaker was holding a pair of those short black double telescopes, and peering out across the ice like all the rest of us.

"Forget him. Forget him," I told myself. "You wish to be a healer, not a striker. You wish to be a help to others."

As if he could hear my thoughts, Kayaker looked down at me and laughed. He spoke to Elisapee, and this is what he said: "Please repeat what Tusks told us—that Shoona is a swimmer, and swimmers do not heal. They know only how to harm."

I narrowed my eyes so that the sun that glared above the ice distorted into wide red and yellow circles of light. Perhaps Kowlee was right. There was something really strange and frightening about Kayaker that made him unlike any white man we had ever known.

"*Kadang*," I called out deep inside me. "*Kadang*—now! Someone come and help me. Now! Give me my strength. *Kadang!*"

As I watched the wide sun circles spin and glaze like fire I heard Kayaker step quickly away from me and felt the hot loon pressing up against my body. I ran my fingers along its feathered necklace and stared into the bright red eye that once more became the sun. I drew back, shielding my own eyes, because I feared the deadly sharpness of its beak.

"Help the trader to get better," I whispered to the loon. "Make him fat again. I did not mean him any harm."

It took the dog team and the hunters until well after midday to reach the ship. There on the hillside we could hear the sailors cheering, and we sent up an answering cheer. We saw the captain lower a sling, which lifted the trader aboard in his canoe, and then the ship's whistle blew, and black smoke and white steam puffed out of her nose, and she let out another roar.

"They are waiting too long," Tusks said. "The tide is running out on them. Go! Go!" he shouted, as though they could hear him. "Take that ship away from that place!"

The boat churned water at her stern as she started pulling herself out from between the blue jaws opening in the ice.

"They're free! They're free!" some of the watchers shouted. I felt proud that my thoughts had helped the trader safe aboard his ship, which was turning in a wide space of open water, trying to set her bow toward the south.

"The tide's running out beneath them," Tusks shouted, and at that very moment the ship's siren began calling. The high-pitched whoop-whoop-whoop-whoop-whoop seemed to scream out in terror above the sharp clear sound of the alarm bells clanging, clanging, clanging! Through the long glass I could see the ship listing slightly, leaning to the west, and she was no longer moving forward.

Old Tusks lay beside me and said, "Let me have a look." Then he whispered, "I am afraid for them. The reef is biting right into the ship's belly." He watched through the telescope and cried out, "Look! Look! She's breaking. She's tipping over. But Sarkak and the dog team are turning around. They're going back to help the ship."

He steadied the glass against the rock. "I can see people climbing down the ship's side. Yes! Some of them are standing on the ice, and more and more are leaving. Look at the black smoke blowing out of her. She is still trying with all her might to pull herself off the reef. Look how her bow and stern are sagging in the water. Oh, I hate to see that! I cannot look," he said, and he closed his eyes and handed me the telescope.

I had almost forgotten Elisapee, until I heard her ask me if the ship was on fire.

"No," I said. "But she's in trouble."

"What kind of trouble? She's making an awful lot of noise."

"She's caught, hanging on the reef. She must be almost torn in half. She's filling up with water. She's sinking! Broken and sinking!"

"Oh, no!" Elisapee wailed. "When you started to walk up here, Kowlee told me you might try to harm the trader."

I stared at her in silence and then hid my face in horror.

"I was only trying to help him," I cried out. "I was trying to help Red Shoes stay alive."

"Did you use that awful word of yours?" she asked in the secret language.

Kayaker had moved close to Elisapee and was listening as though he understood every word we said. Because of him I didn't answer, but turned away and staggered down toward the tents. They were almost totally deserted. Everything about the place was silent except for a cold autumn breeze that flapped the canvas walls.

When I went inside Kowlee's tent and saw her lying on the bed, I could almost believe that she was dead. Her eyes were closed, her face was gray, and she did not seem to breathe. I waited quietly, staring at her, remembering when she had traded the lever-action rifle and the cartridges for me. In those days she had seemed in every way much stronger than most men.

As I turned to go she whispered, "Did they put him on the ship?"

"Yes," I said, "but now the ship is sinking."

"The captain must have bought some useless kind of amulets. They don't make good ones in the south."

"I am sorry Red Shoes is sick," I said.

"Well, don't you try to help him," Kowlee whispered. "You're no healer. You might make him worse."

Those were the last words she said before she went to sleep.

In the evening Sarkak and the hunters and the dog team returned to Trader's Bay. Sarkak was so tired from climbing on the ice that they had to bring him back in the canoe tied on the sled. Pingwa told me that the dying ship had called on the radio to another one beyond the ice, and this second ship was hurrying to pick up the crew, all out safe now, waiting on the ice. As long as there was no wind, they were in no danger. They had plenty of food, and rum, and blankets, and they had begun to set up several tents.

I felt dizzy and depressed, but there was nothing I could do. When I passed people on the way back to my tent, they seemed to shrink away from me, and I fell down on our bed not caring if I slept or woke or ever saw another day.

Later Elisapee shook me. "Wake up," she said. "It's morning. I know you're angry at me, but I have to tell you this. An icebreaking ship is lifting all those people off the ice. It's a good thing, too. The hunters say the tide is high again and that ice they're standing on could break up on that reef."

Later Pingwa came to see me, so tired he could scarcely stand, to tell me everyone had left now on the icebreaker. Then he said: "There's a lot of talk about how it happened. A few are saying you made it all happen, just to revenge yourself on Red Shoes."

"I hope you know I would never do a thing like that," I said. "I was trying hard to help the trader."

"Kowlee says you are not one who can help people. You only have the power to hurt them. Is that true?"

"I think it is not true," I said strongly. "You'll see. The trader did not die. None of those people drowned out there at sea. Only a big red piece of iron went to the bottom. That is not so bad as losing human beings."

Pingwa looked at the ground and said, "I don't believe what people say. I think you are just an ordinary person like all the rest of us. You were sick when you were young, and Kowlee took you. But now you're better. I don't think you can do good or bad things any more than I can. I believe that, and Josie believes that. I don't care what others say or think."

"Thank you," I said to Pingwa, but I doubt that he heard me, for he had flung himself down in one corner of our tent and fallen into an exhausted sleep.

With the rounding of the moon came the enormous autumn tides, and a north wind roared over us, sweeping the seas clear of ice, and lashing rain mixed with flurries of wet snow. People talked of little else except the sinking of the ship, imagining how many whole boxes full of precious rifles and ammunition, and blankets and shirts, and thread and sacks of flour, and tea and accordions, and steel knives and tobacco, sank beneath the waves and lay out there just beyond our grasp. It left us with a feeling of desolation.

Yannee said he believed some other ship might come in

before the new ice formed. But for now, he said, he was the boss, and he wasn't going to give out anything until the ship did bring new supplies and another trader.

He put a padlock on the store, and neither the missionary nor Kayaker could talk him into selling even them a single thing. We waited patiently. We had no tea, no tobacco, and only a handful of cartridges for the hunters' rifles. Ice formed on all the ponds, the weather worsened, and the seals were scarce. But still no supply ship came to us.

Just as we had given up all hope of new supplies, and ice the thickness of a thumb had formed from the shore to a distance farther than a man could throw a stone, we heard a whoop-whoop-whoop, and there, cautiously edging into our fjord, came a small ship with a tall blue nose. It belched gray smoke and live red sparks, and a small brass side snout let off hissing steam that rose in an angry cloud. This ship was like the whites—noisy, boastful, laughable, just right in size and color.

When the first bargeload of strangers came ashore, I was among those who stood waiting there to greet them.

"Kunowipisee," an Eskimo voice called out to us.

We answered, *"Kunoungi."*

A short, broad-faced Eskimo in a sailor's duffle coat and a fine peaked hat stepped off the barge and shook hands with all of us. Then he gestured to a long, lean man who was getting off the barge.

"This is the new trader who will stay here with you," he told us. "On board we have rifles, ammunition, sugar, tea, flour, canvas for tents, thread for women's needles, lamps, trade cloth, traps for foxes, iron hatchets for chopping frozen meat, and every other thing that you desire."

"Ayii! Ayii! Ayii!" people shouted.

"Tell the new trader he is welcome to winter here with us," said Sarkak. "He may stay with us in every season."

We gladly helped the crew unload the ship. Up on the

beach the sailors built two huge fires from wooden packing cases, not knowing, I suppose, how valuable wood was to us here in this treeless place. But we used the firelight to go on unloading through the long dark autumn night.

Wet snow came driving in at dawn and whitened all the beaches. Small children in the tents wept in the cold, for we had little seal oil and not a drop of kerosene. What could we do but wait? We could not go back to our winter camps without supplies.

You have never seen a ship's captain in such a tremendous hurry, and, as if by a miracle, he had all the freight for Trader's Bay totally unloaded before midday. Then the blunt-nosed ship let off a mighty farewell blast of steam, and on the highest tide headed out between the treacherous reefs.

When the supplies were safely piled into the warehouse and the trade-store shelves were loaded, wives and hunters came and swiftly did their trading. Kowlee asked me to help her over. She had to use a stick for walking because she had grown stiff, and the new snow, more than ankle deep, made it slippery underfoot.

"The trader here before you, Red Shoes, was a friend of mine," Kowlee announced to the lean new trader.

"Is that so?" he said. "I never met him." He paused, staring at Kowlee seriously. "Just before our ship headed north from Montreal, I heard that he was dead," he told her.

"*Tokovok?*" said Kowlee, hoping he had used the wrong word.

But he repeated it. "*Tokovok.* Yes, I said dead. I'm sorry."

Kowlee looked at me and said in the secret language, "Did you do that? Did you do that to Red Shoes because of Annee?"

It was long past time for leaving Trader's Bay. Almost every camp had surely missed the walrus hunt, and everyone was short of meat. By this time, too, the new trader had grown bad-tempered with the lot of us.

The widow who did his washing told him that I had put my curse on Red Shoes and sunk the trading ship. He bellowed at the poor old woman, telling her exactly what he thought of such ideas. He was sick and tired of all the talk about Eskimo shamans, and wanted to hear no more of it.

Next time I went in his store, both Kayaker and Elisapee were there. The trader laughed scornfully and pointed at me. "Is this the magic man you all talk about?" he demanded.

Kayaker turned coldly to him and talked for a long time. Only later did Elisapee tell me what he had said—that I had a history of serious fits and that our people believe that in such a fit the hidden soul, the *inua*, leaves the body and goes flying or swimming into some unknown world. He also told the trader how Raven had bought me when I was a boy, and how Kowlee had bought me from Raven, and taught me all her secrets. Then he surprised and angered Elisapee by seeming to sneer at our beliefs.

"They believe there are only a few like Kowlee and Shoona left," he said, "but they live all across the Arctic. I've studied shamanism, and it's a false religion. It has no church, and though it has a sort of priesthood, there's little continuity. Each shaman has to operate apart from all the others except the one that taught him, and the one that he will teach. By now almost every intelligent Eskimo in the Western world claims Christianity."

At that, Elisapee's anger burst out at Kayaker. "Why do you say such terrible words to the trader?" she demanded. "I thought you were truly interested in our old religion, and that is why I helped you. Now you have turned it all around and made it bad. You made Shoona and Kowlee sound evil and insane. Have you forgotten all Shoona did to help you learn?"

Elisapee started crying and turned and ran outside. The trader came from behind his counter and ordered me to leave, too, saying I was the one who had caused all the trouble. He followed me from his store and stood with his hands jammed in his pockets, shouting at me in his own strange language. Elisapee told me later what his words were: "Goddamn your soul, you loony. And you, too, you great witch bitch," he yelled at Kowlee, who was waiting for me in the path with a pail full of seal livers that the west-camp people had given her. "I've heard about the way you scare these people. Go on, the two of you. Get out of here."

He shouted something more at us, but I turned my back and pulled up my parka hood, and Kowlee started hammering on the pail so that we could no longer hear the hateful sound of his voice.

15

I was mortally ashamed because the new trader had insulted us both before so many of our people, and Kowlee was raging mad. She said she hoped that I really did have magic powers and would use them to strike down our enemies. But of course I never did. I went and lay in our tent in misery and listened to the missionary and our local Christians hammering nails into their church. It seemed to me that I had lost almost every friend I ever had.

After the argument inside the store, Pingwa told me I would have to go away from Trader's Bay. Elisapee agreed, but said she had to stay. Pingwa asked me then if I would come away that winter and live far down the coast at Kamakjuak, with just him and Josie.

All my plans for living with Elisapee seemed to have crumbled into pieces, so I thanked Pingwa and said I would like to go out and live on the land, hoping that such a life would change everything for me.

Josie's father lent Pingwa his trap boat, and we left Trader's Bay late one afternoon in the gathering autumn gloom. As I looked back, I could see the missionary and Sarkak and four other hunters hammering long boards on the church's wooden ribs, each stick of bright new lumber standing boldly up against the evening sky.

We slept not far along the coast and traveled next day until noon, when the sky turned black and the wind rose into frightening gusts. We were forced to remain in a small, desolate harbor for three days before the violence of the storm abated, and while we were there we discovered that we had forgotten the small drum of kerosene we needed for our Primus stove. So we had to turn back to Black Whale Mountain.

As we entered the fjord, Pingwa and I made guesses whether the church roof would be on or not. To our shock, we saw no church at all. The whole valley on the other side of Black Whale Mountain had been swept free of any sign of human habitation.

We learned when we went ashore that a storm had come in the night, and although it did not hurt the trader's house or many of the tents, it roared down the mountain and tore the church apart, breaking the lumber and scattering it across the hills and out to sea.

Avo Divio told me that the missionary and Sarkak had rushed over in the darkness to the valley where they were building the church. In their desperation they had driven in more nails. They had even tried to fight the screaming wind by clutching the boards with their hands. A rafter fell and struck the missionary a crippling blow across the back. He suffered such pain he could no longer work.

That was one reason why he had left Trader's Bay so quickly, Avo Divio said. Also, perhaps, he had feared that the newly forming ice would surround his boat and force him to remain the winter, with his own mission unattended.

At first we could scarcely believe the words we heard. But I saw people along the shore turn their heads and stare at me, pointing and whispering. And a woman standing close to our boat said, "He tore it down. Yes, he and that half-white girl he lives with. They hate the missionary."

Sarkak came up in rage, and said, "I don't believe you had the power to tear apart my church, but I don't trust you. I don't like the look of a man with amulets hanging around his neck. Leave this place," he growled at me. "Let us never see your evil face again!"

That night Pingwa put the kerosene aboard, and we slept in the boat. Almost all night long the lanterns glowed too brightly in every tent, so I knew people were afraid. Elisapee, Kayaker, and Kowlee all kept away from me, and we crept away at dawn like thieves.

When we arrived at Kamakjuak, we tried to forget the past and begin a whole new life, grateful to have found such a lonely, sheltered place. I felt sorry for Kowlee, because for the first time she would have to spend a dreary friendless winter in Trader's Bay.

The heavy snow we were waiting for did not come at once, and we used our time to anchor down our tent lines with great huge boulders. It was well that we had done so, for two nights later killing winds came wailing in across the ice-slick sea, lashing our tent with wet sleet that gathered into sheaths of ice against its sides. The violent shaking of the walls sounded like skin boats smashing up against the rocks. Then a blizzard came, howling at us from the inland plain.

We stayed in bed for three whole days, sharing our body heat as we spoke of the past and the present. It is not our custom to plan the future. We never feel convinced that there will be another day for any one of us.

On the third evening the north wind ran away across the frozen sea, and outside there was only awesome silence. We forced open the low door and looked outside upon a changed world, with hard-packed drifts carved into strange shapes like enormous white drawings scrawled across the winter blackness of the rocks behind our camp.

We hurried outside, quiet at first, but we were so glad to see this true snow once more that we began laughing and pushing each other like children. We knew that greater cold would come, and more blizzards, and thick ice would form on the lakes and freeze the sea into its winter thickness. Then the whole world would be ours. We could drive our dog team where we pleased, the trail would be hard and fast, the caribou would make wide tracks to follow, and the seals would keep their breathing holes open in the ice, showing us where to find them.

Oh, yes, I thought. In this year with Pingwa as a hunting companion, I shall myself become a true hunter! Never again shall I sit around a snowhouse like a widowed woman, sewing amulets into skin bags. I will truly be a hunter, and everyone will respect me.

Because the drifts were not yet strong, we could build only half a snowhouse, with our tent stretched across its top, but even that was much warmer than the tent itself. Each morning when I awoke, I saw Josie's and Pingwa's breath rising in white plumes over our bed, spreading and making hoarfrost against the sagging canvas ceiling. Each morning the water was frozen in the kettle and the urine pot, and above the tent at dawn I heard the high thin moaning of the wind. Except for that, there was no other sound, for this whole country, with all its valleys and the hills and frozen lakes and rivers, was possessed by us alone. No other human beings lived near us.

We three had come to Kamakjuak not just because we were running away, but because we were still young, and just beginning a camp life of our own. The best-known sealing coves and reefs, the lakes and rivers with the greatest abundance of fish, had been occupied for generations by families who rightfully held claim to them. This lonely place of ours had once been famous, too, but all the families that knew it then had long since died or moved away.

Josie's uncle had lent me a rifle, and Pingwa gladly showed me how to use it. I practiced shooting four bullets through a piece of driftwood, which seemed a waste, but it was the first time in my whole life that I felt like a hunter taking part in ordinary people's lives. It was as though at last I had found a family of my own.

"This winter," Pingwa said, "we three will live out on the sea ice hunting seals. And that little one will be busy scraping skins, sewing, and keeping everything repaired for us."

"I am ready. Yes," I said. "Oh, yes! I am eager to go."

That night I couldn't go to sleep. I had a hungry yearning for Elisapee that would not go away, even though I tried to fill my thoughts with the new life we would live.

When I awoke next morning, Josie was sitting by the lamp cutting out a pair of duffle stockings, shaping them carefully with her *ulu*. She laughed when she saw me watching her fill her mouth with thread to make it soft for sewing.

"I'm not good at this," she said. "But your old duffles are all patches. You have to have new stockings or your feet will freeze."

She went ahead and made them for me, and laughed again because one foot was somewhat bigger than the other. I told her that I couldn't see the difference, though she was right about not being good at sewing. Since the days I'd first met Kowlee, only famous older women had sewn my clothes.

I carefully eased the newly made knee-length stockings inside my sealskin boots, and did not tell her that I felt the left one split open at the heel. Later, when Josie found this out, she laughed at herself so hard she nearly fell off our bed. Oh, I liked Josie. She had enough love and gentleness for both Pingwa and me.

Soon heavy winter was upon us. We built a full-domed igloo, and Josie carefully heated and glazed the inside with her lamp. We had built a sleeping bench of snow blocks, waist high when we stood before it, that stretched across the whole house.

Ever since we had been living together, Pingwa had slept in the middle, with Josie on one side of him and me on the other. But when we moved into the new igloo, Pingwa put Josie between us, and that's the way we three went into the winter. We were two best friends, hunting companions, sharing one wonderful girl, whom we both cared for, oh, so greatly!

Pingwa, being of a most generous spirit, would on some days rise from the bed early, and when I started up to join him he would laugh and press me back. Taking the rifle and a few cartridges, he would say, "I am going out to look for ptarmigan. You two keep each other warm."

Of course we were not the first to think of such a three-way household, nor would we be the last. In our land there are so few human beings—often not enough young men, sometimes too few young women—that we are forced to find our own solutions, and we do. And in all the days and nights that we three lived together, I do not believe that any of us knew a single moment's jealousy.

One night in bed, when we had eaten all that we could wish, Pingwa said, "I believe that as long as a man goes on giving, he will go on receiving. If he stops being generous, sharing with his neighbors, then the animals will no longer give themselves to him. He will know hunger, and all feelings of contentment will fly away from him, perhaps forever."

I tried hard that winter, but I could not match Pingwa's skill as a hunter. In the February moon we had nine sealskins and only four white fox pelts, but we were out of tea and had forgotten to trade for a second box of matches. So we decided to make the long trip back to Trader's Bay. We could do this only because we had a big bearded seal cached halfway there, and that would give us dog food. But most of all we went because Josie longed for the midwinter dances. And in truth Pingwa wanted to go, too, and so did I.

Because the days were short and our dogs were slow, we had to build two igloos on our journey. Two other nights we slept in winter camps with Josie's relatives. At noon on the fourth day we could see Black Whale Mountain hanging like a faint ice cloud before us.

❈

It was cold and dark when we arrived, and a storm was blowing up. We slept with friends and lay in bed until the following afternoon, talking, laughing, drinking tea, listening to the local gossip. People seemed to have forgotten about our autumn troubles.

Josie's cousins helped Pingwa and me build a snowhouse, and when Josie came back from visiting, she said there was going to be a dance that night. You could tell she was excited by her eyes, and by the quick way she unstitched her canvas traveling bag and snatched out her best white sealskin boots and a blue-flowered head scarf.

I did not visit Elisapee or Kayaker, because I had not been able to swallow all my bad feelings toward them. Nor did I visit Kowlee, because I feared she would be angry that I had forsaken her and would have no pleasant words for me.

When we reached the entrance to the trader's warehouse that evening, our eyes were nearly blinded by the strong white glow of two pressure lanterns that hung hissing from the rafters. What a marvelous place to dance! Almost empty it was, with only enough flour sacks and tea cases along the walls for the old people to lean against. There was no heat, but we'd soon supply that with our bodies.

The Wanderer was there, pressing magical sounds from her accordion, sounds that made you want to leap into the air and kick your sealskin boots together, sounds that compelled even the oldest people to whirl round and round and stamp their feet as if they were young again.

When my eyes became accustomed to the brightness of the lanterns, I could make out the thin new trader, but he would not even look at me. Kayaker and Elisapee were there, too, and stood staring at the three of us without making any sign of recognition. Kowlee sat with her powerful shoulders hunched forward. Her skin looked creased and yellow, and she had dark hollows underneath her cheekbones. When she saw me, she sent the Sinew Puller over to say she wanted me to speak to her.

Many curious eyes watched as I walked across the warehouse floor and squatted down beside her.

"Shooona! Where have you been, bad Shoona?" she said to me in the common language, but in a voice so hoarse and low that others could not hear her.

"I've been camping near Kamakjuak with Pingwa and Josie. I've been living like a hunter. I got a seal myself this moon," I boasted, not admitting that it was the first and only one that I had ever taken.

"Yuuuuuuk!" She wrinkled up her face in deep disgust. "I grow old and close to dying. And what do you do? You leave me and that half-trained mission girl to go off doing anything you please. I am not her teacher. I have no control of her," Kowlee said. "She knows the secret language, but she's not yet a shaman. She lives with that white man, and who knows what she tells him in the bed?"

She took my wrist in a tight grasp.

"You ran away from here like a stupid child without a word to me. Everything I ever taught you has blown out through your nostrils. You took your simple soul and went wandering among the seal holes, not caring if I lived or died, trying to be a killer of the sacred animals that had fed you all your life."

"Perhaps those words are true," I said to Kowlee proudly, and I pulled up my parka to show her that I no longer wore Wolf Jaw's shaman's belt, which she had lent me long ago.

"Where did you leave that belt, you fool?" She tightened her grasp on my wrist even more. "He trusted me to keep it, and I trusted you. You may lose your other amulets or give them away, yet they will go on working for you. It is not the amulet itself that has the power, but the soul of the animal from which the amulet is made. Have you forgotten everything I taught you, you fool?"

"Yes, I am trying to forget," I told her. "For now I live in the best way I have ever known."

Kowlee's grip on my wrist grew so tight I feared she might break it.

"What are you going to do about Elisapee and her teaching?" she snapped.

I did not look at her or answer.

"So, miserable Shoona! You think that you have the power to end all this? Who knows how many shamans before you have struggled to hand down the knowledge of the *angokait*: the amulets, the taboos, the hidden language? You and that thoughtless mission girl," Kowlee cried, "are you going to kill it finally?"

I was trying to think of some good answer when Tusks, who remembered most about the whalers' dances, formed eight pairs of males and females. Kayaker and Elisapee and Pingwa and Josie helped make up the ring, and when the Wanderer started playing, they all joined hands and went stamping round and round, sending puffs of flour dust flying shoulder high, like white smoke billowing from the cracks in the warehouse floor. The dancers' boots went thundering past us. Everybody was laughing, shouting, singing.

I felt Kowlee's grip upon my wrist relax and saw her eyes close. She laid her head against the tea chest at her back. Her face was lean and drawn.

I saw a movement in the shadows. Slowly a form emerged, a creature such as I had never seen. He was not much taller than a child, but his heavy-muscled, sloping wrestler's shoulders twisted into a hunchback. It made him a menacing dwarf figure that you would not wish to touch. I squatted motionless, with my breath caught in my throat, watching him. I do not believe that he was any kind of human being, *Inuit* or white. In color he was that kind of shifting blue one sometimes sees in flames, he seemed to wear no clothes at all, and he had a round skull without any sign of hair. He clutched and unclutched his fingers as he stood and stared intently out of cruelly hooded eyes, at Kowlee first and then at me.

Just then Kayaker called out something to the trader and

walked across the room toward him, passing between me and the strange dark creature. As he did so, the hunchback disappeared.

I rose and went straight to the place where I had seen it standing, but there was nothing there. I shaded my eyes and looked up into the rafters, beyond the glaring lanterns. Again I saw nothing. No such creature remained in that room, but I could not rid myself of the vision, and I shall never doubt that it was real. Oh, yes, that creature had existed.

Only when Pingwa urged me did I join him and Josie and the others in the third round dance. After that was over we were all in such a sweat that we had to go outside, and our damp black hair turned instant white with hoarfrost. To amuse us, Pingwa did his pantomime of an old man dancing like a sand crane. But I did not laugh, because I was nervous and kept turning my head, afraid that I might find that small flame-blue horror standing just behind me.

Elisapee had not danced that round dance, and when she came outside, she locked her arms across her breasts against the cold.

"Shoona," she whispered to me, "why don't you come to visit us? We don't want to be bad friends with you. We live over in the wooden house they built for summer visitors doing research. The government man sent word that Kayaker could use it. I have not stopped helping him. He's still writing down everything about kayaks, and about all kinds of other things as well. He only pays me half of what he did before, because you've gone away. He talks almost every day to Tusks and Tadlo and other older hunters, and he says he'd like to talk to you again. You know, about—the *angokait*.

"Couldn't we all be friends again?" she asked, and then she blushed. "I mean—I don't know what's going to happen. You know, later, after next summer, when he goes away. I mean—" She looked into my face. "I wonder what we'll do then. You and I. Will you still be my teacher?"

⁂

I didn't know what to say. I turned away, but she called out to me in the secret language, "I do not forget you. You are so often in my mind."

As I walked away I said, "Maybe I'll come over and see you later."

I tried. I started out once on a cold, clear night. I could see a candle and a lantern burning, and their two shadows inside the frosted window of the little government house. Just as I got near the door, though, something made me turn away. I found myself hurrying along the snow path to the igloo where my mother and her hunter and his wife were staying, now that they, too, had come to join in the midwinter dances.

My mother's hunter was glad to see me, but she was out, visiting at the nursing station. He gave me half a seal to drag back to our dwelling, and Josie told Pingwa that I was as fortunate a provider as any other hunter.

Soon after that I went to visit Kowlee. She had not risen from her bed that day.

"I'm sick," she said. "So sick that if I did not know so much about the way you two work the weasel, I'd trade you and Avo Divio something valuable to have you cure me. If it was summer and the ship was here, I'd even go to that doctor who looks inside you with his one-eyed box."

When I heard her say that, I knew Kowlee must be truly sick, and I told Avo Divio to take good care of her.

He was sitting in the middle of the bed rolling the sinews back and forth between his fingers. Wolf Jaw was huddled underneath a blanket on the other side of him. I shouted good-bye to the old man, who tried to smile as he peered out at me, but I could tell that his thoughts were drifting and that he no longer knew my face.

::

16

With the coming of the spring moon, we three began preparing for our return to Kamakjuak. I was anxious to leave. I was sick of Trader's Bay and did not want to see Kayaker with Elisapee again.

Pingwa and I worked together for five days, repairing the sled and getting the sealskin lines and harness ready, and Josie made new boots and mitts. We planned to wander out on the vastness of the inland plain, searching for some of our people whom we might join for the caribou hunt.

On a bright clear morning, cold but without wind, when the blue sky stretched from one white horizon to the other, Pingwa asked me to cast the knucklebones. On the second cast they fell out in a half-moon form. It was an excellent sign, and we decided to begin our journey on the second day.

We had good weather and our six dogs pulled well together as a team. Two days later we passed through the coastal hills, and in the evening we saw spread out before us the great plain of the Kokjuak. Up there near the Kikitiwak hills it was almost like summer, and we threw away our heavy winter feelings and breathed in the new warmth of spring. The sun had melted much of the snow, so we looked for little twisting gullies to travel through with our dogs and sled. It was only there in the shadows that the hard-packed drifts remained. On cloudy days we had to set up small stone cairns and sight carefully back on them to keep from traveling in circles. For some time we journeyed on a narrow frozen river, then rested and lay basking on the sled. A pair of rough-legged hawks circled high above, calling "pee-vee, pee-vee," looking for a place to make their nest. The tundra plain stretched on all sides to the round horizon. It was as though the whole world belonged to us alone.

On the sixth morning we saw the sled tracks of two other hunting families. Pingwa studied the way their tracks bit into the snow, and said, "Like us, they have nothing heavy on their sled. They have not taken any caribou yet."

We came up to their camp by evening. Josie was delighted to see they were her cousins from Chorbak, and Munamee and the others were glad to see us, too. Everyone knows that four or five families hunting caribou together more often have success.

We ate trader's hardtack biscuits and some dried scraps of walrus meat, and treasured our true hunger. From that moment forward we all became careful of every move we made, and even of the thoughts that we possessed. If you do not believe, as we do, that animals have a higher sensitivity than man, try approaching any animal or bird with a hidden weapon in your hand and the intention of doing it harm. You will see how quickly it will flee from you. Approach another one without a weapon and no plan at all to harm it; that animal will usually understand and show little fear of you.

Early one morning, when we had been traveling for half a moon beyond our winter camp, I heard Munamee's son come whispering against our tent wall.

"*Tuktualoweet!* Many caribou!"

We rolled out of our wide sleeping bag, dressed as quietly as we could, and jammed everything into our grub box.

Gently we collapsed our tent and rolled it loosely and caught our six dogs and harnessed them, then turned over our sled so they could not follow us. Kusigak, an old woman who had a bad leg, stayed behind with a heavy whip to control them, for we wanted nothing to frighten the wary caribou. There were few places to hide on this wide flat Arctic plain, and the caribou could easily see us.

"They are in just the right place," said Pingwa. "See the line of *inukshuk* stretching far into the northwest? Those stone men lead toward the Mingo River."

The weather was gray and the wind calm over the open tundra. The sun had wiped away almost the last of the snow, and the damp earth gave off the pungent smell of early spring. After we had pitched the tent again, Munamee waved his hand toward the group of women and girls, who were slinging the youngest children on their backs, and the young boys, who were hopping from one foot to another in their eagerness to start the hunt.

"Josie, you should go with all of them," he said. "They will try to drive the dear beasts toward the open river, just below the rapids. That is not an easy task. The men will wait here together until we see what direction they take."

Josie joined the women and children, carrying a woman's knife, a rolled-up sleeping skin, and a length of fish line with a hook. Although they were not many, they spread out into a huge half circle around the grazing herd of caribou, who saw them wandering in the distance but grazed on undisturbed. Sometimes the women and the children disappeared from sight along the dry stream beds, and the hunters had to search out their movements with a telescope.

"Will they not frighten the caribou?" I asked. "When they get closer?"

"Only when they wish to do so," Munamee answered. "That old wife of mine will show the others. She knows how eager young boys are, but she won't let them move too fast."

He led the rest of us inside the tent but left the flap open so we could go on watching the mist-hung plain that hid the caribou.

After a while I said, "Are we just going to lie here? Aren't we going to hunt them?"

Munamee smiled and said, "Not yet, Swimmer. That would spoil everything. We want to meet them at the river. All of us together—those dear beasts, our women, our young boys, and us. Ah, yes. We ourselves hope to be there when the dear beasts come to us."

The sky grew heavy, and rain drove across the tundra in thinly falling sheets, blotting out the *inukshuks*, hiding our boys and women and the whole herd of caribou from our sight.

Munamee and his eldest son went walking in the fog and rain, and when they returned they carried two caribou antlers, one from a big male bull, one from a smaller female, that had been shed some time after the autumn rutting moon. Munamee placed the horns between the tundra and a rock, then knelt gently until his weight caused them to snap. Only when he had enough pieces did he hand them around to the hunters, kindly presenting the first one to me.

We drew out our knives and some old files and began carving. The year-old antler had softened while lying on the dampness of the tundra and was not difficult to shape. Everyone made some form of caribou. Mine was a double image, two caribou heads, facing in opposite directions to represent the true animal and its *inua*.

"Caribou are handsome creatures." Munamee smiled and turned his carving in his hand.

"Yes," said the hunter named Kungo. "The dear beasts have warm coats and such soft and beautiful hair beneath their bellies. Often it is whiter than snow."

"I like best their kind brown eyes," said Pingwa.

And so we five hunters sat comfortably together, thinking

and speaking oh so gently of the caribou, wanting them, prais-
ing them, carving respectful images of them, male or female,
not favoring one above the other.

Munamee even sang a small song to them:

> *"Ayii, Ayii, Ayii, Ayii.*
> Joyous it is
> When wandering time has come.
> Joyous it is
> To hear the clattering of hooves
> On pebble ground.
> Joyous it is
> When wandering time has come.
> *Ayii, Ayii, Ayii."*

"The women will not have trouble finding their places in
this fog," Kungo said, "if those wise lemmings don't double
back on them."

Of course he meant the caribou, but he believed they could
clearly understand his words, even at such a distance, and he
did not wish to give away the fact that our women and the
young boys were very close to them.

We hunters boiled and ate some trout and prepared to go to
sleep.

"What of the women out there?" I asked, thinking only of
Josie.

"Oh, they'll be all right." Munamee laughed. "Women
have a way of resting on the ground half curled around a rock.
If the wind shifts, they shift, too, in a very cunning way. They
teach their daughters how to do it, not their sons."

"And what will they eat?" I asked.

"Oh, there's a little fish lake out there. One or two of them
will find a weak place in the ice, pick it open, and kneel all
night if necessary, jigging for the trout they will share with all
the others. Women are patient fishers."

We slept through that gray-white spring night, and in the

morning the rain had stopped and the ground fog was drifting southward across the tundra. The cloudless sky was tinted yellow in the east. Even I, who did not know the inland, could guess that this would be a strong clear day.

The hunters were impatient, not knowing if the women had already begun their drive. Munamee tested the wind by throwing a tuft of caribou hair into the air, and we watched the way it drifted so we could approach the dear beasts upwind. Then we circled far to the southeast, exactly opposite from the women and children, walking hard until the sun was high. From a slight rise in the ground we could see a dozen stone *inukshuk*, and northward the hollow curves of the gravel river banks.

Kungo, who had the keenest eyesight, took the telescope and lay flat, propping it against a stone. He pointed its shining eye into the northwest and carefully scanned the horizon. No one spoke.

"There they are," he said quietly. "They're moving slowly, grazing, not frightened. I cannot see the *arnait* or *uvikait*," he said, meaning the women and half-grown children. "But they have the dear beasts moving nicely along the line of stone men. Tomorrow in the early morning they may reach the river."

Pingwa and Munamee drew out their knives and sharpened them by drawing one blade cleverly against another until each had a razor edge.

We walked until the sun dipped almost to the long flat horizon of the western plain and turned a full half of sky flaming red. The rifle that I carried across my shoulder seemed seven times as heavy as it had been when we left camp that morning, and I had holes in both my sealskin boots.

We slept heavily and arose at dawn. By now we were in easy sight of the caribou and we crouched low and moved as slowly as if we, too, were grazing. Whenever possible we hid from their view and moved quickly along shallow gullies, hoping to reach the river before they approached their ancient crossing place.

I looked out at the dark silhouettes of the stone men, and was terrified when one of them moved. The nearest pair of caribou saw that movement, too, and turned nervously and came across the plain toward me, followed by a dozen others.

As I stared at the stone, it moved again and disappeared, and it was then that I realized I had seen a person. The women and the children were advancing down the lines of stones, imitating them, and moving in exactly the right way to make the caribou move, driving them in exactly the direction they wished them to go, so that we would all meet at the shallows on the river, well above the rapids.

"Take your pants off," Munamee whispered to me. "Take your boots off, too, and hold them over your head, along with your rifle and cartridge bag."

I did what he said, and we made our way across the river. It was wide and swift, swollen because of melting snow, with a slippery stone bottom that hurt my feet at first. But then, like my legs and groin, they grew numb from the icy water.

When we came out on the opposite side, we hurried up the bank, without bothering to put on our pants, and peered into the two stone hunting blinds that had been made there long ago.

Munamee got the better one and called out to me softly, "Swimmer, come and join me. You also, Pingwa."

His son and Kungo crouched in the other.

"You lie in the middle," Munamee said to me. "You may be able to draw those dear beasts to us if you speak to them softly with those secret words of yours."

Our secret language was only for speaking so that others would not understand, with no magic power in it at all. But still I answered, "Yes, I'll try." I wondered what the word *kadang* might do, but was afraid to use it.

Pingwa looked at me uneasily and said, "You just shoot that

rifle straight, the way I showed you, and you'll see what happens. I want to see you get one, or two, or three, or more," he said, unfolding all five fingers of his right hand.

I saw the first three caribou come down the gravel bank, then pause, staring suspiciously at the river. Others followed, until there were as many in our sight as a man has toes and fingers. Still more came in behind and joined them, and one or two of the boldest waded knee deep into the shallows. But when the others did not follow they returned to the river's bank.

"That's good," Munamee whispered. "We want almost all of them to come together, because our rifles make such a lot of noise."

Pingwa pointed to one of the women who walked some way behind the caribou. "Be oh so careful of the women and children when you point the rifle," he told me in a hoarse whisper.

Now one big male caribou started out into the fast current, and others followed, only a few at first, then all of them. They did not cross on the ford that we had used, but came through deeper water that forced them to swim, moving beautifully, their heads held high, their wide splayed hooves propelling them powerfully through the swift icy water.

"That one is yours," whispered Munamee, nodding toward the big bull caribou that had led them all across the river.

It was kind of him to give me the first chance. I think he hoped that such a generous act might bring us all good fortune.

When I raised myself cautiously up onto my elbows and peered out of the blind, I saw with horror that the big caribou was almost up to us, with others following in single file. Behind them I saw many animals leave the water and shake themselves like dogs.

I aimed at the big caribou's chest. He halted, blowing his nostrils wide as he caught our scent, and his large liquid brown eyes seemed to stare straight into mine.

I tried but found I could not bring myself to squeeze the trigger.

"Go ahead!" Pingwa whispered. "Now!"

Then Munamee nudged me. "*Ataii!* Shoot! Shoot!"

I did nothing, but closed my eyes and clutched the gunstock, causing the barrel to tremble like a person with a fever.

I heard their rifles fire at the same instant, and the big bull and the second caribou went down. I heard many other shots explode and then echo off the river bank, and I looked down at my trembling hands. I did not wish to see the falling caribou. Imagine! I, who had eaten countless haunches of their meat, found that I could not kill one or even bear to see one killed.

When the shooting was over, we rose from our blinds and viewed what had been done. There must have been twenty brown animals lying quietly before us. Those that had escaped our rifle fire had fled out across the tundra. They were scattered at first, but then they rejoined, running away together into the evening shadows.

"I never saw them come so close before," Munamee said.

To me, Kungo said, "I did not hear you fire your rifle."

"That is because I did not fire," I told him.

"Perhaps you were shaking that small caribou image in your hand and asking them to come very close to us. They walked straight to us!" Munamee said.

"*Isumapala*—a strong thought! And look how well it worked," said Kungo. "I have never seen anything like that. Shoona," he said, "I will give you something fine in exchange for that caribou amulet." Then he hurried away to start cutting and sharing the meat.

I could hear the women and the young boys crying out and laughing as they crossed the river and the icy water rose around their thighs.

Josie came running up to me. "You got one or two, did you?"

"He got all of them for us, with magic," Munamee called out to her. "And he did not have to fire one shot."

I knew then that I would never fire a killing slug of lead into the body of another animal. I feared too much the power of their wandering souls.

When we could no longer use our sleds, the women made canvas saddle bags for the dogs and for us, and together we packed out all the meat and rolls of skins that we could carry. We ate not at all throughout the days of walking, but when we rested at night we ate until we felt that we would burst. We lay near one another and listened to the older ones tell certain stories of the past. We watched the full new moon rising, and I would have chosen to be nowhere else in all the earth except with Pingwa and Josie and those I'd known all my life.

By the time we reached the long arm of the Chorbak Inlet, where Josie's cousins had left their big canoe, we had all of us grown thin from walking. No one grows fat on caribou, for it is a lean, delicious meat. It is also known to make families affectionate and good-humored, and that is what it did for all of us.

We had four more days of walking before we reached Trader's Bay. The sea ice had not yet broken from the land, but small starflowers were bursting into bloom, and handsome pairs of pin-tailed ducks came whistling into the ponds, calling "akee-ak-kunuk, akee-ak-kunuk!" That wonderful sight and sound told us that the warmth of summer was reaching northward.

When I went to Kowlee's tent she said, "I would never have recognized you. Your face has grown dark brown from the sun, and you are skinny as a summer weasel. You must have almost starved to death."

"As many caribou gave themselves to us as we could carry," I told her. "It was the walking and the packing of the meat that wore my flesh off." I handed Avo Divio the plump bull haunch of caribou that I had brought for all of them, and said, "I feel stronger now than I have ever felt before."

"How fortunate you are," said Kowlee. "It is not the same with me. I know that I shall never see another winter. I will not even live to see the autumn come."

I looked at her, lying hollow-eyed upon the bed, and I, too, felt that she was dying.

"Swimmer, while you were away I thought of all the good times that we have shared. You are no healer. We both know that. But what are you? I have been counting on these fingers the strange and evil things that have happened here—all perhaps because of you.

"*Sivordlukpak*, first, the death of Annee's future husband. Wasn't that convenient? *Mukolo*, second, the sinking of the ship with the trader who took your Annee. *Pingasut*, third, when that sinking failed to kill him, he died down there in the south.

"Raven, the man you hated, broke his leg, and only I know enough to count that as *sitamut*, number four. But no one here forgets the destruction of the church. *Tidlimut!* That is surely five. Shoona, I believe that you have the rare power to destroy, to do so from a distance without so much as touching what you wish to harm. Last night I heard how you did it with the caribou. You don't need any rifle."

She paused and stared into my eyes. "Shoona, you were like a son to me. Are you now the one who is destroying me?" Kowlee held up the thumb of her right hand. "Will I be *pingasuruktuk?* Number six?"

"*Agaiiiih!* No!" I cried. "I would never hurt you. I am not a destroyer. I have *not* the power that you believe."

"Liar!" she cried, and pointed her bone-thin finger at me. "You are the one who tore the fat flesh off the trader, and now you tear it off me. You are slowly killing me, as you killed Red Shoes. All that I say is true. Ask Avo Divio. We have talked together. He believes every word I have said is true."

I glanced at the Sinew Puller, who sat in misery, saying nothing, staring at his long limp hands.

"Look at him. He's afraid of you, Shoona. He knows that you are a destroyer. Do you hear me, Swimmer? A destroyer! I am only a sick old woman now. But I have one last lesson I will teach you, Swimmer. That lesson is revenge."

17

A feeling of terror gripped me. I went back to my tent and sat alone, and thought about all that Kowlee had said, and about myself. Could it be that I had such power? I thought about those caribou walking straight toward me, almost stepping on me, and the sharp mean sound of rifles firing. Certainly when I was young and Kowlee walled me inside that tiny stinking igloo, I had had dreams and visions. Tusks had told me that all starving people will in time come to suffer hallucinations, but Kowlee said that fasting opens the entrance passage to the unseen world. In truth, terrible happenings had occurred around me. I wanted to believe they were just accidents, as Pingwa had said. It terrified me to think I might possess some power that I could not even understand or control.

I let my mind go blank. *"Kadang, Kadang,"* I whispered forcefully, and I pointed at a bottle from the trader's partly filled with kerosene. "Burst! Burn! Burst! Burn!" I commanded, concentrating until my body trembled. I waited. Nothing happened. I tried a second time. Still nothing.

Cautiously I opened the door of my tent and peered outside. A large black husky with tan spots above his eyes was lying on the tundra, enjoying the summer breeze. I said again, *"Kadang, Kadang!"* and pointed directly at his head, first with my right hand and then with my left. I aimed my loon's beak amulet at him. "I wish you dead," I whispered. "Die, die, die! *Kadang, Kadang!*"

The husky heaved a sigh, yawned, got up and stretched himself, and walked to the stream to lap some water. I watched him for some time. He was absolutely unaffected. Still I went on fearing myself, and I tossed and turned in my bed that night and scarcely slept at all.

In the early morning I heard children running toward my tent. They were screaming, "Someone's floating in the water! A person is down there in the water!"

I jumped out of bed and raced with others down to the beach. The hunter named Tunu snatched a long gaff from Ikhalook's whaleboat. Wading out waist deep, he carefully caught the body and drew it to him hand over hand. It was a woman. Even before he rolled her face up in the water, I knew that it was Kowlee.

Her lips were drawn tight, and all the color was drained away from her wide face, so that her tattoo lines appeared more strongly than I had ever seen them. The breath seemed caught in my throat, but I could hear people gasping around me, and when I turned, a woman from the north camp pointed at me and whispered, "It's him! It's him who drowned her! Shoona is the one who causes all these troubles."

The women huddled together on the beach, their hoods drawn over their faces, and in a single voice they began a long and dreadful female wailing, which is their way of mourning a drowned or murdered person. Their lament lasted as long as it takes a man to draw five breaths, and stopped as suddenly as it had begun. A silence followed, achingly sad and lonely.

Among us all, the Sinew Puller was the first to behave sensibly. He walked off in his crooked way to ask the trader if he had a wooden box in which to put Kowlee's body. The trader gave him a good-sized one, nearly square but strong, and Yannee helped him bring it back.

He and the women bent Kowlee's legs to shorten her,

wrapped her in a blanket, and laid her gently in the box. Old Tusks hammered the lid on.

Those who carried the box up the hill remembered afterward that Kowlee had lost almost all her great weight. But that didn't stop them from piling the heaviest stones on her. Some say we place heavy stones on our dead so that wandering white bears or our own dogs will not get hold of the body and scatter its bones about. Others say we do it so the dead will not get up and roam at night, searching for us in our tents and igloo passages, shivering and moaning like the wind.

Sarkak followed us up the hill, took his black book from a green cloth bag, and started to read from it in Eskimo. Nobody had asked him to do that, and Tusks and Avo Divio and Sea Bird asked him to stop, even though he was a most important man.

"You save those sayings for someone else," said Sea Bird in her high and scratchy voice. "This big woman lying underneath these stones," she said, not daring to utter her name for fear of ghosts, "had thoughts too different from that book. Don't you or any missionary come up here and try to put a white cross on top of her head."

"You are right," the Sinew Puller said. "She wouldn't want a white cross."

I didn't say a word for my old teacher, but when Sarkak turned and left the hill, I went to my tent and got the battered rifle Josie's uncle had lent me. I took all the cartridges, loaded it with five, and put five more ready in my mouth, the way I had seen the hunters do. Then I hurried straight back up the hill.

"Why are you doing this?" I asked myself, and I answered through the bullets in my mouth: "Because all those people think that you are bad."

When I got near the others, I shouted at them, "I didn't do it to her!" My voice came out all crooked through the cartridges in my teeth.

I raised the rifle and fired it over Kowlee as she lay beneath the stones.

"Someone or something else did this to her. I did not drown her," I shouted, and I fired the rifle a second time. People moved back from me and crouched closer to the ground.

"And she didn't drown herself," I shouted. "She had an awful fear of water."

I closed my eyes and fired the rifle a third time. It was only a way to say good-bye to Kowlee and to give warning to the evil thing that had drowned her. This time, I think, I must have aimed the rifle a little bit too low above their heads, for when I opened my eyes, they all had scattered and were running away down the hill.

I laid the rifle on Kowlee's grave and spat the bullets from my mouth, and ran down to my tent and sat huddled on my bed. After some time I heard a scratching at my tent flap, and when I looked up, the Sinew Puller was squatting in the entrance.

"I know how bad you must feel," he said. "I always thought I would go away before her." He sniffed and wiped his nose on the back of his hand. "I'm going to miss her. I don't know what to do with her gone. All I know about is helping her. Pounding blubber for the lamps, making the weasel jump by pulling the sinew strings." In his broken wheezy voice he asked, "What do you want me to do?"

"I'm in too much trouble myself," I told him. "I don't know what you're going to do."

"Let me work for you," he pleaded. "Kowlee wanted me to work for you. No one else. I know that."

"No. She was angry at me. Just at the end she told me I did bad things."

The Sinew Puller stared at his long thin hands and worked his fingers nervously.

"Yes, lots of people say you do bad things." He squinted at me. "Shooting off that rifle so close to people's heads—that was pretty bad. But I could understand how you would be upset."

I said nothing to that. He let the silence draw out between us, and then he told me he could still do all his tricks. But when he tried to show me by making a knucklebone thrust forward like a deadly finger, he dropped it on the ground.

"I'm too nervous today," he said, "and I'm out of practice with that one. But I'll get it going smooth again. I'm still quick at pulling the sinew strings." He tried to laugh, but I could see him working his skinny throat to keep from crying.

"Lots of people here say she was bad. But nothing's ever going to be the same for me. I worked for her half of all my life. She never gave me anything much except a share of food, and she often used to say that I was stupid, too slow and clumsy with the strings. But you've seen those weasels move. Sometimes they looked as real as life, even to me!"

"That's true," I said. "You can make the weasels fly on those strings of yours."

"We can still do it together, Swimmer. We can do it anytime we want. I've still got to take care of that old man. Will you not help me?"

I listened to the mosquitoes humming softly on the sun side of the tent, and I thought about the winter.

"Yes," I said. "Come with me if you want, when I go back to camp. But for now I wish that you would live in her big tent, and take care of the old man, and protect her things from the dogs. If you're afraid she'll come back, you can always change the entrance. Make a false one."

"No," he said, "I'm not afraid of her. She liked me. I'd be glad enough if she came back to visit me. Wouldn't you?"

I shuddered and said, "No. I've had enough."

I didn't really want the Sinew Puller, but that is how he attached himself to me. And when I got him, I got Wolf Jaw, too. He was now so senile that he did not even know Avo

⁑
———

Divio, and he had no idea that Kowlee was gone from us forever.

After her death I was in trouble with everyone but the Sinew Puller. People told me that when the ship arrived again, two policemen in red coats would take me south and put me in an iron cage for killing people. Some said they would grab me just for shooting the rifle too near people's heads. The trader knew all about that and would surely tell the policemen I was far too dangerous to remain among the good people who lived in the lee of Black Whale Mountain.

Josie told me, looking frightened, that her uncle wanted his rifle back. Pingwa said he couldn't understand about Kowlee's drowning, and also that he had hated my firing the rifle so close to everyone. When I said my eyes had been closed and I hadn't meant to aim at anybody, he just shook his head and said, "Never do a thing like that again."

Through all these troubles I had been giving little thought to Elisapee and Kayaker. I did not even find it strange that they had not come to the beach when Tunu pulled Kowlee from the water, or climbed the hillside afterward for the burial. But now word was going round that Kayaker had begun to talk again about rolling his kayak. He was determined to do it this very autumn, people said, before heavy ice formed on the bay.

One day I met Elisapee on the path from Kayaker's tent, and she told me that all this was true. "I have tried to change his thoughts," she said, "but he pays no attention to what I say. Old Tusks tells him about the danger many times over, but he pays no attention to him, either. Shoona," she said, and looked at me pleadingly, as she might have when we still lived together, "maybe he will listen to you."

I felt angry with her then because she had not even mentioned the drowning or my farewell to Kowlee. "Kayaker has not really spoken to me since you both came back from Sharlo,"

I said coldly. "Why should I speak to him? I am the last person he would listen to." And I turned away from her.

Fog lay across the sea for two whole days and nights, wrapping itself around the cliffs of Black Whale Mountain. I heard the raucous sea birds calling, and the sky was like a sheet of lead, through which the sun had no more brightness than a morning moon. Ice had begun to form on the water of the bay, the rocks along the shore were silver slick, and snow clung to the north side of the hills.

When I next saw Elisapee, she told me that Kayaker was furious with himself for having left it so late to roll his kayak over. But Tusks, she said, had laughed and told him that he was fortunate—the early coming of the ice had saved his life. Then, as sometimes happens in the autumn, a warm wind blew in from the southeast, and the weather was almost like that of summer again.

Now Kayaker became like a man possessed. He gave up sleeping and talked of nothing but the roll he planned to make. Every Eskimo joined Tusks in telling him not to do it, but the male nurse and the new trader, who had heard that the Greenlanders could roll their kayaks, urged him on. Elisapee said they were telling people it would be a great sporting event. That's how life is. The people who know the least are the first to offer their advice.

Kayaker was making sure that all the preparations for his roll were made with the greatest care. Elisapee told me he had gathered great lengths of bearded seals' intestines and had paid the older women to split and sew them into a special parka. I think it was because he was so proud of this parka that he came with Elisapee and showed it to me, just as if there had been no long silence between us and we were friends again, the way we were before he took Elisapee from me.

"See," he said, holding the parka up, "now I'm really ready." Light came through the long thin sewed-together strips of seal intestine, but no weather would come through.

The bottom of the parka was made to fit tightly over the kayak's cockpit, and it had drawstring at the wrists and around the facing of the hood. Everything about it was made for keeping out the water.

"Tomorrow, if the weather holds, I'm going to do the roll," Kayaker said, and his cold gray eyes caught mine and held them. We stood like that for a long time, and it seemed to me that we understood each other without the need for Elisapee as interpreter, without the need to speak at all. I knew he was telling me that I already had the answers hidden somewhere deep within my mind.

I cannot say whether I was relieved for Kayaker or spitefully pleased when I woke the following morning and saw the north wall of my tent pressed in with the wind and heard the lashing rain. I laughed and thought that if Kayaker hadn't sense enough not to risk his life, Sila, the weather woman, had saved it for him again.

Two mornings later the dawn crept cautiously through leaden clouds, and the air was finger-numbing cold once more. The black ice that had edged the fjord had now extended almost halfway out, and I judged that it would join together solidly before the moon of autumn disappeared.

When I looked from my tent door across the ice, I saw Kayaker and Tusks already moving out, with the kayak lashed on the old man's dog sled. I hurried down, not wishing to miss anything, and Elisapee came, too, with many other women and children following her. Two strong girls were pulling Sea Bird on a hand sled. Even Annee was coming. I could see her sitting on her father's dog sled, holding her hood in that sly elegant way she had, as though she wished to hide her face. Everybody left in Trader's Bay gathered in the end to see Kayaker do what we considered impossible.

Tusks' dog team stood at a safe distance from the edge of the ice, and Kayaker waited casually, panting from the running, not untying the kayak at first, just standing, staring out over the cold blackness of the water. He held his hands on his hips in the strange gesture that is one of the things that set the whites apart from ordinary men.

When Elisapee arrived, she went straight to Kayaker. He turned nervously when he heard her voice and unslung the camera that he had been carrying around his neck and handed it to her. I saw how close they stood together as he pointed out certain buttons that she should push, and others that she should twist or flip, when she was ready to make a picture. Finally, though, I saw her refuse even to touch the camera and jam her hands deep inside her sleeves.

Kayaker pointed at the trader's sled, which had stopped a safe distance from the ice edge, and Elisapee walked back on the ice, spoke to the trader, and handed him the camera.

The trader hung it around his own neck and took the silver stop-clock out of Elisapee's hand. I could guess that he didn't like Kayaker, but he probably didn't care whether he lived or died as long as he did it in a hurry.

Kayaker looked at the sky and at his black-faced wrist-clock, and then he bent and unlashed his kayak from the long sled. He heaved it up onto one shoulder, took the double-bladed paddle in his other hand, and walked cautiously almost to the edge of the ice.

"Taika," Tusks called to Elisapee, using her Eskimo name, "come and speak to this foolish man for me."

Elisapee went and stood between them. You could tell she did not like being that close to the thin edge of the ice. I didn't either, but still I wanted very much to hear what Tusks would have to say to Kayaker.

"Can it be true," asked Tusks, "that you still plan to get into that kayak and try to roll it over in the water and come up on the other side?"

Elisapee translated and Kayaker simply nodded his head.

"*Ayii*, that's what he hopes to do," Elisapee answered.

"I must tell you that you are trying to do a very dangerous thing," said Tusks. "I, too, have heard that the *Inuit* in Greenland do such a trick. But I say again, their kayaks are of a very different style and shape, rounded on the bottom. That one is almost flat, and I do not believe it will roll up for you."

This time Kayaker spoke, and Elisapee looked desperately at Tusks. "He says to tell you that he's got to roll this one. He will never know unless he tries, and if it doesn't work, he'll swim back to the ice and run to his tent to get warm again."

Old Tusks frowned. "I've seen a man hanging upside down in a kayak. It was so hard for him to get out that he drowned."

Kayaker bent and slid the kayak into the dark water. He held the paddle across the front of the bent-wood cockpit in his customary skillful way and eased himself inside without so much as placing his foot weight on the bottom. He fitted his parka bottom carefully around the cockpit, pulled the drawstring tight, and secured it with a special seaman's knot. He raised the hood and pulled the drawstrings at his wrists and all around his face.

Gathered on the ice, we watched him without speaking or moving.

"I'm ready!" he called out to the trader, who was busy looking through the camera, first at one person, then another.

Elisapee came and stood near me, and she was trembling, but not from cold. Kayaker called out to the trader in English. Elisapee told me, "He wants him to press the button on the stop-clock the moment he pushes off from the ice, and he wants him to call out the seconds to him before he starts the roll, and then later to tell him exactly how long it took from start to finish."

Kayaker pushed off boldly and started moving out before us, circling smoothly, gaining speed.

Elisapee turned her head away, and old Tusks went across the ice, caught the hunter called Ikhalook by the sleeve, and made him stand close. It was only then I noticed the ugly three-pronged seal hook hanging down from Ikhalook's right hand. In his left he held a strong thin coil of cod line.

I myself had no real feelings either way about Kayaker trying to roll a kayak. You might say that I, like the trader, didn't really care whether he lived or died. But seeing Elisapee so tense and Tusks so nervous sent shivers up my spine.

Kayaker stopped rolling the paddle on the hardwood cockpit and held it chest high as he drove hard, gaining speed, turning in an ever-tightening circle.

"Fifteen seconds!" the trader called.

Kayaker increased his speed and swayed his body inward. I could tell that he was preparing to make the roll.

"Ten seconds!" the trader shouted. Now he was holding both the camera and the stop-clock up before his face.

I felt Elisapee's hand on my arm, and it was trembling.

"Five seconds!" yelled the trader.

Kayaker drove his paddle with such power that his kayak left a white wake curving on the smooth gray surface of the water.

"Four seconds!"

"Don't do it!" Elisapee screamed. She whirled around, and as she did, I saw a dark undulating shadow of something as large as a Greenland shark moving out slowly from beneath the ice on which we stood.

"Three seconds!" called the trader.

Men shouted out and children screamed, but whether it was in pure excitement or because, like me, they saw the dreadful creature moving like some great fish out from the thin black ice, I do not know. The only pointing was toward Kayaker, and there were no words I could hear among the shouts and screams. But I myself—I tell you I clearly saw the swimming shadow rise to the surface, just beyond the edge of the ice, causing the water to swirl and boil the way it does when a big fish rises. I saw its long wet hair wave like seaweed on the water's surface. I saw it swimming toward the kayak.

"Two seconds!" cried the trader, and Tusks yelled, "*Tima! Tima!* Stop! Stop!" Did Tusks see that monstrous, fishlike creature following close behind Kayaker?

"One second!" the trader called.

Kayaker cocked his paddle high, dug deep with the right blade, and flung his weight sideways. The kayak tipped, and for a moment I could see its long slim deck reflect the afternoon light. Then he went under.

Elisapee screamed again, and I saw the dark shadow spread its arms and lunge at him. In all the shouting that still went on I could hear no words, and in my own horror I could find no words to say. I closed my eyes, hoping that when I opened them Kayaker would be up again. But Elisapee grabbed me with both hands and shook me so hard that I had to look.

The kayak lay upside down. Beneath it there was a desperate thrashing in the ice-cold water, and then I knew that Elisapee saw what I was seeing.

"Oh, God!" she cried out. "That's not an animal. Look at the face, the mouth, the eyes. It's killing him! It's tearing him to pieces! It's drowning him!"

Whether or not Tusks and Ikhalook saw the creature, too, they ran dangerously close to the thin edge of the ice, determined to rescue Kayaker.

"He's been down for thirteen, fourteen, fifteen seconds," yelled the trader. Then he bellowed, "Come up, man!" as though the struggling Kayaker, hanging in that narrow cockpit upside down, could hear him through the freezing water.

Elisapee screamed again, and I reached down into the neck of her parka to haul up the ancient ivory amulet I had given her. She knelt on the ice and shook it toward the water that churned around the crippled kayak, as though she held a magic weapon.

Ikhalook whirled the three-pronged hook around his head and flung it out beyond the kayak. Hand over hand he pulled

✽

it to him, and when it touched the kayak's bottom he gave a violent jerk. The hooks caught, and Tusks and Ikhalook, then Pingwa, then others helped him drag the kayak back toward the ice, leaving a pink trail in the water.

"No hurry now. It's no use," the trader called to us. "He's been down too long. Much too long. It's been more than sixty seconds. He can't possibly be alive."

However I may have felt about Kayaker, I hadn't wanted anything like this to happen. I, too, took hold of the strong thin cod line and helped to pull in the capsized kayak. It was the only thing I could do.

The women began shrieking again, and we all whirled around. Behind them, where the autumn ice was thick enough to walk on, we heard a shattering sound and saw cracks run shivering in all directions. The ice burst and sent broken shards whirling outward, and through the jagged hole Kayaker's body pressed upward. Head, shoulders, hips, knees appeared before the thrust collapsed and he sagged like a dead man back onto the edge of the broken ice.

Hunters held their hands over their faces, knowing that what they had just seen could not possibly have happened. Elisapee remained kneeling for a moment, paralyzed with horror. As we watched, blood seeped out of Kayaker's parka hood and widened in a scarlet stain across the ice beside the hole.

Old Tusks was the first to move. He ran and knelt beside Kayaker and pulled his legs from the freezing water. Snatching off his mitts, he tugged back the parka hood and held his bare hands across Kayaker's dreadful head wound to staunch the flow of blood. His clothes were torn to shreds. Elisapee ran toward him, and I followed, and the trader moved cautiously sideways after us, one step at a time as he tested the ice.

I bent down, sure that Kayaker was dead or dying. His face was ghastly pale, his eyes, though partly open, held no spark of life, and his head hung limply to one side, as though his neck was broken. When I tried to reach out to him, Elisapee shrieked at me. I had never seen a woman look or sound like that. Her lips were drawn back, showing all her teeth, and her face had turned dark red.

"Don't you touch him!" she screamed, holding her body over him. "I know you! You did this thing to him. This is what a swimmer does to people. You can't heal them! You can only send things to kill them!" And then she shamed me and all the other men, for Elisapee herself dragged Kayaker back to safety, sliding his body across the dark smooth ice.

One of the hunters knelt and felt the ice hole, then stood holding his thumb and forefinger apart to show the thickness of the ice that Kayaker's head had broken.

"No wonder he's dead," said Ikhalook. "The skull of a bull walrus could scarcely break through ice like that."

"But he's alive! He's breathing," Elisapee cried out. "Help me get him on the sled."

The last I saw of them, they were rushing Kayaker across the ice toward the two-bed nursing station. I helped Pingwa and Ikhalook and Tusks drag the kayak from the water. When we turned it over, we found the sealskin covering round the cockpit slashed open as though a huge white bear had tried to rip it into pieces. After we had lashed it on Tusks' sled, the other three squatted on the ice and stared at me.

"Can you explain that?" old Tusks asked in a strange voice.

"No," I said. With the toe of my sealskin boot I tried to cover up the bloodstain in the snow. I could not think how to ask them if they had seen the dreadful creature with flowing hair. Whether they had seen it or not, they might believe, like Elisapee, that I had conjured it from under the ice. "You don't need to worry," I told them. "I'm going away."

"What do you mean?" said Pingwa. "Where can you go?"

"I don't care where I go," I said.

"You told us you'd come and camp with us again," said Pingwa.

"Not after this. You would not want me."

I turned and ran from all of them toward my tent. The Sinew Puller, who was halfway across the ice, turned and ran after me. As I passed Kowlee's tent, the door opened violently and Wolf Jaw thrust his head out of the entrance. He was on his hands and knees, and was trembling violently.

"*Kiageet*. Come, you!" he rasped at me in a hoarse and broken voice.

I could scarcely believe my ears, for I could not remember when I last had heard him speak. Although he was sobbing and shuddering, he spoke again as the Sinew Puller and I ran to help him.

"I tried! I fought with him," said Wolf Jaw, weeping. "I had hold of him like this." He reached out, his fingers hooked like claws. "But he got away—he tore away from me."

"Who got away?" I asked.

Wolf Jaw only stared at me with those unseeing eyes, and he trembled so terribly that we had to carry him back to bed.

"I think he's remembering something from long ago," the Sinew Puller said.

"No! No! Now! Down there!" The old man screamed, pointing to the place on the ice where we had stood.

Those were the last words I ever heard him speak.

The Sinew Puller said, "Kowlee wanted you to have this." He handed me her snow knife. "She said you'd remember it."

I looked across the bay and saw a light come on in the window of the green-roofed nursing station. I knew Elisapee would be inside, helping the male nurse to keep Kayaker alive, with no room in her thoughts for me, even for hating me.

Kowlee was gone. Wolf Jaw had gone mad. From now on Pingwa and Josie would always fear me. There was only one thing left for me to do.

I went into my tent, grabbed the skin pouch from its hiding

place, and shook out the amulets. When they hung around my neck I lashed a caribou sleeping skin tightly around the snow knife and flung the pack across my back.

I went down to the black ice of the fjord and hurried westward, running sometimes to drive away the cold. The early winter midday faded into darkness. I could see fog rising, swirling all along the floe edge. High above me I heard the east wind coldly whistling to the Dog Star.

I moved along the frozen coast like a frightened animal under the white hook of the early winter moon, constantly looking back to see if I was being followed. I knew that if I stopped walking, the cold wind would kill me.

I edged around the shore of every bay, turning far inland to make safe river crossings, haunted by images of setting my foot on thin black ice and falling through into the realm of that monstrous creature I had seen lunging out from beneath the ice. I had seen it, yes, and so had Elisapee, and so had Tusks and Ikhalook.

I walked on, bending from the wind, bewildered, terrified, and shunned by every other human being.

18

My journey down the coast forced me to seek food in several camps. Oh, yes, the people of those camps did share a little meat with me, but in a nervous way, almost without speaking or looking at me, as though I were accursed. None offered dogs or asked where I was going, and I always left them early in the morning.

I forced myself to move, to stay alive.

The winter moon grew full. I found a small, poor camp where the people greatly feared me, but stayed there until they could no longer tolerate me. Then, without asking, I borrowed a caribou skin and a needle case and sinew to repair my worn-out boots and clothing, and left before dawn, believing that one more wrong would not change my fortune. The people there would pass the word that Shoona had also become a thief, but I no longer cared. I now fixed all my thoughts on the task I knew I must perform.

When I was walking eastward a dog-team driver stopped and offered me a ride. His name was Naakalook, and he had just come from Trader's Bay, where he had gone to the nursing station with a wounded hand. He told me that he had himself seen Kayaker, who was still alive, but who lay in bed without opening his eyes or speaking. Elisapee was also there, even sleeping there, to help take care of Kayaker. She told Naakalook she believed that Kayaker was going to live, but the male nurse said no one could be sure whether he would live or die.

He left me at the Nunavak camp, where the people gathered and sang Christian hymns against me, and would not let me sleep in any igloo with them. Next morning, before they woke, I rose and walked away from their freezing meat porch. I seemed to shrink in size throughout that dreadful winter moon, and each snowhouse that I built at night became smaller and more miserable, until at last each one was like the awful stinking prison in which I had spent my fast.

Some distance from the Nunavak camp I found a meat cache built of stones and cleverly sheathed in ice. In my desperation, I smashed it open with a stone hammer. It was packed with rich red walrus meat, frozen and delicious, and when I had taken what I needed, I cunningly replaced the loosened stones. It is a double crime to take food from a family without immediately informing them, but I did so with only the slightest sense of guilt.

Using Kowlee's snow knife, I built a wretched igloo among the rocks nearby. I returned to the cache each night, removed the loose stones, and gorged myself like a wolverine on the meat I stole from others. I had almost lost my human feelings.

One day I grew bold and wandered onto the sea ice until I found what I was searching for. I flung myself down on my belly and stretched out full length on the snow, staring into the dark water of a seal hole. It seemed to me that I caught a fleeting glance of some small image reflected on the smooth surface of the water.

Kowlee had told me that through the seal's round breathing hole in the ice, the sky is joined to the world beneath the sea. Through this magic entrance we may see reflections of our past and of our future—reflections from the other world. I waited for a long time, scarcely daring to breathe lest ripples on the water's surface hide some vision from my eyes. As I lay there alone on the vast frozen sea I wished for neither life nor death, food nor shelter.

That night I could not sleep but lay like an overworked dog, twitching and dreaming. Long before morning I rose, shivering, and with my two sleeping skins around my shoulders I crept toward the cache and stole the last meat. I hacked it crudely into dark red strips, which I hung by a leather thong around my waist.

I made my way westward, following some dog-sled tracks. I was obsessed with the idea of opening the Tunik house ruins and returning the amulets to their rightful place. At last I had come to believe that all the evil started on the day I took them, and that this was the only way I could bring it to an end.

One afternoon, as I lay hidden among the rocks, I watched a dog team moving slowly eastward on the sea ice, coming out from Trader's Bay. At first I did not recognize the driver or the one who crouched behind him. They both sat half asleep, legs crossed, faces buried deep inside their hoods.

Slowly the team drew to a halt, and the man behind the driver stood up stiffly. It was the Sinew Puller. Out from the body warmth beneath his parka he pulled a small accordion, and squeezed from it the most tremendous chords, of the kind we had used to call the people to our séances. After that he stuffed it back in against his belly and shouted, "Shoona! Shoona! Do you hear me, Shoona?"

I stayed hidden behind the rocks and watched the two of them shading their eyes as they searched the hills. The Sinew Puller sat down, the driver rattled a trap chain against his grub box, and the team started moving eastward once again.

I stood up uncertainly, half hoping and half dreading that they would see me. In the end I waved my arms and called out, "Avo Divio! Avo Divio!"

He jumped off the sled and came running back toward me in that crooked way he has.

"I've been out squeezing on this thing and shouting for you

for I don't know how many days." He took me by the arm. "Come on, you've got to come with me."

As the dog team carried us east along the coast, the Sinew Puller said, "You are leaner than I've ever seen you, and your clothes are tattered. Oh, how that man has been searching for you! He says you have to help your mother."

When we arrived at his camp, my mother's hunter was waiting for us beyond the igloos. I shook hands with him but asked nothing, acting in the way of a true shaman, believing that words are worth little and that one who remains silent appears wise.

When we stepped inside the igloo, I saw my mother lying in the very center of the wide bed. Two large seal-oil lamps had been moved in close to her for warmth. She looked at me and smiled, but in a painful way. Her face had an unhealthy flush, and her eyes were bright with fever, larger than I'd ever seen them.

"Each day she seems to have grown weaker," her hunter said. "Because she wasn't well last summer, we stayed up at the fish lakes and let others do the trading for us. Since then she has hardly been able to get out of bed."

"Your mother is dying," said the old grandmother, who sat in her proper place on the right-hand side of the house.

"I know you will do all you can to help her," my mother's hunter said, and his old wife added, "Please help her. She is more than a daughter to me."

"That is not an easy task," I said.

I did not use our secret language when I spoke to the Sinew Puller. I had no need to, for each of us knew exactly what the other thought. I could tell he had real pity for my mother and for me.

"We must carefully plan how we will try to take the sickness from her. It will be very difficult," I said to him.

"Shoona," the hunter's true wife said to me, "you must use all the strength you have. Ask your *sakavok* to help you."

We went into the igloo of their neighbors, who offered us tea and meat. But I found I could drink and eat nothing.

"It is your own mother," the Sinew Puller said. "You're the only one who can do the healing. In the first part I will work the accordion for you, and try my best to do the singing and the chanting."

My hands and my forehead turned wet with fear. "Kowlee used to say that I was a swimmer, not a healer. *Kapiashukunga!* I am afraid," I whispered to him. "Afraid I cannot cure her."

Then I said, in the secret language, "I must tell you that if a ship were in at Trader's Bay, I'd take her to the doctor who healed Raven's broken leg."

It was dark when we began the curing séance. The wind had cleared the sky and all the stars were out. The half moon made a path across the sea ice, which glinted where the wind had blown it clear of snow. I was trembling and afraid.

When we went back into the snowhouse, everyone from the camp, including every single child, was crowded around my mother. One by one the adults stepped forward and shook hands with her, saying *"Tabouotit*—good-bye to you." They told her they had observed her human signs and expected her to die that night or early in the morning unless I performed real magic. For it is our custom to speak the truth before those we believe are dying.

The Sinew Puller rose and brought me the belt of amulets to lay across my mother's chest. I turned my head and closed my eyes, not needing to see what was about to happen, and started calling out the magic words. I took my mother by the shoulders and shook her frantically to break the hold of the sickness that clung inside her. I held her nose, as Kowlee had taught me, and when she opened her mouth to breathe I tried to fan away the evil spirit with a jaeger's wing. I massaged her throat. I laid her crossed hands on her stomach. Nothing seemed to give her strength, and I sensed that she was slipping away from me.

Desperately I knelt beside her, and using secret words, I asked Avo Divio to get the sinew ready. After a while he coughed and sniffed to tell me everything was in position.

I started dancing, weaving in and out among the watchers, to the sound of frightening moans that Avo Divio squeezed from our accordion. Tears ran down my face as I sang to my mother. I did not turn my head when I heard our audience gasp, for I knew that right after the weasel left my sleeve in the cover of the shadows, they had seen it dart between my mother's sealskin boots.

The Sinew Puller whirled around, and as he did, the weasel stuck its head from beneath the collar of the my mother's parka. I let out a roar. It seemed to leap from her open mouth, and I lunged with my hands and caught it. The watchers cried out in horror when they saw it bite me, and the blood spurt from my thumb. They saw me grab it in my anger and snap its neck and violently fling it through the shadows. It disappeared as it went beyond the lamplight to the sound of wails from the Sinew Puller and screams from the accordion.

I laid the second belt of amulets across my mother's waist. She had turned pale as death, with her eyes half closed. I started to rise, but she reached out and took my hand again.

"*Nakoamiasit*—thank you so much," she said, "for coming here, for being here with me. I wish I'd made the boots for you. Oh, thank you, Shoona." She spoke my name in the kindest way I'd ever heard.

The Sinew Puller put his hand on my shoulder and said, "See! You do have the power. She is getting better."

I squatted down and started rummaging among the curing amulets still hidden in our bags.

My mother whispered to me, "I never made those boots for you because—"

Her voice was so weak that I had to lean close to hear her words.

"Never mind the boots," I answered. "You did many thoughtful things for me."

⁑

"No," she said. "It was wrong of me to leave you in that little igloo while I walked south to save myself. If I had kept you with me, Kowlee would never have been able to buy you. Did you have a bad life with her?"

"No," I said, glancing at the Sinew Puller. "We were never hungry. It was not bad for us at all."

The Sinew Puller warmed up the little accordion over the lamp flame, making it give out a soft moaning, groaning sound, perhaps because he did not think it right for others to hear the private words my mother might wish to say.

"Where does it hurt you most?" I asked her.

"Everywhere," she answered. "Worse than that—I am growing numb. I can no longer feel my hands and feet."

I placed my hand upon my mother's chest and pressed gently downward. She winced in pain, and I could see her breathing had turned to slow and violent heavings. Every adult in the tent became alert and watchful, and Avo Divio moved among them, working the accordion, slowly making sounds that would carry my mother, carry all of us, across great distances, send us soaring between the opening in the sea ice and the sky.

"There's no use wasting your time or his," she whispered. "I am going to die. Soon. Almost now, I think. I feel peaceful having you so near me, Shoona. You who have come out of my own body. We have been apart so long, and now you're here beside me when I need you most."

She pointed at her hunter. "He has only been good to me. And his true wife sitting there, she has been as kind as a mother to me. I only wish you could have lived with us. I wish you could have shared the pleasures we've had together. We've had so much singing and laughing in his camps. Don't feel sad, Shoona. My body is dying, but my soul will go on living, dancing, singing."

"Don't talk too much," I said. "Just rest and listen. I will try to sing to you."

✹

"That will be nice," my mother said, and closed her eyes.

I made my healing song go on, and on, and on, and on. Sometimes my mother's hunter and even his old wife joined me in the chorus. My mother's breathing became calm and steady. The sweat dried on her face, and she fell into a deep and peaceful sleep.

Avo Divio and I crept away, exhausted, and lay down in the neighbor's igloo. Just before dawn my mother's hunter came inside and sat quietly beside me on the bed. He took my hand and held it tight in his.

"I have come to weep with you," he said. "She is gone. Your mother has gone to some other place. She has gone away and left us."

We two started weeping quietly together, trying not to wake the others.

"She was a lovely, patient wife to me," my mother's hunter said. He didn't use the word *aviliak* for my mother. He called her *nuliungaapik*—my small wife.

I tried to tell him that she had never been unkind to me, but my voice kept choking, and I couldn't make the words come out the way I wanted.

"Don't take it so," he said. "You two did everything you could."

He asked me to stay with them, and I thanked him but told him I could not. "There is a thing I must do quickly," I said.

He lent us his dog team and a driver and gave us a haunch of caribou. We went east again toward Trader's Bay.

Avo Divio tried to cheer me by telling me everything had been forgotten back at Trader's Bay and asked me to live with him and help him care for Wolf Jaw. But at midday, when our team drew opposite the blunt rock we call Big Toe, I told the driver to halt the sled.

"I am going to leave you now," I told Avo Divio. "I wish to visit Kuni's camp."

"Do you need me to come with you?"

"No," I said, and when he tried to unlash our gift of meat I stopped him. "Keep it. Thank you for helping with my mother."

I watched them moving toward the faint shadow of Black Whale Mountain, which stood far off in the winter gloom, and began walking. But as the trail turned toward the frozen bay at Big Toe I could scarcely make my feet go forward. I crouched behind a snow hummock, trying to work up my courage, and I waited there in the searing cold until the northern lights appeared. The amulets hanging around my neck were burning me.

A shift of wind must have carried my strong smell into the camp, for I could hear the low growling of the dogs. I rose when I saw all fourteen of Kuni's people come out to see who was near. I hobbled like an old man up their snow trail because my right foot had lost all feeling, ashamed because my clothes were soiled and tattered, and I had no dogs, no sled, no food.

Kuni did not greet me warmly, but neither did he bar my path or scorn me.

"Why are you out there walking alone?" he asked me.

When I did not answer him, the others stared at me in hostile silence. Then he and all the rest of them turned away.

I walked toward the igloos, and a woman screamed out, "Are you going to allow this useless devil of a man to live with us? He will gobble down the little food we have."

The hunters kept their backs to me, knowing that such an insult should drive the most shameless scoundrel from a camp. But I, who had no friends, who had come to fear my past sins more than loneliness, stood shivering before the three igloos, my face hidden in my hood.

The woman who had screamed the insult stood defiant, with her arms spread out to bar my way, and another one flung a rusted snow knife at my feet. "Go, make your own house, if you are afraid to leave tonight," she shouted. "Don't build too close to us!"

They waited in silence, all of them, and watched me walk away three times as far as I could throw a stone. There, in a deep, hard drift, I cut out blocks and formed a crude igloo of my own. When it was finished and I had dropped the key block into place, I unwrapped my ragged pair of caribou skins. I reminded myself that I had come here not because I wished once more to live with human beings, but because I could not go on living unless I returned the ancient Tunik amulets that I had stolen six summers past from one of the house ruins.

Oh, I had paid for them by leaving my trade comb and iron knife, but I knew now that those had in no way been enough to purchase such powerful amulets. Even after the mounting trouble at Trader's Bay, when I had begun to suspect they were at the root of it, I could not have mended matters by throwing them away. Even if you try to lose or destroy an amulet improperly possessed, it will go on working against you.

In the morning, when I left my snowhouse, I saw the hunters' sleds only as disappearing specks upon the flat expanse of frozen sea. Without asking permission, I snatched up a large wooden snow scoop and climbed the nearby hill. Before long I found the snow-filled hollows that marked the ancient Tunik houses.

I stood staring at all three of them, trying to remember that summer day when I'd been here with Kowlee. Which way had we walked up from the beach? In which house had we found the shaman's hiding hole beneath the sleeping bench? After walking this way and that, observing the hollows from every angle, I assured myself that it must be the central one.

My digging was made difficult because the winter winds had packed the snow as hard as dried clay, and in the end I used the long snow knife, hacking out blocks the way a hunter builds an igloo. I had little skill, and my wanderings and my hunger had left me weak, but I worked desperately, for the winter night was coming all too quickly. Only when I had finally cleared the front of the sleeping bench did I discover that I was in the wrong house. There was no secret hiding hole there.

"Tomorrow I will find it," I told myself, and as I looked at the other hollows I fancied that I could remember following Kowlee through that open entrance passage and seeing her remove the stone.

I stumbled back down to my dark, freezing snowhouse and crawled inside.

A boy whose face and name I did not even know came over from the igloos, skidding a half seal behind him. He pushed it in my entrance and said, "My mother is your cousin by marriage and that is why she sends this to you." He turned and ran away without another word.

On top of this gift was a small stone oil lamp. With trembling hands I cut the thick winter fat from the seal and pounded it soft and fixed a wick for my small stone lamp. I was shivering hard before I got it going, but by dark the inside of the new house glistened in the lamplight, and I ate the meat, and that helped to warm me. Because of that almost unknown cousin's kindness I felt better than I had since early summer. I knew that tomorrow I would find the hiding place. I could feel so in my bones.

Sometime later I went outside my igloo and saw the three snowhouses glowing faintly in the darkness, and I heard a child crying and dogs whining, and I drew a great breath into my body and thought how good it was to live near this last true relative of mine. I looked up at the sky, and all the stars seemed just above my head, flashing their wordless messages directly down to me. I said to them aloud, "Please let me find the hiding place. Let me put an end to all the troubles."

In the morning I went up on the slope and dug frantically for almost all that day, but still I could not find the hiding hole. When it grew dark in the afternoon, and all the stars appeared, I went back to my igloo. I lay down and made my lamp burn very small, because I wished to conserve the little seal oil I had been given. I drew my sleeping skins around me, and pulled my arms inside my parka, and tried to make my mind's eye find the hiding place beneath the bench.

I slept again—I do not know how long—but when I awoke I heard footsteps creaking across the snow. The walker stopped just outside the entrance. I imagined I could hear the sound of breathing.

When no more happened, I coughed, which was a sign to anyone waiting outside that they were welcome to enter, but now I heard no sound at all. I sat up and listened again, gathered my courage and rose from the bed. Bending low, I stepped outside my entrance.

Standing just beyond the low snow wall that I had built to break the wind, a woman waited quietly. Even though her silhouette was black against the starlit night, and her hood concealed her face, I could tell that she was young, well formed, thin-waisted.

"*Tikipeet?* You arrive?"

She did not answer.

"*Kenukiat?* Who are you?" I asked gently, not wishing to frighten her away.

She shifted her weight from one foot to another, shyly, the way young girls do when asked a question. Being unsure of herself, perhaps, she remained absolutely silent.

Her silence puzzled me, and I did not know what to do.

Meekly she stepped around the wall, and, pulling off her mitt, she reached out and took my hand in hers. It was warm and soft and young, and yet it had a woman's strength that excited me.

"*Ekeerahlook.* It's very cold," I said. "Come inside with me."

Still holding her warm hand, I drew her after me inside my igloo. I made a place for her and we sat down side by side upon my bed. I drew one of the sleeping skins over her back and my own.

***

"Taktooalook," I said. "It's dark in here." For I was ashamed of the miserable flame that sputtered in my lamp.

"Kowmiajualook," she answered softly. "It's bright enough."

She pushed back her hood and knelt gracefully to tend my lamp, using the tip of my snow knife to shape the wick and regulate the flame. She tilted the whole lamp gently to her, causing the warm seal oil to flow and burn clear white without a hint of smoke.

Only then did she turn and look full face at me. I tell you, she was beautiful, with wide, clear cheeks that burned bright red in the lamp's warmth. Her even white teeth flashed when she smiled at me. Her thin eyes glistened black beneath alluring lids. Her nose was small, and so flat that when she turned her profile to me I could see both bright eyes glittering, reflecting in my lamplight. Her handsome, rounded forehead gave her the elegant look that our high-born Baffin Island women sometimes have.

I said nothing, but I thought how truly beautiful she was. Imagine such a girl out wandering alone at night! Perhaps she had been lying with some young hunter, not having asked permission from her husband, and now she was an outcast, running desperately back to the safety of her father's camp.

"I don't care who you are, or how you got here," I whispered to her. "I will be oh so grateful to have you lying close beside me." I ran my hand along her back and said, "You must be cold."

Still she did not answer, but I could feel her tremble the way a woman does when she's excited.

"Come," I whispered. "We'll warm each other in this bed."

She looked at me and smiled, her dark eyes shining in the light. In one smooth motion she drew off her long-tailed parka and spread it over us. As I lay back, staring at her naked torso, I, too, started shuddering with uncontrollable desire. Her breath rose in the frigid air, and yet she seemed to feel the cold not at all. I watched her reach up and gracefully unbraid her hair.

⁑

"Will you comb it out for me?" she asked in her soft warm voice.

Eager to please her in any way, I reached up with my fingers hooked and I tried to run them through her hair.

"Not that way." She laughed and stopped my hand. "Use this."

She drew from her hood a delicate ivory comb, dark brown with age, narrow, with long teeth, a kind women used for decoration when they wore their hair in topknots. Carved in the ivory was a double image—two white bear heads staring in opposite directions.

I raised my hand and gently drew the comb down through her long blue-black hair. As I pulled off my clothes, she reached out and touched the ancient ivory amulets strung around my neck.

"Oh, there they are," she said, and sighed contentedly as she snuffed out most of the lamp, leaving only a match-sized flame alight.

I could feel myself trembling when this strange girl lay down beside me. I could feel her wriggling as she stripped off her fur pants and boots. She drew my winter caribou skin around the two of us. She was smooth skinned and warm all over. Her long hair tickled softly, rippling across my body in a way that left me with no other thought than to possess her.

It was ecstasy to find myself lying beside this naked unknown woman, perhaps unmarried, perhaps a hunter's wife. Among our people, secretly taking someone's wife is an act that demands revenge. Yet that ever-present danger of losing your life seems to bring out strange lusts and uncontrollable desires. Is it the awesome thrill of touching forbidden flesh that makes one dare to lie so close to life or death?

Women who join you in a secret act, oh, they are the ones to be remembered—those who run out and meet you in the hills or make love hurriedly against a snowhouse wall. Those are the ones to be remembered through all the winters of your life. I shall never forget the soft curves of her body as she wriggled against me, and I drew my arms around her, and possessed her fully, in a way that made her like no other woman I had ever known.

After that we lay quietly together. As I basked in her warmth I had a feeling of pure contentment, as though all my aimless wanderings and my loneliness had been washed away.

Perhaps I slept a while. What roused me from my contentment was a shivering sensation that seemed to run up through my thighs. It felt at first like a cold wet hand. Then I could hear a faint, yet terrifying, humming, which seemed to rise from within the woman who lay beside me.

Cautiously I raised my head and stared at the dark outline of her face. Her eyes gave off a green glow, like that from a pair of starfish mating in the sea at night. A dampness spread from our loins and rose up around me, and the strange woman whose legs entwined me grew clammy cold. I could feel her flesh stretching beneath my fingers, and shrank away in horror as she arched her back and drove her pelvis passionately toward me. I could feel powerful coils of muscles flex and roil beneath her skin. Her thighs seemed to grow like a pair of giant salmon. Her hair was wet and shining in the lamplight. Her whole body had the salt smell of the sea.

This female thing that I had thought a woman clutched me in a terrifying grip, and when I tried to pull myself away she drew me to her all the more powerfully. Her arms encircled me, her webbed fingers moved passionately across my back, and as I opened my mouth to try to suck in air, I felt choking waves wash over me. I could no longer breathe, and I knew that I was lost.

The last thing I remembered was the sight of her opening wide her jaws as if to scream, then slowly, hungrily, clamping them over both my mouth and my nose. I struggled as I felt the wetness rising all around me. Desperately I tried . . . to draw . . . my brea . . . th . . .

::

THE
NORTHERN SERVICE
OFFICER'S REPORT

CANADA

Okoshikshalik Camp
South Baffin Island
Northwest Territories, Canada

From inside my tent I heard Nylak's voice call out that two dog teams were approaching across the frozen sea, and moments later her uncle hurried in to make sure I was awake. By the time I pulled myself together and went outside, the first sled had arrived. The man unlashing a big pack from it must be the one Shoona had called Kayaker. The woman who stood beside him, stamping her feet to drive away the cold, paler than most Eskimo girls and taller, would surely be Elisapee.

As soon as they saw me they began moving toward my tent, Elisapee in the lead. I sensed a holding back, a sort of physical reticence, in the man, and in the woman a tension that had nothing to do with the cold.

"Shoona?" she asked, barely above a whisper.

"Sleeping now," I said. "You've had a bad journey."

She agreed with the smallest motion of her head and said that the other team had run into trouble in the rough ice. One of their dogs had been caught and killed, and that had delayed them. "But they will be here soon," she told me.

"Let's wait in Nylak's house," I suggested, turning them toward it. "It's warmer than mine, and cheerier." Just after I had ushered them in, I heard the second team and went back out to greet Corgy and the other two drivers, and thank them for coming.

"Sweet Jesus!" Corgy grunted. "A Northern Service officer must have deep-frozen brains, living in such a place as this. I've never traveled in these parts in January before, and I hope to God I never shall again." He shivered and said, "Where is he? The sick man, what's-his-name?"

He jerked open the grub box lashed to the front of the long sled, using his mitted hands like a robot with a pair of frozen pincers, and pulled out a brand-new plastic medical bag.

"Look at that!" he said. "The sides are splitting in this bloody cold." He held the bag together and hung it on his shoulder. "Come on. Let's get the hell inside that little castle of yours."

I went first, with Corgy close behind. Kayaker, who had followed me out of Nylak's house, came, too, but slowly, and once inside he stayed back in the shadows, close to the door, as if he wanted to dissociate himself from what was taking place. Out of the corner of my eye, as I bent over Shoona, I saw Elisapee join him.

I rose and said to Corgy, "He's still asleep. I think his temperature is down."

Corgy pulled off his mitts, blew his nose, and asked me to hold the lantern closer for him. He took just one look at Shoona, and then, without even having touched him, turned and stared up at me.

"He's dead, for Christ's sake! You must know that."

I felt as if the room were spinning around me, and looked automatically at my watch that didn't work. "But he was all right—weak, sure, but all right, alive, no more than—" I fought the dizziness, wondering if time itself had stopped working. "He was talking to me no more than twenty minutes ago."

Corgy reached out and pressed his fingers against Shoona's cheek. The prints stayed there, indented. He pulled back the eyelids and examined the pupils closely. He lifted one arm and tried to flex it. When he looked up this time, his whole face flushed with anger. "Don't you try to make a bloody fool of me," he said. "This man's been dead a week. At least that. If it weren't so Christ-awful cold in here, you'd smell him."

I felt a futile, answering rage. "I swear to you he was talking to me just a little while ago," I heard myself shouting. "Half an hour at most."

"The hell he was." Corgy stood straight and glared at me across the body. "Listen, you! I used to work in the London city morgue. I worked in the morgue in Montreal. It takes days for a dead man's pupils to dilate like that. Rigor mortis. Have you never heard of rigor mortis, for God's sake? You brought us down here on a wild-goose chase. Four wind-blasted bloody days of travel on that ice in January. Is that your idea of a joke?"

To stop the room from spinning again, I moved across to Elisapee and made myself speak calmly to her. "Would you please go get Nylak's uncle?" I asked, ignoring Kayaker, who quite as steadfastly ignored me. Elisapee turned and went out again. It wasn't possible to guess her feelings.

When she returned with Nylak's uncle, I said to Corgy, "Leave me out of it. Ask *him* when he last saw Shoona alive."

"All right. Go ahead and tell me. When?" Corgy demanded.

Elisapee translated the uncle's answer from the shadows.

"I talked to him this morning, just before you all arrived. He asked me for tobacco and a mug of tea. He was lively then, although he didn't look too good. Are you sure he's dead?" He stared suspiciously at Corgy and said, "What did you do to him?"

While Elisapee was still translating, Corgy said, "Sure I'm sure. He's been dead for a week or more."

But Nylak's uncle stubbornly repeated what he had said before: "I was talking to him just this morning."

Corgy hunched his shoulders. "What shall I write to

Northern Health Services? That you two are crazy? Or that I am?"

I asked him if he wanted to take the body to Trader's Bay, and he said, "No, hell no! I wouldn't even take a dead man on a trip like that." He blew his nose again. "You know something? If everything wasn't all frozen up everywhere, I'd tell you that man died from drowning. Six days ago, maybe eight."

"Drowning." I remembered asking the men who brought Shoona in if he had been in the water. "But it isn't possible."

"I know, I know. That sounds crazy, out here in January. But all the indications—" Corgy pressed down hard on Shoona's rib cage and listened. "Hell, yes. He still has water in his lungs."

His hard eyes looked straight at me. "We'll both be making reports. You write your version and I'll write mine." He drew a long breath, and when he went on he sounded less belligerent. "You can tell the hunters to bury him—put the stones on him, I mean. Anywhere around here will do. He'll freeze and keep. If the police want to dog-team over here and confirm the death, they're welcome. But I don't recommend the trip."

He drew the canvas up to cover Shoona's face. Glancing at me afterward, he managed a smile of sorts. "Sorry if I blew my stack. I guess we've all been under quite a strain—us out on that frozen bloody trail, and you in here cat-napping and talking with a corpse." He paused. "He really does show all the signs of drowning. That's what baffles me."

"Why don't we go over to Nylak's again?" I suggested. "She'll be glad to give us all a cup of tea."

"I'm for that," said Corgy, and headed for the door.

Nylak's uncle went next, and then Elisapee. Kayaker stood without moving, just inside, where he had been from the start, and I paused when I reached him, to let him go first. He gave me a slight nod, almost like Elisapee's, and did move on ahead. Outside, he just touched the sleeve of my parka, and spoke directly to me for the first time.

"I need fresh air," he said, "and a chance to think about everything that has happened. It isn't—simple."

"No." I grimaced at the understatement. "There's a lot I don't understand myself. Maybe you can tell me—"

He said, "Please. Go on with the rest of them and have that tea." He turned his back and stared at the cold black fog that hid the sky beyond the ice.

Corgy was waiting for me, just outside Nylak's door. "Odd bugger," he said. "He spouted a lot of nonsense when his head was split. A bad concussion. Took thirty-eight stitches to sew him up. To tell you the truth, I don't know how he stayed alive. He ought to be dead, too." He looked at me. "The Eskimos at Trader's Bay are talking a lot of nonsense about what happened."

We finally had our tea with Nylak, but Corgy went on seeming restless and soon set his empty mug down. "That man Morgan, or Kayaker, or whatever you want to call him. He must be damn near frozen solid, standing out there. Let's go talk sense to him, or try to."

He thanked Nylak for the tea. *"Mawr ddiolch am y tê,"* he said, winking at me as he hung the ruins of his medical bag on his shoulder. "I often speak to them in Welsh. They understand it just as well as English."

Elisapee followed us from Nylak's house out into the wilderness of Okoshikshalik.

"Where is he?" said Corgy.

I jerked open the door of my tent, but Shoona's body lay alone, in awesome stillness, in the dank gray freezing cold.

"His pack is gone," Elisapee said. "He's gone, too. He's gone for good." I thought she was about to weep and said, "Why not go back inside with Nylak? I'll find him for you." I gestured toward the sleds. "He can't be far away."

I soon found a set of wholly distinctive footprints in the hard-packed snow, leading off between the rocks to the ridge that lifts behind the camp. They had to be Kayaker's. No one else in all the north country had boot soles that would leave prints like those.

When I reached the top of the ridge, a wind with a razor's edge was driving hard. It had swept the big red granite boulders clear of snow, and there the footprints ended. I looked east and west along the coast. I'd judge that I could see at least a mile or more before the ridge disappeared in freezing fog and the gathering winter gloom, and there was no sign of any human being, no movement at all except for the whirling ice crystals.

"Hello! You! Morgan! Kayaker! Ka-yak-er!" I shouted into the wind. "Hellooo!" I wondered how he could possibly have got himself beyond my sight.

But he was gone. I stood looking at the place where his footsteps faded into nothing. Were they covered by drifting snow, or was he carefully stepping only on the rocks?

I climbed up onto the highest boulder and studied every course he might have taken, inland or along the coastline or out across the frozen sea. Range after range of low hills in the distance turned from cold steel blue to gentle gray and then to palest silver. I stared along the ridges and the valleys, hoping to see some sign of him. But there was nothing. The wind rose and drove thickening clouds of ice fog in from the sea, and even the nearest hills began to fade from view.

As I climbed back down toward the sea, our own camp disappeared in whirling snow, but I found it easily, walking loose-kneed toward the mournful howling of our dogs.

Elisapee stood outside the snow wall around my tent, alone in the driving snow. Her hood was up, her shoulders hunched, her bare hands hidden in her parka sleeves. Tears had left frozen white streaks on her face.

She said, "I knew you wouldn't find him."

"Come inside," I told her. "It's hard enough on you— losing Shoona first, and now this Victor Morgan. But—can you tell me why he would leave in such a damned great hurry?

Where would he go? How can he get anywhere without dogs and a sled and a rifle?" As I studied her face I somehow knew she would not weep again. She seemed once more composed.

"*Iyonamut*. It can't be helped," she whispered. "Poor Shoona's dead. And Kayaker . . . he only did what he was sent to do. Can you understand that? Kayaker doesn't need me, or shelter, or dogs, or a rifle. And I know now that I would never have been allowed to go with him. Not where he was going."

A LAST WORD

The unresolved seed of this story has haunted me for almost thirty years. The truth is that an unknown white man was indeed seen by the Eskimos walking alone on a desolate part of West Baffin Island without any life support. I immediately reported that to the government in Ottawa. All our efforts, including help by the Eskimos, failed to locate that man. The matter remains a mystery to this day.

Shoona was a shaman of the northern Paleo-Asiatic type, one of a long line of shamans so ancient that we can only guess when their order first began or even when its adherents crossed the land bridge out of Asia from their caves, perhaps as far away as France and Spain and central Europe, moving eastward through Siberia. Their language today is linked to Hungarian Magyar and the more northern Finno-Ugric. Their powerful religious beliefs have been almost lost in Europe, Asia, and America, smothered by the waves of later religions.

I had the luck to live with the Baffin Island *Inuit*, these splendid and untrampled people, winters and summers for more than a dozen years. All the events and shamanistic practices recounted here were not unusual. (See Knud Rasmussen's three "Intellectual Culture" volumes of the Fifth Thule

Expedition.) I have thought it prudent to change the names of all the people and places and sometimes to shift the sequence of events. Identification of the characters in this novel with actual individuals, alive or dead, would be totally coincidental.

The validity and values of these religious practices are matters of tradition and most especially of faith. The true meaning of this story I leave to my readers, and wish them God's good help in their solution.

James Houston
FORMER NORTHERN SERVICE OFFICER
BAFFIN ISLAND
NORTHWEST TERRITORIES, CANADA

Old folk declare that when a man sleeps, his soul is turned upside down, so that the soul hangs head downwards, only clinging to the body by its big toe. For this reason also we believe that death and sleep are nearly allied.

—KNUD RASMUSSEN
"Intellectual Culture of the Iglulik Eskimos,"
Report of the Fifth Thule Expedition, 1921–24,
Vol. VII, No. 1, Chap. 4, p. 93
(Gyldendal, Copenhagen, 1929).